Shying Away

Kate Sherwood

Published by Kate Sherwood

Cover Art by Catt Ford

Print ISBN #978-1-988752-17-4
ebook ISBN# 978-1-988752-18-1

Second Edition Issued 2019

CHAPTER ONE

THE beat of the music was pounding into Quinn's body, pulsing against him and around him and into him, making it hard to think, or even to feel anything other than the primitive rhythm. It was exactly what he wanted. It would be nice if it was a little bit louder, enough to make conversation totally impossible instead of just difficult, but other than that, it was perfect.

He wasn't dancing, just leaning against the rail of the balcony, watching the bodies writhe on the floor beneath him. There were more women than usual, he decided, which was a bit of a nuisance. They kept him from getting a clear view of the male bodies on display, and if he couldn't see properly, how could he make his selection?

His inspection was interrupted when someone pressed in too close behind him, grinding into his ass. It would be easy enough to go along with that invitation, but he wanted to choose, not be chosen. There wasn't much in his life that he had control over, but this—this was his. He shifted forward, making his rejection as clear as possible without actually having to turn around and interact with whomever it was. Not that easy, though.

"Quinn. Hey, baby." The guy eased away from Quinn's ass at least, but instead of leaving entirely, he shifted over to stand next to Quinn at the railing. "It's been a while. Where've you been?"

Quinn turned his head enough to see the guy's face, then turned back. He recognized him, but couldn't think of a name. He also couldn't think of a reason to care. "I've been around." Surely that was dismissive enough.

There was a bit of a pause, as if the guy had to regroup. "Well, you're here now, right? Can I buy you a drink?" Something about the way the guy said it jogged Quinn's memory. He remembered the lavish apartment, right downtown, with the incredible view over the city and the ocean. They'd been drinking something, champagne maybe, something the guy seemed to think Quinn should find impressive. And maybe there'd been coke—not Quinn's favorite drug, but not something he'd turn down, either. But he couldn't remember much else, and that wasn't a good sign. Quinn might not be able to recall every fuck he'd ever had, but he liked to think he remembered the good ones.

He took another quick look at the guy's face, and then down his chest. He was handsome enough, with a sort of aristocratic look and a long, lean body that would probably feel just right pinned under Quinn's shorter, more muscular frame. But there was no flash of attraction, none of the instinctive pull that he liked to put his trust in when selecting partners.

"I'm good, thanks." He angled his body slightly away. He wasn't trying to be rude, but he wasn't worried about it, either. There are those who pull the bandage of rejection off fast, and those who pull it off slow; Quinn liked to pull it fast. It gave both him and the other guy lots of time to find somebody more interesting. Or interested.

But this clown really wasn't getting the message. He eased in closer, the front of his body rubbing against Quinn's side, and when he spoke, instead of raising his voice to be heard over the music, as he'd been doing, he leaned in and spoke quietly into Quinn's ear. "I've missed you. I've been looking for you. Waiting for you."

That was too much, and Quinn jerked away. Apparently he'd have to spell it out. "I'm not interested, buddy. Find somebody else to stalk."

The man looked stunned, and Quinn noticed the reaction. The guy was hot, but not scorching, so he must have a hell of a lot of money, or something else going for him, to be so confident. Quinn wracked his brain, trying to remember the sex. He really didn't think it had been too outstanding. So the guy was either rich, or maybe deluded. Either way, Quinn wasn't interested. Hell, "deluded" could be a good time, maybe—it was "rich" that was making Quinn's blood run cold. "Seriously, man. I appreciate the thought, but it's not going to happen."

"You appreciate... you appreciate the *thought*? Are you kidding me?" The man's expression was changing, anger starting to replace the surprise.

Quinn felt his body want to flinch away, but he forced himself to stand still. The guy's expression was too familiar, too soon, but Quinn had never been a victim and he'd be damned if he'd start acting like one now. This shithead had just better have the sense to back down, because Quinn sure as hell wasn't going to. "I'm not kidding. I'm just not interested." He turned to face the man. Quinn was a little shorter, maybe, but the other guy was a twig; Quinn was a stone, and he let all the cold hardness show in his eyes as he stared the man down.

It worked.

Instead of letting the anger grow, the man's expression shifted back to surprised, and then to hurt. Quinn was glad he'd seen the anger first, so he didn't have to feel bad. When the guy spoke, his voice was uncertain. "But—we had a good time, didn't we?"

"I have lots of good times, man. It doesn't guarantee a repeat." It was too bad, because Quinn liked his location, liked the view he had over the club, but discretion was the better part of valor, so he decided that he'd better find somewhere else to stand. "Cherish the memory."

That last part was a bit smart-ass, he thought as he turned and let himself melt into the crowd, but life was too short to be careful all the time. That philosophy had gotten him into trouble on more than one occasion, but he didn't think this was going to be one of them. He was in a crowded, open place, and the guy had just been arrogant, not evil. Everything would be fine. Well, maybe not "everything," in a cosmic sense, but this guy shouldn't be a problem.

He forced himself not to turn around to check if he was being followed. He wasn't a rabbit, trying to evade the fox. He was a fox himself. Or maybe a wolf. Hell, he was a tiger. The fox had better not mess with him. Quinn smiled to himself as he worked his way into the crowd around the bar. Yeah, his imaginary animal spirit could beat up anyone else's imaginary animal spirit. That was a mature outlook.

He caught the bartender's eye and raised his empty beer bottle, showing the label so he'd get the right kind as a refill. He wasn't really too picky about beer, but bartenders always seemed to want him to care, so he tried.

He paid for his drink and then turned to survey the crowd at the bar. It was quieter here, away from the dance floor, and people were having actual conversations rather than just yelling lines at each other. There were some half-familiar faces mixed into the crowd, and he nodded at Wade, down at the far end. They weren't friends, exactly, but they were—something. If neither of them had found anything better by the end of the night, they'd probably go back to Wade's place together. The sex wasn't usually outstanding, but it was reliably good, and they both knew exactly what to expect from the other. There was no need to worry about Wade getting too attached, or thinking he had a claim on Quinn's attention, or any of that crap. He and Quinn were two of a kind, and they both had sense enough to recognize it.

Quinn ran his rough hands over the smooth wood of the bar, and moved his gaze farther along through the crowd. He was trying to pick up on that hint of attraction, trying to find someone who could excite him, pull him out of himself at least for a while. He'd almost given up, almost decided that he should just go buy Wade a drink and call it a night, but then there was movement in the shadows at the end of the bar. The want and need were twisting through Quinn's stomach before he even fully understood what he was looking at.

The kid was beautiful. Tall and rangy, his shoulders taking up so much space that he was twisted around sideways, leaning into the wall in order to not crowd the man next to him. He was fair, with light skin and a disorganized thatch of blond hair, and Quinn had always liked the way that his own tanned body looked against someone paler. He liked the way it felt, even, his skin seeming warmer, as if it retained some of the heat from the sun that had darkened it. But that wasn't what was drawing Quinn in; there were plenty of well-built, fair men in the bar. This guy, though. There was something else about him, and Quinn pushed himself away from the bar and started working through the crowd, trying to get closer.

Nobody was talking to the kid, or even seeming to notice him. And that didn't make sense, because maybe he wasn't flashy, but he was definitely good-looking, by any standard. He seemed to be hiding in the shadows, as if he didn't want to be seen, and against all the bolder displays in the room, he was just fading away. Quinn himself wouldn't have noticed him if he hadn't moved at just the right time, and Quinn had been looking pretty hard.

Just as Quinn arrived, the kid moved again, setting his beer bottle down and pushing himself to his feet. Damn, he was tall. Quinn was almost six feet, and this guy was towering over him. And broad too, with those shoulders. He was wearing a simple, black button-down and loose jeans, so Quinn couldn't get a good view of his body, but he bet it was good; there didn't seem to be any fat on any of the parts that were visible. But the guy was moving again, shifting around as if trying to get past, and that spurred Quinn into action.

"Hey. You leaving?" The words weren't smooth, but they were the best he could come up with on short notice. He tried to make his tone do the work for him, hoping that he sounded seductive rather than startled.

The kid shifted his eyes toward Quinn and then dropped them. When he looked back up, it was as if he was forcing himself to do it. "I was going to. Yes."

Jesus, maybe he was just shy. Quinn normally didn't like that crap, didn't want to have to jump through extra hoops to get where he wanted to be, but somehow, on this guy, it was kind of adorable. "What's wrong? You not having fun?" The kid didn't look like he knew how to respond, so Quinn stuck his hand out. "I'm Quinn. Why don't you let me buy you a drink? I can introduce you to some people, if you want." He sincerely hoped the kid took him up on offer number one, but not offer number two.

The kid grasped the extended hand automatically, and Quinn could feel the warm strength in his grip. Damn. The guy had big hands. He still didn't seem too sure, though, and again it seemed like he was forcing himself to interact. "Hi. I'm Aaron."

"Aaron, huh? Like the aardvark?" Quinn didn't know quite what he was doing—he'd wanted to put the kid at ease, but who would be at ease when talking to someone spouting random crap like that?

The kid surprised him, though. "Yeah, like the aardvark. I don't fly an airplane, though."

"Damn—I wasn't even sure what I was talking about. But you're right—Aaron the Aardvark, flying an Airplane. What the hell is that from?"

"It's a kids' book. Like an illustrated alphabet, I think. Aaron, aardvarks, airplanes—they're all about the letter A." Aaron eased himself back down onto the barstool. He still didn't look entirely comfortable, but at least he wasn't getting ready to bolt. And this aardvark thing was actually kind of interesting.

"Yeah, that's right! There were, like, I don't know, bunnies, maybe?" Quinn was trying to trace the memories down inside his tangled brain. "Well, and aardvarks, obviously."

"Just the one aardvark, I think. Just Aaron."

And that seemed like an opportunity to get this back on the track it was supposed to be on. As soon as Quinn had thought of the bunnies, he'd realized that he probably didn't want to spend too much time chasing down that memory. "Yeah, maybe. Just the one. Just Aaron. Sitting all alone, at a bar...."

The lighting wasn't great, but it was enough that Quinn could see the blush creeping up Aaron's face. Yeah, the kid was shy. And, yeah, it was pretty damn adorable. "What are you drinking, Aaron?"

Aaron looked down at his hands as if hoping they held some clue, and then back up to Quinn. "A rum and Coke?"

It felt like a kid pretending to be all grown up, and not sure he was carrying it off. "You *are* of age, right? I'm not going to be corrupting a minor, or something?" Quinn smiled to show that he was mostly kidding, but he kept an eye out for a response even as he caught the bartender's attention.

A shy half-smile as Aaron said, "I'm twenty-two."

"All right, then." Quinn looked at the bartender. "A rum and Coke, and another one of these." He held up his half-empty bottle. He was pretty sure the kid wasn't going to be a fast drinker, so he might as well have something to keep himself occupied. Something to distract him from staring at Aaron's succulent bottom lip, or the strong tendons that led from his wrists up under his sleeves, up to hidden skin, skin that Quinn wanted to uncover. Damn, this kid was getting to him. He needed to get things back under control. "You live around here, Aaron?"

"Yeah. I just moved in, a few blocks away."

"Don't tell me you just came down for a drink, and didn't know what kind of bar you were going to...."

Another blush, but Aaron didn't look down this time. When he spoke, his voice was firm. "No. I knew where I was going."

Quinn nodded slowly, and decided that it was time to press his luck. He didn't know quite what he'd do if he got shot down, but he might as well find out; his strength was his looks, not his small talk, so if the kid wasn't hooked by now, Quinn was probably not going to get anywhere. "And did you have something specific you were looking for, here? Or just a drink?"

This time, the look was bolder, as if the kid was warming up and getting into his act. "No. Not just a drink. I was looking for something specific."

The bartender was back, then, and Quinn paid for the drinks, torn between being pissed off at the interruption and glad of the chance to regain his cool. This wasn't like him, getting so worked up over a simple hookup. He was Quinn Donahue, and this was what he was good at. He was a tiger, damn it! He wasn't going to get flustered by a cute little rabbit. Or even by a cute *big* rabbit. He watched Aaron's fingers curl around the glass of dark liquid, and brought his own bottle to his lips. He took a deep swallow as he watched Aaron's cautious sip. By the time he'd brought the bottle down to rest on the bar, he was back in control. "And this specific thing you're looking for—any chance you've found it?" Quinn had to force himself to stop talking, to not babble about damn aardvarks or something, and he was rewarded, after an agonizing few seconds, with Aaron's slow nod.

"Yeah. I guess maybe I have." Aaron's quick grin showed straight white teeth. "Or I guess maybe it found me."

That was an excellent answer, but Quinn forced himself not to jump up in the air and start waving his arms over his head in a victory celebration. Instead, he returned Aaron's smile, slow and easy. "Well, all right. You want to get out of here?"

Somehow, though, things had changed between them, shifted somewhere that Quinn wasn't used to. He wasn't supposed to be the one sitting there, waiting and hoping. And damn it if the kid didn't feel the shift in power too. Aaron had set his drink down on the bar, and he reached for it slowly, lifting it to his lips and taking another thoughtful sip, his eyes never leaving Quinn's face. He set the drink back down on the bar and waited for another several seconds before his head moved almost imperceptibly up and then down. "Yeah. Okay. Let's go."

Quinn fought to keep his cool. If nothing else, he had a reputation to protect. He took another long swallow of his drink before placing the half-empty bottle on the bar next to his earlier unfinished drink. Then he stepped back far enough to give Aaron room to move. "Your place? I'm not too far, but I'm more than three blocks." And he didn't bring hookups back to his apartment, not ever. He didn't want people to know where he lived, and he didn't want strangers in his space.

Aaron stood up as he said, "Yeah, okay." Then he waited, and Quinn started for the door. He only hoped that Aaron was behind him, and for the second time that night, he forced himself not to look backward. He wasn't sure what the hell had happened to his animal symbolism—when would a tiger hope that somebody was following him? He would certainly never care about a damn rabbit—but maybe he'd want to be followed by another tiger. In mating season, at least.

Quinn made it to the door before letting himself slow down and look back over his shoulder. Aaron was still there, thank God. He froze when Quinn looked at him, but then smiled nervously and edged forward. Quinn would have loved to be able to laugh at the guy for being nervous, but he was pretty damned edgy himself. "All right?" he managed to ask. When Aaron nodded, Quinn pushed the door open and stepped outside.

It was a warm night, and clear, and both of those were rare for Vancouver in late September, so Quinn took a moment to breathe in and appreciate the mild weather. Neither he nor Aaron had jackets, and there wouldn't be too many more nights that they'd be able to get away with that. He glanced over and saw Aaron watching him. "Sorry. You're ready to go?"

"Don't be sorry. It's a beautiful night." Aaron stepped a little closer. "If there weren't all these lights, I bet the stars would be really clear."

Quinn glanced up at the sky, but it was just a dark backdrop to the neon of the bar's signs and the bright streetlights. "I guess." He looked back at the street, and then at Aaron. "Which way?"

Aaron wordlessly led him along the crowded sidewalk. They were on Davie Street, the heart of Vancouver's gay village, and the area was alive with other men, all out enjoying the unexpectedly warm weather. Normally, Quinn would have been distracted by the skin on display, the beautiful faces smiling and laughing and flirting all around him. He was having no trouble keeping his focus on Aaron, though.

They stopped in front of one of the tall, concrete buildings that punctuated the more common low-rise structures of the area, and Aaron punched a code into the keypad. "This is it," he explained belatedly. Quinn was pretty sure he'd been in the building before, with some other resident, but he couldn't remember details. He followed Aaron inside, and then into the elevator.

They still didn't talk as Aaron pushed a button for the sixteenth floor. The walls of the elevator were mirrored, and Quinn had to fight the urge to pull the emergency stop button. It would be delicious to undress Aaron in there, with the mirrors displaying every angle, every inch of skin, but Quinn didn't think the kid would be into that kind of public display. He didn't think he'd be into it himself, if it came down to it, but it was fun to think about. He let himself smile a little, and he knew Aaron noticed. He hoped he looked sexy and enigmatic rather than psychotic.

Another punch code got them inside the apartment. It was a bachelor, but a good-sized one, at least by downtown Vancouver standards. There were all the expected furnishings: a kitchenette in one corner, a two-person table, a brown leather couch facing a TV hung on the wall, and over toward the big window, a dresser, a bedside table, and a bed. Everything looked immaculate; the covers on the bed were even folded down, like they were in a hotel.

"Did you just move in? Or are you actually this tidy?" Quinn took a few steps into the room and looked around for any sign that the apartment was lived in. The only things that even hinted at actual habitation were the two pairs of boots lined up by the front door. They reminded him of his younger sister; she'd been deep into horses, the last he'd seen her, and she'd had boots like those. Much smaller, of course.

Aaron was watching him uncertainly, and when he spoke he sounded like he was justifying himself. "I've been here a few weeks. But, you know—I tidied up before I went out tonight."

Ah. "Because you knew you were going to bring somebody home with you."

"Well—I didn't *know*. But, yeah, I thought I might."

"So how come you were leaving, when I saw you? You'd given up?" It still didn't make sense that this kid would have any trouble at all picking up, not if he put any sort of effort into it.

Aaron dropped his eyes, and the newly familiar blush made another appearance, creeping up from the neck of his button-down. Quinn took a step forward; he really wanted to see if the kid's chest had the same beautiful pinkness. He stopped moving when Aaron looked back up. "I just felt sort of stupid, you know? I mean, I didn't know anyone, and I was just sitting there."

"You don't dance?"

Aaron's laugh was more like a snort, but he controlled himself. "No. Not—not in a way that would make anyone want to talk to me. Possibly they'd want to sedate me, and get me back to the asylum."

"Yeah, okay." Quinn took another step forward, so close now that he could reach out and touch the kid, if he wanted to. And he absolutely wanted to. Aaron stood frozen as Quinn lifted his hand toward his face. Quinn slowed down, although he hadn't been going all that fast in the first place. "You okay? This is what you wanted, right?"

Aaron nodded jerkily. "Yeah. It was. It is." He lifted his own hand and brought it tentatively toward Quinn's chest.

Quinn shuffled forward enough that Aaron didn't have to stretch very far, and they felt the first brush of contact, the tips of Aaron's fingers against the cotton of Quinn's shirt. Quinn wanted more, and he wanted it as soon as possible, but he was pretty sure Aaron needed things a bit slower. He curled his fingers around so that he could brush the side of the kid's face with his knuckles instead of the work-hardened skin of his palms. Aaron's eyes slid shut as if he'd been hypnotized. Hopefully that was a good thing. Quinn stretched his fingers out, rested them along Aaron's jaw, and then curled them gently in, suggesting but not insisting.

Aaron responded, leaning down, letting himself be guided, and Quinn felt his already hardening dick throb a little more. He reached forward and gave a gentle kiss and felt Aaron's lips move as he kissed back. Quinn deepened the kiss, and Aaron responded willingly, enthusiastically even. All of a sudden Quinn found himself being pushed backward, spun around so that he was the one with his back to the wall, and Aaron was the one on the outside. Aaron took advantage of his new freedom and moved until Quinn was shoved up against the wall by Aaron's whole body, long and hard and strong. There was no break in the kiss, not as Aaron moaned, not as he arched his body into Quinn's, and not as his hands raced all over Quinn's torso, feeling his chest, his sides, then out to his arms. It felt frantic, as if Aaron wasn't sure Quinn was real, or as if he thought he might disappear at any moment. Apparently the kid didn't need things slow after all.

And that was just fine with Quinn. He pushed off the wall, and damn it, the kid was strong, but he wasn't fighting Quinn, exactly, he was just a solid mass that needed to be moved. Quinn put a little more muscle into it and then Aaron was going along, letting himself be guided. This time it was Quinn's turn to spin them and slam into the wall. But Quinn wanted to do more than just feel Aaron's body through his clothes, and he pulled his face away while keeping their lower bodies lined up. They were both hard, pushing against their jeans. Quinn let his hips grind in. Aaron's eyes were still shut tight, but he made a little whimpering sound that was far better than any soulful gaze could ever be. Quinn's fingers attacked the buttons of Aaron's shirt, twisting them loose. He had to pull the bottom out from where it had been tucked into Aaron's jeans; he could see the effect that even that little bit of extra friction had on the kid's cock.

Once the buttons were taken care of, he shoved the fabric aside, and he got his first look at the chest in front of him. The kid was ripped, and the flush from his face was spread down over his chest, but it was arousal, now, not embarrassment. Quinn wanted to taste every inch, but he also wanted to keep staring, keep enjoying the view.

Aaron squirmed as if begging for attention, and Quinn brought his lips down to the warm skin in front of him. The kid tasted good, but the best part was the way he reacted to every kiss, every lick, every gentle nip that Quinn gave him. One of Aaron's hands found its way to the back of Quinn's head, not guiding, just encouraging, and when Quinn found a nipple and gave it a hard suck, the fingers tightened in his hair as Aaron gasped. Quinn had never gotten all that much pleasure from his own nipples, but he loved finding guys who were sensitive there—it made things so easy. And it was hot, seeing the reactions he could get from Aaron. Quinn gave each nipple some attention while his hands were busy unbuttoning his own shirt. He shrugged the fabric off onto the floor and then straightened, bringing his bare chest into contact with Aaron's. It was skin on skin, more contact than they'd had so far. It felt perfect, especially when Aaron bent down and found Quinn's mouth, pulling their tongues together into a writhing tangle.

Then they were spinning again, and Quinn was back up against the wall as Aaron pushed in, just on the limits of too hard. Quinn shoved Aaron's shirt the rest of the way off his shoulders and then went to work on the kid's belt buckle, and then his fly. Quinn pushed the loosened fabric out of the way and eagerly felt for Aaron's cock, as big and hard as the rest of his body, straining through the thin cotton of his underwear. The initial contact was enough to make Aaron gasp away from Quinn's mouth, his breathing jagged and rough. Quinn didn't release his loose grip, but he needed a little information. "You're right on the edge, aren't you?" Aaron buried his face in the hollow of Quinn's neck, still gasping, but Quinn pulled him back so they were facing each other, and for the first time since they'd gotten started, Aaron opened his eyes. His pupils were huge, staring at Quinn like he was seeing a miracle, and okay, it was a pretty good ego-boost.

"What's your recovery time like?" But Aaron seemed to be beyond words, and Quinn figured he could take a chance. The guy was young, he was obviously horny, he could probably get hard again pretty fast. And if he couldn't, what were they going to do, sit down and have tea until he calmed down a little? "Okay, man, I'll take care of you." He eased Aaron around so that the kid was leaning against the wall again, and then dropped to his knees and used one hand to reach in and support Aaron's cock while the other pulled his underwear down.

Quinn had the same conflict as before, torn between admiring from a distance and tasting from up close, and he made the same decision, leaning in and letting his lips gently close around the head of Aaron's cock. The kid's moan was more like a shout, and Quinn tried not to worry about neighbors. Instead, he pulled off, a wet, sloppy kiss, and then opened his mouth and went for it, bobbing down as far as he could go at that angle, then back up, fast and tight and almost rough. A few more times and Aaron was keening, his fingers back in Quinn's hair, tightening, twisting, and Quinn pulled off far enough that he wouldn't choke as Aaron arched his back off the wall, his whole body spasming as he came.

Quinn swallowed while he kept his tongue and his mouth working. The kid's climax seemed to go on forever. It was exciting, feeling this sort of power over somebody else; and it was good to do something that somebody appreciated. Finally, Quinn figured he was done, and he gently moved away and then stood up. Aaron's fingers stayed in his hair as he straightened, and as soon as he was upright he was pulled in for a kiss, Aaron's lips loose and relaxed now, sloppy and easy instead of hard and demanding.

And that was all right as far as it went, but Quinn had his own interests to pursue, and he maneuvered around to bring his groin into contact with Aaron's hip. Hopefully the kid just needed a reminder.

But Aaron seemed totally oblivious, kissing gently like he wanted to just make out for a while. Quinn figured it was lucky they were standing up or the bastard would probably be falling asleep on him. He rubbed his hard cock a bit more firmly against Aaron's hip. "You still with me, here?"

Aaron's eyes flew open, and there was that blush coming up again, and that made it pretty difficult to hold a grudge. "Shit! I'm sorry. I—uh—what should I do? I mean... I'm not very good, you know, but...."

Okay, this was more like it. Quinn was a pretty firm believer in the idea that even a bad blow job was still pretty good, but if the kid was open to other options, maybe they should be explored. "What do *you* want to do?" Aaron gave him a blank look, so Quinn decided he needed to elaborate. "Do you want to fuck?"

Aaron's blush got deeper; Quinn wouldn't have thought it was possible. The kid wasn't looking at him anymore, his eyes back down, staring toward the floor. Staring toward his own softening cock, actually, and Quinn wasn't surprised when Aaron shifted enough to get his hands free, then reached down to start doing up his pants. It was a bad sign, damn it. Quinn was going to get shut down entirely, just because he'd said what he'd been thinking? "Dude, before you get too offended about something coming out of my mouth, why don't you take a second to remember what just came *in* my mouth."

Aaron's eyes lifted. "I'm not offended! I just—I don't know. I guess...." He took a deep breath, and then blurted, "We can if you want. You know—we can 'fuck'."

This was getting annoying, and Quinn pulled his body away

a little. He was getting the distinct feeling that he wasn't going to be getting off, so there was no point in continuing the tease. "Yeah, you sound really into it—that'd be a great time. Jesus, Aaron. So you suck at sucking, and you don't want to fuck. What are we looking at, then? Hand jobs? I can reach my own dick, man, I don't need you for that."

Aaron looked... damn it, he looked hurt. He was the one who'd just come his brains out, he was the one trying to weasel out of reciprocating, and Quinn was the bad guy?

Aaron stared up toward the ceiling, as if he was trying to draw strength from above. "It's just—it's my first time."

The words were so quiet Quinn wasn't sure he'd heard them, and when they eventually registered, they took a while to sink in.

When they finally did, he jerked away, leaning back against the door that led outside. "Your first time—your first time at what? Like, you've never fucked before?"

Still no eye contact. "I've never... anything. With a guy. I've—you know—done stuff with a girl. But with guys, this is... you're it."

Quinn felt cold. "Jesus Christ, Aaron. You should have told me that!"

"Oh, yeah, in all our long conversations, as we were really getting to know each other. That's when I should have told you?"

"But that's—that's the whole point! If you're a fucking *virgin*, for Christ's sake, you should be taking it slow! Getting to know somebody, trusting him—all that shit."

Now Aaron's eyes were on him, and they were fierce and angry. "Fuck you. You just admitted that you don't know me, so don't try to tell me what I *should* be doing!"

Okay, that was a pretty good point. And why was Quinn the one acting outraged here? He wasn't the violated virgin. He tried to calm down. "Yeah, okay. You're right. Sorry." The pressure of his dick against his fly was almost gone, now—if he ever needed an anti-aphrodisiac in the future, he should remember this moment. "Okay, well... not a bad night for you, then. Right? I mean, you got off, you got a bit of experience—everything's okay. Right?" Quinn didn't know quite what he was looking for; he didn't know why he was so worried that he might have brought some sort of trauma into Aaron's pure, virginal life.

"I'm not—I didn't say I wanted you to go. I didn't say we couldn't do... whatever."

"No, you didn't say it. But, you know, I was just looking for—for something simple. This is—this is over my head. You need somebody else for all this stuff."

"All *what* stuff? I'm not... *you're* the one who says I need some sort of deep emotional bond, or something. That's not me. I—I'm not looking for something complicated. I'm not."

Quinn might have believed him if it hadn't been for that final "I'm not." The rest of it had sounded all right, but just at the end there, it had seemed like the kid was trying to convince himself, not convince Quinn. And then Aaron looked at him again, blue eyes trying to be sincere, and Quinn felt the same twist of lust in his stomach that he'd felt in the bar, felt his cock twitch hopefully. He needed to get the hell out of that apartment before he did something that would destroy what little self-respect he had left.

"I gotta go, Aaron. You take care of yourself, okay?" Quinn had the door open and was easing through it, and Aaron didn't say anything more, didn't try to get him to stay. Once he was outside and the door was safely shut, Quinn took a moment to collect himself and then started down the hall. He wondered if Wade was still at the bar. He needed something to distract himself from blue, trusting eyes, pupils wide, staring at him with wonder. Somehow he doubted that Wade would be enough to erase the image entirely, but maybe he could at least help.

CHAPTER TWO

AARON moaned and his fingers gripped tighter, Quinn's mouth soft and wet around his cock, swallowing him down, sucking hard and deep. Quinn's fingers moved back, tugging gently on Aaron's balls, and then farther, back into the crease of his ass, gliding smoothly, and then inside, where no one else had ever touched him. Aaron felt the orgasm building from his spine, then washing over him in wave after wave. His come spurted out over the wall of the shower, over his own hand, and imaginary Quinn faded away even before Aaron's body relaxed into the warm heat of the spray.

He let himself recover for a few moments, then lathered up and rinsed off his body. His favorite thing about living alone in the huge, impersonal apartment building was absolutely the shower time. Nobody to yell at him about hogging the bathroom, nobody to make smart-ass comments about how he wouldn't have to shower twice a day if he'd just get himself laid—his family was great, but they were not big on boundaries, and Aaron really appreciated the privacy he'd found in his new home. And it wasn't like he still didn't see all of them almost every day.

He gave his body another quick lather and rinse before turning the shower off and stepping out into the steamed-up bathroom. It was almost nine o'clock at night, and normally he'd be thinking about a bit of TV and then bed. But things weren't normal anymore, not since he'd met Quinn. He was trying to be rational about it, trying to remember that it was just one guy, a guy who seemed pretty damned determined to not have anything to do with Aaron or his issues. But rationality couldn't hope to compete with the memory of Quinn's beautiful, angular face, his dark hair just long enough to curl a bit behind his ears, his strong, solid body, and God, his mouth. Aaron had dated Sara for almost four years, and she'd been a more-than-enthusiastic partner in whatever they'd gotten up to, but none of it had ever felt right to him. In all of those years, it had never felt anything like those few unforgettable minutes with Quinn. So, yeah, the part of his brain that was telling him to let go—it wasn't really being heard by any other part of his body.

He pulled on clean jeans and a T-shirt, then a sweater. He'd need a jacket too, because the fall rains had absolutely hit the city. He didn't mind getting a little wet, though, not if it gave him a chance of running into his target.

Ten minute later he was back at Candy's, the same club where he'd met Quinn. It was a Tuesday, so it wasn't too crowded, and the music wasn't as loud as it was on the weekends. He shed his jacket and then his sweater before finding his favorite seat at the bar. The stool was out of the way, and he had a good view of the door.

"Aaron, man, you're getting to be a regular." Paul, the bartender, slid the rum and Coke across the bar without even waiting for him to order.

"Yeah, I guess so." Aaron took a sip. He didn't really like the drink, but that was part of the plan. He drank beer too fast, and then spent half the night in the bathroom. Time spent in the bathroom was time *not* spent watching the door, waiting for Quinn to appear.

"You're sure you still want to hold out for him? I told you, man—he's not predictable. He'll be in every night for a week, and then not again for a month or so." Paul made a face. "And, dude, every night that he comes in, he goes home with a different guy. I really don't think he's looking for...." He waved his hand vaguely in Aaron's direction. "For whatever you're looking for."

"I'm—I'm just looking for *him*."

The bartender looked at him for a moment before smiling regretfully. "Yeah, okay. Good luck with that." He went off to serve his other customers, and Aaron went back to watching the door. It had been nine days since he'd met Quinn, and he'd been back to the bar eight of those nights, with no sightings.

"I'm not saying he's not hot." Damn, Paul was back. How long had Aaron been staring at the door? "But there are other hot guys here, you know. I could introduce you to some of them."

Aaron shook his head. "No, thanks, really, I—" He broke off.

Quinn was there, standing in the doorway, his dark hair wet from the rain and glistening in the club lights. His shirt was damp too, and it was clinging to his muscular shoulders. Aaron could remember the way Quinn's body had felt beneath his hands, and the way he'd moved, powerful and balanced. He wondered if the raindrops were still cool where they rested on Quinn's neck, or if his skin had already warmed them. He wanted to taste the rain and the skin and anything else he was allowed to get near. But somehow he was having trouble pulling himself off of the barstool.

"You're not going to pussy out, are you?" Paul looked half-amused, half-concerned, an expression that made Aaron think of his older brother.

"No. I'm—I'm good. I'm going to do it." But he stayed still, watching. Quinn stood just inside the door and slowly surveyed the room, then started moving, over toward the bar where Aaron was sitting. He hadn't spotted Aaron, though, that was clear. He was just coming to get a drink.

"You want to play this cool?" Paul asked.

"I don't know. Maybe. What would that mean?"

"Buy his drink. When he tries to pay me for it, I'll just nod over at you and say it's been taken care of."

That did sound cool. Like, James Bond cool. Probably more than Aaron could live up to, really, but it was a start. "Okay, yeah. Let's do that. Thanks, man."

Paul shook his head. "Don't thank me, Aaron. It's totally against my better judgment." But he moved over anyway, took Quinn's order, and reached into the beer cooler behind him, finding a bottle that he opened and placed on the bar. Aaron waited, and saw the bartender nod in his direction, saw Quinn swivel his head and see Aaron—and saw Quinn look back down at the bar, without even a smile. Something twisted around deep in Aaron's stomach. For a second he thought maybe he was going to be sick.

Paul came back, his face carefully neutral, and Aaron shoved a few bills at him. He wanted to go home and bury his head under the covers and hide, but he'd waited too long for this moment. He'd been waiting his whole damn life, it felt like. He couldn't give up. So he slid off the bar stool and worked his way over to Quinn.

"Hi, Quinn," he tried, and immediately felt stupid. Why couldn't he have thought of something better to say, something more decisive, or memorable?

"Hey, man." Quinn didn't even look at him. "Thanks for the beer."

"Yeah, no problem. I, uh—I wanted to thank you for the other night. I mean, I didn't... you know. I didn't return the favor, or whatever." Aaron had never considered himself sophisticated or a smooth conversationalist, but this had to be a new low. Still, he pressed on. "And I just wanted to say—you know. If you're interested, I'd totally be interested in... in whatever. Seriously. I was a bit of a freak the other night, I guess, but that was—it was nerves, or a misunderstanding, or something. I absolutely want... whatever you want."

Finally, Quinn looked up, but his expression was closed. "Jesus, kid, you can't even say the words."

"No, I can say them." Aaron was hardly a choirboy when it

came to swearing; he'd curse like a pirate if he stubbed his toe or something, but this felt different. He summoned his resolve. "If you want to fuck. That's what I want. With you."

Quinn just looked down at his beer bottle, and Aaron knew he wasn't going to like what he was about to hear. "Sorry, man. I don't think it's a good idea."

"No." That response was a bit of a surprise to Aaron, and from the looks of things, to Quinn as well. "I mean—it *is* a good idea. I'm sorry about the last time, I really am, but I promise it won't happen again. And, you know, it wouldn't have happened last time, if you'd stuck around. I just got nerves. I would have gotten over it. Absolutely."

Quinn shook his head. "That's not what I'm worried about. You're.... Look, Aaron, you're a nice guy. You're young, you've— for whatever reason, you've held out this long. So, you know— hold on a little longer, and find somebody you really care about. You know?" He took a long swallow of his beer. "You really don't seem like the kind of guy who wants his first time to be a one-night thing with somebody he picked up in a bar."

"I want it to be with *you.*" Aaron barely recognized his own voice; he sounded so young, and almost petulant.

"No. Trust me, man. You don't. I'm an asshole. You want somebody who's going to wake you up the next morning with fresh coffee, and take you out for brunch, and then for a walk on the damn beach, or something. Seriously, man, I'm not that guy."

"I don't...." Aaron caught himself. He *did* want all that, now that he heard it described, and he was pretty sure he couldn't lie well enough to fool Quinn. "I don't *need* that." That was closer to the truth. "Or, you know—you could maybe give me a tiny bit of it?" He tried to look cute. "Like, the coffee, maybe? If I did all the grounds and stuff the night before?"

"Do you like your coffee at two in the morning? 'Cause that's when I'd be leaving, if I even made it that long." Quinn finished his beer. "Thanks for the drink, Aaron. Now, go find somebody else.

This isn't going to happen."

And there it was. Aaron had made his pitch, and he'd been turned down. He was done. What else was there to say? He stepped back slowly, then back forward quickly. "Come on. You...." He tried to remember what Quinn had said to him that first night. "You didn't just come here for a drink, right? I mean—you came here looking for something?"

Quinn nodded slowly, and finally he turned to face Aaron head-on. "Yeah. I came here looking for something specific. And, I'm sorry, man. It's not you." He spun his stool halfway around and stood up, and he walked away.

Aaron stood there watching, still close enough to hear every word, as Quinn eased in behind a man at the bar, then ran his hand up over the guy's lean back and around his shoulder. "Wade. Hey, man—you want to get out of here?"

The guy turned around. He was good-looking, maybe not as gorgeous as Quinn, but absolutely attractive. He glanced over at Aaron before looking back at Quinn and smiling lazily. "Yeah? You just got here—you sure?"

"Yeah, absolutely."

Wade nodded and gulped the last of his drink. Then the two of them were moving toward the door, not touching, not looking at anyone, just smooth and relaxed and purposeful. Aaron couldn't think of anything to do other than just watch them go.

AARON parked in the driveway of his parents' house and hurried toward the barn. He'd had another sleepless night, only one of several in the week since Quinn had shot him down, and after he'd finally dozed off he'd slept through his alarm. His brother Danny was cleaning manure out of one of the outdoor rings, and checked his watch ostentatiously when he saw Aaron.

"Third day this week, Aaron. Not good."

"Shut up. It's, like, five minutes." This could be useful—Danny was annoying, but he was a distraction, and that was exactly what Aaron needed. "Is Carol even here yet?"

"It's not your job to get here before the client; it's your job to get here on time." Danny was clearly enjoying himself.

"Well, it's not your job to supervise me; it's your job to shovel shit. So, you know, carry on...." Aaron pointed his chin to the far side of the ring. "I think you missed a couple bits over there."

"You used to be a nice, respectful young man, Aaron. Whatever happened to you?" Danny stepped closer and peered into his brother's face. "Is the abstinence thing finally getting to you? I'm telling you, man, the monk's life is not a happy one. It's time for little Aaron to get some loving."

"Jesus, Danny, leave it alone." And maybe his brother caught the extra edge in Aaron's voice, or maybe he was just distracted by the car pulling into the parking area, but either way, he stopped teasing.

"That's Carol now."

"Yeah." Carol's summer convertible had been switched for a winter-appropriate Mercedes SUV, but as soon as she was out of the car, her long, straight frame and silver hair were clear identifiers. She was pushing fifty but in better shape than just about any other boarder, and her undyed hair and practical clothes made her a particular favorite of Aaron's mother, whose appearance was similarly matter-of-fact. Carol was not a woman that Aaron wanted to disappoint or annoy, so he needed to get his mind back on his job. Sexual frustration and an unrequited crush were problems for his own time, not for his workday.

So he met Carol at the barn and stood with her as she groomed Titan. The family had bred and trained the horse before selling it to Carol, so Aaron knew all of his strengths as well as all of his tricks. And Carol tended to want to spoil him. That combined with the horse's naturally dominant personality to create a potential problem.

"Carol, that's your space—don't let him push you around like that."

Carol frowned. "But he's just looking for some love—he wants his face scratched."

Well, the damn horse wasn't the only one feeling a little affection-starved, and not the only one with an itch he couldn't scratch himself. But Aaron forced himself to stay good-natured. "But you're not his scratching post. Push him back into his own space, and then if you want to give his face a rub, on your terms, that's fine. But if you let him push you around down here, don't go acting all surprised when he thinks he's the boss under saddle, as well."

Aaron needed to save that idea and think about it later. Had the problem been that he'd invaded Quinn's space? Was the guy determined to be dominant, and he'd just pushed Aaron off to make a point? The first time they'd met, Aaron had been sitting still, and Quinn had moved into his space—but, damn it, Aaron needed his face scratched! How was he supposed to get what he wanted if Quinn wouldn't let him make the first move? He had a new sympathy for poor Titan.

"He's a mean man, isn't he, honey?" Carol cooed to the horse, but she had pushed his head away from her, so Aaron decided to take the victory. Carol went back to her grooming, but apparently it didn't take all of her attention. "Ooh, Aaron, I meant to tell you—my hair stylist is back on the market!"

"Jesus, Carol, please...."

"No, Aaron, you are way too sweet and good-looking to be sitting around at home! And he's a catch—really handsome, and funny, and he owns the salon, so, you know... not poor. He's a bit older than you, but that can be good, right? I mean, a little experience...."

"Carol, I beg you to stop." Aaron had never come out to his family, and had certainly never told them he was a virgin— they had just known. Probably because Sara, his ex-girlfriend, was friends with his sister-in-law and was *not* known for her discretion. So she'd probably told Stephanie, who'd probably told the rest of his family—and apparently they'd had no hesitation about telling others. But just because *they* were open about it all, it didn't mean that *he* had to be. Especially when he was counting on work to get his mind off his love troubles.

"I'm going to go set up the arena—bring him in when he's ready, okay?" He didn't wait for an answer, just headed off down the aisle.

His mother was in the barn office that was attached to the viewing lounge, and when he walked by, she waved him in. Her close-cropped hair was more gray than its natural red, but otherwise she could have passed for a woman half her age. Not as lithe as Carol, maybe, but just as fit, with muscles built from hours in the saddle, followed by even more hours with hay bales and the manure fork. And she'd always been careful of the sun, replacing her riding helmet with a baseball cap as soon as she was off a horse, so her skin was still quite smooth, with only smile lines to indicate all the years that she had lived and laughed through.

Today, though, there was a frown creasing the space between her eyes. "Baby, I need you to cover my next class, I think. Danny set up the interviews this morning. I don't know if he's deliberately saying that he doesn't need my opinion or if he just forgot that I had lessons. Doesn't matter, though, because I want to at least meet them all, if they might be going to work with my horses, and you can cover the classes, right?"

Aaron looked at the board where the day's lessons were noted. "Not Marion and Alexis, Mom! You'll be back in time for them, right?" Some aggravation might be a welcome distraction, but Marion and Alexis were more than *some* aggravation. They'd been around the barn for years, never getting too serious about their riding but never actually quitting, either, and they seemed to confuse seniority with actual competence. Aaron sometimes wanted to ask them why they were still taking lessons, since they already knew everything there was to know about horses, but he didn't think his mom would appreciate it. And they did seem to recognize *her* expertise, generally—it was Aaron they had a problem with.

His mother just laughed at him. "No, I wouldn't set them loose on you again, not this soon. I think Danny's still cleaning up the blood from the last mauling."

"More than just blood, Mom. I think they took actual chunks out of me."

"Oh, don't be such a baby, Baby." His mother smiled at him brightly as she sorted through the sheets of paper on her desk. "And stop getting here late—you're the one who wanted to move into town, so don't even think about using that as an excuse."

"Five minutes! There was traffic!"

"Oh, no, sweetie, you misheard. I said *don't* use that as an excuse." She gathered whatever papers she thought she needed and headed for the door. He was behind her when she stopped and spoke to somebody out in the barn. "Oh, we're ready? Excellent. I'm Wendy Miller, the owner and head coach. Come on in here." She turned around, and Aaron backed up to get out of her way. She checked the top page of her stack of paper and continued speaking toward the door. "You've already met Danny, our barn manager, and this is my other son, Aaron. He trains our horses and does a little teaching. You're Quinn?"

Aaron stared at the man in the doorway, and saw his equally surprised reaction. Quinn recovered quickly, but Aaron stared for far too long, and he knew that his mother and brother both noticed, but he didn't care. Quinn was there.

"Do you two know each other?" Aaron's mother was not a fan of subtlety.

Aaron wasn't quite ready to answer that, but Quinn filled in smoothly. "Kind of—we live in the same neighborhood."

His mother didn't look completely satisfied with that answer, and Danny was obviously aching to get Aaron somewhere for a grilling, but they kept it businesslike in front of Quinn. Aaron was thankful for small mercies. His mother glanced down at the paper she was holding. "So, Quinn, you're applying for a job in a horse barn, but you don't have any experience working with horses. Why do you think you'd be good at this?"

Quinn looked a little less smooth, but he still handled the question better than Aaron could have. "I'm a hard worker, and a fast learner. I don't have much experience, but that means I won't have a lot of bad habits or wrong ideas about how things should be done. And I like animals, and I'm not nervous around them, or anything like that."

Wendy nodded and glanced over at Danny for the next question. He said, "Why are you leaving your current job?"

"I'm working construction now, and I'm just getting really sick of the noise. I go home and my ears are ringing for hours every night. I figured a barn would probably be quieter, most of the time." Quinn seemed exceptionally casual, as if he didn't care much about his answers. Aaron realized with a start that the guy was assuming he wouldn't be getting the job. He thought Aaron was going to veto him.

"Okay, thanks." Wendy looked at Danny. "Why don't you take Quinn around the property, introduce him to a couple horses and give him an idea of what the job would be? I need to help Aaron get the arena set up for Carol."

Aaron didn't actually need help and his mother was perfectly aware of that, so he knew he was heading for an interrogation. He didn't really want to let Quinn out of his sight, but he comforted himself with the thought that the man's contact information must be on his job application, so he wouldn't be lost forever. Well, he wouldn't be lost if Aaron was willing to compromise his ethics by misusing information that Quinn had released for a totally different purpose. And Aaron was pretty sure he was more than willing to do that. So he stood quietly as Quinn followed Danny out into the barn, and completely ignored the curious looks his brother was shooting his way.

"So—you live in the same neighborhood. That's why you were staring at him like he was your personal messiah?" His mother waited, but didn't seem too surprised when Aaron said nothing. "So would you have any reason to object if we decided to hire him?"

"No!" Aaron tried to modulate his tone. "I mean, no. I wouldn't object. No reason to. No."

She raised an eyebrow. "And would you object if we hired him and I decided to start enforcing the 'no dating co-workers' rule?"

"What? Since when have we had that rule? Danny *married* a co-worker, for God's sake!"

"So can I take that as, yes, you would object?" She smiled softly. "How well do you know him, Baby? He's very good-looking, obviously, but... is he someone you think you might be serious about?"

Aaron had learned to be cautious about confiding in his mother. She was a good listener, but she sometimes had trouble accepting that listening was all she was required to do. She didn't want to just know about her children's problems; she wanted to solve them. Her way. He didn't like to think how that approach might be applied to his current predicament. He was saved from needing to make a decision when he looked through the viewing window into the arena and saw Carol doing her pre-mounting tack check. "I need to get in there and get things set up." His mother's voice stopped him before he reached the door.

"Just be careful, Aaron. Good looks are nice, but good hearts are a lot more important."

He couldn't argue with that. "But what if he's got both?"

"If he's got both, Baby... then he's a keeper." She smiled again as she brushed past him out into the barn aisle. "For a guy like that, I would be willing to make an exception to the 'no dating co-workers' rule."

"That's not a real rule!" he called after her, but she ignored him. He turned toward the arena and caught a glimpse of Quinn and Danny, touring around the edge of the barn toward the back paddocks. Aaron had no idea how he was supposed to concentrate on a lesson with Quinn so close by, but he knew he had to try. He remembered his theory that maybe Quinn was like a dominant horse who didn't react well to having his space invaded, and he resolved to try to play it cool. He wasn't sure how long he'd be able to maintain the façade, but he had no other ideas. And he really, really wasn't ready to give up.

He managed to pay some attention to the lesson, but his mind was definitely elsewhere. When Quinn returned from his tour, he spoke to both Danny and Wendy for a few minutes, and then headed out toward the parking lot. Aaron fought the urge to chase after him. He wasn't sure if his "dominant horse" theory made any sense, and he wasn't sure what that meant, really, if Quinn *did* turn out to be wired that way. Was Aaron looking to be dominated? Not in a Dom/sub way, he was pretty sure, but if it turned out that the only way to get what he wanted was to let Quinn take the lead, Aaron could handle that. He thought he could, at least....

"Aaron? Am I doing this right? He seems like he's hanging back a little." Carol's question brought Aaron's mind back to business. Damn it, he should have been the one pointing that out, not the rider.

"Yeah, good, I'm glad you noticed that yourself. I was hoping you would." A little bullshit could be good fertilizer, his mom sometimes said. "What do you think the problem is?"

Aaron kept his mind on his job for the rest of the lesson, managing not to stare at the other candidates who appeared for their interviews. It wasn't easy, though. He was practically dancing with impatience by the time he was able to tell Carol to cool Titan out. He would usually stay and chat with her while she walked the horse around, but there was no way he had the patience for that, not with Danny and his mother standing in full sight inside the viewing room, obviously talking about the people they'd interviewed.

Aaron tried to be cool as he opened the door, and forced himself to pour a cup of coffee before turning to join the conversation. "So, anybody good?"

Apparently his efforts to sound casual were not totally successful, because Danny's face split into a huge grin as soon as Aaron spoke. "Anybody good-*looking*, you mean?"

"No, I could see if they were good-*looking* for myself. I wondered if there was anybody who would be good for the job." Aaron didn't think he'd convinced either of them, but at least he hadn't totally admitted defeat.

"There were a couple strong candidates. Lots of experience, and a good way with the horses." His mother was watching his reactions closely. "But—Quinn wasn't bad. I mean, he knows nothing, but at least he admits that. And Danny said he was good with the mares—gentle, but didn't let them push him around."

Jesus, that was a beautiful mental image for Aaron. He liked the idea of Quinn being soft, but firm. Calm and experienced. He needed to get his mind off that, because he really didn't want to get hard in front of his mother. "That sounds okay."

"Whatever you're up to, Aaron, is it going to get in the way of the barn? I mean—he'd be okay for the job, probably." Wendy was pretty demanding of her staff, so that was about as glowing a judgment as Aaron thought she would give to anybody. "He actually seemed like the fittest of them all, and after Dennis and his endless injuries, I'd be happy to have someone who was in shape to do the job. But I don't want you mooning around after him. And I don't want you crying, either, if it doesn't work out. And I really, really don't want the barn slapped with a sexual harassment lawsuit, or something." Aaron could see her talking herself out of the idea.

"When's the last time you saw me crying, Mom? And, seriously, I'm not really the harassing type."

Of course Danny couldn't stay out of the conversation. "When's the last time you let a rider take a totally unbalanced horse over a jump four times in a row without saying anything? I wouldn't have said you were the absentminded instructor type, either, but apparently things change." He was mostly teasing, but that didn't mean that the truth of it didn't sting.

And when Danny stung Aaron, Aaron fought back in true little-brother fashion. "Go shovel shit, Danny. That's your job. Don't worry about the actual lessons—I can take care of the hard stuff."

"Aaron!" His mother's voice was hard. "Watch the attitude. If this is the way you're going to act, then I don't think we need to worry too much more about your opinion, or about trying to please you." She nodded her head toward the door. "We're short-staffed until Danny decides who he wants to hire, so you need to chip in more than you have been." She turned toward her older son. "Danny, should he get started on the stalls, or is there something more important for him to be doing?"

Danny couldn't even do Aaron the favor of looking smug. "Stalls would be great, man. Thanks."

Aaron didn't fight it. He'd been mouthy, and for no good reason. His brother was secure enough to not be hurt by it, thankfully, but that didn't mean that Aaron should be a snotty bastard. Sexual frustration was apparently a fact of his life, and he needed to just get used to it and keep himself under control.

He set his coffee cup down on the counter and headed out to the stalls. He tried to focus on the job, but it wasn't easy. The two people in the office behind him were deciding his fate, and he really wasn't sure that they were going to give him what he wanted.

CHAPTER THREE

As SOON as Quinn got in the door of Candy's, he headed for the bar. That was his usual pattern, but as a rule he was looking for a drink. This time, he was looking for the bartender.

The guy was there, polishing glasses, and he came over cautiously when Quinn leaned over the bar. "Hey, man—what can I get you?"

"Did you send me out there on purpose?" Quinn didn't know whether to be angry or confused. "Did I just take a day off work to go waste my time applying for a job that they're never going to give me?"

"Why wouldn't they give you the job?" Damn, the bartender was pretty good at looking innocent. Quinn really couldn't tell if he was faking or not.

"Are you saying you didn't know that the kid's family owned the barn?"

"'The kid'? Aaron, you mean? Yeah, I knew it was his barn. He's the one who told me about the job. So what?" The guy leaned back and placed the polished glass on the counter behind him, then picked up another and continued his work. "Is there some reason Aaron wouldn't want you working at the barn? I mean, you've treated the kid fair, right? You haven't been an asshole to him, have you?" And there it was, the glint in the bartender's eye that let Quinn know that the whole thing had been a setup.

"Fuck you, man. I haven't done anything that wasn't for his own good."

"Yeah? You think going home with Wade the other night, right in front of him—you think that was for his own good?" At least the bartender had gotten over his passive-aggressive bullshit.

"Yeah, I do. The kid had a crush, and he needed to get over it. I tried the gentle way, and it didn't work. So it was time for the hard way."

"He needed to get over it because it would be good for him, or because it would be convenient for you?"

"Both." Quinn might have had more to say, but his phone rang and vibrated in his pocket, and that was a bit of a distraction.

He clicked the phone open. "Hello?"

"Quinn? This is Danny Miller—from the barn this morning?"

Shit. This was going to be embarrassing, getting rejected in front of the asshole bartender. Quinn turned away from the bar. "Yeah, hi."

"So, we'd like to offer you the job, if you're still interested. And if you're still available to start tomorrow, because we're really jammed up out here."

That was a surprise. Maybe the kid wasn't out to his family, or couldn't tell them why he didn't want Quinn hired. But it put Quinn in an interesting position in terms of the bartender. He turned back to face the man, and smiled sweetly. If the guy hadn't liked Quinn rejecting Aaron in the bar, how was he going to feel about hearing Quinn reject his whole damn family over the phone?

It was too bad, though, because the barn had been really appealing. The people seemed solid, and the horses had been great. And Quinn was getting really, really sick of his current job.

"Quinn? You still there, man?"

"Yeah, sorry." Quinn had never really trusted his instincts

about anything other than sex, but he'd never really had much luck with taking the time to think things through, either. "Yeah, okay. Sure, I can start tomorrow. Thanks. What time should I be there?" Quinn might be getting himself into a really awkward situation, but at least he had the satisfaction of seeing the smug look slide off the bartender's face.

QUINN arrived at the barn early the next morning, following a pickup truck along the winding road and into the parking area. It was Danny who climbed out of the truck, not Aaron, and Quinn told himself that the weird twist in his stomach was relief, not disappointment.

He climbed off his motorcycle and undid the helmet. It wasn't raining out, but it was misty, and he was glad to have the water-covered visor out of the way.

"Hey, man. Nice bike." Danny's smile was genuine. "They don't make 'em like that anymore."

Quinn was inclined to agree. "Yeah, it's not bad. And considering how old it is, it's pretty low-maintenance."

"That's the Beemer for you, huh?" Danny circled around the bike, and Quinn got out of the way. It wouldn't hurt to have his new boss think he had good taste. "An R-75/7, right? What year?"

"Damn, good eye. It's a seventy-six. Do you ride?" Quinn looked around the barn area. "Bikes, I mean."

Danny just shook his head. "Nah, not any more. Not bikes *or* horses." He headed for the person-sized gate in the fence that separated the parking area from the barnyard. Quinn followed him. "The wife doesn't approve."

"I've heard of guys who aren't allowed to ride bikes, but you work in a barn and your wife won't let you ride *horses*?"

"Well, 'won't let' is a little strong. But she's so worried the whole time that it's not really worth it." Danny seemed pretty philosophical about it all.

"Damn. She's always felt that way?" Quinn wasn't sure what the polite way was to ask his new boss why he'd married the neurotic mess.

"Nah. And *she* still rides. But I broke my back a couple years ago and it freaked her out."

"You broke your *back*?" They were at the barn now, and Danny reached out and pressed a green button on the wall. The garage door in front of them slid up, and they were facing the main aisle of the barn.

"No boarders or anyone else allowed unless staff is here, but there'll be days when you're the one to open the place, once you get trained. As a general rule, boarders shouldn't show up until eight, but we've got a couple exceptions, for people who want to get in a ride before work." Danny stepped inside and started down the aisle. "And, yeah, broke my back. Now my spine's fused in a couple places, and I can't really ride all that well anymore with it like that. So it's not a huge loss." He cast a quick look at Quinn, as if trying to decide whether to say anything more. "To tell you the truth, I was never much of a rider. Nowhere near as good as Aaron. So it's not altogether bad to have an excuse for staying on the ground—it'd kinda suck to get my ass kicked by my baby brother."

This was a lot of information. Quinn was intrigued. "Horse or bike? When you broke your back?"

"Hell, horse. Motorcycles are safe compared to these bastards." Danny's smile was quick, but in the context, Quinn wasn't sure if it was comforting or actually a little creepy.

The next several hours were spent learning the barn routine. They fed the horses, checked supplies, and made seemingly endless trips to various paddocks, turning the horses out for the day. Quinn knew that Danny was giving him the quieter horses and then monitoring him closely, but he was still pretty pleased that there were no mishaps. The animals were huge, but they were willing to be guided, even by somebody who didn't know what the hell he was doing.

Then it was time to start cleaning the stalls. Danny showed Quinn how to do it and then watched for a while before wandering away, leaving Quinn to work. When Quinn's peripheral vision picked up a tall, blond shape standing in the doorway of the stall where he was working, he assumed Danny had returned. "You've got thirty-two stalls? This is a pretty big job, every day. Couldn't they wear diapers?"

"I'm not sure anyone's tried that." The voice was familiar, but clearly not Danny, and Quinn turned quickly toward the stall door.

"Aaron. Hi." Quinn felt like he'd been caught trespassing. He wasn't sure if he should play it cool or be up front. He decided to try honesty, for a change. "I, uh... I hope you don't mind that I took the job. I wasn't sure if you'd be okay with it, but I figured you could have said something to your family, if you didn't want me here." That wasn't exactly true, of course. Mostly Quinn had figured that taking the job would piss off a smug asshole of a bartender. But he didn't think he needed to share that with Aaron.

"No, of course I don't mind. I'm glad you're here." His smile was just as shy and sweet as Quinn remembered. "Is everything going okay? Did Danny show you around?"

"Yeah, everything's good. Thanks."

"Except that we have too many stalls to clean."

"I was just kidding about that. I mean—if you didn't have all the stalls, you probably wouldn't need to hire extra help, right? So I shouldn't complain."

Danny's voice called from farther down the barn. "Aaron—take Quinn with you when you go to get the ponies, okay? Show him how it's done?"

"Okay," Aaron replied. Then he turned back toward Quinn. "I

was just going to go down now, if you've got time."

"Yeah, I don't think the shit's going to go anywhere without me." Quinn leaned his manure fork against the stall wall, and maneuvered around the wheelbarrow to get to the door. "It's okay to leave it like this?"

Aaron nodded. "If it was just the fork, you'd want to put it away, because somebody might not notice it and they could put a horse in the stall with it. And horses are really good at injuring themselves in creative ways—a fork would be like Christmas morning for some of these dolts. But with the wheelbarrow there, you're fine."

Aaron led the way to the tack room, where they grabbed halters and lead ropes, and then out toward the back of the farm. The drizzle had stopped, and it was almost sunny, so Aaron didn't seem interested in hurrying. He gave Quinn a tour as they went, and a lot of the information was a repeat of what Danny had already told him, but it was interesting to get the different perspective. And it was nice to hear Aaron talking about something he clearly loved. He was calmer than he'd been with Quinn before. The alternating shyness and ferocity were gone, replaced with a quiet confidence, and it was enough to make Quinn start thinking of the guy as less of a kid, more of a man. Of course, he was still a virgin, and still almost certainly looking for more than Quinn was willing or able to give. Quinn needed to remember that.

Aaron stopped walking when they were beside a gate leading into a small paddock. The grass was worn away right around the gate, but it was lush and green everywhere else. Aaron nodded at the tall, black horse standing in the middle of the paddock. "This is Oscar. He's just arrived from the track, and we're giving him a little time to get used to the place before finding him friends to get turned out with."

"The racetrack? He's a Thoroughbred?" Quinn wasn't sure if that was a stupid question or not, but there was no point in pretending he knew more than he did.

Shying Away

"Standardbred, actually. A trotter." Aaron whistled and the horse raised his head briefly to look at them before returning to his grazing. "We usually do the Thoroughbreds, but I wanted to give this guy a try."

They continued along the gravel path to the next paddock. It was larger, and there were several horses in it. The grass was shorter in this enclosure, and there was hay piled in a couple of places near the gate. "We buy our hay from out in the valley," Aaron explained. "Any halfway flat land we've got, we put horses on it. A good part of our property is foothills, and we back right onto the Lower Seymour Park. Nice for some interesting trail rides, but not a lot of space to waste."

Quinn nodded. That made sense, and it was kind of interesting. "I grew up out in Calgary. We can see the mountains, there, but it's not like here. We're not right *on* them." It had taken him a while to get used to feeling so geographically restricted in Vancouver: sea to the west, mountains to the north and east, and the border to the south. The mountains that were remote and scenic in Calgary had felt too close, like they were looming over him, when he'd first moved to Vancouver.

"Yeah. They're beautiful, but they're not really the easiest places to build." Aaron smiled companionably and they continued walking.

Quinn wasn't usually a big talker, but he found himself wanting to keep this casual conversation going. "I worked on a house up in West Van, one time. They'd built it right on the side of the mountain but the foundations weren't good enough. The whole damn thing was sliding down the hill." Maybe that sounded a little too dramatic. "Not fast, or anything. Just a couple inches a year. But it was enough to pretty much wreck the house—they aren't really meant to be mobile."

"Don't get Mom started on all that—how we're pushing into areas we should stay out of, and how the mountains should be left the hell alone. She'll talk your ear off."

–39–

"You don't agree?"

"No, I totally do. It's just... she gets pretty fired up about it."

They had reached another gate, by then, this one opening onto a large field. "This is where we keep horses that live outside. It's mostly retirees, so all we have to do is come down once a day and check on them, and the rest of the time they're on their own. But we're a bit overcrowded right now, so we stuck a few of the lesson ponies back here as well." Aaron shrugged. "Honestly, ponies on all this grass—it isn't ideal. That's why we bring them inside for the day, put them in stalls without much hay. We just sent the bigger ones back, and none of them are likely to founder, but they're still getting pretty fat. We need to get rid of some horses, make some damn space." He hit the buckle of one of the halters against the metal gate, and a loud clanging broke the peace of the morning. "They know that sound—always carry some treats down with you, bang the halter, and then give them the snack once they get to the gate. Otherwise you'll spend half your life chasing the little bastards around the field."

They slipped through the gate, Quinn closed it behind them, and they stood waiting as a cluster of horses appeared from over the peak of the hill. "Don't give treats to the retirees—we don't want them coming for the snacks. Just the ponies. That one's Buster, with the light mane? And the black one is Dumbledore— no idea why. The two brown ones that look the same? Genghis and Attila."

Quinn nodded. He was feeling a bit overwhelmed with all the information, but it was interesting. He had no idea what "to founder" meant, but he hoped he wasn't really expected to know. He also hoped he wasn't about to find out why two innocent-looking ponies were named after bloodthirsty conquerors. He tried to focus on what Aaron was saying, but it wasn't easy, not with the kid standing there, beautiful and confident, practically glowing in the dim, watery sunshine. Damn it, Quinn didn't want this to be a problem. He just needed to keep his discipline.

They caught the ponies and Aaron showed him how to lead two at a time. Then they headed back up to the barn. Wendy was there when they arrived, and she took over Quinn's instruction, walking him through the right way to groom the ponies and tack them up. Most of the riders would do that themselves, but Quinn should know how to help.

By the time Quinn was done trying to shove all that new information into his brain, Aaron was back, leading a huge gray horse into the barn. Quinn tried to ignore their arrival, just focusing on his work. He wasn't expected to clean all the stalls himself, thank God, but he was certainly supposed to be getting as many done as possible. He wasn't there to moon over the hot, young son of the owner. It wasn't fair to his employer, it wasn't fair to Aaron, and damn it, it was stupid for Quinn to do it to himself. He knew the kid was off limits, so he'd be much better off to just get that message to his dick and stop getting worked up.

All his resolutions meant nothing when Aaron appeared at the door of the stall Quinn was working on. The kid was stretched out, his hands gripping either side of the wide doorway while he leaned his body in, letting his arms reach back behind him. It should have looked awkward or strange, but for Quinn it just highlighted the size of the guy, and the quiet, effortless strength of his body. "Want to come meet Casper?" Aaron asked, and Quinn was moving before the question was even finished.

Aaron seemed proud of the horse, and Quinn had to admit that he was beautiful. Apparently the dark spots on his otherwise almost white coat were called dapples, and he was a Hanoverian, and Aaron was going to work on dressage with him, because the horse was being trained as an eventer and they needed to be good at dressage as well as cross-country and show-jumping, and....

"Are you in information overload, man?" Aaron was looking at him with amused concern. "Your eyes are kinda glazing over." Then the blush started. Quinn realized that it was the first time he'd seen that coloring at the barn. "Or am I just boring you to death? I'm sorry, I just—I don't know. I forget that not everyone's into all this."

"No, man, I wasn't bored. Just... like you said. A lot of information. I think possibly my brain's full."

"Yeah, sorry." Aaron looked sheepish, even though it was Quinn who'd just admitted to a weakness. "You don't really need to know all that stuff, not right now. Sorry."

"I appreciate you taking the time to tell me," Quinn started, but Aaron was already backing away.

"I'll just get on with tacking him up."

Well, that wasn't what Quinn had meant, but it wasn't really his place to tell the guy how to spend his time at work. And it wasn't like Quinn didn't have plenty of his own work to do.

Danny came by shortly after and suggested that Quinn take some time for lunch. It was still only about eleven, but Quinn had been at work since seven and was more than ready for a break. And Danny seemed to approve of Quinn's stalls, so he didn't feel like a total slacker. They sat together in the viewing lounge, eating their packed lunches and watching Aaron ride. The finer points were well beyond Quinn's understanding, but he was beginning to get the idea that the whole "riding" thing was a bit more complicated than he had thought. And apparently Aaron was pretty damn good at it.

"So, you're living down in the West End?" Danny asked, and Quinn turned away from the window and nodded. "Right in Davie Village?"

That was a pretty polite way of asking whether Quinn was gay. Of course there were straight people living down there, but they were in a minority. "Yeah. About a block south of Davie."

"My wife and I live just down the way—the blue house, third from the highway?" Quinn didn't think he was really expected to have noticed the house. This was just Danny's way of letting Quinn know he was straight, he figured. Off limits, so don't try any of your fag come-ons around here. It wasn't like Quinn would have been remotely interested, anyway. Danny did look like Aaron, in size and coloring, but his face had none of the delicate sensuality of his brother's. Not to Quinn's eye, at least. But he wasn't here to rate his boss's attractiveness, so he nodded noncommittally and took another bite of his sandwich.

"We've got two kids," Danny continued, and Quinn wondered if the guy was still trying to prove his heterosexuality. But then the questions started. "How about you? Are you living alone?"

Quinn had a mouthful of food, and he was glad of it. He wasn't entirely prepared for this conversation, maybe. So he just nodded again, pointing to his full mouth as an explanation for his reticence.

Danny seemed happy to carry on. "I've never actually lived alone. Parents' house, then roommates, then married. I don't know if I'd like it. You don't get lonely?"

And the bastard had caught Quinn with an empty mouth. "I'm not home that much, really."

"Yeah, fair enough. Work, and that bike—you must get some great riding in. And a social life, of course. There's some excellent bars down there, huh?"

Danny's tone was nothing but friendly, but Quinn still didn't know quite what to do with this conversation. How little could he say without seeming churlish? "Yeah, they're okay." That felt like he needed a bit more. "It gets old after a while—the same places, the same people." Damn it, that was maybe a bit closer to the truth than he'd planned on getting.

"Well, you get *some* fresh blood, right? Innocent farm boys moving down to the big city for a little adventure?"

And there it was. This little talk hadn't been about warning Quinn away from Danny; it had been about Aaron. But what message was it that Danny was trying to send, exactly? Maybe it was time for Quinn to stop working to decode Danny's signals and try to send one of his own. "I guess there are, yeah. I guess if the kids can't handle themselves, they'd be better off staying at home."

That caught Danny's attention. He nodded in slow agreement. "Yeah, maybe so. Maybe it's all a part of growing up, eh? Getting in over your head, getting caught in the current and coughing up a little water, and coming out of it stronger."

Quinn wanted to object, wanted to say that not everybody got in over their heads, but he couldn't. Gay or straight, probably everybody got their hearts at least bruised. Which made him wonder why he was treating Aaron like he was so fragile. Yeah, Quinn would end up hurting the kid; that was pretty much a given. But if Danny was right, Aaron was going to get hurt by somebody, sooner or later, so why not by Quinn? God knew the attraction was there—Quinn had been jerking off thinking about Aaron's wide shoulders and tight ass since the first time they'd met.

Danny was busy packing up the remains of his lunch, so Quinn allowed himself to look out through the viewing window to watch Aaron taking directions from his mother. He looked relaxed, but serious, as if he was really concentrating on what she was saying. Instead of the familiar churning of lust, Quinn felt a wave of affection for the kid. He was so genuine, so sincere. He was too trusting, but Quinn liked that about him. So maybe Danny was right, maybe it *was* just a matter of time before Aaron got in over his head. But Quinn didn't want to be the one holding the kid beneath the water.

So Quinn would focus on being Aaron's friend. It was for the best, especially now that they were working together. That didn't mean that the kid wouldn't still get him hot, though—Quinn knew himself too well to imagine that he'd ever be immune to that attraction. But he'd just practice a little self-control, and get the hell away from the barn before he found someone to help him quench the flames. It wasn't perfect, but it was the best Quinn could do.

CHAPTER FOUR

"WHAT are you even trying to do?" Aaron had been watching Quinn for quite a while now, and he couldn't figure it out.

Quinn's head swiveled around quickly. But he took a moment before he spoke. "Shit. I can barely even remember anymore. She—she wouldn't lift her foot. And so I tried to shift her weight off it, like you said, and then she wouldn't shift her weight either, so I tried to get her moving, and then... I don't even know." He had been looking frustrated, but that was fading to sheepishness. "I just—you said I had to be the boss. I couldn't let her win."

Aaron moved out of the office doorway and into the aisle of the barn, where Quinn had the mare standing. "Yeah, you've got to be in charge. But, you know, don't be a dick about it." He lifted his hand to the mare's neck and gave it a gentle scratch. "Which foot was she being stubborn about?"

"Back left," Quinn said, stepping toward the wall for a better view of the whole show.

Aaron ran his hand gently down the mare's neck, along her spine, and down over the curve of her rump. He firmed his grip a little as he slid down her leg, and when he reached her foot, he gently leaned into her hip with his shoulder, and then lifted. The foot came up easily.

"Son of a bitch," Quinn said, and Aaron tried not to grin. Quinn had been a good sport about all the lessons he'd had to learn since he'd started at the barn, and he didn't usually mind being teased a little, but Aaron didn't want to push it.

"I swear to God, I did all that, and she just wouldn't move it."

"Well, she's a mare. You know, they can be a bit moody." And, okay, Aaron had tried, but he couldn't resist entirely. "A stubborn horse needs a confident, calm handler. A horse like Chloe, here, she needs to feel a certain level of maturity from her riders." Quinn was already giving him a dirty look, but Aaron decided to keep going and make it all perfectly clear. "I'm not quite sure *why* she feels that from the, you know, the *eight-year olds* who handle her on a regular basis but not from you. Maybe something you should think about for a while."

Wendy's voice called out from the office before Quinn could respond. "Quinn, you about ready to go?" A quick glance told her that he wasn't. "What's the matter? Getting cold feet?"

"I've had cold feet since you first suggested it." Quinn moved over to take Aaron's place by Chloe's side. "But, no, I'm still working on it."

"He was having a bit of trouble with the grooming, Mom. Maybe he's not quite ready to ride, yet." Aaron watched for Quinn's reaction, and was pleased with the dirty look he earned.

"Get moving, Quinn. Aaron, stop distracting him." Wendy sounded good-natured, still, but Aaron moved to obey anyway. She was his mother, *and* his boss. Her word was law.

"If you need any more lessons, Quinn..." he started as he moved away.

"What was that last one, man? 'Don't be a dick', I think?" Quinn nodded as he leaned over to pick up the mare's hoof. "Good lesson for everybody, probably. Right?"

Aaron smiled to himself as he walked away. Everything was fantastic with Quinn being at the barn. It had only been a couple of weeks, and already it felt like he'd always been part of the team. He'd been a little reserved at the start, maybe, but once everyone had gotten to know each other, he'd opened right up. And he was great with the horses—a real natural. It made it that much sweeter when Aaron could find something to lecture him about, of course.

Everything was just as Aaron had dreamed about, right up until the end of each day, when Quinn drove off on his insanely sexy black motorcycle and Aaron climbed into his truck, alone. Then Quinn was off doing whatever the hell he did, and Aaron was at home, jerking off until his dick was raw without even getting temporary relief from the sexual frustration.

He wasn't really sure what he'd thought would happen. Quinn wasn't a dominant damn horse, fighting to protect his autonomy. If he *had* been, then Aaron's plan of being nonaggressively welcoming would have worked by now. No, Quinn wasn't dominant; he just wasn't interested. Aaron needed to accept that. He and Quinn were not going to happen. They were friends, though, and that was valuable. Aaron needed to be sure he didn't mess that up by pushing too hard for something more.

He forced himself to be slow and patient with the ground training he was giving Oscar, the off-the-track Standardbred. The horse had pretty good manners overall, but there were a few things that were different in a boarding barn, and it was Aaron's job to make sure the horse understood. That meant Aaron had to be consistent, which was a bit of a problem lately. His mother had already spoken to him a couple of times about keeping his mind on his work, and he had to admit that she was right. He had been pretty distracted since Quinn came to the barn. At least Quinn didn't seem to notice; or maybe he did, and he was just generous enough to not embarrass Aaron by commenting.

So Aaron stayed with Oscar until he was behaving like a proper horse should, and then turned him out into his field and practically ran back to the outdoor ring. He was almost too late, but Quinn was still there, and he was still on the horse. It was a bit frightening for Aaron to realize that he was apparently capable of a whole new level of lustful thoughts, above and beyond the pinnacles he had already reached. But seeing Quinn on a horse, sitting strong and tall, balanced and comfortable—it was incredibly appealing.

But that wasn't what Aaron was supposed to be focusing on. He was trying to be just a co-worker, and a friend. "Looking good, man!" he called, and gave a "thumbs up" sign when Quinn glanced in his direction.

"He's doing pretty well," Wendy agreed, speaking loudly enough that both men could hear. "For a first lesson." She walked over to stand next to her son, Aaron outside the railing, her inside, both of them looking in Quinn's direction. "Keep working on your steering," she called. "Try to use your legs and seat more than your reins."

"You're starting him on that already?" Wendy had a fairly set pattern for instructing new riders, but apparently she was jumping way ahead of things with Quinn.

"He's got good balance, and good hands—and he's really paying attention. I thought I'd give it a try. Save him from having to unlearn a bunch of stuff later on." Wendy kept her eyes on her student.

"'Later on'? I thought... you were talking as if this was a one-time thing. Letting him get a feel for what it was all about. But now you're thinking about 'later on'?"

The feigned nonchalance of Wendy's shrug would have fooled someone who didn't know her. "Well, we'll see." She called out to Quinn, "Good. Take her around the cones once more, and then we'll call it a day." She glanced over at her son and spoke casually. "I think he can handle something more than Chloe. I was thinking about putting him on Clay next time."

Aaron didn't know how to react. Clay was Wendy's own horse, retired from competition but still trained beyond any other animal in the barn. "You barely even let *me* ride Clay!"

"Well, *you* get carried away sometimes. I think I can trust

Quinn to follow directions." She started to walk toward the middle of the ring. "Okay, Quinn, bring her in here and you can dismount. Good ride."

Aaron just stared after her. His mother was always enigmatic, but this was a new level of opacity. Why was she being so nice to Quinn? Did it have anything to do with Aaron? What could she possibly be up to? But he knew from experience that there was no way he was going to get her to talk until she wanted to, so apparently this was just one more thing for him to put out of his mind.

He watched Quinn dismount and give Chloe's neck an affectionate pat. Then horse and rider started off toward the barn, and Aaron forced himself not to follow. He had work to do, and he wasn't going to get over Quinn if he spent all his time mooning around after him. So he controlled his body, but he didn't even try to fight his eyes, and they enjoyed the sight of Quinn and his mount until they were out of view.

AARON forced himself to leave the barn that afternoon with only a casual good-bye to Quinn. They were co-workers. Friends. That was all. Aaron needed to control his fantasies and accept reality.

But that left him right back where he'd started: a virgin, with no prospects of more. Actually, he was both better and worse than when he'd started, and both were because of Quinn. He was better because he'd actually had some experience. One earth-shattering blow job might not be much for some people, but for Aaron, it had been huge. If nothing else, it had made him absolutely, positively certain that he was gay, where before he had just been pretty damn sure.

On the other hand, Aaron's encounter with Quinn had made his situation quite a bit worse, because it had shown him that

Quinn was right. Aaron *would* be more comfortable if his first time was with someone he really cared about. But the only person he'd found that he cared about wouldn't give him the time of day. So where did that leave him?

He stepped out of the shower he'd been trying to relax in and rubbed the steam off the bathroom mirror. He stared at his reflection. "Option One: don't have sex until you find someone you really care about." That sounded okay, except he couldn't imagine finding someone he cared about while his entire mind and body were focused on lusting after Quinn. "Option Two: have sex with someone you don't care about." It wasn't appealing, but it was looking like his only option. Maybe if he could just get laid, he'd go back to being his calm, reasonable self. Maybe he'd be able to see Quinn as a pushing-thirty party boy with nothing but a string of dead-end jobs to his name. And a hot motorcycle.

Damn it! He'd been doing all right until he thought about the goddamned motorcycle. Now he had to think about Quinn riding it, the way the bike would hum and throb between his legs as his hands caressed the gears, the way Quinn would be able to coax just the reaction he wanted from the sleek black machine, leaning into the corners, revving the engine when he wanted more power....

Ten minutes later, Aaron was back in front of the mirror. "Okay. That was a setback, but you can still do this." He opened up the medicine cabinet and pulled out the eyeliner pencil. He'd bought it on a whim his first day in the Village, some sort of declaration, he supposed, although he really wasn't sure just what he was declaring. Gayness, he guessed. He was here, he was queer—it was just too damn bad that nobody seemed to care.

He'd worn the eyeliner around the apartment a few times, but he'd never been brave enough to take his act outside. But if he was going out to get laid, which he was pretty sure he was, he needed all the help he could get. A little eyeliner wasn't much, but it was something. It made him feel sexier, more confident, less like an innocent farm boy and more like....

More like an albino Adam Lambert. He'd put on way too much. He smudged the creamy line under his lashes and it blurred nicely, giving him a sort of smoky-eyed look. He repeated the process on the other side and squinted at his reflection, then made his eyes wide. Not bad. He hoped.

He pulled on the same black button-down shirt that he'd worn that first night with Quinn. He wasn't sure if he should consider it lucky or unlucky, given all that had happened, but at least it had gotten him noticed. And he could still remember the way it had felt under Quinn's sensitive fingers, the way the fabric had dragged across his hard cock when Quinn had untucked the shirt, the way....

Damn it, no. He was not going to do that again. It was time to get the hell out of the apartment.

He made it down to the street and started walking. It was drizzling, of course, so there weren't many people outside, but he was sure the clubs would be as crowded as ever. He thought about trying somewhere new, but his feet took him toward Candy's. If nothing else, maybe Paul would be working, and he'd have somebody to talk to. Maybe Aaron would take the guy up on his offered introductions.

The club was loud, as usual, and Aaron could feel what little confidence he'd had deflating under the musical assault. Instead of working his way over toward the dance floor, as he'd been considering, he headed for the bar. His usual seat was occupied, though, so he weaved through the crowd until he was in front of the bar.

"Aaron, hey." Paul was already pouring Aaron's rum and Coke, which kind of wrecked his plan to order something different. "You haven't been in for a while."

"No, I guess not. I got kind of busy." He accepted the drink and handed over enough for payment and a generous tip.

"Yeah? Like, *busy*, busy? That guy got the job at your barn, right? Quinn?"

"Yeah, he did. Thanks for sending him up, I guess." Aaron hadn't known how to feel about Paul's interference when Quinn had first told him about it, and he still wasn't sure. "But, no, not *busy*. We're just friends."

"Good. I didn't want to have to tell you that he's been in here practically every night for the past couple weeks. Leaves with a different guy each time."

"You didn't want to tell me that, huh?" Aaron tried to choke back the bitterness. It wasn't Paul who was whoring around, it was Quinn. And whoever it was, it wasn't any of Aaron's business.

Paul looked cautious. "Well, you know—I didn't want you to be upset *when* I told you."

Aaron nodded and took a long pull of his drink, holding the ice back with his teeth. "So, you said maybe you could introduce me to some people?"

"Yeah, absolutely." Paul smiled happily and looked around the bar. When he looked back at Aaron, his face wasn't so happy anymore. "But maybe not right now. I don't really see anybody you'd want to spend time with, I don't think."

Of course. So Aaron was on his own. He took another pull from his too-sweet drink and then set the empty glass on the bar. Paul moved to make him another, but Aaron found his voice. "No, wait. Give me...." What would be suitable? What did a desperately horny virgin drink? What magical elixir would keep Aaron from thinking about his cock-tease slut of a co-worker going home with a different guy every night for the past two weeks while Aaron was sitting at home jerking off to his memory? "Tequila. Please. Just a shot." Paul raised his eyebrows but moved to comply. "No, wait. Two shots. And a beer."

"Gonna be one of those nights, huh?" The voice was right in his ear, and for a moment, Aaron thought it was Quinn. But it wasn't, and he realized that even before he turned his head.

The guy was beautiful. Muscular, like Quinn, but taller, and fair instead of dark. But there was something about his eyes, the way he was watching Aaron like he was the only guy in the room, that was just like Quinn. Like Quinn had been the first night, before he'd decided that slow, virginal Aaron wasn't worth his time. Aaron found his voice. "Uh—yeah, maybe."

"You ordered two shots. You planning on sharing?"

Well, he hadn't been. But, okay, maybe that was the way these things were handled. Aaron tried to find his inner flirt. He remembered his eyeliner, and that helped. "I could maybe be persuaded."

The guy nodded slowly, his eyes never leaving Aaron's. "Well, we're in luck, because I can be *very* persuasive." He moved in a little closer, and Aaron forced himself not to back away. He wanted this. He did.

Paul was back with the drinks, and Aaron paid without making eye contact. He didn't really want Paul's judgment on this guy. Instead, Aaron lifted one of the glasses and held it out, halfway to the other man's lips. "All right, then—persuade."

The man smiled, and Aaron could feel it now, the same predatory vibe that he'd gotten from Quinn that first night. Well, maybe not quite the same, but similar. Close enough that when the man slowly raised his hand to grip Aaron's forearm, Aaron didn't resist. And when the guy gently moved Aaron's arm out of the way and moved his body closer, Aaron didn't move away. He let the man kiss him, smooth lips gentle at first and then more demanding, the stranger's tongue slipping between Aaron's uncertain lips and circling, probing, before withdrawing. The man leaned back, obviously pleased with himself, and looked meaningfully at the shot glass still in Aaron's hand.

Aaron passed it over. He didn't know quite how he felt about whatever was going on, but he didn't really think he needed the cloud of two shots of tequila to add to his confusion. The man accepted the glass but didn't drink it, not until Aaron reached over and claimed the second glass from the bar. "Nice to meet you," the man said, raising his glass in a toast. Aaron raised his own in reply before bringing it to his lips and knocking the shot back.

He reached for his beer as a chaser and took a long swallow. When he brought his head back down, the man was staring at him, and Aaron offered the bottle. He had no idea if that was what the guy was after, but it seemed polite. And it seemed a little late to be worrying about swapping spit. The man accepted and drank a little, then edged in next to Aaron at the bar. He nodded to Paul. "Two more, please."

So much for Aaron's decision that he didn't really need multiple shots of tequila. He took a nervous sip of his beer. If this was going where it seemed like it was going, how did he feel about that? He honestly had no idea.

"I'm Brendan," the man said, and Aaron nodded. Considering that they'd just been making out, it made sense to exchange names.

"I'm...."

"Not for you." A new voice, and this time Aaron knew that he recognized it. What he *didn't* know was why Quinn was interfering.

Aaron resolutely didn't turn toward Quinn, speaking to Brendan instead. "I'm Aaron. It's nice to meet you."

Brendan was looking back and forth between Aaron and Quinn, an amused smile playing across his lips. "It's nice to meet you, too, Aaron. Quinn—good to see you again. I don't mean to be rude, but Aaron and I are having a private conversation, here. Maybe you'd be happier somewhere else."

Quinn ignored Brendan and spoke right to Aaron. Not that Aaron was going to turn around to look at him. "This isn't the right guy, Aaron. Trust me, he's an asshole."

Okay, maybe Aaron *was* going to turn around to look at him. "I remember you saying the same thing about yourself. Damn, I guess maybe I have a type."

"Okay, yeah. I mean, he's more of an asshole than I am, but neither one of us is a good choice, man. Seriously."

The new shots had arrived, and Aaron didn't wait for any rituals, just grabbed his and gulped it down. A swallow of beer soothed the burning in his throat, but did nothing to cool his temper. "It's really not your call, Quinn. Paul says you've been pretty busy the last couple weeks—maybe you should go back to whoever it is you came here for."

"Yeah. Fucking *Paul*. I'm sure he had a lot to say. But it's none of his damn business, Aaron. Come on, man—you know me, right? Trust me. Brendan, he's... he's not who you want."

And that was too damn true, but if Aaron let himself think about it, he'd be right back where he'd started from. Instead, he reached out for the still-unconsumed shot waiting on the bar and drank it quickly, then finished his beer. He needed to get this show on the road. He turned, reaching for Brendan's shirt. He could still remember how that had felt, touching Quinn for the first time, brushing his fingers against his hard chest. He wanted that feeling again, and Quinn had made it crystal-clear that it wouldn't be coming from him. But this time, instead of touching his partner's strong chest, his fingers ran into Quinn's back.

Quinn had insinuated himself between the two of them, rubbing up against Brendan's body like he was in heat. And he was saying something, whispering in Brendan's ear. Whatever he trying to sell, Brendan seemed to be buying it. He was smiling, his hand wrapped around Quinn's back, pulling him closer, and then sliding down to his ass and squeezing, hard.

Aaron had no idea what to do. He wasn't prepared for this, not for any of it, and the tequila was starting to make its presence known, a strange, wavy heat flowing out from his stomach all the way to his muddled brain. "Hey," he tried, but neither Quinn nor Brendan paid any attention to him. "Hey!" he tried again, a little louder, but the only reaction was Quinn leaning farther into

Brendan. Aaron could see that he wasn't whispering into his ear any longer, he was sucking on his neck… long, slow kisses that made Aaron's knees threaten to give out. Although that could also have been because of the tequila. "Hey," he said again, but it was to himself this time, because Quinn and Brendan were already moving away, heading toward the door. Aaron couldn't think of a single thing to do other than fall back onto his bar stool and watch them leave.

"That sucks, man," Paul said, and Aaron really wanted to hit him in the face. He didn't need the obvious to be pointed out to him. "Weird too. I mean—with their history, and all."

Aaron didn't know if he could stand to hear about Quinn's history with another man, but he knew that his curiosity would kill him if he didn't ask. Quinn had been right—Fucking *Paul*. "What history?"

"You don't know? That guy put Quinn in the hospital the last time they hooked up."

The words didn't make any sense. Aaron swiveled on his stool, trying to focus on Paul's face. "What—what are you talking about?"

Paul shrugged. "I guess he likes it really rough. Didn't take no for an answer. Quinn ended up… I don't know the details, but he was pretty messed up."

Aaron's world was spinning, and it wasn't just the booze. "But—if he's—if you know he's…. If you know the guy's abusive, or whatever, why do you let him in the place?"

Another shrug from Paul. "Well, you know—who's to say it wasn't Quinn's idea? You know, something kinky that went too far? Like I said, I don't know the details."

"But—Quinn's out there with him!" Aaron was starting to panic.

"Yeah, that's what I said, it's weird. But I guess it proves that he did like it, last time…."

But Aaron wasn't listening anymore. How clueless could Paul be? Quinn was out there with a—a rapist, practically, and it was all because Aaron had been too stubborn to listen to his friend's advice. Quinn had sacrificed his own safety in order to keep Aaron from getting hurt. He lurched toward the door and made it outside, but there was no sign of Quinn or Brendan on the street. And Aaron didn't know where either of them lived. He cursed the tequila that kept his brain from functioning properly before pulling himself together enough to find his phone and hit a speed-dial number.

When Danny answered, he sounded like he'd just woken up. "Aaron? Are you okay?"

"Yeah, I'm fine. But I need Quinn's address. And his phone number. Whatever you've got, I need it."

"What's going on, Aaron? You're sure you're okay?"

"Fuck, yeah, I'm fine! But I seriously need Quinn's information. I'll explain tomorrow. For now, please just trust me." That was what Quinn had said to Aaron. Trust him. And Aaron hadn't, and that meant that this was all his fault. But Danny was apparently a better person than Aaron, because he was on the job.

"Okay, I've got to go down to the office. This had better be worth it, Aaron."

"It's seriously important. Honestly." And, damn it, Aaron could hear the slur in his voice himself. He should have known better than to keep talking.

"Did you just say 'honeshly', Aaron? Are you drunk?"

"Yes, I'm drunk. But that doesn't mean this isn't important."

"You're not going to go over there and make a fool of yourself, are you? I mean, I tried to let him know that you were available, and that it wouldn't be the end of the world if you guys hooked up. But if he hasn't made his move by now...."

Aaron didn't know if he could stand the embarrassment of hearing how his brother had gone about trying to fix him up.

Luckily, he had more important things on his mind. "Danny! The address and phone number! Please."

"Okay, okay." There was a pause. Aaron closed his eyes and tried to imagine his brother making his way to his small home office and then turning his computer on. It was a laptop, at least, so Aaron didn't have to wait through the whole start-up.

"All right—oh. Shit. The address is a PO box. That probably won't help, huh? You're not looking to mail him a letter? But there's a phone number—do you want that?"

"Fuck. Yes, though, give me the phone number."

Danny said it twice, and then Aaron hung up without saying good-bye. He couldn't afford to let his drunk brain get distracted from remembering the number. He dialed, and almost slammed the phone against the brick wall next to him when it clicked over to voice mail. "Quinn? It's Aaron. I need to talk to you. About Brendan. I didn't know. I made a mistake. Please don't go anywhere with him, okay? Quinn? I'm really sorry...."

Aaron let the phone click shut as he leaned back against the wall and then slid down it until he was sitting on the sidewalk. He wasn't really that drunk, but he somehow didn't have the energy to stand upright. He'd been mad at Quinn for being who he was. It wasn't like the guy had ever denied that he slept around—hell, given the way the two of them had met, it was pretty damned obvious.

But Aaron had somehow thought that he had a claim. And he'd gotten jealous, and that had made him stupid, and now Quinn was the one paying the price. Quinn, who had known exactly what he was getting into, and had gone ahead anyway, all in order to help Aaron out. To save him.

That was friendship. Whatever other stupid ideas Aaron had been playing with, he couldn't let himself forget that Quinn was his friend. A good friend. And Aaron wanted to be a good friend back. He buried his head in his hands. He only hoped he'd have the chance.

CHAPTER FIVE

QUINN took one more quick look in the bathroom mirror. He didn't look too bad, all things considered. If he kept his face angled right, the bruise along his jaw could just seem like a shadow, or some dirt. And everything else was covered by his clothes. He was sore enough that he was dreading just the ride to work and really trying not to think about the pain of a full day of physical labor. Still, not too bad. And it had absolutely been worth it.

He took the stairs down to his bike more slowly and carefully than usual, but otherwise, everything was going smoothly. And the ride out to the barn was okay, with only a few twinges going around corners. He was pretty sure his ribs weren't broken, but they were definitely bruised. Maybe sprained—he'd heard of sprained ribs, but wasn't really sure what that meant. It sounded right, though. It sounded like a good description of the way he was feeling. He wondered if anyone was ever diagnosed with a sprained *body*.

Danny's truck was in the barn lot when Quinn pulled in, and that was a little unusual, because Quinn was pretty sure that he had been asked to open the barn that morning. But the more alarming sight was Aaron, storming out to the parking lot like a furious Viking. Shit. Quinn had known the kid would be mad about the man-stealing, but he'd hoped they'd be able to keep it out of the barn. The presence of Danny's truck seemed a bit more sinister now. Quinn had realized pretty quickly that Aaron didn't keep much from his brother, and it was hard to miss Danny's protective streak. Maybe he'd come in early to fire Quinn for being an asshole to poor little Aaron. At least that would give Quinn an excuse to crawl back into bed and heal for a couple days. And whether Aaron liked it or not, Quinn was sure he'd done the right thing the night before—right for Aaron, and right for himself too.

Quinn was barely off his bike before Aaron was grabbing him by the arm. There was no time when Quinn would like to have his shoulder wrenched like that, but this day was even worse than usual, and he jerked away. Aaron barely seemed to notice the rebuff, charging on without pause.

"Are you okay, Quinn? I tried to find you last night, but I couldn't—why didn't you answer your phone? And we need your real address, not a PO box!"

It took Quinn a moment to regroup. This wasn't what he'd been expecting.

"What's going on? Did something happen?"

There had been a time in his life when Quinn had lived in dread of the midnight phone call telling him that something had gone wrong, but that time was over. He really couldn't imagine what Aaron was so upset about.

"Did something... did something *happen*? Jesus, Quinn! Paul told me that the last time you went home with Brendan... he said it went really bad."

Oh. Fucking Paul, with his big mouth, chipping in after it was too late to do any good. If Paul had known that Brendan was a violent psycho, why the hell had he stood there and let the guy move in on Aaron? "Everything's fine, Aaron. Paul's an idiot. You shouldn't listen to him." Quinn tried to shift to the side and move around the kid, but apparently Aaron didn't think they were done talking.

"So nothing happened? I mean, nothing bad?" He peered closely at Quinn, who was glad that his mirror time had helped him figure out the best angles from which to be seen. And it was still mostly dark in the parking lot, which helped. "I tried to call you—I left a voice mail. Did you get it?"

Quinn patted the pocket of his jacket, but he didn't feel the familiar weight. "I didn't get a message. Honestly, I don't even know where my phone is. It might be here at the barn, actually...."

"So everything was fine with Brendan? But, then, why were you so worked up about me going home with him? I mean, if he's an okay guy...."

"He's not an okay guy. He's an asshole. And, yeah, the last time wasn't good, but that was because I was drunk and he caught me by surprise. This time—sober, and prepared. So everything was fine."

Aaron fell back a little at that, and Quinn took the opportunity to deke around him and head for the barn. He started to half-turn in order to call back over his shoulder, but his ribs objected. So he looked straight ahead but raised his voice loud enough to be heard. "Sorry if you were worried, Aaron. Paul should have kept his mouth shut."

"But...." Quinn could hear Aaron following close behind him. "What happened? I mean...." Aaron caught himself, as if he'd realized that he maybe didn't want to know the details of Quinn's night.

And it would probably be better to leave it at that, but for some reason, Quinn stopped walking and turned to face his friend. "Nothing happened. I mean—no sex. There was never any way that was going to happen. I just wanted to get him the hell away from you." He started walking again. "Seriously, Aaron. You want to get some action, that's fine. But you should find a nice guy. And you should trust your friends when they tell you that somebody's bad news."

"I'm sorry about that. Sorry that I didn't listen, I mean."

Quinn didn't want to look at the kid's face, but he certainly did sound genuinely regretful.

"I was just... I was mad. And it made me stubborn."

That was a new twist. "Mad? You were mad at me, or at somebody else?"

"No, at you."

Quinn shot a quick glance at the kid and saw his miserable face.

"Paul told me—he told me you'd been in a lot lately. And going home with lots of people. So, you know—I was—I was jealous, or whatever."

Shit. Quinn *had* been going home with a lot of guys. He'd been fucking anything that moved, trying to get his mind off Aaron. But.... "Why the fuck would Paul tell you that? I mean—he's a bartender, not a goddamn detective. It's none of his business."

"And it's none of my business, either." Aaron's voice was dull and resigned. "I realize that. I mean, I don't own you."

They were inside the barn now, and the conversation stopped when Danny came out of the office. "Quinn. You're alive." He didn't sound too surprised. "Aaron was overreacting. What a shock."

Quinn wondered what Danny would say if he pulled up his shirt and showed the rainbow of bruises that Brendan had left all over his torso. Aaron hadn't been overreacting by that much. It had been a fight, this time, instead of the abuse Quinn had taken the time before, but that didn't mean he hadn't felt the hits. Still, he was glad he'd done it. He could have found some other way to get Aaron away from the guy, probably, but there was no substitute for the satisfaction he'd felt as his fist connected with the asshole's face. Repeatedly. Quinn was not a rabbit, running scared. He was a predator himself, and just because he'd had one off night didn't mean that he was going to let himself start thinking like a victim. He'd known that, mostly, but he'd still needed to prove it to himself. And, just as importantly, to

Brendan.

Aaron was still looking at him, his alarm fading into confusion. Quinn tried a smile, sending it toward both of the brothers. "Well, I appreciate the concern." And he did. It had been a long time since Quinn had felt like anybody cared whether he lived or died. "But, seriously, it's no big deal. I'm good." He shrugged his jacket off and hung it on the wall above his knapsack, in what had become his spot. "You already did the hay, right? Have you done the feed yet, or should I do that?"

Danny looked at him closely, and Quinn realized that his bruised jaw was probably visible from the angle Danny was standing at. Damn it. His mirror practice hadn't prepared him for the scrutiny of two people in different locations. Thankfully, Danny seemed to decide not to mention the mark. "I fed already. Aaron had me convinced there was going to be an apocalypse or something, so I came out pretty early." He looked over at his brother. "Aaron, why don't you figure out who stays in for lessons and who goes out? Quinn and I can go back and grab the ponies."

Aaron looked like he was maybe going to object to the division of labor, but Danny was already starting for the door, and Quinn made sure to be right on his heels. He didn't need any more scrutiny from Aaron.

They walked through the arena and out the wide doors that led to the paddocks. The sun was rising, casting the farm in a warm glow. "Clear day, for a change," Quinn said.

"I'm sure it'll cloud over soon." Danny didn't say anything more for a few moments. Then he asked quietly, "You're okay to work today? If you're not up to it, I can cover for you."

It was the surprise that did it. It wasn't that Quinn was a suck—he wasn't the sort to get emotional about stupid stuff. So it was just that he hadn't been expecting the quiet expression of concern, the willingness to help out without demanding details as payment. That was the only reason he felt the sudden surge of emotions, actual tears welling in his eyes. He fought them back, and managed to answer before he embarrassed himself. "No, I'm okay." He kept his gaze resolutely forward. "Thanks, though."

Danny nodded. "Is this... is this something I should be worried about? With Aaron, I mean?" He lifted his baseball cap off his head and resettled it in the exact same position. "I don't mean—I don't want to judge, but is he hanging out in places where he's likely to meet people... you know, people who might not be safe?"

That was kind of a tricky question. Quinn had heard enough assholes equating gays with perverts or pedophiles; he wasn't interested in contributing to a whole new insulting stereotype. But he couldn't deny that sometimes people got hurt.

"I think—I mean, gay or straight, there's violent people out there. Violent men, mostly. So... you know. If you had a younger sister, you probably wouldn't be crazy about her going out to bars alone and picking up strange guys." That was true, but Quinn wasn't quite sure it was the whole story, so he kept trying. "Aaron's big, and he's fit and strong. So, you know, it's not like he's helpless. And he doesn't generally drink a lot, that I've seen, so that's good." Quinn wasn't sure how much more he had a right to say, but he decided to push it a little. "But, yeah. I'd be happier if he was trying to meet people some place other than in a bar. Seems like there's got to be somewhere better."

Danny nodded thoughtfully. "He tried the Internet, I know. When he was first... whatever. Coming out, coming to terms with all this. But he said he couldn't get a feel for what people were really like. He arranged to meet one guy, and I guess he was nothing like he'd seemed online. And there was another guy, Aaron met him and there was no... no chemistry, or whatever. But I guess, for the other guy, there was. He made a total nuisance of himself, following Aaron around to all the chat rooms and whatever. Trying to stake a claim, or something."

Quinn could see how that could put somebody off. "Yeah, that'd suck. But, you know, nobody actually gets *hurt*, online. Like, a nuisance is—it's just a nuisance. It's not a beating."

They were at the gate to the ponies' field, but Danny didn't open it. He looked out at the grazing animals and spoke quietly. "That's what happened to you? Last night? A beating?"

"No. Not last night." Quinn wasn't sure how much of this he wanted to get into with Danny. Danny with his wife and two kids and his house in the suburbs. "The first time, a couple months ago... it was pretty bad. But last night was just a fight. He got worse than he gave, I'd say. He was the one who ended it."

"The first time, though. He beat you up?"

Quinn looked down at his hands, and saw that he'd wrapped one of the lead ropes around his fingers so tight that they were turning purple. He forced himself to relax his muscles. "We should get those ponies in." He clanged the metal snap from one of the halters against the gate, and the discordant sound rang out across the dew-damp pasture. The ponies lifted their heads, and after a moment's thought, Genghis started ambling toward them. The other three followed.

Danny opened the gate and the two men slipped through. "What did the cops say? I mean—they couldn't charge him with anything?"

"I didn't call the cops." There it was. It had seemed reasonable at the time. He'd been humiliated and angry and hurt and maybe even afraid, and he'd just wanted to forget about the whole thing. But seeing Brendan in the bar the night before, Quinn had realized his mistake. By not reporting the son of a bitch, Quinn had left Brendan free to do the same thing to somebody else. Quinn had stepped in to keep the guy away from Aaron, but how many other guys had Brendan taken home since Quinn? How many more would there be before somebody finally stopped him? "I should have. I wish I had."

Danny didn't say anything until the ponies arrived. He was fastening Dumbledore's halter when he said, "It's not too late, is it?" He turned to face Quinn. "I don't mean to push, man. I know it's none of my business."

"It would have been your business if Aaron had gotten hurt." There were so many things that Quinn would never be able to forgive himself for. He'd thought he was past that—he'd thought that if he could keep himself from caring about people, he wouldn't have to live with himself after letting them down. He'd done the right thing by Aaron, keeping himself from acting on his attraction; how had it turned out that he'd still screwed up? How had a decision that he'd made before he'd even known the kid led to something that could have gone so horribly wrong?

"But Aaron didn't get hurt." Danny sounded serious. "You took care of him, and I appreciate it. A lot. I just—you know, if you want to help out some other people too, this might be a good time." He left it at that, leading the way up to the barn with the ponies.

Aaron seemed to have calmed himself down in their absence, although he still looked a little anxious. Quinn was careful to keep his face turned in the best direction, and he got to work without giving Aaron a chance for further conversation. The kid took the hint.

It was harder to work with sore ribs than Quinn had expected, and even more challenging once he realized that both Danny and Aaron were monitoring him pretty closely, looking for any signs of weakness.

He forced himself to keep going until his usual mid-morning break, trying to ignore the way the pain was starting to spread out from his ribs. It was just bruising. And he was using his muscles in weird ways, trying to avoid stretching his torso, and that was why he was sore. It wasn't a big deal.

He and Danny and Aaron usually took their break together, hanging out in the viewing room, or outside if it was a nice day. It was just casual, though, and when he saw Danny busy with one of the boarders, helping her put stable bandages on her warmblood, he grabbed his apple and headed into the feed room. It was quiet in there, and he could sit down, and that was all he needed. Just a little break.

He was sure he hadn't fallen asleep, but maybe he'd zoned out a little, because he didn't hear Aaron come into the room. The light touch on his knee startled him so much he almost tipped off his perch on top of two hay bales. "Jesus, Aaron! You should wear a bell around your neck, or something."

But Aaron was staring at Quinn's jaw. "He hurt you. Again. Because of me. Because I was too stupid to listen to you." The kid sounded like he was about to cry, and Quinn fought to keep his heart from breaking.

"No. He didn't hurt me—not bad. And it wasn't your fault, anyhow. If I'd reported him after the first time, none of this would have happened. But it's not a big deal, Aaron. Seriously."

"You're such a liar, Quinn." Aaron's voice broke, and there were tears in his eyes. Not out yet, thank God, not actually crying, but still—not something Quinn ever wanted to see.

He hopped down off the hay bales. "No, it's okay." His voice was quieter than he'd planned, and he was closer to Aaron than he should be. Way closer. Still, he didn't back away. "It's okay," he said again, and he had no idea what his hand was doing on Aaron's shoulder. His neck, almost.

God, his neck. Quinn could remember the way Aaron's flush had spread up from his chest, the way his pale skin had glowed with arousal. Quinn felt his fingers moving now, and the skin they found was so warm, so smooth. Aaron was standing still, frozen, but with the first contact, the first touch of skin against skin, no fabric between them, Aaron swayed forward. He exhaled, and Quinn's fingers spread out, letting himself feel the way Aaron's chest moved.

Aaron leaned forward, slowly, jerkily, and bent his head down a little. Quinn couldn't resist. Didn't resist. He tilted his neck back, and let their lips meet. It wasn't even a kiss. Just a brush of skin, an exchange of breath, and it was enough to make Quinn almost dizzy with desire. His fingers tightened on the spot where

Aaron's neck met his shoulder, holding onto the only still thing in the world that was swirling around them both. And then a horse neighed somewhere in the barn, and Quinn came back to himself.

His hand jumped away as if Aaron was on fire. "Fuck!" Aaron looked startled. "Shit. Sorry."

Aaron's face fell. "No. No, please, don't be sorry." He took a tentative step forward, but stopped when Quinn backed away. "It doesn't—" He swallowed hard. "It doesn't have to be a big deal. It doesn't have to mean anything."

At those words, Quinn's arousal disappeared as quickly as it had developed. For the first time, he wondered whether he was staying away from Aaron in order to protect the kid, or to protect himself. "I gotta go," he said hoarsely, and he didn't worry about being too rough as he pushed past Aaron and made his way out of the feed room.

DANNY hadn't given him a hard time about taking the rest of the day off. He'd seemed to assume that Quinn was going to go home to bed, and that was certainly tempting, but he had something more important to do.

It wasn't easy to go inside the police station, and once he made it in it was hard to explain why he was there. But he pushed past all that. The first cop he talked to didn't seemed too interested, but he called somebody else down, and the new guy took notes, and went to check on something, and came back to see if Quinn could stick around for a while. So Quinn sat on one of the hard plastic chairs lined up in the hallway. Then he was moved in to sit in a slightly more comfortable chair in a glass-walled conference room.

He waited there for quite a while, wondering what the hell he thought he was doing. Who he was trying to impress. Not Aaron, he was pretty sure. Maybe Danny, but that didn't seem right either.

A youngish woman wearing a sleek business suit opened the glass door and poked her head into the room. "Quinn Donahue?" When Quinn nodded, she came the rest of the way into the room. She extended her hand and he half-stood as he shook it. "I'm Amanda Clarke. I work as a Crown Counsel, and I've been assigned the Brendan Underwood case."

Quinn sat back down in his chair as Amanda pulled out a seat across from him. "I don't understand. It's—you've been assigned already? That happened pretty fast."

"Not really. We got our first complaint about him almost three years ago." She made a face. "I'm sorry, but—we've had trouble with witnesses. He seems pretty good at choosing people who...." She stopped, then started again. "The first alleged victim refused to cooperate with police. We only knew about the incident because the hospital called us. The second alleged victim was willing to give a statement, but he disappeared halfway through the investigation. No reason to suspect foul play; he was essentially homeless to start with. Third alleged victim gave contradictory evidence—we couldn't put him on the stand." She looked down at the thick file in front of her, then back up at Quinn. "And so on. You're number seven. That we know of. And I'm here to see if we can finally get this bastard behind bars."

Quinn didn't have the courage to ask whether any of the other assaults had happened in the time since he had failed to report the crime. He just nodded, instead. "Okay. Yeah. Well, however I can help...."

Amanda shuffled through the papers near the top of her file. "I've read your statement. I need to ask you a few questions. Please understand that nothing I say is meant to make you think that I personally disbelieve your story, or that anyone else associated with the prosecution disbelieves it. We're just trying to find the weaknesses before Mr. Underwood's attorneys do. You understand?" Quinn nodded, and braced himself. She gave him a sympathetic smile before looking back down at her notes. "You left the bar—Candy's on Davie?—willingly."

"Yes."

"And—I'm sorry, I know you've already been over this, but one more time—you went to his home, and you had a few drinks. And at some point, you realized that you were inebriated?"

"At some point? Well, when I got dizzy and passed out, I had a clue." Quinn couldn't even remember why he'd been drinking so much that night. It wasn't like he ever needed a real reason.

"But we don't have any blood tests on that. No way of knowing just how intoxicated you were, or how much alcohol you'd consumed." Quinn didn't say anything. He wasn't going to argue this with her. She waited, and then smiled softly. "All right. And when you woke up, you were restrained, and gagged." Quinn nodded. "Is this something completely outside the realm of your usual sexual experience?"

He wished he had a drink right then. "Not completely. It's not really my thing, but I've tried some stuff. But—" He wasn't sure if he wanted to say this, but he pushed on anyway. "Not both. Not gagged *and* tied up. Never that."

"Because you wanted to be able to object, either verbally or by moving away." He nodded, and she jotted a note down on her page.

"So, you were bound and gagged, and he had intercourse with you. Anal penetration?" She kept her eyes down on her notepad, but she could apparently see his nod with her peripheral vision. "But you left the bar with him, with the intention of having sex. So are we looking at sexual assault here, or was it just a date that didn't end quite the way you wanted it to?" She didn't sound judgmental, just businesslike, but Quinn's skin crawled anyway.

"I don't know. You're the fucking lawyer."

She waited, so he tried to come up with something more useful.

"I didn't—I didn't want to have sex with him. Not after being tied up and gagged. If I hadn't been gagged, I would have told him to fuck off, and if I hadn't been tied up, I would have beat the crap out of him. So you can call that what you want to."

She nodded. "I guess I can. Candy's—this is a bar that you frequent?"

"Yes."

"And about how many men would you say you've gone home with? Say, in the last year?" Quinn didn't answer right away, and she looked up from her papers. "Mr. Donahue?"

"A lot. And this son of a bitch is the only one I've ever gone to the cops about. So I might be a slut, but that doesn't mean that I'm crying wolf." He refused to look down, and she didn't look away from him. After a moment, she smiled.

"Well, all right. Thank you, Mr. Donahue." She nodded, and her smile widened. "The bastard miscalculated a little when he chose you, didn't he?"

Quinn didn't know what to say to that. He'd been one of the ones who hadn't come forward, so, no, really, Brendan had made a good choice when he picked up Quinn. His mistake had been the night before, when he'd chosen Aaron. But there was no need to go into all that. Instead, he just shrugged, and waited for the lawyer's next question.

CHAPTER SIX

"This is a shitload of pumpkins." The weak October sun wasn't giving them much warmth, but there was no breeze, and Aaron could see the sweat glistening on Quinn's skin as he spoke. It made it kind of hard to pay attention to the actual words.

"Uh, yeah. We need a lot." Aaron shuffled forward along the row of vines and used his pruning shears to cut off the next gourd.

"No, man. Nobody *needs* this many pumpkins. I mean, maybe a canning factory, or something. But no single family. It's insane."

"I've told you before. This isn't a single-family event. It's huge. The boarders, and a lot of the students, and the neighbors. And, of course, the loyal staff."

Quinn didn't say anything, and it was enough of a change in the rhythm of their conversation that Aaron looked behind him. Quinn was focusing a little too hard on lifting the mid-sized pumpkin into the wheelbarrow. "You're going to be there, right? Quinn, it's a tradition!"

"It's not *my* tradition." Quinn didn't sound like he was making an argument; he was just stating a fact.

"Well, okay, but it could be. I mean, you work here, now—you could hang out with us a little, you know." Aaron tried not to sound hurt. He knew that he wasn't the only member of his family who had made an effort to get Quinn more involved in their social activities. But he was the only one who seemed to take it so personally when Quinn politely declined, as he always did.

"Dude, I spend all day with you guys. I don't want to outstay my welcome, right?" Quinn put a final pumpkin in the wheelbarrow and then straightened his back and grabbed the handles. He started back along the row of vines, nodding as he passed Danny, who was returning to Aaron with an empty barrow.

"Cut faster, little brother. Will and Meg are on their way, and you know how much work we'll get done once they're here." Danny started scooping pumpkins into his wheelbarrow.

Aaron sped up obligingly. Danny wasn't joking; his kids were sweet, but at five and two years old, they did tend to get in the way of any serious labor. "We're almost done." He glanced over at his brother. "I don't think Quinn is going to stay for the carving."

Danny looked back at him, then shook his head. "Of course he's not going to stay, Aaron. Get over it." He heaved a large pumpkin up into the wheelbarrow. "I hate to say it, man, but... get over *him*."

"No, it's not about that." At least not entirely. "I just—don't you get the feeling that he *wants* to stay? Like, he just doesn't think that he should?"

"He's a big boy, Aaron. If he wants to stay, he will." One more pumpkin and Danny's wheelbarrow was full. He started back toward the hay wagon that they were loading the gourds onto, and Aaron watched Quinn as he approached.

Quinn had lifted the first pumpkin into his wheelbarrow when Aaron finally said, "We don't bite, you know."

Quinn let out an exasperated sigh. "I know that, Aaron."

"So why won't you stay? I mean, at least to give it a try. If it's no fun, you can head out, and I won't say a thing."

"Come on, Aaron. What the hell am I going to do at a—a pumpkin-carving block party?" Quinn straightened up and quickly stretched his back. "I have literally never heard of anything more wholesome and chock full of family values."

"Well, that's where you're wrong!" Aaron wasn't quite sure on his facts for this, but he was willing to try a little creativity. "Carving faces into pumpkins is actually an ancient pagan ritual. Some people still say that it's satanic and evil."

Aaron was watching closely, so he saw the grin Quinn tried to hide. "Well, I'm not actually all that into Satanism, either. I mean, yeah, it makes the whole thing a bit more interesting, but still not a party I really want to go to."

"Quinn...."

"Aaron...." Quinn's imitation of Aaron's whine was actually pretty good. It made Aaron wonder just how often he'd been using that particular tone of voice. It really wasn't too manly.

He decided to try another approach. "I just thought maybe we could hang out. But okay, if you're not up for it... I guess I could just spend a little time at the carving, and then go down to Candy's, or somewhere." For a couple of days after the incident with Brendan, Aaron had shied away from any mention of the bar. But it had been more than a week now, and while Aaron hadn't been back to visit the place itself, he wasn't above bringing it into conversation.

"Jesus, Aaron." Quinn heaved the next pumpkin so hard it almost tipped the wheelbarrow over. "Did you think about any of the other places I suggested?"

"The *church*? I'm not religious, Quinn. And even if I was, I don't think it would be a great place to pick up guys!"

"But that's the wrong mindset. You're not looking to pick up, right? You just want to meet people, get to know them, see if anyone knows anyone else who might be right for you—that's a good thing to do at a church, isn't it? I mean, they're *rainbow* services, for fuck's sake. Seems worth a try."

"I'm not going to start going to church just to meet guys. It's—I don't know, it's disrespectful or something." Aaron thought it was a bit weird, for him to be spending all this time talking to the guy he *did* want about how to meet a bunch of guys that he was pretty sure he *wouldn't* want, but at least he and Quinn were talking. And about something vaguely related to Aaron's sex life.

"Well, how about the volunteering, then? That sounded good."

"What possible skills do I have to volunteer for a gay community center? What am I going to do—tour around to high schools and tell gay kids that they should be happy with themselves? I can tell them that they'll never get laid, once they come out, but, still—happy, happy, happy!" Aaron didn't even have to look over in order to know the expression that would be on Quinn's face.

"Well, you could probably just volunteer to help out. You don't need to go in as an expert at something. But, okay, Captain Snarky, if you don't like those ideas, how about... hockey!" Quinn sounded genuinely pleased with himself.

"Hockey? Like, what?"

"Like strapping blades onto your feet and chasing around after a little chunk of rubber—hockey."

Danny joined them, and Aaron could see the interest in his expression as he heard their topic of conversation. Aaron just frowned at him, then turned his attention back to Quinn. "I don't get the connection. Are you saying that there's a gay hockey league?"

"Nah, not a whole league. But there's a gay team. I found it on the Internet." Quinn looked proud of his detective skills. "You said you played, right? When you were a kid?"

"I haven't worn skates for, like—seven years, maybe?"

"So? It's just a rec league. You don't have to be Gretzky. Go to a couple free skates to get warmed up, then give it a try. I don't think they even have tryouts—you just make the team if you show up."

"That sounds all right." Aaron didn't know why Danny thought his opinion was needed, but Aaron's disinterest had never kept his brother quiet. "You could just meet some guys. Not a big deal, just a casual thing."

Quinn nodded enthusiastically. "Take it slow, see if anybody seems interesting."

Aaron couldn't think of a new way to point out that he'd already *found* somebody interesting. And maybe Quinn was right; it wouldn't hurt to meet some new people. "You think this is a really good idea? Something I should do, for sure?"

Quinn's face turned cautious, as if he was vaguely aware that Aaron was trying to set some sort of trap, but wasn't sure just what it was or how exactly to avoid it. "Well, yeah. I think it could work out."

Aaron nodded. "Yeah, okay. I just—you know, it can be scary to try new things. I think I'd really—I'd really feel a lot more comfortable with something like this if I had a role model. You know, somebody to show me that trying new things is good. You know?"

Quinn still didn't get it. "Okay, maybe. What are you saying, exactly?"

Aaron could see Danny's grudging smile out of the corner of his eye. His brother knew what he was up to, and he approved, and that gave Aaron confidence as he spoke. "I'm saying that I'll give the hockey team a try... if you stick around for the pumpkin carving."

Quinn's head swiveled almost comically. "Come on, Aaron— are you serious?" He shook his head. "I'm just trying to get you to meet some people, to get to know them and see if there's a chance that you might want to get laid."

Aaron nodded. "Yeah. And I'm trying to get you to meet some people—to get to know them even though there's no chance of you getting laid. Some people have 'friends and acquaintances' as part of their social circle."

"I have friends...."

"Yeah? Who? And don't say Wade. Give me the name of

somebody you socialize with who you don't have sex with."

Quinn frowned, and looked over at Danny, who kept his face carefully neutral. Aaron followed his lead and didn't push, even though he wanted to. Finally, Quinn groaned in defeat. "Okay, yeah. I'll stick around for a bit. And you'll go give the team a try?"

"Absolutely." Aaron tried to hide his smile, but Danny caught his eye and Aaron couldn't help himself. Danny had thought Aaron should give up on getting Quinn to stick around for socializing? He grinned smugly at his brother. Danny had clearly underestimated Aaron's powers of persuasion.

There was a happy squeal from the direction of the house, and the men turned to see Meg, Danny's two-year-old, running down the row toward them. Quinn took a quick look at her and turned to Aaron. "Okay, if costumes are part of the deal, I'm out."

"Oh, come on, man, it's part of the fun," Aaron tried, but he knew Quinn wasn't going to believe him, so he gave up.

Meg arrived and was scooped up in her father's arms in a manner that totally disregarded the care that had gone into constructing the bright orange pumpkin around her torso. She gave her dad a quick, enthusiastic greeting, and then swiveled in his arms and reached out toward her uncle. Aaron stepped forward for his own hug, and by the time that was taken care of, Meg's mother and brother had arrived with their own greetings. It took Aaron a while to realize that their group was one person smaller than it should be. He looked around and saw Quinn down at the end of the row, transferring pumpkins from the wheelbarrow to the hay wagon. When he was done, he turned to look at them, and Aaron waved his arm vigorously. "Come here, man! You know Stephanie, right? And Meg and Will?"

Quinn raised his own arm in greeting, but kept his distance. "Yeah, hi," he called. He jerked his head toward the barn. "That's the last of the pumpkins—I can get started on the feeding, now, if you want...." He kept his head turned to wait for instructions from his boss, but his feet were already carrying him toward the barn.

Aaron was about to object, but Danny beat him to it. "That'd be great, man. But don't forget to come over to the house when you're done, all right?" Quinn nodded and turned away.

"I should go help him," Aaron said. "It's not fair for him to be working when we're all goofing off." He started to head for the barn, but he felt his brother's hand reach out and catch his shoulder.

"Give him a little space, Aaron. You got what you wanted— let him do it his way." Danny could obviously sense that Aaron wasn't quite convinced. "What, you think he's just going to take off?" His voice was teasing now. "Or disappear back to Magical-fantasy-hot-boy Land?"

Aaron could feel himself starting to blush, but this was just Danny, so he tried to be honest. "Not the first, no. But sometimes— yeah, sometimes I feel like the second could happen...."

Stephanie was busy reshaping Meg's pumpkin costume, but she looked up at him with a gentle smile. "You are just head over heels, aren't you?"

He thought about denying it, but he didn't think he had a prayer of pulling it off. Instead he just shrugged, and he felt Danny's arm wrap around his shoulders in an affectionate half-hug. "He's a good guy, Aaron. But that hockey thing—that sounded like a good idea, right? I mean, just to broaden your horizons, or whatever?"

Aaron nodded reluctantly. He wasn't crazy about the plan, but he couldn't think of a real reason to object. And with Danny and Quinn presenting a united front, resistance was futile. "I'll give it a shot, yeah." He shrugged loose of Danny's arm and bent down to swoop Will up into the air. "Did you get that, Will? A *shot*. Like, hockey? A hockey shot?" He took a firm grip on Will's ankles and flipped the boy around, dangling his fair head over the top of the pumpkin vines. "Did you get it, Will? Did ya?" Will screamed in delight, but Aaron was pretty sure that it was because he was being hung upside down, not because he had a keen appreciation of bad puns.

"All right, funny guys, let's get the rest of these pumpkins in." Stephanie ruffled Will's hair as Aaron carefully set him down on the ground, and Danny grabbed the handles of the remaining wheelbarrow. Together, they started off toward the house.

There was a flurry of activity once they arrived, and Aaron was so busy getting the bonfire started and setting out the pumpkins that he didn't have much time to wonder about Quinn. By the time the work was done, people were arriving, and there was plenty more to do.

Once the carving got started, there was a bit of a lull, and Aaron found himself looking toward the barn more and more often. It reminded him of sitting at the bar at Candy's, waiting and hoping that Quinn would arrive. The parking lot was between the house and the barn, and the cars were like the crowds of people that had sometimes obscured Aaron's view of the club's door.

It was strange; in some ways, he felt like they'd come a long way. He saw Quinn almost every day, and they were friends. At the same time, the dynamic hadn't changed much at all. It was still Aaron sitting and waiting, anxious and wondering where Quinn was, what he was doing. It had been almost two months since they'd first met, and Quinn was just as much of an enigma as ever.

But he was an honest enigma, Aaron realized as he saw Quinn appear from behind a large pickup truck. He looked hesitant, rubbing his hands on the sides of his jeans and coming to a complete halt when there was a particularly loud burst of laughter, but he started moving again right away. His eyes were searching the crowd, and when they met Aaron's, he smiled, and Aaron felt something strange and new swell up in his chest. He smiled back and worked his way across the lawn, dodging enthusiastic carvers with every step.

"You made it."

"That was the deal, right?"

"Yeah, I just—you took so long. What were you doing, feeding them each piece of grain individually?"

"What? Isn't that how you're supposed to do it?"

Aaron smiled, and nudged Quinn sideways. "There's beer and snacks and stuff over here." They walked toward a long folding table, covered with an array of potluck dishes. There were metal tubs filled with ice at each end of the table, and Aaron reached into one and pulled out two bottles. "You like Pale Ale, right?" Was it stalkerish to remember the beer that Quinn had ordered at the bar? Maybe a little, but it was too late to play coy. And it wasn't like Aaron hadn't already totally embarrassed himself on that front.

"Yeah, thanks." Quinn took the beer and twisted off the lid as Aaron did the same with his bottle.

There was a pause as they both surveyed the chaos before them. "You ever had any amputations at these things?" Quinn asked, and Aaron tracked his eyes to see a fairly small boy hacking away at his pumpkin with a large knife.

"Not so far, but...." Aaron set his beer down in preparation for going to help the boy cut a little more safely, but then the kid's mother arrived. That was all right, then. "You want to carve one?"

Quinn took a long swallow of his beer. "I don't know—I guess. That's what we're supposed to be doing, right?"

"It's not meant to be a punishment, man. We can just watch, if you want."

Another long swallow, and the beer was gone. Quinn set the bottle down on the table firmly. "No, I'm ready to carve. Let's do this." He rolled his shoulders like he was warming up for a fight.

"Okay, uh—go grab us a couple pumpkins, then, okay? I'll get knives and spoons."

"I'll carve with the knife—you can use the spoon."

"It's to get the seeds out, smart-ass. Seriously, if you're this much of a carving rookie, you'd probably better follow my lead." Aaron headed off for the other table before Quinn had a chance to respond.

When he returned with the tools, he found Quinn sitting on the ground just outside the main circle of carvers, two pumpkins next to him. But he wasn't alone. Aaron's dad was sitting in front of him, cross-legged and relaxed. Quinn, on the other hand, looked as if he was facing an interrogator. Aaron knew that the two men had met before, at the barn, and this had always been Quinn's reaction. It was a bit strange, but Aaron wasn't sure what to do about it all. His dad was laid-back and funny, and everybody liked him. Everybody but Quinn, it would seem.

Both men looked up at Aaron when he arrived. "Hey, Aaron," his dad said. "Quinn and I were just talking about family traditions. Well, I was doing most of the talking, I guess." He gave the innocent, clueless smile that Aaron had grown to realize meant that he was up to something. His dad's first name was George, and it hadn't taken long for the family to stick the label "Curious" in front of his name. He was a social worker by profession, and Aaron could see how, in that capacity, it would be important to make sure he had the full picture. It would be nice if he knew when to switch out of inquiry mode, though. Still, talking about family traditions didn't seem too offensive.

Aaron settled down on the grass and passed Quinn a knife. "Traditions, huh? Like your insane squash recipes every Christmas?"

"Well, I hadn't got to that one yet—and, really, I think I'd prefer that we refer to that as culinary creativity. Let's face it, none of us like squash anyway, so it's not like I'm messing with a favorite." He leaned back on his hands and watched as Quinn inspected his pumpkin. "You know what you're doing there, Quinn?"

Quinn looked up. "I think so. It's been a while, I guess, but— just cut the top of his head off and scoop out the brains? And then carve a face?"

"Make sure you cut the lid on an angle; otherwise it'll fall in." Aaron was glad to have at least a little wisdom to offer, and Quinn nodded seriously.

"Yeah, right. I'd forgotten that. Good tip." He looked down at the pumpkin as if he still wasn't quite sure how to proceed.

George didn't have a pumpkin of his own, so he had no distractions. "So, what about you, Quinn? Any fun family traditions?"

Quinn didn't even look up, and Aaron realized that he had known the question was coming. Apparently George had been telegraphing his intent pretty clearly. But Quinn kept his voice bland and level. "Not really, sir. And from the sounds of the squash thing, I don't think I'm missing out too much."

"Well, that's the fun of traditions, of course. It's not the action itself, it's the repetition, and the way it gives people a common bond. I bet you have some you haven't even thought of." George smiled. "Do you have family here in town?"

"No, sir," Quinn said, and then he rose gracefully to his feet. "I'm going to get another beer—can I get anybody anything?"

Aaron lifted his almost-empty beer bottle to indicate that he'd like another, but George shook his head. As soon as Quinn was out of earshot, Aaron turned to his father. "What are you doing, Dad? He obviously doesn't want to talk about all this. I had to work my ass off just to get him to come at all—why are you trying to grill him about stuff?"

"Aaron, it's hardly a grilling. And don't you wonder what's going on with him? I mean...." George had the grace to look a little unsure of how to proceed. "I realize that you and he aren't dating, exactly, but... you're obviously interested in him. It's my job as a parent to try to get to know him a little, and to see if there are any challenges that might come up in your relationship."

"*Challenges in our relationship?*" Aaron tried to keep his voice down. "Jesus, Dad, the biggest *challenge* in our *relationship* is that he's not interested! There IS no damn relationship. He thinks I'm totally innocent and don't know what I want—and you acting this way, *you* acting like I'm a stupid kid who can't pick his own friends—it's really not helping, Dad!"

"Now, nobody thinks you're stupid, Aaron."

"Well, I notice you didn't say nobody thinks I'm a kid. I moved out for a reason, you know. I'm trying to still be a part of the family, and come to stuff like this, but you need to give me a little space. I mean, if I make a mistake, I make a mistake. It'll be MY problem."

It sounded like a pretty good argument to Aaron, but his father just shook his head. "Wait and see, Aaron. Wait until you're a father, and see if it's that easy to just walk away and see your kids getting hurt."

"Nobody's getting hurt, Dad. Quinn's a good guy. I don't need to know every detail about his background to know that. And like I said, it's not like it's going anywhere, so... no need to worry about anything."

George looked like he was mustering a counterargument, but then Quinn was back, handing a bottle of beer wordlessly to Aaron before sitting down in front of his own pumpkin. "All right, Jack," he said. "Brace yourself—it'll only hurt for a minute." He plunged the knife into the pumpkin, at an angle as Aaron had instructed, and focused on his work. Aaron got back to his own pumpkin, and they labored in silence for a while.

Eventually, George stood up and rested a hand gently on Aaron's shoulder before saying, "I think I'll go check on the bonfire."

Once he was gone, Aaron felt like he should say something, but wasn't sure what. He decided for the direct approach. "Sorry about that—if he was being nosy, or whatever."

"Don't worry about it, Aaron." Quinn lifted his pumpkin up and swiveled it so that the face was toward Aaron. "What do you think? Bigger mouth?"

"Yeah, maybe a bit bigger," Aaron agreed, and they got back to work. Quinn was quiet, but that wasn't too unusual, and he seemed fairly content, working away with more care than Aaron had expected. Danny came by with the wheelbarrow to pick up finished pumpkins before Quinn was quite done.

"Damn, you're doing a good job, for a rookie." Danny leaned over to get a better view of Quinn's work. "I was expecting three triangles and a circle. But you've got a real artistic sensibility going on here."

Quinn looked almost startled, and set his knife down quickly, wiping his hands on the grass. "No. He's done." He stood up. "Do you want some help collecting them?"

"There's no rush, man, if you want to do some more," Danny said.

"And I can help Danny, if he needs it." Aaron stood up as well. "Seriously, if you want to keep carving...."

Quinn looked at them as if they were insane. "I cut a face into a pumpkin. You're going to set it out in a field for a couple days and then toss it on the manure pile. I don't think I need to worry about perfection."

"Well, that's a pretty hard way to treat poor Jack," Aaron said, reaching out to gently lift the pumpkin off the ground where Quinn had left it.

"Nah, I carved him tough. He can take it." Quinn picked up Aaron's pumpkin and added it to the pile on the wheelbarrow before turning back toward the others. "We ready to go put them in the field, or do you guys want to wrap them in little blankies or something?"

Danny snorted, and turned toward Aaron. "Your boy's got a bit of an attitude, doesn't he? Carves one jack-o'-lantern and thinks he's king of the pumpkin patch."

Aaron tried to ignore Danny's choice of words. Quinn wasn't

"his boy," and there was no point in pretending that he was. "Some people are just born arrogant, I guess. But, yeah, let's go lay them out. I'll wheel—Danny, you get more beers."

"Not for me," Quinn interjected. "I've got to drive soon."

"Not for a while." Aaron didn't want to sound like he was whining again, but he wasn't sure he could manage to restrain himself. He tried to sound less emotional, more reasonable. "It's not even dark yet—you need to see them all lit up in the dark."

Quinn checked his watch. "What, another half-hour, maybe? That's not enough time to get another beer out of my system."

"More for me and Aaron, then," Danny said, and headed over toward the table.

Aaron gripped the handles of the wheelbarrow and started toward the hill where the pumpkins would be displayed. He was, as always, aware of Quinn's presence, even though the other man was following behind him without a word.

They had placed all of the pumpkins from their load along the sides of the walkway before Quinn finally spoke. "You guys do this every year?"

"Well, yeah." Aaron wasn't sure what Quinn was getting at.

"It seems like a lot of work. I mean... you're all really into Halloween?"

Aaron shrugged. "Not really. I mean... it's like my dad was saying, it's a tradition. It's just nice to see everybody. It's not really about Halloween." He wasn't sure if it would be more awkward to ask a personal question or to keep himself from asking when it seemed so obvious that he should. He decided that he'd take the option that might get him a bit more information. "You're not close with your family?"

For a long moment, Aaron thought he wasn't going to get an answer, but finally Quinn huffed out a quiet laugh. "No. Not close." He glanced over at Aaron, and in the fading light, his face looked beautiful, and sad. It seemed like he was about to say more, but then he caught himself. "Long story. Kinda messy."

Then Danny was there, handing Aaron a beer and Quinn a can of Coke, and they got back to work.

The other jack-o'-lanterns started arriving, carted in wheelbarrows, carried in the arms of adults and children, and one small one carefully harnessed to the back of the neighbor's Saint Bernard. Everyone was busy with candles and placement and last-minute adjustments, and Aaron lost track of Quinn. When George called everyone's attention and the lighting was about to begin, Aaron realized that Quinn wasn't in sight. He felt almost panicky. He didn't know why it was so important to him, but somehow it was. He wanted Quinn to see this, wanted him to understand that it wasn't about the pumpkins, or about Halloween; it was just about everyone working together, and making something beautiful and odd and surprising, just for the sake of doing it.

He stepped back and began to turn, ready to hunt Quinn down, but then he was there, a shadow in the darkness, his white teeth showing in a quick smile. "Ready for the big moment?" he asked, and he was teasing a little, but it was gentle.

Aaron smiled back. "Yeah. You?"

Quinn held up his lighter. "I guess so."

At George's command, they all bent and lit the candles in their jack-o'-lanterns, and then stepped back. The crowd shifted easily down the hill until they were far enough away to see the full effect, the flickering yellow glow of the candles shining out like a hundred tiny beacons.

Aaron was watching the man beside him, and he saw that Quinn's smile was easy and genuine. "Hey, that's not bad. They really cast a good light, huh?"

"You can see it halfway to the highway, if you look for it. People drive by on Halloween night, just to see them."

Quinn nodded. "Nice." He glanced over at Aaron. "It's a nice tradition, man."

Aaron smiled back. He was tempted to try one more time, to reach out and take Quinn's hand. He could feel it, the way the cool of their fingers would blend into a shared warmth, and how they would hold on, not tight, but secure. He wanted it so much he could almost believe that it would happen, but he managed to restrain himself. Wanting wasn't the same as having, and he couldn't afford to push his luck. He'd gotten Quinn to stay for the carving; that would have to be enough for the time being.

CHAPTER SEVEN

"GET your heels down. If you keep digging my horse in the ribs, I will haul you off and make you walk him back to the barn!" Wendy sounded serious.

"Sorry." They were working in the outdoor arena, so the barn was only a few steps away, but Quinn really didn't want the humiliation of being ordered off his mount. And he didn't want to keep kicking poor Clay in the ribs. "It's just a lot to keep track of."

"I know." Her voice was kinder. "And your hands are great—you haven't dragged on his mouth once. And your weight is good, mostly. You're not flopping around and bouncing on his back. But the heels count too."

"Yeah." He ran over his mental checklist, and tried to keep himself from tensing up in the saddle. It was hard to put in that kind of concentration and still keep his body relaxed. Clay's easy walk was helpful, though, and Quinn let his hips roll with the horse's motion.

"Good. When you're ready, ask for a slow jog. Get your balance perfect, get him framed up, and ask for a lope. Remember to release your leg pressure as soon as he gives you what you've asked for—you're not a boa constrictor up there."

"Okay, yeah—good tip. I'm not a snake." A gentle squeeze was all it took to get Clay jogging, a slow, smooth movement barely bouncier than his walk. Quinn hadn't understood the difference, at first, but the more he learned the happier he was that Wendy had decided to start him out riding Western. Aaron said it was harder, in a lot of ways, but Quinn didn't care. He was happy to have the slower gaits and the deeper seat in the saddle.

"No smart comments, now," Wendy warned, but Quinn knew she wasn't really upset. She'd been finding time to give him a riding lesson almost every day he had worked, and they'd gotten to know each other reasonably well, at least within the boundaries of their worker/boss, student/teacher relationships. He knew what he could get away with, and he respected her too much to push anywhere past that line.

He asked for the lope and Clay shifted easily, the rolling motion gentle and controlled. Another reason to be grateful to Wendy—letting him ride Western, *and* letting him ride Clay. Not to mention taking the time to give him lessons at all. The more he thought about it, the more he wondered just why she was being so nice to him.

"Damn it, Quinn, your *heels!*"

"Shit, sorry." He adjusted his position immediately, and tried not to let his mind wander again. Wendy was being nice, but not *that* nice. He made it around the ring once with what he thought was a fairly respectable leg position, and apparently she agreed.

"Okay, fine. Good. Bring him to the walk, and cool him out." Wendy strolled out to the middle of the ring and watched as Quinn and Clay walked around her. "Pretty good lesson. You should start riding on your own. If I don't have time, just take Clay out and do the same things we do in a lesson—but watch your heels. Seriously, he's too good of a horse. I won't see him treated poorly."

Quinn felt guilty. "No, absolutely. I mean—maybe I shouldn't ride him. Not when you're not around."

"You should ride him. You should just do it *with your heels down.* I think you can manage that, Quinn." She took a drink from her water bottle. "If Aaron's got time, you could get him to watch you too. You two spend enough time just hanging around—you might as well be doing it with you on a horse." She looked thoughtful. "Or you could both ride. He's just doing flatwork with a couple of the youngsters. He could keep half an eye on you."

And there it was, another totally logical reason for him to spend time with Aaron. More time. More time sneaking looks at the kid, more time trying not to think about his huge, strong hands, or the way his shirt stretched across the hard muscles of his broad back. But lately, it hadn't even been the body that had been distracting Quinn from his job. He'd been finding himself working to earn a smile, wanting to see the way Aaron's eyes lit up when Quinn said something he liked. And it was good to get Aaron talking too, his voice warm and affectionate, or sometimes rough and teasing, but always perfect. Every casual touch made Quinn's skin burn, every meeting of eyes made his heart beat faster. And Wendy thought he should spend *more* time with him? Quinn was just barely surviving at the current rate of contact.

"Uh, yeah, maybe."

Wendy obviously sensed his reticence. "What, you guys are having a fight or something?" She peered up to see Quinn's face, and shook her head. "He doesn't bite, you know."

"I know! Wow, why do you guys keep telling me that people don't bite? I—" He caught himself. He'd been about to say that he'd never been bitten by a human, but that wasn't *quite* accurate, depending on the way "bite" was being defined. But he didn't think he needed to get into that with Aaron's mother. He also didn't really want to get into the reasons why he was less than eager to spend more time with her precious baby boy. And he should keep his mind on his damn job, and the fact that she was his boss. He smiled. "It's a great opportunity... you know, to ride a horse like this. I appreciate it. And all of your time with the lessons—I know you're busy, but it's been really useful." It was easier to kiss up when he actually believed what he was saying.

She gave him a look that showed that she was aware of the

topic change, but apparently she decided to let it go. "He's a treasure." She reached out a hand and Quinn let the horse stop walking long enough to get an affectionate neck scratch from his owner. "He means a lot to me, but I trust you with him—and you're doing fine. A bump or two from your heels won't kill him, or even do any real damage." She grinned. "But don't get in the habit!"

"No, ma'am, I'm working on it." Heels aside, Quinn was beginning to wonder if she was trying to send him a message about something more than the horse.

"I know you are. And, remember, he's gentle, but if it came down to it, he could hurt you a lot worse than you could ever hurt him." And maybe the hidden message wasn't intended, but if it was, she was getting a little too close to the truth.

"I know that—believe me. I'm being careful."

She nodded slowly, and then stepped back to let Quinn continue walking the horse. "I know you are." When Quinn was back out on the rail, she started walking toward the gate. "Walk him 'til he's cool, then bring him in."

Quinn nodded, and then went back to concentrating on his riding position. Clay was cooling out, but that didn't mean Quinn got to take a break.

He didn't even notice Aaron's approach until he heard him call, "Heels down!"

Quinn didn't even need to double check. "They're down, you jackass. Don't make me paranoid."

Aaron's laugh made Quinn feel warm even in the cool of the November day. "Yeah, okay. Seriously, you're looking pretty good. And you've got Clay moving well, so you must be doing more than just *looking* good."

"Well, your mom gives some pretty clear instructions."

"Yeah, clear and loud—we heard some of that at the front of the barn. She should just get a recording of herself yelling at people about their heels. It would save her vocal cords from all the strain."

"Well, it's good to know I'm not unique."

"Not even close, man."

"Aaron!" Danny's voice called out from the barn door. "You're out there for a reason."

Aaron just waved an arm dismissively. To Quinn, he said, "Let me cool him out for you—Danny wants your help with the Deere."

"Yeah, I heard it backfire again, earlier. Clay spooked a little."

"Yeah, and that was from far away. I thought Sunny and Casper were going to bust out of their paddock. We can't use the damn tractor until we get that fixed. Imagine if it went off when we had a bunch of little kids riding around."

"Yeah, okay." Quinn wasn't a mechanic, but he liked tinkering, and he'd had a lot of experience keeping his bike in shape. Of course, a diesel tractor was a bit different, but most of the principles were the same, and it was nice to find an area of the business where he could actually contribute something more than brute strength. Still, he didn't want to get overconfident. "I'll have a look, but, you know, might be time for a pro."

"Well, give it a try yourself, first. Mom hates spending money outside of the barn, and it's a pain to get the tractor into the shop."

"Yeah, okay." Quinn brought Clay to a halt in front of Aaron and swung his leg over before dropping to the ground. He held out the reins. "Now, you know your mother has only trusted *me* to ride him, so you'd probably better cool him out from the ground."

Aaron's laugh was quick. "The sad thing is, that's true—I don't know how you did it, but you've got her thinking you can do no wrong."

Quinn didn't like the sound of that—too much pressure, and too much disappointment when he did, inevitably, screw up. "I'm good at hiding the evidence, I guess."

He left Aaron walking the horse and headed toward the front of the property, where the tractor was parked in the drive shed. Danny was standing there, staring at the machine as if he hoped that it might just speak up and explain itself. He barely looked up when Quinn entered. "You got any ideas, man?"

"We can just do the basic stuff—air and gas filters, check the plugs. It was running for a while before it got cranky, right? It was good cold, and then bad once it warmed up?" Danny nodded. "I don't know—maybe the coil. That'd be next on my list."

"Well, I don't have a list at all, so let's try yours."

They worked companionably for a while, only speaking as needed for the job. Eventually, Danny said, "Aaron had his first game on Tuesday, you know. Hockey. They heard he used to play goal, and they practically offered him the keys to the Zamboni." Danny straightened and stretched his back. "They went out for drinks afterward. He said he had a good time."

Quinn had been trying not to think about that too much. "Yeah, he mentioned it."

Danny paused before he said, "He'll do it, you know. Eventually. I mean, he's a stubborn son of a bitch, but he's not totally stupid. Sooner or later, he's going to find someone. He's going to get over you."

Apparently Danny wasn't aware of the "trying not to think about it" plan. Or maybe he was aware, and just didn't give a damn. "That was the idea, Danny. He needs to find somebody.... "

"Somebody what?" Danny said when Quinn didn't finish his sentence. "Somebody who'll care about him more? I don't know who you're trying to fool, man, but we can all see that you like him. A lot. I don't know why you think he'll find more of that somewhere else."

"Come on, man." Quinn didn't want to even think about any of this, and he sure as hell didn't want to have a damned conversation about it. But the expression on Danny's face made it pretty clear that he wasn't going to give up. Quinn sighed. "It's not about—I mean, yeah, sure, I like him. He's a great kid. A good guy. Whatever." It didn't seem totally appropriate for Quinn to go on about Aaron's broad shoulders and tight ass. He stared into the exposed engine of the tractor. "It's not about me not wanting him. He just—he can do better. A lot better."

Danny didn't really respond to that. He walked over to the doorway of the shed and looked out at the farm. When he spoke, his voice was quiet. "Why didn't you report that guy? That—the one from the bar."

Quinn jerked his head up. "I did! I told you this—they arrested him. He's out on bail, but, you know—I'm going to testify. I'm going to follow through."

Danny turned toward him. "No, man. Not after Aaron. Why didn't you report him the *first* time? After *you*?"

Oh. Quinn had hoped that Danny was giving him a free pass on that mistake. But he should have known better. "Yeah. I know, I should have. I'm sorry." It wasn't enough, didn't begin to make up for allowing Aaron to be exposed to that kind of danger, but Quinn was already doing everything he could to make up for it with the police and the lawyers "Sorry" was all he had left for Danny.

But it didn't seem like enough. "Shit, Quinn, I'm not saying—this isn't about Aaron, and it sure as hell isn't about me! I meant why didn't you report him, for you? He hurt you, and you just let him go? Why?"

Oh. "A lot of guys did. The Crown Attorney, she said—it wasn't just me. He was good at picking... I don't know. Losers, I guess." Quinn guessed nobody really wanted to use that word in reference to themselves, but he had to admit, it seemed to fit. It was probably a bit unfair to the other guys, though. "You know, I'm sure they all had good reasons. Not losers, maybe, just...." He really didn't want to get into some sort of deep self-analysis. "Fuck, man, can we just work on the damn tractor?"

Danny obediently returned to the machine. He picked up the spark plug he'd been cleaning, but he just held it in his hands. Quinn decided to ignore him and get on with the job, but Danny shifted around and looked him in the eye. "You're not a loser, man. Aaron likes you, and he's not stupid. And I like you—in a different way, I guess, but still, I like you—and I'm practically a genius. Mom likes you enough to let you ride Clay, and that's huge. And pretty much every boarder and student in the barn is trying to think up ways to talk you out of this stupid 'gay' phase you're going through so they can have your beautiful babies." He grinned, but his eyes were sincere, and they didn't leave Quinn's. "You're a good guy, and Aaron would be lucky to have you. And you'd be lucky to have him." Danny tossed the spark plug up in the air and caught it neatly. "And I'd be lucky if the two of you would stop mooning around after each other and get on with it already."

Quinn didn't know what to say. He didn't want to even let himself start thinking about Aaron as a possibility. For as far back as he cared to remember, he could only think of two things he'd done that he was almost proud of. He'd finally gone to the cops about Brendan, and he'd walked away from Aaron before the kid got hurt. Changing his mind on that now... it wouldn't just make him the bastard who gave Aaron his first broken heart, it would take away one of the few things he'd ever done right. But it was so, so tempting.

He'd done bad things before, and he'd managed to survive. Surely he could survive this too. And he was probably exaggerating to think that there was anything within his power that would actually hurt Aaron. The kid was strong. Stronger than Quinn, he was pretty sure. So maybe it would just make things neutral. He wouldn't be doing anything all that wrong, even if it would eliminate the credit he thought he'd earned by doing something right. But then, if Aaron *was* strong, and hadn't been going to get hurt in the first place, then Quinn had been stupid to be giving himself credit for that anyway.

His head was spinning. He needed something concrete to focus on, and it was hard to get much more solid than a broken-down tractor. "Are you done with the plugs?"

Danny gave him an exasperated look, but he got back to work on the spark plug, so that was something. Quinn tried to turn his brain off, or at least to turn off the parts that weren't trying to figure out why the damn tractor was getting too much fuel, or not enough air, or whatever else might be causing the backfiring. That was his job; that was how he was able to contribute.

They worked on the tractor for most of the rest of the afternoon, until Quinn's list of ideas was exhausted. Aaron was busy in the barn, doing all the chores that they were neglecting in order to play mechanic, but he came outside when he heard the tractor roar to life. Danny was at the wheel, so Quinn was free to visit, and he couldn't really keep himself from wandering over to where Aaron was standing in the doorway.

"It's about time you got done—you're about two hours past your quitting time." Aaron said, and Quinn just shrugged. Aaron looked back toward the barn. "Sounds good so far."

"It hasn't warmed up yet. We did a bunch of stuff, but we didn't find anything that was totally wrong, so... who knows."

"Excellent optimism, there, Quinn. Keep up the positive attitude."

Quinn tried not to think about a world where he could respond to Aaron's teasing the way he wanted to. A world where he could pin the man up against the wall of the barn and kiss the smirk off his face, and then kiss until it came back again. He tried not to think about what his hands would be doing while his mouth was busy, where they'd be allowed to wander, how Aaron would respond....

God, maybe he could have it. Not forever, but maybe for a little while. It would cost him his job, of course, once things went bad, and he liked the job, but if he got to have Aaron, even temporarily— he could find another damn job. But then he wouldn't get to see

Aaron at all. Was it better to have a bit of Aaron for a long period of time or all of Aaron but only for a while? It was an impossible choice. But it was getting increasingly difficult to see the guy and *not* have him, so maybe the decision was going to take care of itself.

The tractor's engine revved, and Quinn looked back toward the shed. Aaron shifted a little, and his arm touched Quinn's shoulder, just a quick brush that was enough to have Quinn's whole body wanting to give in to the magnetic pull. "He's just going to stay in the shed?" Aaron asked. "He's not going to do anything?"

It took Quinn a moment to even remember what the hell Aaron was talking about. "Uh—oh, yeah. We figured it was safest in there, if it *did* backfire. Furthest away from the horses. And he's staying with it so he can turn it off in a hurry if it starts going bad."

"It's not really too interesting to watch." Aaron sat down on the wooden bench that rested against the barn wall, and Quinn followed him. "Hey, did you see the pumpkin carnage today?"

"Can I say how disturbing it is that you guys did that? I mean, it's like one of those crime labs, where they leave human bodies out in the weather to see what happens to them. Poor Jack deserves better."

"Nah. You said Jack was tough. He's happy to be part of the circle of life, I'm sure."

"I could barely even see which one he was, with them all piled together. And he's starting to... melt, or something."

Aaron nodded gleefully. "They all are. It's totally gross."

"Some poor kid is going to stumble across it and be scarred for life."

"Aw, Quinn, was there a pumpkin trauma in *your* childhood? Is that why you're so anti-Halloween now?"

"I'm not anti-Halloween."

"And don't even get me started on your problems with

Thanksgiving."

"I don't have problems with Thanksgiving."

"Is Christmas going to be bad too? Did Santa do you wrong? Or is Rudolph the guilty party, for this one?"

"Okay, well, the joke's on you, because Rudolph isn't real. He's just a story."

Aaron clapped his hands over his ears. "La-la-la-la, I can't hear you," he began, and Quinn laughed. He glanced over toward the shed and saw Danny watching them, and even from a distance, Quinn could feel the commentary in Danny's gaze. Quinn and Aaron, together. Laughing, relaxed—happy. It felt so good, so natural. It felt the way Quinn wanted to feel for the rest of his life.

An unfamiliar car pulled into the parking lot, and Quinn watched it idly. Aaron, on the other hand, seemed to recognize the driver. He stood up, took a step, and then looked back at Quinn. "Okay, well... I didn't think you would still be here, by now. I, uh—there's a guy from the team, he said he really liked horses, and I just—you know, just to be friendly, I said he should come by some time. But, I'm not sure why... he took me up on it. So don't be an asshole to him."

Quinn tried to keep his face still. "Why would I be an asshole?"

"No, you wouldn't," Aaron said quickly. "But, you know— Danny's over-protective enough. I don't need two big brothers looking over my shoulder and trying to intimidate people."

Quinn's stomach churned. He'd been thinking about Aaron, obsessing about him, pretending that it was somehow up to Quinn whether the two of them got together. God, where had he gotten so deluded? As if Aaron would have been pining over him all this time. Quinn was lusting after the kid, and Aaron was thinking of him like a big brother. Well, not a brother, maybe, nothing that close—just someone who might be stupid enough to try to take on the more embarrassing, annoying aspects of the big brother role. Quinn was an idiot.

"Quinn? You're not going to, right?" Aaron looked anxious. "You'll be good?"

Quinn stood up. "No, man, it's fine. I'm on my way out, anyhow. I'll go take over from Danny, let him come meet the guy."

"No, please don't! It's not a big deal—nobody needs to meet anybody. I just said I'd show him around. I said maybe we'd go for a ride."

The guy was inside the gate, now, walking toward Aaron a little hesitantly, as if wondering why he wasn't being greeted. Quinn stepped backward, angling toward the doorway to the barn. "Do you want me to bring in a couple horses for you?"

"No, it's fine. Don't worry about it. We can just—you know, we'll probably just hang out, or something."

So that meant Quinn had no excuse to go into the barn. And the new guy was between Quinn and the drive shed. There was no escape, and the guy was approaching fast.

"Aaron, hi," he said, and Quinn forced himself to look over at him. The newcomer was tall, almost as tall as Aaron, and he looked pretty fit, although his face wasn't too great. Good, but not outstanding. Not in Aaron's league. He had a good smile, though, warm and genuine as he said, "I'm not early, am I? Is this a bad time?"

Quinn bit back his own answer and listened as Aaron said, "No, right on time. Uh, Mitchell, this is Quinn. Quinn, Mitchell."

Mitchell held out a hand, but Quinn raised his own in front of him, showing the grease and grime. "Sorry, I've been working."

Mitchell didn't seem too taken aback. "Oh, okay. Looks like you've been taking care of mechanical stuff, not horses."

Quinn nodded toward the drive shed. "Just trying to sort out a tractor." He turned toward Aaron. "I'll go check in with Danny, see if he needs anything else—otherwise, I guess I'll head home." He forced a half-smile in Mitchell's direction. "It was nice to meet you."

"Yeah, you too," Mitchell said, and then he smiled at Aaron. "It's beautiful up here. How far back does your property go?"

Quinn willed himself to keep his hands from becoming fists as he walked over to the drive shed. This wasn't about him, it was about Aaron, and Aaron seemed happy. The guy seemed nice. Everything was good, and Quinn was either an idiot or an asshole if he let himself feel any other way. He couldn't really meet Danny's eyes when he got to the barn, but he kept his voice under control as he spoke over the dull rumble of the engine. "It seems okay—maybe we fixed it."

Quinn focused on the tools he was tidying up, but he knew Danny was watching him pretty closely. "Maybe," Danny agreed. "Who's that talking to Aaron?"

Quinn wished there were more tools to pick up, but they'd been pretty tidy while they were working, and it would be too obvious to keep looking away, so he forced himself to glance up to where Danny was sitting. "Some guy from the hockey team." He tried for a smile. "You were right. Are you psychic, or did you know he was coming?"

Danny left the tractor running but swung down to stand next to Quinn. "Neither. I just know my brother."

Quinn tried not to let his wince show. He hadn't thought that old scar was still so tender, but maybe he was just feeling sensitive for other reasons and had let his defenses too far down. "Yeah, okay. So, if the tractor seems okay, maybe I'll head out? You can run it a while, and if it goes off, we can look at it again tomorrow?"

Danny nodded. "Yeah, okay. Or, if you want to stick around for another few minutes, until you're sure it's good—do you want to go get a beer? Or you could come down to the house. Steph would love to see you, I'm sure. And the kids are always happy to have a new person to climb all over. You could stay for dinner, if you want."

Spending time with happy families was uncomfortable for Quinn at the best of times; it would be torture under the current circumstances. Still, it was nice that Danny asked, even if his hospitality was only motivated by pity. "Thanks, man, but I've got plans. I'm actually running a bit late. So if it's okay...."

Danny looked disappointed, but not surprised. "Yeah, of course. We'll see you tomorrow, then? I'm here to open, so you can come in a bit late if you want to, to make up for tonight going so long."

Quinn shrugged. He didn't really need to sleep in, but he guessed the barn didn't want to pay him overtime for his inexpert mechanical efforts. "Yeah, okay. I'll see you tomorrow."

He had to go back to the barn to trade his work sweater for the leather jacket he wore on the motorcycle, and to pick up his keys and helmet. He walked quietly, trying to hear where Aaron and his friend were, hoping to avoid any further contact. He felt a bit stupid about the whole thing, being so melodramatic. If he wanted to keep his job, he was going to have to get used to seeing Aaron with other guys. Jesus, maybe even talking to Aaron about it—what if the kid wanted advice, or something?

But that probably wasn't likely. Aaron had a solid big brother to bounce ideas off of; he wasn't likely to need the opinions of a loser bar-slut. Maybe if there were specific technical issues, but even on that topic, Mitchell looked like he was old enough to have some experience. So Quinn would be spared the need to get into all that, at least. And he'd get over the awkwardness, the feeling of emptiness. He would. Or maybe not get over it, but at least push it down to a less noticeable place. Not comfortable, but not a total distraction from the business of getting by.

Yeah, that would happen eventually. For now, though, Quinn would like a little time without having to deal with it all. He tried not to look sneaky as he walked cautiously down the aisle of the barn. Several horses had their heads swung out over their stall doors, and Quinn stopped briefly to greet Clay. The gelding stuck his nose out in a way that made it clear that he'd welcome a treat, if Quinn happened to have anything handy, but he wasn't demanding. It made Quinn wish he had something to give him, but his pockets were empty, and his hands were too dirty to even offer a good scratch. "Sorry, buddy. I've got nothing for you." And damn it, there was that melodrama sneaking its way back in, reminding Quinn that he had nothing for anybody.

He pushed the emotion down ruthlessly. He just needed to get laid, probably. He hadn't been to Candy's since the night with Brendan and Aaron, and he hadn't bothered to find anywhere else, either. That was way too long without sex; Quinn didn't know what the hell he'd been thinking. Of course that was the problem. He just needed a hookup, and everything would go back to normal. He didn't really feel like going to Candy's, especially not if that asshole bartender was working, but there were plenty of other bars. Or he could go for a real quickie, and head over to Stanley Park. It was a bit chilly for the great outdoors, though, and he generally preferred to combine sex with alcohol. His two favorite painkillers, conveniently wrapped around each other. Yeah, that was the best plan.

"You stay cool, Clay. I'll bring you something good tomorrow. It's apple season—I'll stop by the market and get a nice juicy one, okay?"

"Are you bribing that horse, Quinn?" Wendy's voice came from the direction of the office.

Quinn leaned out far enough to see past Clay's head. "Oh, hi. And... yeah, absolutely. Is that not a good training method?"

"No, I think it's an excellent idea. He's doing good work for you, so whatever you've been doing... keep it up." She smiled as she walked toward him, and reached out her own hand to rest on Clay's neck. It was comfortable, both of them admiring the horse, until she said, "You met Mitchell?"

That was an unpleasant but necessary return to reality. "Yeah, briefly." She seemed to be waiting for more. "He seems nice."

And that was all he was giving her, so she could just stand there and keep waiting, if that's how she wanted to play it. She didn't hold him for too long, though. "Long day for you—any luck with the tractor?"

Quinn shrugged. "We're testing it now. I'm heading home, but Danny's got it running, so—we'll see." He shifted around, ready to head for the office to pick up his gear. If he said he was heading home, maybe it was time to start heading.

But apparently Wendy had a different idea. "Why don't you come up to the house for dinner? I started a roast in the crockpot this morning, and I was just over there and it smelled great. There's lots."

Yeah, probably enough for Aaron and his new friend too. Quinn really liked Wendy, but her husband made him nervous, with all the questions and the long pauses, as if waiting for Quinn to start spilling his guts. And breaking bread with Mitchell was out of the damn question. Luckily, Quinn already had his excuse ready. "I've got plans, actually. Thanks, though."

Wendy didn't seem any more surprised than Danny had been. "I'll make you a sandwich from the leftovers—for your lunch tomorrow."

"You don't have to do that."

"Obviously I don't *have* to." And that was that. She turned and headed for the door. "Have a good night, Quinn. We'll see you in the morning."

Quinn nodded, but she wasn't looking at him anymore. And there was no sign of Aaron or Mitchell, so that was good. Something was finally going Quinn's way. Until he started wondering where exactly they were. There was the walk to the back pasture; it was a daily nuisance for Quinn, now, but he could see how it could be sort of romantic, to fresh eyes. And that was the best-case scenario. What if they weren't out in the open at all, but somewhere private, maybe up in the loft, Mitchell leaning Aaron against the wall, or sitting him on a stack of hay bales, Aaron's legs wrapping around Mitchell's waist as they kissed....

Damn it. Quinn practically ran to the office to grab his gear. He needed to get the hell out of the barn, off the farm, and out to a damn bar. There were plenty of guys out there, and most of them came without any of the complications that Aaron had. And there would be alcohol too. Maybe even something a little less legal, something that had a little more power to shake Quinn out of the way he was feeling. He had all the ingredients for a hell of a night, and the sooner it got started, the better. He headed out of the barn and barely waved to Danny. He wanted to be on his bike, he wanted to be somewhere else. He wanted to be some*one* else, if he was being perfectly honest, but that didn't seem likely to happen, so he'd just have to forget himself using other means.

CHAPTER EIGHT

THREE dates, if you counted the first visit to the farm. And quite a bit of time spent in non-dating contact, practicing or playing or hanging out with the team. So surely that was enough time. Surely Aaron was giving this thing a fair chance. It wasn't his fault that it just wasn't working. Or maybe it was his fault, but not because he wasn't trying.

Aaron startled when he felt the cold, wet bottle press against his sweaty neck. He glanced up and saw Mitchell smile at him before handing the beer over. "Damn, you were miles away—how do you get that distant in a bar this crowded?"

Aaron shrugged. "It's a gift." He waited until Mitchell sat down opposite him, and they drank together. "So, was it who you thought it was?"

"Yeah, it was. I went to high school with him. It's weird, because we both came out in college, not high school, so neither one of us really expected to run into the other in a gay bar. He and his partner are engaged now. They're getting married in the spring."

"Wow." Mitchell was a couple years older than Aaron, but only a couple. How were people his age getting married, while Aaron was still just trying to figure out the basics? "How long have they been together?"

"That's the crazy thing. Only a few months. He said they just clicked." Mitchell took another drink of his beer. "I wouldn't have said I believed in that, the whole love-at-first-sight, one-perfect-person-for-everybody thing, but... they seem pretty damn sure."

Aaron decided not to think about that, and certainly not to consider the implications of one person being convinced while the other was totally disinterested. If he was being honest with himself, he would have to admit that there was a part of him that had been hoping Quinn would come around. That he'd see Aaron with another guy and realize that it wasn't right. But Quinn had shown no reaction at all to Mitchell. He'd been polite, like he was with pretty much everyone, and that was it. In case Aaron needed any more evidence to convince him that Quinn was never going to be with him, that should have been it. But he still couldn't forget that one almost-kiss in the feed room when they were dealing with the aftermath of Quinn's fight with Brendan. It hadn't been much, but it had felt real. It had felt like Quinn wanted Aaron just as much as Aaron wanted him. But obviously Aaron was fooling himself, because there had been no other signs of interest whatsoever.

They finished their beers, and when Mitchell suggested they head out, Aaron didn't argue. They didn't really discuss where they were going; Mitchell just started walking, and Aaron went along with him. They talked a little, about nothing important, and it was fine. It was comfortable, but unexciting. It was nothing like being with Quinn.

They turned down the street that led to Aaron's apartment, and finally, he started getting a little nervous. They had hugged good-bye after the time at the barn, and kissed a little after their second date, standing on the sidewalk outside Aaron's apartment. But they hadn't spent any time alone together, in private, and Aaron wasn't sure of the rules on these things. No, not the *rules*—that wasn't right. He knew that the rule was that he wouldn't do anything that he didn't want to. That was easy enough. But he didn't know what the standards were. He didn't know what to expect, or, more importantly, what Mitchell was expecting.

Obviously Quinn had been operating at a much faster pace than Mitchell; Quinn had been ready for sex after two minutes of conversation and a beer. So his standard wasn't the same as Mitchell's, so he was no use. Aaron had heard girls talking about the "third date rule," but he didn't know if it applied to guys. If it did, was he ready? Was it time for him to just get the whole thing over with?

Maybe he was just obsessing over Quinn because he was the only guy that Aaron had ever really *been* with. Maybe if he gave Mitchell the chance, and found the same pleasure with him that he'd found with Quinn, then maybe this whole thing would start to seem more exciting.

It wasn't a sure thing, but it seemed like the best option. When they got to the door of Aaron's building, Mitchell stopped walking, but Aaron summoned his nerve and caught Mitchell's hand, then pulled a little. Mitchell gave him a curious look. "Come up?" Aaron managed.

Mitchell looked surprised. "Up? Yeah?"

"If you want...."

"Yeah, sure—I want." Mitchell's smile was real, and when he leaned forward and kissed Aaron, it felt good. But not great.

Still, Aaron had decided. He punched in the code for the door, and when they were inside the elevator and Mitchell leaned in for another kiss, Aaron didn't pull away.

They made it out of the elevator and down to Aaron's apartment before Aaron's nerve broke. Once they were inside, though, once he was standing in the same place he'd stood with Quinn, the whole thing seemed like a bad idea. But he was tired of waffling, tired of being stuck in limbo.

"Do you want something to drink? A beer or something?" He was mostly buying time, but the thought of a little more alcohol wasn't totally unwelcome. He wondered if it was time to break out the bottle of vodka he had in the freezer. Or maybe it would be a bit insulting—he shouldn't make it too clear that the only way he could go through with this would be with the help of alcohol.

Apparently he'd already made it clear enough, though, because Mitchell was giving him a strange look. "We don't have to do anything, Aaron." His voice was calm, almost amused.

"We don't—no, I know that. I mean... I want to. I do." He hoped he sounded convincing, but he wasn't totally sure.

"Yeah, your enthusiasm is pretty overwhelming, man." Mitchell's smile was soft. "It doesn't have to be all or nothing, you know. We can just fool around a bit, if that's better for you."

That sounded perfect, but Aaron didn't want to fall into the trap. "But, you know—I don't want to be a cocktease... I mean...." Mitchell was watching him like he wasn't making any sense, but Aaron knew that he was. "I've heard people talking. I mean, I'm a guy too. I know what it's like...."

"Yeah, you're a guy. Does that mean you want to have sex with people who don't want to have sex with you?" Mitchell shook his head. "Or do you think you're special somehow? More sensitive than the rest of us?" He seemed a bit impatient, but not angry. "And whoever you've 'heard talking'? Maybe you should just stop listening to assholes." He took a deep breath. "Okay. Sorry—I get a little worked up. How about that beer?"

Aaron moved toward the fridge automatically, most of his mind still busy thinking about Mitchell's words. They made sense. And if he thought about it, he had to admit that he liked this version of things better. He could see why Quinn had been impatient with him their first night—he'd been looking for a quick, simple hookup, not a relationship, and Aaron's inexperience had complicated things. But this was what Quinn had been talking about: having his first time with someone who cared about him, who didn't mind going slow. He pulled two bottles out of the fridge and turned to hand one to Mitchell. "I, uh—yeah. That sounds good. You know, if it's okay with you."

Mitchell just smiled, and let his fingers brush Aaron's as he accepted the bottle of beer.

Aaron smiled back. "Do you want to sit down?" The bed felt like a huge, awkward presence in the room, now that he wasn't feeling pressured to fall into it, but Mitchell didn't seem fazed. He just crossed over to the beat-up leather couch and lowered himself easily onto the cushions at one end. One hand rested on the padded end of the couch, holding his beer, but the other arm stretched out along the back of the sofa. It looked casual, but inviting, and Aaron forced his suddenly reluctant feet to cross the floor. He wanted to curl up at the far end of the sofa, but managed to plop himself down somewhere near the middle.

Mitchell let his hand fall off the back of the couch and onto Aaron's shoulders, but he didn't move it any farther, just lightly kneaded the tight muscles. "Jesus, Aaron, relax. We don't have to do anything at all, if you don't want." He took a swallow of his beer, and then asked quietly, "Do you want me to just go?"

Aaron had no idea how to answer that question. He decided it was time for absolute truth. "I like you. But I'm—I don't know what I am. I'm kind of obsessed, I guess. With this other guy."

Mitchell nodded. He didn't seem even a little bit surprised. "Does he know that? I mean, what's getting in the way?" He pulled his hand away from Aaron's shoulders and placed it over his own heart in melodramatic dismay. "He's not *straight*, is he?"

Aaron surprised himself with his laugh, rocking some of the tension out of his body. "No, nothing that bad. Just... I don't know." He shrugged, and that got rid of a little tension as well. "At first, he was sort of... protective, I guess. He didn't want me to lose my virginity with a one-night stand. And now...." Aaron trailed off. He wasn't actually sure just what Quinn's current objection was, other than more of the same. "I guess he's just not interested." It hurt a bit to say it, but it wasn't exactly a new idea. "I started playing hockey as part of a deal to get him to spend time with me, and then I figured that if I got some experience with another guy, he might be more interested." He smiled apologetically. "In my head, it didn't sound so much like I was just using you."

Mitchell didn't seem too worried about that. "I've enjoyed spending time with you. And, you know, it's not like you were really fooling me about whether you were into me or not. Actually, you had me wondering whether maybe you were just experimenting with the gay thing, and weren't sure you were going to go for it."

"No, I'm—I'm sure on the gay thing. There's no way I could be going this mental over Quinn if I wasn't really gay."

"Quinn?" Mitchell smiled. "The guy at the barn? Damn, man, you've got good taste—he's hot. I didn't get a real 'gay' vibe from him, though. Is that totally confirmed?"

Aaron's mind flashed to Quinn's mouth, hot and demanding on Aaron, the way he'd slid down his body, the tight, perfect warmth of his lips around Aaron's cock. He dragged his mind back to the present. "Yeah, it's confirmed," he almost squeaked.

"Nice." For a moment, it seemed like Mitchell was enjoying his own memories of Quinn, and Aaron felt a flash of hot jealousy. He knew Mitchell had noticed when he said, "So, if he's not into you—does that mean he's available?" The smile was immediate, and Aaron punched his shoulder.

"No! Keep your grubby mitts off my imaginary boyfriend."

"Maybe not all that imaginary." Mitchell looked thoughtful. "I mean, like I said, I didn't really get a gay vibe off of him. And my gaydar's not bad, usually. So if I didn't pick up on it, maybe it's because he wasn't scoping me out, at all." He nodded as if he liked the theory he was constructing. "Honestly, I got a bit of a hostile feeling from him. I just figured he was another homophobic redneck, but maybe he was actually pissed that I was going after his boy."

But Aaron couldn't let himself listen to that, couldn't let himself be convinced that there was even a shred of a chance. "I've been throwing myself at him on a pretty regular basis. And, you know—he's not exactly shy about going after what he wants."

"Yeah, but if it's a 'wants but doesn't think he should have' situation, then... you just need to convince him that he *should* have you, right?"

"Okay, can I just ask... are you not even a *little* bit pissed off that I'm not interested in starting something with you? I mean, I appreciate you being so understanding, and everything, but it's getting a bit insulting." It was a good way to change the topic, at least. And now that he thought about it, Aaron *was* a little hurt about how easy it was for someone to get over him.

Mitchell just laughed. "I told you, man—you're not a very good actor. I was just wondering how much longer we were going to be dragging this out. I mean, you're a good guy, we can still hang out, but... you know, the 'take it slow' thing would have been okay, but the 'I'm totally not into you' thing—that's kind of a deal-breaker." He laughed again. "Actually, the whole situation has got me thinking that I owe a serious apology to my high-school girlfriend. She was a sweetheart, but I wasn't into it, and I thought she didn't know. But now that I'm on the other side of things—I think she knew. Maybe not the reason, but definitely the general vibe."

"Yeah. Sara—my high-school girlfriend—she was the one who first asked me if I was gay. I guess I should have known better than to try this again." Aaron sighed, and leaned back into the couch cushions. "I'm sorry. I thought—I don't know, I hoped that maybe it would just hit me, you know? Like, if I went through the actions, the emotion would follow?"

"Well, it was a good test, then, right? And, you know, I'm quite a catch, so if I'm not enough to tempt you, then the barn-boy must be pretty damn excellent."

"Yeah, he kind of is." Aaron frowned. "Not that *he* thinks so. I honestly... I'm not even sure that he wants all the anonymous bar sex he has. It's like he thinks that's all he deserves, or something. Does that make sense?"

"Well, yeah, maybe. But, you know, don't knock anonymous bar sex. Some guys are perfectly happy with that." Mitchell raised his hands defensively. "You know him a lot better than I do, so you're the better judge, for sure. Just—make sure you're not projecting, or whatever. Like, just because anonymous sex isn't what *you* want, that doesn't mean that nobody else could possibly want it."

"Yeah, okay." Aaron swallowed the last of his beer and glanced over at Mitchell's bottle. "You want another?"

"I don't know—am I staying? Like I said, the 'take it slow' offer is kind of off the table, but if you want to just hang out, that's cool."

Aaron lurched to his feet and headed for the fridge. "Jon Stewart's on in five minutes—you can stay for that, at least, right?"

"Absolutely. Beer me."

Aaron got two fresh bottles and returned to the couch. This might not quite fit Quinn's plan for Aaron's hockey team contacts, but he bet Danny would approve. Making friends, broadening his horizons... that was all good. It didn't help him get over Quinn, but he was beginning to wonder if anything really ever would.

CHAPTER NINE

Quinn couldn't remember if he was supposed to be a tree, stretching his roots down through the horse's legs to the ground, or a balloon, floating weightlessly on the horse's back. He had a nagging suspicion that he was somehow supposed to be both, simultaneously, and it was making him a little crazy. Wendy had been really enthusiastic about lending him all the books, and there were a couple that she regularly quoted from during their lessons. So he'd taken them home, and he'd tried to read them, tried to remember what it felt like to study and to want to learn. But he'd apparently gotten pretty rusty. Everything would seem clear while he was in his apartment, sitting at the kitchen table and staring at the book, but as soon as he got on Clay's back, nothing made sense.

He saw Danny walking by, leading a horse out to the pasture. Quinn had worked the early shift that day, and it was kind of fun to still be around after work, seeing somebody else do the chores that would normally be his. "Hey, Danny! Am I supposed to be a tree or a balloon?"

"If you try really hard, someday you'll be a *real* boy. Until then... I have no idea what you're talking about." But Danny stopped walking and looked as if he was willing to continue the conversation.

"From the books—*Centered Riding*, and all that."

"Oh, yeah. I never read the books, man. Mom and Aaron go

on about that sometimes, but I was more of a get-on-and-figure-it-out kind of rider. You know—instinctive. Almost a spiritual thing, with me...."

"Yeah, okay." Quinn grinned. "How's the back feeling these days?"

"Feels like I should have been trying a bit harder to be a balloon. Or a tree." Danny started walking again, the horse obediently following. "Keep reading, young Quinn."

"And don't worry if it doesn't all make sense at first." Quinn turned to see Wendy at the gate of the riding ring, holding the reins of one of the young horses she and Aaron were training. "Just let it percolate around in your brain, and when you need the idea, it'll be there." She unlatched the gate and led the horse into the riding area.

"Do you want the ring? I don't have to ride right now." Quinn had been taking advantage of Wendy's offer to work with Clay even when she wasn't available for lessons, and he'd ridden with boarders a few times, but never with Wendy herself.

She shook her head at him. "We can share the ring, Quinn. But actually, it's such a nice day, I thought maybe you'd like to go for a ride along the trails. Clay loves hacking, and once you know the ropes, you can take him out there to cool down."

"Really? Yeah, that'd be great. If you have the time."

"Absolutely." She brought her horse to stand next to the mounting block, and Quinn waited while she effortlessly swung into the saddle and patted the horse's neck. "Misty's still green, so I want her to have a calmer horse along with her on the trails. You'd be helping me out."

Quinn somehow doubted that was true, but he didn't argue. He'd been dying for an opportunity to ride along the trails. He felt like he and Clay were just going around in circles in the ring, practicing, getting better, but with no actual goal in sight. If he was now good enough to be trusted in a less controlled environment, that could be his reward.

He began to wonder whether Wendy had a slightly different agenda, however. They were barely out of the ring before she was talking. She'd told him to ride in front, so that her younger horse would be able to gain confidence from Clay's leadership, so some of what she was saying was just directions, since he had no experience on the trails. But she didn't seem to content to leave things at that.

"So, you've been living in Vancouver for quite a while now?" Her voice was casual, but Quinn was instantly on guard. They didn't usually make small talk while he was riding. But maybe this was just how things were done, on the trails.

"Yeah, quite a while. Aaron said you're one of the few people actually born here—does it feel like we all invaded?" Quinn turned his head to the side in order to be heard without yelling.

"Sometimes it does, to be honest. I mean, individual people that I know, of course I want you all here! But it's not a great location for a huge city, in my mind. There's just not enough room, and it makes people build in stupid places. Not like Calgary—that's where you're from, right? It's pretty flat there, isn't it?"

That seemed safe enough. "Yeah, compared to here, at least."

"So, what brought you out to the coast?"

Quinn was beginning to see how well she'd laid her trap. Back at the barn, he could have just walked away from this conversation. Even in the middle of a lesson, he could have faked an injury, or something. But out here, where could he go? He'd just have to try to bluff his way through. "'Go West, young man.' Isn't that the line?" He couldn't see her, but he was pretty sure she wasn't going to be satisfied with that. "Why did everybody else come out here? It's Vancouver, right? As warm as you can get, in Canada. And it's beautiful, and all that."

She didn't answer right away. When she did finally speak, she seemed to have accepted his reticence. "Go left, along that path.

The hill's pretty steep, so give him his head, and put your weight in your stirrups and lean forward."

Quinn did as he was told. This was a whole new kind of riding, and he was starting to understand a lot of the seemingly pointless work he'd been doing in the ring. It was nice to be confident in his ability to control the horse and balance himself, now that he needed to. The novelty was enough to take his mind off Wendy's invasive questioning, and by the time they were at the top of the hill, he was relaxed and happy again.

They were on a sort of plateau, big enough for their two horses to stand comfortably, but not with much room left over. The trail continued on the far side of the clearing, but Clay stopped walking before Quinn even realized that he had given the signal to the horse. He wanted a moment to absorb the view.

Wendy brought her horse to stand beside him. "Not bad, eh? When I was a kid, growing up on this farm, only about a quarter of that was developed. The rest was still forest and farmland. We were way out in the country, then—now we get most of our business because we're practically in town."

"I can see why you're not crazy about the changes. It must have been beautiful."

Quinn could see Wendy's shrug out of the corner of his eye. "This is beautiful too, in its own way. Especially at night, with the lights. And I do love going into the city, and experiencing all the different cultures, meeting all the new people from all over the world. It's not bad, just... different."

That was a bit more philosophical than Quinn thought he'd be if he were in Wendy's place, but he admired her for her attitude.

When Wendy spoke next, there was a strange new tension in her voice. "Being a mom—that's my most important job. It's... it's the most important thing in the world, to me."

Quinn had no idea where she was going with this new topic, but he tried to give her what she might want. "You seem really good at it. Both Aaron and Danny chose to work for the family company, and they both seem pretty happy. That's a good sign, right?"

"It is. I—I can't imagine how I would feel if something happened to either one of them."

Quinn felt the twist in his stomach that meant it was time to escape. He turned in his saddle to look at the path. Was he supposed to ride back down the way they'd come, or go in the other direction?

"Stop for a second, Quinn." Her voice wasn't loud, and it wasn't an order. It was a request, almost a plea, and it froze him in place. She waited a moment, then took a deep breath before speaking. "George—my husband—he's a social worker. He does a great job, he has a lot of contacts all through the system, trying to find ways to help people. And he's got good instincts too. He somehow just seems to know when something's up. When somebody needs his help."

Quinn had no idea what to do. He didn't want to say anything to encourage the conversation, and he didn't know how to shut it down.

When Quinn said nothing, Wendy continued. "He asked around, about you. Dug some information up. I know it's an invasion of your privacy, and I told him not to say anything to Aaron or Danny, or anybody else, and he agreed. But, Quinn... I'm a mom. I just needed to talk to you, just once. I know I haven't heard the whole story. But... your mother. She lost one son, Quinn. She—I can't imagine how she feels, not knowing where you are."

Clay shifted nervously, and Quinn realized that his legs were tightening like a vice around the poor animal. None of this was Clay's fault. Quinn tried to relax, but it was only partially successful. He looked out at the view and tried to lose himself in it. He fought to imagine how it had been when Wendy was a girl, looking out and seeing farmland and trees and a little town. The city that he'd always found beautiful seemed malignant now, just one more corruption of something that should have stayed wild and pure. But that thought wasn't helping him to relax. He threw his mind back to the old standbys: alcohol and sex. They hadn't been working as well lately as they used to, but they were all he had left. He needed to get off this hill, off this horse, and into a damn bar.

"Do we go down the way we came, or over there?"

Wendy didn't answer right away. When she did speak, her voice was gentle. "I won't bring it up again, Quinn. I promise. But if you need to talk to somebody about it, please think of me." She waited, but he didn't say anything. Finally, she gave up. "We can go down along the other path. It's more gradual. But there are steep parts, so be ready to lean back a little, keeping your weight off his forehand."

He tried to pay attention to the new technique, for Clay's sake if nothing else, but he couldn't keep himself focused. He hadn't been prepared for all of this to come up, and he didn't think he was going to be able to handle himself if he didn't get some space. At least Wendy kept her word, and didn't speak to him about anything but riding directions as they worked their way back to the barn.

They'd been walking the whole way, although Quinn had been resisting a pretty strong urge to kick poor Clay into a full gallop, so there wasn't any need to cool the horses out. Quinn had Clay untacked before Wendy had even brought her horse into the barn. A quick hoof-picking and a once-over with the dandy brush, and Clay was ready to go out to his field. Quinn snapped the lead rope onto Clay's halter, then undid the cross ties. When he turned back around, Danny was coming down the barn aisle toward him.

"Hey, man. Aaron's almost done with Casper. We were going to go get beer and wings, watch the game. And you've got tomorrow off, so it's not like you need to worry about getting your beauty sleep. You in?"

Danny sounded casual, just like he always did, but Quinn wasn't so sure. Wendy had said that she hadn't told anybody anything. She'd said that she'd told her husband to keep his mouth shut too. But people lied all the time—maybe Danny knew all about everything. And it didn't matter anyway, because being around Aaron was exactly the last thing Quinn needed right now. He was looking for cheap, fast sex, not frustration at watching Aaron flirt with his new, perfect boyfriend. It had been hard enough for the last couple weeks, trying to deal with that. Quinn had no reserves of self-control left for this new assault.

"I've got plans, man. Thanks anyway." Quinn tried to get Clay moving, but Danny's hand shot out and caught his shoulder.

"There's something going on with Aaron. He's been weird for a couple days now, and I'm trying to get it sorted out. I could use the backup."

Quinn's laugh sounded ugly, even to his own ears. He pulled his shoulder free. "I'm really no good for that. Maybe your mom could help. Or your dad." Quinn knew that his tone wasn't too friendly, but at least he hadn't let loose with a string of curses, so he'd call it a win.

He was kind of blowing his cover, though. He didn't think he was ever going to be coming back to the barn—he wouldn't be able to avoid Wendy, considering that she owned the place, and he really couldn't handle her poking at him and watching him and thinking she knew something about him. And as much as it would hurt to not see Aaron again, it would hurt just as bad to see him moving on with somebody so much better for him than Quinn could ever be. So this was almost certainly his last day there, which meant that he didn't really have to worry about pissing people off. All the same, it would be nice to go out with as little drama as possible, so he needed to put a lid on things. He tried to lighten his voice. "I'm sure Aaron's fine. And if he's not—you're the guy, right? You're good at this stuff."

Danny didn't look convinced, but he let Quinn go. It was a bit hard to make himself turn Clay out into the field, though. The horse had been generous with Quinn, and taught him so much, with no expectation of a reward other than an occasional neck scratch and a few apples. It hadn't been perfect, but it had been one of the better episodes in Quinn's recent life, and he was sorry to be letting it go. Still, it wasn't like he'd ever let himself believe that it could be permanent. "Take care of them, okay, buddy?" he said, and Clay nuzzled his head into Quinn's shoulder as if he understood the words. That was a bit too much. Quinn took the horse's halter off quickly and latched the gate behind him, then returned to the barn.

He wasn't quick enough, though, because by the time he returned Aaron was in and had Casper in the cross ties. Quinn had really been hoping to get out of the barn without seeing the kid. It had been hard enough to say good-bye to his damn horse.

But Clay hadn't known that Quinn wouldn't be back, and there was no reason for Aaron to know it, either. Quinn had walked away from bad situations before, and he'd never felt the need to make an announcement of his intentions. There was no reason for him to do things differently this time.

He ducked into the office and traded his barn coat for his leather jacket. He caught himself before he replaced the barn coat on its hook. It would maybe make his departure a bit obvious, if he walked out with it, but it was still in pretty good shape, and it wasn't like he was made of money. He couldn't really afford to be careless with his belongings.

Aaron walked into the office while Quinn was hesitating. "Hey, Quinn. You coming out with me and Danny? Beer, wings, hockey—sounds good, doesn't it?"

Quinn forced a smile onto his face. "Sorry, I've got plans." He tried not to look at the kid; he wasn't sure he'd be able to walk away if he had a fresh memory of Aaron's face.

"Come on, man, you always say that. And then when we talk you into staying, it's not like the world ends, or anything. Your plans aren't too serious, right?" Aaron had moved a little closer, near enough that Quinn pretty much had to at least glance at him, and it was just as hard as he had known it would be.

"They're fucking vital, tonight." He brushed past Aaron and headed out of the barn. He had his coat; whatever else he might have left lying around he'd just have to get along without. He'd made a mistake, thinking that he could keep working there without getting too attached, and now he was paying for it. These people had crawled in under his skin, and they were starting to make themselves at home. It hurt to scratch them out, but better now than later, when they were in even deeper. He just needed to find a bar and get to work on distracting and anesthetizing himself.

He had to slow down to open the gate to the parking lot, and he heard somebody in the barn calling out his name. He couldn't be sure if it was Danny or Aaron, but he was far enough away that he could pretend he didn't hear whoever it was. He shut the gate behind him without turning around, then strode over to his bike. He focused on getting himself out of the laneway and onto the road, and he didn't let himself turn to look behind.

Chapter Ten

AARON had no idea what he was doing, following after Quinn. It was totally insane, not something that he would normally even consider. But the look on Quinn's face as he'd pushed past Aaron and practically run out of the barn... it had made it clear that there was something wrong.

When he'd looked toward his mother for an explanation, she'd looked as upset as he could remember seeing her. "I made a mistake, Aaron. I pushed him too hard—go and make sure he's okay."

So it wasn't only Aaron's instinct that had inspired him to jump into his truck and take off after the motorcycle. And normally his mom was even more even-keeled than Aaron, so if they were both thinking the same thing, then maybe they were both right.

Or maybe they were both wrong, because Aaron couldn't decide whether he felt like a total idiot or a creepy stalker. Neither was really an appealing way to think of himself. He wasn't sure if he was supposed to try to catch up to Quinn and get him to pull over to the side of the road, or just trail him home. He didn't really have to decide, though, because Quinn was driving fast, pushing his bike through any hole he could find in the highway traffic. Aaron was doing his best just keeping the guy in sight, so there was no way he'd be able to pull him over.

They headed over the bridge, and for once Aaron wasn't distracted by the view. He'd driven behind Quinn before, when they'd both left work at the same time, so he knew that the motorcycle was being pushed harder than usual tonight. Harder than seemed safe, in Aaron's judgment. Did Quinn know Aaron was behind him? Was he trying to shake the tail? Or maybe Aaron had just been watching too many cop shows.

Quinn took the Hastings Street exit, as usual, but they were barely off the highway before Quinn pulled the bike over to the side of the road, wedging it in between two parallel-parked cars. It didn't leave too much room for either car to get out without dinging the motorcycle, and that was another sign that Quinn wasn't acting like himself. He loved that bike.

Aaron watched just long enough to see Quinn head into a cheap-looking chain restaurant. Was the guy just picking up dinner? Aaron decided that whatever Quinn was up to, this was an opportunity to stop stalking. He could just go in, say hi, make sure everything was okay, and then deal with things from there. He found a parking spot down the street.

Aaron knew there was a problem as soon as he stepped inside the restaurant. Quinn was standing at the bar, face to face with a belligerent-looking middle-aged man. Then again, if Aaron was being honest, Quinn was looking pretty damn belligerent as well.

"I have already told you—this is not that kind of a place!" The man was almost shouting.

Quinn's voice was much quieter, but somehow just as intense. "Not what kind of a place? The kind that sells drinks? You have a BAR, asshole!"

"We have already sold you drinks. We are not the kind of place for you to get drunk. We are a family restaurant."

Quinn half-turned, surveying the room. "You're an EMPTY restaurant. Who the fuck am I going to scare away?"

Aaron wasn't sure what to do, but he figured he'd better intervene. Quinn wasn't wrong about the place being empty, but the man really didn't seem to care too much. He tried to sound casual. "Hey, Quinn. There you are. Ready to go?"

Quinn looked confused as he turned. "Aaron?"

"Yeah, hey, sorry I'm late." Aaron didn't have any idea why he was making up a cover story. Aaron saw four empty shot glasses on the bar beside Quinn—a lot for the two or three minutes that Quinn had been in the place, but not enough to make him drunk enough to believe Aaron's lies. And who cared what the other guy thought? Still, he'd started, so he charged on. "Have you paid your tab? We can go now."

Quinn just stared at him. The other man said, "Yes, he has paid. I made him pay before I handed over the drinks. Now, both of you, go!"

Quinn looked like he was gearing up to restart the argument. Aaron covered the ground between them in a few long strides and wrapped an arm around Quinn's shoulders. "It's good to see you, man. Let's go find someplace better."

For whatever reason, Quinn let himself be guided out of the restaurant, but as soon as they were outside, he shrugged violently and pushed Aaron's arm away. "What the fuck are you doing here, Aaron? Did you—" He cast his eyes down the street and saw the truck. "Did you *follow* me?"

"Uh, yeah. Sorry. Mom said you were upset about something, and you seemed weird to me, so... yeah. Sorry. I followed you."

"Jesus Christ." Quinn looked like he was about to say more, but instead he turned and started walking purposefully down the sidewalk. He didn't even turn his head as he called, "Go home, Aaron."

That was actually kind of tempting. Aaron had no idea what was going on, and he wasn't sure he wanted to know. But he couldn't just leave Quinn there.

It occurred to him that Quinn was walking away from his bike. That was a relief, actually, so they wouldn't have to have the drunk-driving fight, but it was a bit confusing, as well. "Quinn?

Are you—where are you going?" Quinn didn't turn around, and Aaron jogged after him. When he caught up, he asked again, "Where are you going?"

Quinn stopped short. He looked frustrated, and maybe angry. He made his voice very slow. "Aaron. Go home. This isn't about you."

"It's about *you*, though. And you're my friend. So that makes me involved." Aaron was getting a bit frustrated himself. "What's going on, Quinn? You were fine, and then you went for a ride with Mom, and she said something she shouldn't have... that's all I've got. What the hell did she say?"

"Nothing!" Quinn's voice wasn't as controlled anymore. "But I've got plans for tonight, and they don't include looking after a fucking tagalong kid. So go *home*."

"What plans? Where the hell are we, Quinn? Did you honestly pull over at the first place that looked like it would sell booze? Come on, Quinn. Does that sound healthy to you?"

Quinn almost laughed. "Who the fuck told you that I was *healthy*? Is that what imaginary Quinn is? The one you wanted to give you your first fuck? Was he *healthy*?"

Quinn leaned in, closer than he'd been for weeks, and even with the anger on his face and the alcohol on his breath, Aaron could feel the pull of attraction.

Quinn gave a disgusted snort. "Wake up, Aaron—that guy doesn't exist."

Aaron was at a loss, but he didn't think he could give up. He didn't know what was going on, but he was pretty sure it was important. "Just talk to me, Quinn. If you don't want to tell me what happened at the barn, just talk to me about now. Where are you going? What's the plan?"

Quinn moved fast. Aaron felt his back hit the brick wall a fraction of a second before Quinn's body came into full contact with his. Quinn was pushing in, too fast, too hard, his fingers twisting in Aaron's hair and pulling his head down for a kiss that was more like a protracted bite. Quinn's other hand was pressed between them, grabbing at Aaron's cock, fast and rough, almost painful. Aaron didn't know what Quinn was doing, but he let it happen. He couldn't make his body relax, but at least he didn't fight back. And God help him, he could feel himself hardening under Quinn's insistent hand.

Then Quinn pushed away, as quick and as hard as he had started. "*That's* my plan, Aaron. I'm going to get drunk, and I'm going to get fucked. And I'm not—" He caught himself, and when he spoke again, he sounded tired. "I can't babysit you tonight, Aaron. Not tonight. So go home."

"Quinn, I've been trying to get you into bed since I first met you. Do you really think you're going to scare me away by offering sex?" Aaron was still a little breathless from the kissing and grinding, but he was pretty sure he had a point.

Quinn just stared at him. "That's how you want your first time to be? Like *that*?"

"I want my first time to be with somebody I care about. You were right about that. And I care about you. So... if that's what you need, tonight, yeah, okay. I can give that to you."

Quinn's face was doing strange things. For a moment, Aaron thought the guy was maybe going to cry. But then he took a deep breath, and huffed it out. "Jesus, Aaron, you're killing me." He ran both hands through his short hair, and grabbed hold just above his ears, as if he was trying to keep his head from splitting open. "I can't be that guy, Aaron. I can't be that much of an asshole. Please don't let me do that to you." He was almost whispering, by the end.

Aaron was still confused, but he was beginning to think that he was actually in better control of the situation than Quinn was. His lips still felt swollen from the assault of Quinn's mouth, and that was a sensation that he wanted to remember, but he needed to put it out of his mind for the time being. "Okay. So, no sex tonight. You *aren't* that much of an asshole." Quinn was watching him with an unreadable expression. "But I can't just walk away from this. I mean—I know, you got along just fine before you met me, you're big strong Quinn, you don't need anybody, you don't need friends, blah blah blah." He knew he was pushing his luck, but Quinn hadn't walked away, yet. "But I can't go through another night worrying about you, and wondering whether you're getting hurt because of something I did, or something my mom did, or... for any reason, really. So, please." Please—what? Aaron was totally without a plan. He had Quinn's attention, but he didn't know what to do with it.

He remembered his earlier theory, about Quinn being like a dominant horse who needed to have his space respected. But that approach hadn't worked at all, and now Aaron had another theory. Maybe Quinn wasn't dominant—maybe he was the exact opposite. "Get in the truck, Quinn." He kept his voice soft and persuasive; he hoped it would be enough of a compromise that Quinn's pride would allow him to follow the order.

And it looked like it was actually going to work. Quinn took half a step backward and then cut a quick look at Aaron. "Why?"

Aaron tried to make his smile reassuring. "You've been drinking, so you can't take the bike, and there's no good bars around here. So we might as well get moving."

Quinn frowned as if he was trying to come up with an objection, but finally he turned and started toward the truck. "This isn't the plan. At all," he muttered loudly enough for Aaron to hear, but he didn't resist. Aaron was glad he had a button on his key fob to unlock the door before Quinn got there—he didn't want any delays, any glitches that might give the man a chance to change his mind.

Aaron tried not to look rushed as he moved around the truck to the driver's side. Quinn was sitting quietly, staring out the window, as Aaron got in and turned the engine on. He was just about to ask Quinn where he wanted to go, but he caught himself.

He thought it might be best to keep working on the new, pliant Quinn for as long as possible. So he pulled out into traffic and tried to drive as if he had a destination in mind.

Quinn didn't seem to be paying any attention to him. The almost frantic energy that he'd had in the bar was gone; Aaron didn't miss it, exactly, but he wished that there was some middle ground between that manic level and the current apathy. He decided to push his luck a little. "So, I thought we could go to your place. I've never been there, and we could order in or something. Thai would be good."

Quinn looked startled. "My place? No, I don't think so." He looked outside as if trying to determine where they were, and Aaron cursed himself for not letting the sleeping dog lie. "You could just let me out up at Burrard. That'd be good."

"You don't live on Burrard, Quinn." Aaron tried to keep his voice level and calm. "We don't have to go to your place, though. We could go out for food, or you could come to my place." Danny and Stephanie did that with the kids, made them feel like they had control by giving them choices, even though both options were carefully preselected. Aaron had no idea if the strategy would work with slightly drunk, totally erratic Quinn, but it seemed worth a try.

Quinn didn't answer right away. Finally, he said, "You should just drop me off. This isn't your problem."

"Quinn, I don't even know what the hell the problem *is*. But you're my friend, so, you know—your problemo es my problemo."

Another pause, and then Quinn quietly said, "Su problema es mi problema."

"You speak Spanish?" This seemed like a safe topic to defuse the situation a little.

But Quinn just shrugged, so Aaron went back to wracking his brain for ideas. He didn't really think it was a good idea to let Quinn out of the car just yet; he was still being weird, and Aaron thought that a contained situation was the best. He just needed to get Quinn to agree. "Do you want to go for a drive? Maybe up to Whistler—there's still enough light to see the views, and we could get dinner up there."

Quinn didn't answer immediately, but when he did, his voice was firm. "Aaron, I appreciate the thought, but... we're not friends like this. I don't *want* friends like this. I don't want your whole family pushing in where they don't have any damn business and trying to... trying to make me be like you guys. I'm not like that. I'm glad it works for you all, I am. But it's not for me." He turned his head, the first time he'd looked at Aaron since they got in the car. "So let me out at Burrard."

"Friends like *what*, Quinn? I don't understand what the hell is going on here! You—you barely knew me, and you took a beating to stop some guy from hurting me. That's okay, but me driving around for a bit, trying to figure out what's going on with you— *that's* out of line?" They stopped at a light, and Aaron took the opportunity to turn and look Quinn in the face. "Please, Quinn. I'm going crazy, I need you to help me understand. Tell me what's going on." He knew that it was a bit unfair, appealing to the protective instinct that Quinn so clearly had and so clearly tried to repress, but Aaron was getting desperate.

But it seemed to hit a little harder than Aaron had expected. Quinn's face paled, and he turned and stared out the front window. The truck was moving again, otherwise Aaron was pretty sure Quinn would be scrambling out the door. Instead, he stared at his boots, and said, "I can't be that guy, Aaron. I'm not... I'm not any good at that—not any good at all."

Aaron made a quick decision and turned the truck right, heading for Stanley Park. He couldn't let Quinn loose like this, and he needed somewhere that he could park and concentrate on the conversation.

They drove in silence, Aaron's brain running over what little information it had, trying to figure out an explanation, or at least an approach to Quinn that might lead to some answers. Quinn didn't say anything when Aaron pulled off into the park and then turned right again. He knew just where he wanted to be, the parking lot that looked out over the yacht club, and finally something was going smoothly, because there was a spot available when he arrived. They had a view of all the boats, with the city in the background, and Aaron always found the spot relaxing. He could only hope Quinn felt the same way.

Aaron turned off the engine and they sat in silence for a while. Then Quinn said, "I could walk home from here. And there are a *lot* of bars on the way."

Aaron sighed. "Yeah, you could. And, you know—if that's what you want, if you're fine the way you're going and you really don't want any help, or anyone to talk to, then that's what you should do. I'm not going to drive you there, but I won't try to stop you, either." Every muscle in Aaron's body was thrumming with adrenaline, but he made himself sit still.

Quinn was still, as well, and the two of them sat in a stalemate for longer than Aaron thought he could stand. Finally, Quinn's hand moved to the door handle, and Aaron fought to keep himself from tackling the guy and forcing him to stay. But Quinn only opened the door a little before saying, "Can we walk, or something? I don't want to sit here."

Aaron scrambled out of his side of the truck, and Quinn frowned at him before reaching back inside and pulling out the barn coat that he'd been carrying. "You're going to freeze. This is big on me, so it might fit you."

Aaron took the coat and tried to be subtle about the way he savored the scent, horses and hay and Quinn all mixed together. It made him feel safe, and made him want to find a way to help Quinn feel the same way. "Where to?" he asked.

"I don't know, man. I thought you were the one taking charge."

So Quinn had noticed the attempt. Aaron smiled sheepishly. "How about just along the sea wall? Oh, but stay here, I've gotta get a parking ticket."

"I can do that," Quinn started, but Aaron was already running toward the ticket machine. He tried not to look over his shoulder too many times as he waited for the family in front of him to figure out how to work the technology and then took his own turn. When he turned to go back to the truck, Quinn was still there, leaning against the front bumper and looking out at the boats. So apparently the flight instinct had been controlled, at least for the time being.

They walked for a while without talking. Aaron tried to sneak a few looks to see if Quinn was relaxing, but it was pretty hard to tell.

Finally, Quinn broke the silence. "It's not a big deal, man. I just—I don't like it when people push into my… I don't know. My life, my—stuff."

"Yeah, okay." Aaron wasn't sure what else to say. "I guess we're not too good at that. At minding our own business. It's not—nobody's trying to hurt you, you know? We just… we like you. We want to know more about you." He jostled Quinn's arm playfully, but Quinn pulled away instead of pushing back.

"No, you don't."

Aaron reached out and gently grabbed Quinn's arm, pulling him around so they were facing each other. "Yeah, we do," he said softly. "You don't have to be a hero, or something. You're just… Quinn. That's enough."

Quinn shook his head, but he didn't argue. Aaron fought to keep himself from leaning down and going for the kiss. It seemed natural, and it was all his body wanted. His could still feel the bruising pressure of Quinn's lips against his, the force of their bodies colliding, and, of course, the rough, hard contact with his cock. Aaron wasn't sure that he'd liked it, the way Quinn had come on so strong; but he wasn't sure he *disliked* it, either. It had been overwhelming—way too much, way too fast—but if Quinn could just slow it down a little…. But that wasn't what they were doing, not tonight. As far as Aaron could tell, sex was easy for Quinn; it was the friendship part that he had trouble with. And friendship was what Aaron was pretty sure Quinn really needed.

CHAPTER ELEVEN

QUINN felt stupid. He could still remember the cold desperation that had churned through his stomach when he'd left the barn, the almost panicked feeling of being too exposed, too vulnerable. At the time, all he'd been able to think about had been getting away, physically and emotionally. It had felt so real, and so sickeningly familiar.

But somehow, walking along the seawall with Aaron, it all seemed far away. It was a like a bad dream that he'd been woken from; he could still feel the emotions, but they weren't important any more. There was no real danger.

A part of his brain was screaming that the feeling of safety was just a trap of the most insidious sort. At some level he knew that Aaron, in his well-meaning innocence, was at least as much of a threat as Wendy, with her pointed questions. But Quinn was tired of running, and it felt good to just walk. Especially with Aaron beside him.

He could think of quite a few other things that would feel good with Aaron, but he tried to keep himself from dwelling on them. Quinn was lucky to even have Aaron as a friend; he shouldn't let himself dream of being something more. He shouldn't let himself imagine that he'd ever be the sort of person who would deserve to be with Aaron.

It was almost dark, the lights of the city bright across the harbor, and Quinn decided he'd probably dragged Aaron away from his life for long enough. "It's getting kind of cold—do you want to head back?"

"If you want. Or do you want your jacket back?"

"Yeah, so I could have two and you'd have none. That's not good math, Aaron."

Aaron just shrugged, and they turned around and walked quietly for a while longer. Then Aaron said, "Why were you bringing the jacket home with you? You usually leave it at the barn, right?"

Quinn didn't say anything. He didn't know how to explain the instinct to run away, and he wasn't sure that the urge wouldn't return, once he was away from Aaron's calming presence. It seemed better to just let the whole thing go.

But Aaron apparently didn't agree. "Were you going to leave? Like... quit?" He sounded as if he'd been thinking about the question for a while, and was braced for the answer.

Quinn didn't want to confirm the guy's low opinion, but he didn't want to lie, either. "I don't know—maybe."

"Just because my mom pushed into something that wasn't her business? Come on, Quinn! Just tell her to back off."

"Yeah, why didn't I think of that?" Quinn shook his head. "Jesus, Aaron, how many times have I tried to get all of you to leave me alone?"

Aaron was quiet for a while. "Even tonight," he said, as if he was just realizing it. "You wanted to do your thing, and I chased after you and made you hang out with me."

"No, man, it's...." Quinn wasn't sure what he wanted to say. "I mean, yeah, I guess. Technically. But—you know, I appreciate the thought. I just... I shut doors for a reason. I don't need somebody else coming along and opening them all up again."

They walked without talking until Aaron asked quietly, "It was pretty bad, then? With your family?"

Quinn's first instinct was to snap at the kid. They'd *just* finished talking about leaving Quinn alone. But there was a strange new impulse twitching through his brain. He almost wanted to talk. He wondered what it would feel like, to just say it all. He didn't know what reaction he could expect, or what reaction he'd *want*, even. Maybe he'd built the whole thing up in his mind, and Aaron would just think he was a pussy for letting himself get all wrapped up in old pain. Would it be good or bad if Aaron felt that way?

He took a deep breath. "My brother...." But it had been too long. He couldn't say the words. Aaron was waiting patiently, though, so Quinn tried again. "I used to have a brother. Now I don't." It almost felt worse, saying it that way, but he pushed on anyhow. "My family didn't handle it well, and I didn't handle it well, and—we just... it seemed like maybe we'd handle it better if we weren't together. That's all. It's not some huge thing. It's just—I don't really need it all dug up again."

Aaron's hand was gentle on his shoulder. "I'm sorry, Quinn."

Quinn nodded. He didn't really trust himself to use his voice, and he didn't have anything to say, anyhow. They started walking again, slower now, with Aaron's hand still a light warmth on Quinn's shoulder. Quinn had talked, and the world wasn't ending. And he wasn't sure yet, it was still too new to be positive... but he thought maybe he felt a little better. Not as much better as he would if he were drunk and getting fucked, of course, but it was a start.

"He was older or younger?" Somehow, from Aaron, it didn't seem like an intrusion; it just seemed like somebody trying to understand.

Quinn gave himself a moment to be sure his voice would work. "Younger. By nine minutes."

Another pause for Aaron to digest. "Identical, or the other kind?"

"Identical." Quinn was surprised to find himself almost smiling as he stopped under a street lamp and turned enough to point to the small scar above his left eye. "I got that when we were seven, and I thought they were going to give me a medal or throw me a party. Up until then, we'd been pretty much impossible to tell apart." It was the first happy memory of his family he'd had in a long time. He was tempted to try for another, but he didn't want to push his luck.

He thought about his alternate plans for the night. It was barely dark yet—still plenty of time to head down to the bars and get back on schedule. The shots from earlier had pretty much worn off, so that had been a waste of money, but he was sure he could find someone to buy him drinks. The alcohol and sex combination was time-tested: it shut his brain off when nothing else could.

But it never lasted. Sometimes he'd go a week or two feeling okay, but other times he'd be crawling out of his skin by noon the next day, before the hangover had even faded away. Maybe Aaron was right, and it was time to try a different approach.

"You think you could drop me off at my bike? I know it's not on your way home, but I shouldn't leave it out there overnight. I did a shitty job of parking it."

Aaron smiled. "Yeah, I noticed that. And, sure, I can drop you off." He checked his watch. "But it's only been an hour and a half. You shouldn't drive yet, should you?"

Quinn felt okay, but he guessed Aaron had a point. "Maybe I should walk out—by the time I got there, I'd be good, right?"

"Or we could get something to eat, and I could drive you out after. I could still go for Thai."

Quinn wasn't sure if he liked calm, in-control Aaron. "You're a bit of a smug bastard, you know that?"

Aaron's laugh brought his body around toward Quinn, and the light from the streetlight shone just right on his face. It made him look beautiful, almost magical. Quinn didn't realize his own body was moving until they were facing each other. Quinn's hand found its way to Aaron's chest, his fingers closing gently on the fabric of his own barn coat. He could feel the hitch in Aaron's breath, even through the layers of clothing.

Aaron bent his head as if hypnotized, and Quinn lifted his chin with the same lack of thought. The kiss was gentle this time, slow, and it just felt right. It felt like they should have been doing it for months, and like they should keep doing it forever. Aaron's cold fingers snuck into the warmth of Quinn's neck, and their bodies leaned together. Normally, Quinn would have been thinking about the next step. Getting more contact, shedding clothes— whatever it would take to keep things moving. But this time, with Aaron, he was perfectly content to just enjoy the moment.

Unfortunately, the moment didn't last. Aaron stiffened as if he realized what he was doing, and Quinn immediately pulled his head back and let Aaron move away. What the hell had he been thinking, taking advantage of Aaron's compassion that way? "Sorry, man," he started, but Aaron cut in.

"No, I'm sorry. You said no sex, and I said okay, and I meant it. I did. I'm sorry, I shouldn't be.... You're not on your game, you don't want this."

"Of course I want it, Aaron, don't be an idiot. I just—you're seeing that... that Mitchell. And he's a good guy, right?"

"I'm not seeing him anymore. But yeah, he's a good guy." Aaron gave Quinn a quick look, as if deciding how much to say. "He was really sweet when I told him that I was still totally hung up on somebody else, and the whole 'trying to move on' thing wasn't working out."

Quinn had no idea what to say. He wanted Aaron. He knew that, and he knew that for the first time in a long time, he wanted more than just sex. But he was nowhere close to good enough for the kid. If he gave in now, if he let the kid act on his ridiculous crush—how long would he have before Aaron came to his senses? Would the pleasure of that time be enough to make the pain of the breakup worthwhile? And how would the whole thing affect Aaron? He was strong, and he'd get over Quinn, but maybe he would regret it if his first time was with somebody so meaningless. Quinn really didn't want to be one of Aaron's regrets.

Aaron shuffled impatiently. "So, you've just got nothing to say to that? You're just... that's it? We're back to where we started." He shook his head, and when he continued, his voice was less aggressive, and almost sounded like he was pleading. "I mean, I'm going crazy. I can't get over you. I dumped my first almost-boyfriend, and the only thing that was wrong with him was that he wasn't you. Is that what you want to hear? Does that make you happy?"

"Yes." Quinn hadn't known he was going to say it, and he almost wished he could take it back as soon as it was out of his mouth. Almost, but not quite, because, God, he wanted this so much. "I mean—this is a bad idea, and I'll do my best but you're going to regret it, eventually. I should—I should get my ass kicked for even thinking about you, but...." He took a deep breath. He didn't know where he got the nerve, but he said, "Yes, that's what I want to hear. Yes, that makes me happy."

Aaron stared at him long enough that Quinn started to wonder whether he'd totally misunderstood what the kid had said. Or maybe he'd just called Aaron's bluff, and when confronted with the actual, messy reality of Quinn, Aaron had finally realized how crazy he was being. But then Aaron moved, and he wasn't running away. He shuffled a little closer to Quinn, and his frown made him look as if he was just as unsure about his understanding as Quinn. "So... what does that mean, exactly?"

Quinn edged backward, because that was a good question, and it was pretty much impossible for him to think clearly with Aaron so close to him. "I don't know. I mean—you're making me crazy too. It's—it's like I said, I don't think there's a damn prayer that this is going to end well. But... I want it. I want you—you know, not just for sex. I want... whatever. Whatever you want."

Aaron shuffled closer again, and this time Quinn didn't move away. Aaron's smile was tentative, but beautiful. "Like, if I want you to wake me up in the morning with fresh coffee, and take me out to brunch? And then we could go for a walk on the damn beach? Is that—if that's what I want.... Can I have that?"

Aaron was close now, way too close for Quinn to be coherent. "Yeah," he choked out. "You can have that." Aaron leaned down, slow but steady, and then twisted his head a little. Instead of kissing Quinn's lips, he found the soft, sensitive skin just below his ear. A shiver ran through Quinn's body, and his fingers reached out involuntarily, finding their way inside Aaron's jacket to the warm flannel that covered his ribs. Quinn could feel Aaron's lips curve into a smile, but then, inexplicably, he was pulling away.

"And we can take it kinda slow?" Aaron whispered.

Quinn groaned. "Jesus, Aaron, you're killing me."

"You said 'not for just sex'. You said 'whatever you want'—that's what you said." Aaron was watching for Quinn's reaction.

"No, I was lying. I'm not all that into you—I'm still undecided. I need to be persuaded." Quinn knew he wasn't even close to keeping a straight face, so he gave up trying and let his smile spread as wide as it wanted. "You need to work for it, buddy...."

Aaron's head darted in for a quick kiss, but when Quinn tried to lean after him and keep things going, Aaron brought his hands up and braced them on Quinn's shoulders. "I've been working for months, man. I think it should be your turn." His face got more serious. "And we said no sex, earlier. Because you were in a weird mood. This whole thing, it could be, like, a strange reaction on your part."

"Are you kidding me?" Quinn said, but he wasn't really all that upset. Actually, he wasn't upset at all. If Aaron wanted to take it slow, Quinn could do that. Happily.

Aaron seemed to be taking it a bit more seriously though. "You said you didn't want to be an asshole. That's what you said."

"Yeah, that's what I said." Quinn shook his head. "So—what, then? Thai?"

"Yeah? Like... a date?" Aaron edge in close enough to give Quinn a gentle hip check as they started back toward the car. "You paying?"

"I could, yeah. Or—shit! You were supposed to be going out with Danny tonight. Wings and the game—is it too late for that?"

Aaron looked startled by Quinn's vehemence. "It's not a big deal. He's probably at home and changed into his sweatpants by now. And once he's in his sweats, he doesn't change back into real clothes."

"He was worried about you, he said. He thought you were acting weird, and he wanted to figure it out." Quinn wasn't sure if that was supposed to be a secret or not.

"Weird, huh?" Aaron seemed to be thinking about it. "Maybe just about breaking up with Mitchell. I hadn't told him about that yet." He glanced over at Quinn. "Am I allowed to tell him about you? Like, you and me?"

Quinn didn't like the sound of that, but it wasn't his place to tell Aaron how to relate to his brother. "Do you want to? Or could you hold off for a while, let us get things sorted out?"

Aaron nodded. "Yeah, okay. But, you know, he's practically psychic. Like, if he says something to you, don't go assuming that I told him something I wasn't supposed to. He's just—observant, sometimes."

"You can tell him what you want to, Aaron. He's your brother." Quinn didn't think he imagined the apologetic, sympathetic look that Aaron gave him. He didn't regret telling Aaron, but he hoped the kid got over that pretty soon. "So, Thai? Have you got somewhere in mind?"

Aaron accepted the change in topic, and they walked on toward the car.

Quinn had no idea what he was doing, or how he felt about the whole thing. He knew how he felt about Aaron—that part was easy. But letting something get started between them? That was a different story. It could go bad in so many different ways, Quinn didn't think he could even start to guard against them all. The whole thing was a bad idea, a total mistake, but all he had to do was glance over at Aaron, and all the worries disappeared. Yeah, it was a disaster waiting to happen, but he didn't care. Whatever time he got to spend with Aaron, he'd call it a win. Everything else would just have to look after itself.

CHAPTER TWELVE

AARON stopped by his parents' house before he went to the barn the next morning. He wanted a chance to talk to his mom in private. He knocked at the back door before opening it and sticking his head inside, and there were both of his parents, eating eggs at the breakfast bar. It looked very cozy, and Aaron wondered for the first time whether they were just as glad as he was that he'd finally gotten the hell out of the house.

"Aaron—good. Danny said you blew off dinner with him, so I assume you caught up with Quinn yesterday?" His mom looked interested, and maybe still a bit apologetic.

"And there's eggs in the fridge, and bagels by the toaster, if you're hungry," his dad offered.

Aaron had already eaten, but he could always find room for a bagel or two. And now that he was in front of them, he wasn't quite sure how to start the conversation that he wanted to have. Really, all he wanted to do was dance around like an idiot and sing a happy song about how Quinn had finally decided to give him a chance, but that didn't seem appropriate. Especially since Quinn wanted to keep things as quiet as possible.

Aaron checked that his boots were reasonably clean and then crossed over to the toaster. With his back turned to his parents, he let himself smile a little as he thought about the night before. He and Quinn had eaten dinner, and then Aaron had driven Quinn back to his bike, as they'd planned. They'd made out for a while in the cab of Aaron's truck when they got there, slow and easy, until some homophobic asshole banged on the hood and shouted an insult at them. That prompted Quinn to launch himself across the bucket seats until he was practically in Aaron's lap, and the kissing got a little hotter and a little less gently affectionate, for a while. But Quinn calmed down once the guy stormed away, and when Aaron suggested that maybe they weren't in the world's greatest location, Quinn had reluctantly agreed. One last, sweet kiss and Quinn was out of the truck. Aaron had watched him walk down to his bike and give it a quick check to make sure that no damage had come to it, and then Quinn had climbed on and driven it away, just a quick wave as he passed Aaron's truck.

That had been the last Aaron had seen of Quinn, and he'd manfully resisted the urge to call him that morning. He didn't think he'd have been able to hold off if he'd thought there was a chance that Quinn would actually pick up his damn phone, or even that he would know where it was. Aaron knew it was pretty early in the relationship for him to be thinking of ways that he'd like to change Quinn's behavior, but his disregard for telecommunications really had to stop. Maybe there was some system of positive reinforcements Aaron could devise. He thought of a couple of rewards that he was pretty sure both he and Quinn would enjoy, and he was blushing when his mother cleared her throat and called his attention back to the kitchen.

"Baby? The bagels will toast even if you're not staring at them. Did you catch up with Quinn last night?"

He knew his face was still pink, and he knew she'd misinterpret that as an answer to her question, if she saw. Well, not a total misinterpretation, but not about *quite* what she'd think it was. So he kept his face turned away and moved over to the fridge as he spoke. "Yeah, I did. That's why I came by this morning." The cool of the fridge was welcome, and he took his time hunting around for jam.

Finally, he stood and turned around. "He said you'd brought up some stuff that he didn't really want to deal with." Aaron stepped closer to his parents. "He was ready to leave, Mom. He took his stuff with him. He really—he doesn't want to talk about any of that."

His father frowned. "Did he tell you what happened?"

"He told me about his brother. And he said he and his family didn't do well together, after it happened, so they don't see each other anymore." Aaron shrugged. "I mean, I'm sure there's more to it, with his family, but... it's his business." Maybe it would be Aaron's business, someday, but he really didn't think his parents had any reason to be pushing their noses in.

"It is." Aaron wasn't used to quite that level of unqualified agreement from his mom, and he looked at her suspiciously. Sure enough, there was more. "I just—as a mother, thinking about that poor woman. One son kills himself, the other disappears.... I think about you and Danny, and I just...."

Aaron tried to hide his surprise at the mention of suicide. He didn't know what he'd been thinking—he guessed he'd assumed an accident, or maybe cancer or something. Suicide must have been even harder for Quinn to deal with. Aaron tried to focus on the part that he knew something about. "The way he talked, it sounded like it had been a mutual decision—for him to stop spending time with his family."

"He didn't just stop spending time with them, Aaron." His father's voice was gentle, but firm. "He cut off all contact. They filed a missing persons report, and they've had private investigators looking for him."

"Private investigators? Really? I mean—how hard is he to find? He's right here, living in the open."

"I don't think they even knew to look in Vancouver. It was one of the possible locations listed in the missing persons report, but there were a lot of other possibilities. I guess he was living down in Boston when his brother died. And he had an Argentinean boyfriend, from the sound of things—there was mention that he might have been down there, or all the way over in Europe."

"How did you see all this? I mean, isn't that sort of stuff supposed to be confidential?" It was easier to think about his dad's investigations than about Quinn's Latin lover.

"I asked around. I know people on the police force, and we do each other favors all the time."

"Yeah? Do you help *them* to stalk innocent people? I mean, he hasn't committed a crime, right? He's not a fugitive or something. We have no idea what went on with his family—obviously, it wasn't too good if one kid killed himself and the other took off. Maybe his parents *deserve* to be alone."

"They're not alone. Quinn has a younger sister, and she's still living in Calgary." His dad wasn't arguing, exactly, but he wasn't agreeing, either.

"Okay, well—just because she didn't take off doesn't mean they have a good relationship. And it doesn't mean that Quinn has to spend time with them."

"No, it doesn't." His mom's voice was calm. "And I'm sorry I brought it up. I didn't know that it would be so painful for him, but I knew it would be difficult. I thought it was worth the risk." She nodded behind Aaron. "Your bagel is toasted."

Aaron took his time spreading the jam on his bagel, using the opportunity to refocus himself. He had come over to the house for a reason, and he needed to be sure he didn't get distracted. He put the bagel on a plate and turned around. "Just don't push him, okay?" He tried to sound firm, not aggressive or, worse, whiny. He was pretty sure he managed it. "He talked to me a bit last night, and if he wants to talk more, he knows where we are. I just—I think he needs a bit of time."

Aaron didn't miss the look between his parents. His father cleared his throat before he spoke.

"He may not get that, Aaron." He lifted his hands defensively. "It's not because of anything we did. But when he filed the police report, about the assault, that got him back on the police radar.

It's not exactly a top priority—like you said, he's an adult, and it's an old case. But they did a background check on him, they found the report, and they want to close the case." He lowered his hands. "Apparently they'll be contacting him about it. He can keep the police from telling his parents where he is—you're right, he's entitled to privacy. But the police have to contact the family and say that he's been found, at least. And it'll be the Vancouver cops who make contact, so it won't be too hard for the family to figure out where Quinn's living."

"And then... what? I mean, Vancouver's a big place. They won't just drive out and find him, right?"

"No, but they've already spent quite a bit of money on private investigators. I assume they wouldn't mind spending a little more. It might take a while, but I expect they'll find him." Aaron's father seemed less like an opponent now, and more like an ally. "It might be best for him if he took the initiative. You know—if he made first contact, he'd have more control over the situation. Or... Aaron, if there's a real reason why he doesn't want to be in touch with them—if there was abuse, or something like that—there are steps we can take to protect him. His family may have a lot of money, but they don't have more than the Province of British Columbia, and we can mobilize a lot of resources if we need to."

Aaron's head was swimming. Quinn's family had a lot of money? They'd been looking for him for years? His brother had killed himself? There was too much new information, and not enough Quinn. He set his untouched bagel down on the breakfast bar. "I'll talk to him about it."

"You and Quinn—you're getting pretty close?" His mom was watching him assessingly, and Aaron tried not to flinch. Quinn had asked him to keep things quiet, and Aaron was on the verge of blowing things after a five-minute conversation with his parents.

He shrugged, and tried to look cool. "I don't know... he's a friend."

His mother didn't smirk, exactly, but there was something

almost smug in her look. His father, on the other hand, was frowning. "You're being careful, though, right? I mean—your mother likes him. And she's a good judge of character. But he's obviously been through a lot." His frown deepened when he saw Aaron's expression. "Aaron, listen to me for a minute, here. I'm not saying he's a bad guy." He took a deep breath and let it out, then another before he spoke. "I don't talk about my work much. And there's a reason. Your mother and I have worked hard to make this home a safe place for you to grow up. We've tried to shelter you from some of the harsher realities of life. But now, you're out on your own, and the truth is, somebody doesn't have to be *trying* to hurt you. Sometimes they can hurt you just by being who they are." He looked over to his wife as if for support, but Aaron was gratified to see that the look was met with a frown. Maybe her expression wasn't as fierce as Aaron's was, but still, she clearly didn't agree with what George was saying.

He continued anyway. "You're young, and inexperienced. He's older, and from a few things Danny's let slip, I'd say Quinn is beyond 'experienced'."

Aaron wondered what Danny had said, and in what possible context, but he didn't have much time to consider it, since his dad was apparently not finished with his speech.

"He's recently been a victim of sexual assault, and that alone, with none of the other history, would make me worry about his stability. Honestly, the fact that he seems so unconcerned about that—it makes me wonder how much other damage has already been done to him, if he's able to ignore such a traumatic event." He looked over at Aaron again, and looked regretful when he saw Aaron's expression, but he seemed determined to keep going anyway. "Issues like AIDS aside—and, I'm sorry, son, but that can't be put aside permanently, not in this day and age—Quinn may not be emotionally ready for a real, committed relationship. Or, no judgment, but he may just not be interested in that. I think... I think he did a good thing, encouraging you to join the hockey team. I think he recognized that he wasn't a good match for you. Shouldn't you be looking for someone closer to your own age, and from a more similar background?"

Aaron tried to keep his temper under control. He wanted to yell at his father, and tell him how great Quinn had been the night before, how he'd agreed to do things at Aaron's speed. He'd said that he wanted more than just sex—what more proof did Aaron need? But it had been Aaron himself who'd suggested that Quinn's way of dealing with things wasn't healthy, and he'd said it to Quinn's face, not just hinted at it in a family conversation. Still, Aaron knew how he felt, and he wasn't going to give up on this before it even had a chance to get started.

"First, he's twenty-nine. It's not like he's fifty or something." His dad looked like he had a response to that, but Aaron charged on. "And, okay, yeah, he's got some stuff that he's a bit messed up about. If he'd been through all that and wasn't messed up, you'd probably be all concerned about *that*, saying that he didn't have proper emotions, or something. I mean, you're trying to use what some asshole did to him to prove that there's something wrong with *Quinn*? There's something wrong with the other guy, but Quinn's... Quinn's the one who kept that guy away from me!" Aaron was breathing hard, and he realized that he'd been yelling. So much for keeping things under control.

His father, on the other hand, was totally calm. "I'm not saying that Quinn isn't a good person. I'm not saying he doesn't deserve our compassion, or that you shouldn't stay friends with him. But if this is going beyond that... I'm sorry, Aaron, but I have some serious concerns."

Aaron didn't know what to say. He felt resentful of his father, and protective of Quinn, and confused by the whole situation. But somehow through it all, one thought came to him, and as soon as it did, he felt calm. "It doesn't matter," he said. He looked at his father. "I appreciate your concern, but this is my decision." He smiled. It seemed strange to be saying it so early, and it seemed crazy to be saying it to his dad before Quinn, but maybe it was the only way to make himself understood. "I love him." It made everything make sense, as long as he kept that idea in the center of things. "If he wants to be with me, then I want to be with him."

His dad's face froze, but his mom's smile was soft and genuine. She stood up and stretched, and he bent his head enough so that she could kiss him on the cheek. "My Baby," she said in a choked voice.

"Mom...."

But she was already moving on. "You'll take care of yourself, of course. And everything your dad said—that's all true. But... you're right too. If you love him, then it doesn't matter." She stopped. "Except for the HIV. That matters. You tell him to get tested, and even if he comes back fine, you'll be careful, right?"

"Mom, yes, fine!"

"Condoms, Aaron! Every time, no exception."

"I know." He grabbed his bagel off the plate and headed for the door. He'd had the condom conversation with his mom for the first time when he was thirteen, and periodically ever since. He needed to get out of the house before she started in on how they really didn't affect sensation all that much, and even if they did, maybe it wasn't that bad of a thing.

His dad's voice stopped him at the door. "Aaron." When Aaron turned around, his dad was standing next to his mom. "We love you, Aaron. We want you to be happy."

Aaron nodded. "Yeah, I know. I love you guys too." He thought about Quinn, leaving his family behind. It was hard to imagine anything that would bring Aaron to that point.

"And we should have him over for dinner," his mother added.

"Mom, you see him practically every day. You don't need to have him over for dinner."

"Not to get to know him—just to enjoy his company. And make him feel welcome."

Aaron shook his head. "Wait until things calm down. I'm

serious, he was ready to leave and not come back yesterday. He doesn't need any more prying." Aaron still hadn't totally come to terms with the fact that Quinn had been ready to walk away. It would have been just like after their first meeting, with Aaron pining over him and not knowing how to find him, but so much worse this time, now that Aaron felt so much more. And while he was thinking about that.... "And, you know—the whole 'love' thing. That's—I haven't said anything about that to Quinn. So, you know, if you could not mention that, if you're talking to him...."

His mother gave him another gentle smile. "Of course not." She glanced at her watch. "Now, get down to the barn. With Quinn off today, Danny will need your help."

So that was that. Aaron guessed he'd been expecting a bit more fanfare, somehow, for his first declaration of love. But he guessed he was doing pretty well, under the circumstances. His father hadn't dragged him away and locked him up in a tower somewhere, and he hadn't declared a blood feud on Quinn and his family, so... it could have been worse.

He checked his phone for messages on the way down to the barn, but nobody had called. Aaron wasn't sure if Quinn even had his cell number; he'd certainly never used it. So Aaron wasn't being too realistic, expecting Quinn to turn into a fully domesticated, attentive, frequently calling boyfriend overnight. A tiny part of Aaron wasn't even sure that Quinn hadn't gone out to the bar after Aaron had left him the night before. They hadn't actually discussed monogamy, after all. Just because it seemed natural to Aaron didn't mean that Quinn automatically felt the same way. Damn, he really didn't want to think about that, not now.

Aaron resisted the impulse for most of the walk, but when he was just outside the barn door, he dug out his phone and punched in Quinn's number. He tried not to consider it pathetic that he knew it by memory, even though he'd never spoken to Quinn on the phone.

When he heard Quinn's groggy, "Hello?" he was so surprised that he almost hung up. "Hello?" came again, less groggy and more cranky. This was not a good start.

"Quinn? Hi, sorry, it's Aaron." He felt like an idiot. "Did I wake you up?"

"Almost." There was no further explanation. Cryptic Quinn made Aaron a little nervous.

"Uh, sorry. I mean—wait, what? Are you saying that you weren't asleep, or that you aren't awake?"

"Hang on a second." There were some muffled sounds on the other end of the line, then a thud, and then Quinn was back, sounding a bit more alert. "Hey. What's up?"

"Uh, not too much." Aaron still wasn't sure what the hell was happening on the other end of the line. "How about with you?"

"Oh, not too much. I just thought I'd give you a call, check in."

"No, wait—I called you." Aaron wondered whether it was possible that his phone call had reached an alternate universe.

"Oh, yeah, good point. So... *what's up?*"

Aaron was pretty sure Quinn had already asked him that, and there was a little more emphasis on the words this time around. He wasn't sure what it meant when somebody who sounded that sleep-addled was outsmarting him. Probably nothing good. He tried to get his head back in the game. "I, uh—I just thought I'd give you a call, check in."

"That's nice. Everything's good here. I was just sleeping in a little. I don't know if you were aware, but it's my day off. Most days I have to get up really early to drive up to the North Shore and feed a bunch of spoiled horses, but not today. Today I get to sleep in!"

"Is there any chance at all that we could start this whole conversation over? And, you know— maybe later? I could call back around noon, maybe?"

"Too late now, man. I'm awake." And he didn't really sound too grumpy, Aaron decided. Actually, teasing-Quinn tended to be happy-Quinn, so maybe everything was okay.

"Sorry. But, uh... I actually wondered whether you have some time tonight. I need to talk to you about something." Aaron just hoped that Quinn wasn't going to see the police or the crown attorney before then.

There was a pause, and when he finally spoke, the teasing was gone from Quinn's tone. "Yeah, okay. Like, a phone call, or you want to meet somewhere?"

"No, meet, if we could." Aaron really wanted to have Quinn face-to-face, so he could get a better read on his reactions. Phone-Quinn was kind of hard to figure out.

"Okay. When and where?"

"Uh, I have late lessons tonight. I could be down there by eight thirty, probably, if that's okay. And wherever you want is fine." Aaron had the distinct feeling that something was going wrong, but he had no idea what it was.

"How about the coffee place two doors down from Candy's? You know the one?"

Aaron didn't really want Quinn to be that close to a bar and casual sex, just in case he took the whole thing badly, but he couldn't think of any way to phrase that objection. "Okay, sure. At eight thirty, then?"

"Yeah, okay. See you, Aaron."

"See you," Aaron said, but he was pretty sure that Quinn had already hung up. A strange conversation, all around. Maybe there was a reason Quinn didn't like to use his phone, if things always went this poorly. Aaron tried to put it out of his mind, and continued on into the barn.

CHAPTER THIRTEEN

Quinn didn't think it was a good idea for him to have a third cup of coffee, but it was that or duck out to Candy`s in search of something harder. Either in liquid or male form, he didn't really care. So he ordered another coffee. Sure, it would be more efficient for him to start the sedation process before Aaron showed up to do the dumping, but that was too pathetic, even for him.

Quinn wished he'd never picked up the damn phone. He should have known better; phone calls were never good news. And once he'd made that first mistake and *had* picked up, he wished Aaron's voice hadn't thrown him into such an instant, obvious good mood. If he'd done the smart thing and kept himself emotionally neutral, he wouldn't have had so far to fall once he heard Aaron's plan.

He'd spent the day trying not to think about the meeting, but of course that hadn't worked. It was painfully obvious that Aaron had some sort of bad news to give Quinn, and what was there besides a breakup? If you could even call it breaking up, after they'd barely gotten together in the first place. He guessed the kid thought he was being stand-up, wanting to break the news in person, but Quinn wished he'd just said it over the phone.

He checked his watch as he returned to the table in the back of the café, fresh coffee in hand. Aaron was late. As if Quinn hadn't had enough trouble filling the hours between the call and the meeting, Aaron had decided to give him a little more time. Quinn tried to dredge up some resentment over the kid's behavior, but he couldn't do it. Of course he had come to his senses and realized that he and Quinn were a bad idea; Quinn had known that was going to happen eventually, although he hadn't expected it to be quite this fast. And he couldn't get upset about the lateness, either. Aaron was driving into town, so there was bridge traffic to deal with. And he might have gotten hung up at the barn, or something. No, none of this was Aaron's fault, and Quinn had to remember that. He just needed to get through whatever torture the kid thought was required, and then get his ass up the street to Candy's. This whole experiment with being emotionally mature had been a disaster, and the best thing to do was get back to his old habits as quickly as possible.

He saw Aaron through the big window at the front of the café, red-cheeked from the cold wind and from hurrying. He looked beautiful, and sweet, and it hurt to think that Quinn had almost had him. It hurt even more to realize that he never would.

But he shoved all that down and stood up casually when Aaron came inside. Aaron's smile was sweet but tentative, and Quinn knew that he'd been right about the reason for the meeting. But of course Aaron had to be civilized about it, and he stopped off at the counter to pick up a coffee of his own before heading back toward Quinn.

Quinn hadn't been going to stay standing that whole time, and the table was wedged over far enough into the corner that he was fairly obviously inaccessible, so there was none of that awkwardness about shaking hands or hugging or, God forbid, kissing hello. Well, there shouldn't have been any of that awkwardness, but Aaron still managed to hover indecisively for quite a while before he finally lowered himself into his chair. "Hey," he said. "Sorry I'm late."

"No problem. I was a little late myself." Quinn had no idea why he was starting all this with a lie, but he guessed it couldn't really hurt.

"Oh, good. I, uh—Casper came up lame, so I had to deal with

that."

Oh. That was why the lie wasn't a good idea; Quinn had to come up with an excuse of his own. Things were starting to spiral. But maybe he could deflect. "Is he okay?"

"Probably. It looks like his hoof. We're hoping for just a stone bruise." Aaron fiddled with his mug. "So, you had a good day off? Do anything interesting?"

Quinn didn't think there was any reason to stop the lying pattern now. "Yeah, it was good. Just got a lot of stuff done, you know. Groceries, and laundry. Went to the gym." He gave a quick, dismissive nod to the guy over by the cash register who'd been trying to get his attention. Yeah, Quinn recognized him, probably from the bar. Big deal. Maybe in ten minutes, after the dumping, Quinn would track the guy down. Right now, though, he should be focusing on Aaron. And maybe he should be helping the kid out a little with this whole attempt at conversation. "How about you? Other than Casper, I mean."

"Uh, yeah, it was okay. I had breakfast with my parents."

"Yeah?" Maybe that was the impetus for all this, then. Seeing their happy, domestic lives might have been enough to help Aaron realize what he wanted, or, more to the point, what he didn't. "They're good?"

"Yeah, they're fine." Aaron looked impatient as another guy walked by and brushed Quinn's shoulder in a casual greeting on the way to the bathroom. "You know that guy?"

"Uh, yeah, I guess. Not well." So maybe this hadn't been the best place in the world to suggest they meet. Or maybe it was all right, to make it clear to Aaron that Quinn had plenty of other options.

Aaron nodded. "Okay, yeah." He paused, and seemed to be having an internal conversation of some sort. "So, what I wanted to talk to you about... I mean, it's good to see you, and everything. But, uh...."

Quinn figured he should jump in and help the kid out, but he didn't think he was going to. It wouldn't kill him to start working on his dumping skills. That much, at least, Quinn could help him to learn.

"I saw my parents this morning."

"Yeah, at breakfast. Got it."

"I went over to tell my mom to leave you alone—you know, about all the family stuff."

"Don't worry about it, Aaron." There was no way Quinn was going back to the barn, not after the dumping, so there was no reason to worry about Wendy.

"Yeah, but... my dad, he's the one who dug up the information in the first place. He's—protective, I guess. Sorry."

Quinn was tired of reassuring the kid, so he just sat there, and finally Aaron continued.

"So, the thing is... apparently your parents filed a missing persons report? A long time ago. And hired private investigators, and stuff. I don't know if you knew all that."

The shift in the conversation was kind of confusing. Quinn had been braced for one kind of news, but not for all this. "Uh—no, I didn't know that."

"Yeah, I guess if they didn't find you, there's no way you would have. But the thing is... when you filed the police report, that got your name back in the system. So everything kind of kicked back into gear, you know?"

This was absolutely not the conversation Quinn had anticipated. He tried to collect himself. Was the dumping off the table, or was that phase two? And how did he feel about phase one?

Aaron was watching him anxiously. "So, my dad said they'll probably be able to find you now. Your family. He said maybe you want to get in front of it, and contact them first. You know, so you control the situation a bit better."

"I, uh—Jesus, Aaron, this is not what I thought you wanted to talk about."

Aaron looked confused. "Sorry. Did you—did you want to talk about something else?" He sat up as if alarmed. "You're not going to call it off, are you? I mean... us? You're still okay with giving it a try, right?"

It probably wasn't Quinn's most sensitive moment, but it felt good to laugh. "Yeah, I'm still good. I thought you were backing out."

"Me? Quinn, that doesn't even make sense. I've been the one saying that I want this. For, like, months."

"Yeah, but sometimes you think you want something, and then you get it, and you realize that it wasn't what you wanted after all." Quinn wasn't sure he was expressing this properly. "Like... buyer's remorse, you know?"

"No, I don't know. I don't get buyer's remorse. I'm not stupid, Quinn—I know what I want, and I'm not going to change my mind overnight." Aaron stood up and leaned over the table. It was a terrible angle, and Aaron had to twist himself into a pretty strange position to keep his balance, but the kiss was absolutely worth it.

When Aaron finally lurched his way back over the table, Quinn realized that the murmur of conversation in the coffee shop had stopped. He glanced around to see a room full of faces smiling at him and Aaron.

"Guess that means you're not going to be at Candy's tonight, Quinn?" It was the guy from over by the cash register.

"Yeah, I guess not," Quinn agreed. He looked at Aaron and smiled. "Definitely not," he said more quietly.

"Damn right," Aaron said, and the hint of a growl in his voice went straight to Quinn's dick. This whole night had turned out a hell of a lot better than he'd been expecting. Then he remembered

Aaron's actual message. Not as bad as a breakup, but, still not good.

"Maybe they won't be interested anymore." Aaron looked confused, so Quinn added, "My parents. I mean—you said they filed the report a long time ago. Maybe they just figured it was the right thing to do, or something. It doesn't mean that they actually want anything to come of it."

Aaron frowned. "I don't know—I mean, I don't know anything about all of this. If you want to just think out loud, that's fine, but if you actually want me to have an opinion, or to try to help you figure it out, I'd need more background, I think."

Quinn sighed. That made sense. And he absolutely could use any help he could get. But he didn't want to talk about all of it. And he really didn't want to confess to Aaron, who seemed to actually think he was an okay person, how wrong he'd been, and how many people he'd let down. Maybe they could at least delay the conversation. And based on that kiss, Quinn could definitely think of some very attractive delaying tactics. "Do you want to get out of here?" He looked over at Aaron's barely touched coffee. "Or we could stay...." but Aaron was already on his feet.

"My place?" Aaron suggested.

Quinn stood up. "Yeah, absolutely. Have you eaten? Do you want to pick something up?"

"I ate at the barn—you?"

"No, I'm good." Quinn was almost nervous, although he couldn't imagine why. How many times had he gone back to someone's place without even a second thought? But this was different, he realized. He remembered how he'd felt when he'd thought it was over with Aaron, cut off before it even got started. He needed to remember that feeling, and do whatever it took to delay having to feel it again. He still didn't see any way for this to work out long-term, but at least he'd know that he'd done everything he could to make it work. He wouldn't let himself hold back, wouldn't let himself hide.

Aaron waited for Quinn to work his way out from behind the table, and then reached out and took his hand, as if it were the most natural thing in the world. Quinn knew the coffee shop crowd was still watching them, and a part of him wanted to pull his hand away. He wasn't embarrassed about being with Aaron, exactly. It was more that he didn't want witnesses to his momentary insanity, his brief flirtation with romance rather than sex. The more people who saw this, the more people who could laugh at him when it all went to hell. But what kind of an attitude was that? It was the exact opposite of the resolution he'd made just moments before. He let his fingers curve around Aaron's, warm skin gripping tight, and it felt perfect.

They left the café and walked silently through the almost-empty streets. It was windy and cold, and halfway to Aaron's place, it started to rain. They quickened their steps, but they didn't release their hold on each other's hands. Pockets might be warmer, but that wasn't important to either one of them, apparently.

They made it to Aaron's building still attached. It felt strange to be there again, retracing the steps they had taken months ago, back when Aaron had just been an intriguing stranger. The mirrored elevator was just as tempting as it had been the last time, but just as the doors were closing somebody called out to hold the door, and Aaron, of course, obliged for the stranger.

But when he got closer, he apparently wasn't a stranger. "Aaron, hi!" The guy was okay-looking, a vaguely granola-flavored hipster-type, but Quinn decided there was something unlikable about him. Unfortunately, Aaron didn't seem to agree.

"Tim, hey! You're back."

Aaron sounded genuinely excited about this, and he dropped Quinn's hand in order to shake the new guy's. And then the new guy leaned in and turned the handshake into a hug. Quinn had to step back to get out of the way.

"How was New Zealand?"

"Pretty good, pretty good." Tim twisted around to punch his floor button on the elevator panel, and Quinn had to step back a little farther. "We should get together sometime—I've got some excellent stories. And some pictures. There are some places that totally reminded me of South Africa, and others that were almost like Scandinavia."

Quinn wished the guy had stayed in New Zealand. Then Aaron's hand reached out as if to reclaim Quinn's, and he turned his head when he realized that Quinn was no longer right beside him. The bell sounded and the doors slid open on the sixteenth floor. Aaron stepped halfway out of the elevator and then leaned against the edge of the doors, keeping them from closing. "Tim, this is Quinn," he said, and Quinn eased his way out of the elevator. As soon as he was close, Aaron reached for his hand again, and Quinn let it happen. It still wasn't a gesture he was totally comfortable with, but he could see how it had some value, especially as a way to tell creepy world-travelers to stay the hell away from Aaron. He tightened his fingers a little, and Tim gave him a noncommittal smile. Quinn tried to return it with the exact same level of disinterest.

"Nice to meet you," Quinn said.

"Yeah, you too."

And finally Aaron stepped out of the elevator doorway. Maybe Quinn could have waited a little longer before he pushed Aaron up against the wall and pulled his mouth down into a deep kiss, but if Tim didn't want to see that, then he shouldn't have yelled for Aaron to hold the damn elevator. Neither of them paid much attention to the doors as they slid shut.

They kept kissing, but Quinn didn't really appreciate the way that Aaron's smile was twisting his mouth around. He tried to work through it, but finally he pushed away and frowned, and Aaron laughed out loud.

"Damn, Quinn, territorial much?" He reached out and grabbed the front of Quinn's shirt. "I'm not complaining, man. I've got other neighbors I could talk to, if it's, like, a kink or something."

Quinn resisted the pull of Aaron's hand, and the even stronger pull of his lips. "He was coming on to you, Aaron. 'Getting together for excellent stories'—yeah, okay."

Aaron released the pressure of his hand, but his smile stayed bright. "I guess I didn't notice. I was too busy thinking about you." He gave a slight pull with his fingers, and Quinn gave in, leaning forward for a kiss.

"That was an excellent answer," he whispered.

He wasn't really expecting Aaron to laugh again. Once he got control of himself, Aaron looked apologetic, and a little embarrassed. He gave Quinn a quick glance as if deciding how much to share, and then fixed his eyes on Quinn's neck as he spoke, so quickly and quietly that Quinn had to strain to hear. "I actually had it all worked out, from a daydream. You were being all possessive, and I was calming you.... We were at the beach, though—I don't know, I guess I fast-forwarded to next summer. Or maybe we went away at Christmas." He brought his eyes back to Quinn's, and he looked like a little kid waiting to see if he would be rewarded or punished.

This whole thing was pretty damn overwhelming, but Quinn was apparently getting into it, because he brought his hand up so he could support Aaron's head and kiss him deep and strong. They didn't break apart until a bell announced that the elevator was back to their floor. Even then, Quinn barely noticed, but Aaron was apparently a bit more alert and pulled his head away. "Respectable building, Quinn," he gasped.

Quinn didn't know why he was supposed to care about any of that, but he let Aaron peel himself off the wall and lead the way down the hallway, the fingers of one hand still tightly entwined with Quinn's. They were inside the apartment with the door safely closed behind them when Aaron apparently decided that it was his turn to initiate things. He shoved Quinn against the wall and leaned in, so tall and wide-shouldered that Quinn felt surrounded, in the best possible way. Well, maybe not quite the *best* way. Which was probably something they should discuss. Quinn's dick was up and ready for action, and if it wasn't going to get any, he should break the news to it as soon as possible. Not that it was likely going to make much of a difference, not with Aaron so close and so available. "Just how far are we going here?" he asked between kisses, lowering his head so that his mouth wasn't right next to Aaron's. Aaron's body shifted, and he looked at Quinn with concern. Quinn really didn't like that expression. He leaned up for another kiss. "It's fine, whatever, I just—you know. If we're only going so far, it'd be easier if I knew that up front."

Aaron looked at his feet, then at the wall they were leaning against. "This is almost the same place we were the last time we had this conversation." He smiled quickly. "I hope it goes a bit better this time."

"It will. Seriously, I don't want to push. But, just—if you've already got some limit figured out, let me in on it, okay? If there's a brick wall up there, I'd like to know it's coming before I run into it."

"There's no brick wall." Aaron looked bashful, and it probably wasn't going to help Quinn's sanity that he found the expression so irresistible. If Quinn got totally turned on by the way Aaron looked when he was shutting things down... it just seemed like a recipe for frustration. "But, you know, it was your idea that I take it a bit slow."

"Yeah, I know. But I also said that you should be taking it slow with some other guy, so—we're not following the plan too closely here." He hooked his fingers into the waistband of Aaron's jeans. "Can we do stuff we've already done?"

"I was the only one who got off, last time." Aaron unhooked Quinn's fingers and held them in his hands. "If we're going that far, you need to let me take a turn. I mean... I told you, I won't know what I'm doing. But you could teach me, right?"

Another shy look, and Quinn started to wonder whether Aaron was doing it on purpose. "Yeah, I could teach you." His voice sounded low and husky, even to his own ears, and his cock was positively twitching in anticipation. Still, this was supposed to be about Aaron's needs, not his. "But you don't have to. If you don't want."

"No, I want." Aaron's kiss was gentle, but his tongue wrapped around Quinn's in a way that suggested that he might have some serious aptitude for the lesson he was asking for. "Can we take off some clothes?"

Quinn nodded. Stupid question, really. Still, he should try to do this right. So instead of shedding fabric with his usual efficiency, he returned his hands to Aaron's waistband, letting his fingers tickle along the warm skin beneath the denim. "Shirts off?" he suggested, and Aaron lifted his arms obediently, letting Quinn slide his hands up along Aaron's torso, then pull the fabric off over his head. Aaron's chest was flushed again, like it had been that first night, and Quinn brought his mouth in to taste the warmth. He found a nipple, and sucked hard before nipping it gently. Aaron's breathing got ragged; this was going to be easy.

But, he reminded himself, Aaron wanted things slow. And that probably meant they should get more than five feet away from the front door. He straightened and nudged Aaron backward. "Bed?"

Aaron's eyes were already a bit glazed over, but after a moment's processing time he nodded and turned. Quinn followed after him, enjoying the way the flush from his chest was also visible on his back, and the shift of his muscles as he moved, even doing something as simple as walking across a room. The kid was beautiful, and Quinn was beginning to think that this whole "going slow" thing might be a good idea. It would be nice to have the time to explore all that skin.

Aaron paused when he reached the bed, as if unsure how to proceed. Finally he turned and perched on the edge. It would have been more efficient to take his jeans off before he sat down, but Quinn reminded himself that this wasn't all about efficiency. Still, he took the opportunity to pull his own shirt off before he dropped to his knees and eased Aaron's thighs apart, making room for himself between them. It was a high bed, so Aaron's head was still above Quinn's, but that wasn't really a problem for what he wanted to do. He returned his mouth to Aaron's chest, focusing on the other nipple this time, while his hands ran over the kid's legs. He could feel the muscles trembling through the denim, and Aaron's breathing was ragged again, with a quiet gasp, an almost musical sound, coming with each inhalation. Jesus, it was going to be a bit hard to take things slow if the kid got this worked up this fast. Quinn had been planning on working his hands in toward Aaron's cock, but he was pretty sure that even a brush of contact at this point would result in an anticlimactic climax. Maybe they needed to de-escalate for a while.

Quinn stood up, and Aaron's eyes followed him. "Swing your legs over, Aaron. Lie down on your back."

Aaron obeyed, but the flush on his face was more than arousal when he blurted out, "I'm not going to last. I'm sorry, it's—it's just like last time. I can't...."

Quinn hoped it was okay to laugh, because he really wasn't able to stop himself. "No shit, Aaron." He eased himself down on the bed, lying on his side with a breath of space between their bodies. "But don't worry about it. Depending on what you end up doing—like, topping or bottoming— coming easily isn't necessarily a bad thing. Especially if you can get it up again fast afterwards." He wanted to touch, wanted to keep going with what he'd started, but apparently this was a big deal for Aaron. "And this is just new. You'll probably calm down a little, once you're used to it."

Aaron threw an arm over his face, his nose in the crook of his elbow, and mumbled, "This is not how I planned it. I was going to be way cooler this time. Not nearly as much of a spaz."

Damn, it was hard to be this close and not be able to touch;

Quinn could actually feel the heat coming off of Aaron's body. He took a calming breath, then lifted his hand carefully and pulled Aaron's arm away from his face. Surely that couldn't be a turn-on. "You're not a spaz. And, honestly—this is hot as hell. You're making me feel like a total sex god."

Aaron snorted, but it was amusement, not self-disgust. "Yeah, by comparison to the total loser."

"Hell, no! By achievement. I make guys come in their pants, without even trying. That's pretty impressive."

"Okay, I have *not* come in my pants." Aaron was starting to get some of his fighting spirit back.

"Not yet." Quinn let a little growl slip into his voice. "But I'm not going to just lie here forever, so if you want to keep that statement true, you'd better shed a couple layers."

Aaron barely hesitated. His hands flew to his fly, but once it was undone, he paused. "Just jeans, or underwear too?"

"It's your laundry, Aaron. As far as I'm concerned, the less clothes the better." He smiled, and let one finger reach out to trace the line of hair from Aaron's navel down to the waistband of his boxer-briefs. "But it's your call. I'm fine regardless."

"You've still got *your* pants on," Aaron pointed out.

"But I'm not shy about taking them off. I just figured, you know—there's only so much stimulation your poor little body seems able to take."

Aaron laughed. "Yeah, maybe you're right." He took a moment to think, and then his fingers hooked under his boxers and pushed them down with his pants. He had to ease the fabric over his hard cock and lift his hips in the air to get the pants down past his ass, and the whole maneuver, combined with the newly exposed skin, had Quinn thinking that Aaron might not be the only one who should be worrying about coming too early. He tried to distract himself by scooting to the foot of the bed and tugging Aaron's pants down over his feet, but helping to undress a beautiful man really wasn't a good way to calm down. And the new location gave him a fantastic view of Aaron in his glory, tall and rangy and stretched out on the bed, waiting for Quinn. Damn it.

"I—I can't not touch you, Aaron." He swung a leg over so he was straddling the kid's legs. "Let me make you come, okay? *Then* we can go slow, if you want. Okay? But I can't... I can't just look, and not touch."

Aaron's eyes were wide, as if he was amazed that Quinn was being affected at all. Jesus, what did the kid think he was, straight? He nodded slowly. "Okay."

But Quinn hadn't waited for the word. As soon as he'd seen the first vertical motion of Aaron's head, he'd been in action. He pushed his body forward, letting himself almost land on Aaron before extending his arms and bracing them on the mattress. But he wanted his hands free, so he shifted to an awkward sprawl, mostly on Aaron's legs, partly on the bed, but with the important parts lined up. Aaron's cock looked huge from so close up, and it hadn't looked exactly small from farther away. Quinn took just the tip in his mouth, running his tongue around the head as he found Aaron's balls with one hand. The other hand ran over the hard muscles of Aaron's thighs, and he could feel them twitching as Aaron fought to stay still. The kid wasn't going to last, though, that was the whole point of this, so Quinn abandoned any efforts at finesse and sunk his head down, his lips wrapped tight around Aaron's shaft. He got most of the way down the first try, then changed the angle and got even further, and that was it. Aaron was groaning something incomprehensible, and his cock jerked in Quinn's mouth, then again, and again, and Quinn pulled off enough that he'd be able to swallow.

The kid came hard, and when he was done, he lay there on the bed as if he was dead. Quinn remembered this lassitude from their previous encounter. It was still frustrating—Quinn was so hard it hurt, and he'd like to get on with finding his own release. But this time, it was nice too, getting to see the relaxed, happy smile on Aaron's face, and knowing that he was the one who'd put it there.

He slid up Aaron's naked body and nestled in beside him, and when Aaron turned his head, they kissed, slow and easy. Quinn let himself sink into those sensations, tried to relax his body and apologize to his dick. He was actually a little startled when he felt Aaron's hand, tentatively rubbing along his fly. Startled, but absolutely ready to go along with whatever Aaron was up to.

"This okay?" Aaron asked softly. His smile showed that he already knew what the answer was going to be, so Quinn didn't bother. He just shifted a little to give Aaron's hand more room.

But Aaron didn't seem satisfied with that, and he pushed Quinn's shoulder to keep him moving until Quinn was the one lying on his back, with Aaron on his side, propped up with one elbow on the bed, the other arm free to explore Quinn's body. And explore he did.

Quinn had no idea how long they stayed like that. Aaron shifted as needed, touching every inch of Quinn's exposed skin, with lips or tongue or fingertips. He returned to Quinn's lips regularly, kissing softly one time, hard and deep the next. Eventually, he nudged Quinn to roll over onto his stomach, and Quinn obliged, allowing Aaron to continue his attentions along Quinn's back. It was a strange mix of sensations—Quinn's muscles were relaxed and pliant, but his cock was still rock hard.

"What's this from?" Aaron asked quietly, his fingers tickling along a scar that ran from Quinn's shoulder blade down toward his spine.

"Uh—there's another one, right? Down below it?" Aaron kissed along the second scar in acknowledgement. "I can't remember which is which. One of them, I was riding my bike and I bent over to go under this sort of... like a bridge, up to a tree house? But I didn't bend far enough, and there was a bolt sticking out of the bottom of the bridge."

"Ouch," Aaron said softly, and kissed both scars. "And the other one?"

Quinn had his standard lie all ready to go, but he caught

himself. Aaron seemed to think he wanted to know about Quinn's family. Maybe he needed a quick taste of reality to understand why it wasn't something that there was any point in dwelling on. "My brother stabbed me with a pair of scissors." There was no immediate reaction, and Quinn wondered whether he'd spoken too quietly. Then Aaron bent and kissed each scar again, harder than he had the first time.

He didn't ask for any details, though, and Quinn wasn't sure if Aaron was just being polite, or whether he really didn't want to know. But it wouldn't be fair for Quinn to leave that statement out there, making his brother look homicidal or something.

"It wasn't his fault. Connor—my brother—he was always on a lot of medication. His brain was... I don't know. They never got a real diagnosis for it. They'd label him as something, and then the next doctor would say, no, it was something else entirely." Quinn twisted his neck so he was looking away from Aaron. All the lovely relaxation was gone from his muscles, but he'd started this—he might as well finish it. "So they tried him on a new drug, and he reacted really badly. It was supposed to be antipsychotic, but it went the other direction. He didn't even remember doing it, afterward." That had hurt almost as much as the physical injury, the fact that Connor hadn't been able to remember the event. He'd stabbed his own brother, and Quinn had really wanted to know why. He knew it wasn't Connor's fault, but he'd wanted to understand what was going through Connor's head, how his thoughts had been twisted enough to make it seem like he needed to kill his twin. But he'd said he didn't remember, and Quinn believed him. They'd never lied to each other—not until the very end.

"On the plus side, it made them start listening to me more, about him. I'd been saying for days that things weren't right, and they didn't believe me. But after that, they realized that I could be useful. I could talk to him when nobody else could, and he'd tell me stuff he wouldn't tell them."

Aaron nodded. He wasn't really exploring anymore, just lying half on the mattress, half on Quinn, giving an occasional kiss to the shoulder that was closest to him. "How old were you?"

"Uh... grade eight. What is that, thirteen, maybe?" Aaron didn't say anything, and Quinn didn't like the silence. "Apparently puberty was part of the problem. They'd gotten him more or less stabilized on the kid drugs, but then his chemistry started changing, and they had to hunt around and find something that would work for a teenager. And then for an adult."

"Did they ever find it?"

Quinn shook his head. "They kept thinking they had, but he was never right. And the ones that calmed him down the best, they made him like a zombie or something. Every now and then, you'd get a glimpse of real Connor...." Quinn had to stop. They had always broken his heart, the moments of clarity and freedom that Connor had sometimes been able to find. He'd always wanted to race around, and do everything that he was missing when he was drugged, and he'd always wanted Quinn to go with him. So of course Quinn had. Amusement parks, funny movies, and, later, girls and road trips and parties. Connor frantically tried to fit in every experience; Quinn watched and waited, the anxiety gnawing away at his stomach, ready to step in and pick up the pieces when his brother inevitably fell apart.

"Hey, Quinn." The kisses on his shoulder got a bit more demanding. "Quinn." A nip that time. "Quinn!" and Aaron pushed in toward Quinn's neck, rubbing his stubbled jaw against Quinn's sensitive skin. "Quinn, Quinn, Quinn!"

"What are you doing, you maniac?" Quinn was laughing, and he squirmed away a little, but not too far.

"Trying to get your attention. I did it again, didn't I? I got off, and I haven't returned the favor." Aaron nuzzled in further, nudged at Quinn's head until he turned it far enough for their lips to meet. "Sorry, Quinn. I'm sorry." He said it more softly than he would have if all he was talking about was sex.

But Quinn didn't have to acknowledge that. "It's okay, Aaron."

He let the kiss deepen, and let Aaron roll him over onto his back again. He wasn't really turned on any more, but it seemed important to Aaron that they keep going, and he was pretty sure he could get it back. Jesus, he was damn sure he could, if Aaron kept kissing like that.

But he didn't keep kissing. Instead, he squirmed around until he was kneeling, straddling Quinn, their cocks lined up just about perfectly, and it looked like Quinn had been right to expect a fast recovery time from the kid. Aaron saw where Quinn was looking and his blush came back, but he didn't move to cover up, and Quinn brought his hand down to wrap around Aaron's cock.

"No, wait—I want you naked, at least, this time."

"So... if you don't like the jeans, do something about them."

"Yeah? That easy?" Aaron's hands started toward Quinn's fly.

"That *is* my reputation." He still wasn't totally into this, but he was getting there. He was hard enough that he wasn't worried about hurting Aaron's feelings if his jeans came off, so that was all that really mattered. The rest would take care of itself.

Aaron had Quinn's fly undone, and he looked up, uncertain again. "Underwear too?"

"Jesus, Aaron, this is your show. You decide. Anything's fine by me."

"Yeah? Anything?" Aaron had a devilish look in his eye, but Quinn really wasn't too worried. And, sure enough, Aaron grinned and cast his eyes down. "Can I take a rain check?"

"It's not a special sale, Aaron—it's an open offer. Anytime, anywhere."

"Yeah? Anywhere?" Aaron leaned down for a kiss, his fingers still tickling and pulling at the hairs beneath Quinn's fly.

"You got somewhere in mind, cowboy?"

"I'll let you know," Aaron promised. "But at this point, I'll go with now, and here." He hooked his fingers under Quinn's underwear and pulled.

Quinn helped, and when he was naked, Aaron crawled up his body and stretched out on top of him. "This okay?"

Quinn laughed. "I swear, Aaron, stop asking. If you want to wrap seven quilts around yourself, cut a hole for your dick, and rub oatmeal all over me, that'd be okay." He let his hands run down Aaron's back, and over the curve of his ass. "It'd be fucking weird, but okay."

"Is it wrong that that's kind of a hot image? The oatmeal part, at least." Aaron nuzzled in and kissed along Quinn's neck.

"It's not wrong. But it's fucking weird. You are a strange, strange person."

"I don't know." Aaron kissed down Quinn's throat to his chest. "It'd fit into all the hollows. This line, here," and he kissed the valley between Quinn's abs, "it'd be full of oatmeal. And the high parts, like here, and here," he said as he kissed one of Quinn's nipples, and then the other, "they'd be clear, with maybe just a sort of film over them, where the oatmeal had slid off. And maybe I could move it around a little." He dragged an imaginary pile of oatmeal up to the high point of Quinn's ribcage, and then ran his fingers down to show how it would slide and trickle, lower and lower, until it got tangled in the top of Quinn's pubic hair. Aaron bent and sucked gently at the spot, then looked up, licking his lips. "Mmmm... brown sugar."

Quinn didn't know whether to laugh or moan. "That is a vivid imagination you've got going, there."

"I'm a twenty-two-year-old virgin. My imagination and my right hand have had a pretty good workout." Aaron looked up at Quinn, and then his face got serious. "Okay, I won't ask any more, but if I do something totally wrong, you'll tell me, right?"

Quinn smiled, and let his fingers trace over the angles of Aaron's face. Aaron turned enough to catch Quinn's fingertips in a kiss, and then he stretched out and kissed the head of Quinn's cock. Finally.

Once he'd started, Aaron apparently decided that it was time to get down to business. He shifted around to a better angle, and then gripped the base of Quinn's cock with one hand and used his mouth on the rest. He slid down the sides, he licked the slit, and he sucked the head right into his mouth, where he gave it generous attention from his tongue. It wasn't intense, more playful than passionate, but Quinn was pretty sure it was going to get the job done.

"Hey," Quinn said. "Aaron, hey." Aaron looked up, but didn't remove his mouth from Quinn's cock, and Quinn wished he had a camera. He gave himself a moment to capture the image in his memory, then said, "Come up here."

Aaron obliged, looking sheepish. "Was that not good? I told you I didn't know what I was doing."

"It was excellent. I just—want you up here. We can use our hands, okay?"

Aaron gave him a quizzical look. "Okay, last time, you said you could give *yourself* a hand job, and if I wasn't going to do more than that, I was wasting your time."

"Well, sometimes I'm an asshole. Hand jobs are good." Aaron didn't look convinced, though, so Quinn forced himself to say the rest. "There's lots of guys who are good at sucking me off. There's not many that I want to kiss."

Aaron looked surprised, but then he smiled. "Oh. Okay." He let Quinn shift them so they were both lying on their sides, facing each other. "But I can do blow jobs *sometimes*, right? I mean—I want to get really good at it. Like you are. I want to learn how to make you feel good."

"You already make me feel good, Aaron."

"Okay, well, I want to make you come until your eyes bulge right out of your head, then."

"Yeah, okay, if it's that important to you, I guess I can let you get really good at blow jobs."

"Excellent." Aaron brought the arm next to the mattress up to pillow his head, and Quinn mirrored the action. Then Quinn took Aaron's free hand and moved it down. Quinn squirmed over until their cocks were lined up, and then laced his fingers with Aaron's and wrapped their hands as far around their two cocks as they could manage.

"Okay?" Quinn asked, and Aaron just grinned, and kissed him.

They lay there like that, kissing slow and deep, working their hands like they had all the time in the world, teasing, playing, until the mood gradually shifted as they got closer to climaxing. Quinn came first, and it was almost too intimate, to have Aaron staring at him, watching the sensations wash across his body, across his face. He had to force himself not to hide. He didn't even shut his eyes, although he lost his focus at the peak of his orgasm, and when he came down and was able to understand what he was seeing, he was rewarded by the look of awed affection in Aaron's eyes.

Aaron returned the favor shortly after, when it was his turn to come. Then they kissed for a while, soft and easy, and finally drifted off to sleep.

CHAPTER FOURTEEN

AARON woke with the clock radio, blaring the typical morning drive nonsense. He didn't like it, but it was annoying enough to generally force him out of bed. He opened his eyes, and frowned. He was on the wrong side of the bed, and the sheets were all messed up. The events of the night before came back to him in a wave, and he looked around for any sign of Quinn. He saw nothing, but stood up to get a better look, and he saw the note left on the little table by the kitchen. He managed to not trip on the sheets as he raced across the floor, but it was a close call.

> *Aaron—*
>
> *I had to go—I need to get changed before work, and I'm on the early shift today. I'll see you at the barn. I've got my phone, so call me if there's a problem.*
>
> *Also, I set up the coffee maker for you. I didn't turn it on, because I figured you wouldn't want hours-old coffee. Does it still count?*
>
> *-Quinn*

Aaron wandered over and switched the coffee maker on. It was nowhere near as good as having Quinn there with him, but it was better than nothing. He opened the fridge and saw that his box of cornflakes had been moved from its home in the cupboard and placed next to the carton of milk. There was another note tucked inside the lid of the cereal, and Aaron smiled as he opened it.

Brunch?

-Quinn

It was nice to think of Quinn moving around the apartment, making himself at home. Well, nice, but also a bit creepy, because Aaron knew he was a sound sleeper, but this was a bit extreme. Quinn could have rearranged all the furniture, probably, and Aaron would have slept right through it. He wondered what the "hours old" meant in the coffee reference—what time had it been when Quinn left? But that was less important than the fact that he had left a note, Aaron decided. Quinn hadn't just taken off; he'd had somewhere to be. That was fair.

Aaron checked his watch. Quinn should already be at the barn. It was tempting, but Aaron resisted the urge to call him. He'd just hurry into the shower and then get to work himself, so he could see Quinn in person. And maybe try to find somewhere private, for a while. Maybe the storage loft, or the hay shed. Or one of the back fields, although that was a bit riskier. Quinn *had* said anytime, anywhere, and Aaron already had a location in mind to put that promise to the test.

He got to the barn and parked next to Quinn's motorcycle. It wasn't the most convenient spot, really; Quinn always parked his bike in a tiny corner that was too small for a car, and parking next to it left the tail end of Aaron's truck sticking out into the driveway, but he didn't care. He liked the idea of their vehicles spending the day together.

Aaron walked into the barn and was immediately set upon by two boarders, one of whom had found heat and swelling in her Thoroughbred's pastern, and the other of whom wanted him to give her detailed instructions about getting her horse off his forehand, although she apparently wasn't interested in paying for a lesson on the topic. He looked around for Quinn, but didn't see him.

He managed to satisfy the boarders and was heading out to see if Quinn was in the back fields when his mother appeared and gestured him into the office. He went in and she shut the door behind him, which wasn't a good sign at all.

"What's up?" He tried to sound casual.

"I just got a call from your father. He's been talking to his friend at the police department, and apparently Quinn's family has been notified that the missing person's case is closed. And they've gone a bit crazy—private investigators, lawyers, the whole thing. It sounds like this is going to happen fast. They're going to find him." She shook her head. "I can't understand why he wouldn't want to be in touch with them, but... there must be a reason, right? Has he talked about it with you?"

Aaron wasn't sure how much was confidential and how much was for public consumption. "He told me a bit about his brother, and it sounded like Quinn and his parents weren't too close through it all. But he didn't say anything that seemed too horrible. Maybe we're blowing it out of proportion. He didn't seem happy, when I warned him that they might be coming, but he didn't panic or anything." Aaron tried to remember the conversation. "He said he thought maybe they'd just filed the missing person's report because it seemed like the right thing to do. He didn't seem to think they'd really be all that interested in finding him."

"Well, I'd say they're interested, all right." She looked undecided for a moment, then snapped back into gear. "He's fixing the gate on the third paddock—it keeps getting stuck. Why don't you go give him a heads-up about all this?"

Aaron was more than happy to have an excuse to look for Quinn. It was raining a little, so he grabbed one of the communal slickers from the hook in the lounge and pulled his baseball cap down over his eyes. He headed out to the paddocks and saw Quinn, wearing an identical slicker with the addition of a beat-up old cowboy hat that somebody had abandoned in the loft. Aaron felt an almost physical rush of emotion. He wanted to be with Quinn, always. He wanted to laugh with him, and cry with him, and protect him from whatever it was that made him feel threatened. He knew it was way too early to start talking about love, and he almost regretted having used the word with his parents, but he wasn't going to try to lie to himself. There was no point. He was in love. He wanted to shout it from the rooftops, or at least say it to Quinn, but he would hold off as long as he could. When Quinn glanced up and saw him, and smiled with a hint of uncertainty, Aaron was pretty sure that he wouldn't be able to resist the temptation for too long. But for now, he had other business to attend to.

"Hey," he said as he approached. "Thanks for the coffee, and brunch. Now I'm just waiting for my walk on the damned beach, right?"

Quinn glanced up at sky; it was gray in all directions. "Maybe we could wait for better weather?"

"Yeah, maybe." He really wanted to kiss Quinn, but he settled for reaching out and rubbing his arm. It was stupid, and awkward, but he was pretty sure Quinn got the message. Now it was time for the other message he needed to give. "Uh, listen—remember yesterday, when I said your family might be on their way? It sounds like that's happening. Pretty fast, maybe. I guess they're serious about finding you."

Quinn's face froze in a careful, neutral expression, and he turned slowly and leaned his forearms on top of the gate he'd been working on. Aaron felt awkward. He didn't want to crowd Quinn, but he couldn't just walk away. So he waited. Finally, Quinn spoke, although he kept his face turned to the pasture. "They have some fucked-up timing. I mean—I'm trying to... I don't know, trying to do something *real* here. With you." He glanced over and smiled a little, but then turned back. There was more silence, and then a quietly explosive, "Fuck!"

"Is it—how bad is it? I mean, how much do you *not* want to see them?" Aaron had a dozen half-assed plans running through his mind. They mostly involved him and Quinn going on the run, traveling across the continent incognito. Maybe they'd go to Mexico—Quinn already spoke Spanish, although Aaron really didn't like to think about the person who might have taught it to him.

"It's not.... Fuck!" But now there was a hint of laughter in Quinn's voice. Self-deprecating and bitter laughter, but at least a start. "It's not a huge deal. I'm being a loser. I just—things were starting to come together. I finally feel like maybe there's something good going on. I don't want any changes, or any distractions. I just want—" He looked over at Aaron and smiled, a mix of shy and mischievous. "You remember those seven quilts, from last night? I want you to *not* cut a dick-hole in them, and I don't want oatmeal involved at all, but I want to hang a couple of the quilts up to make a fort and then I want to wrap the two of us up in the ones left over. And I want to stay in there forever. Or at least for a very long time."

Aaron liked that plan even better than his road trip idea. God, he really wanted to touch Quinn. But they were totally in the open, and it had been Quinn's request that they keep things quiet. It wouldn't be fair to force their relationship public at the same time that Quinn was going through all the stress from his family. So he tried to distract himself, a little. "If we had the oatmeal, we could stay in even longer, because we wouldn't have to worry about getting hungry...."

Quinn grinned, and that made it totally impossible for Aaron to stay so far away. He tried to look casual, just eased his way over to lean on the gate next to Quinn. Quinn didn't run. Instead, he shifted over a little closer, and reached his far hand over to wrap in the fabric of Aaron's shirt, just above his belt. Aaron realized that the slickers were wide and draping, so that it would be hard to see where one began and one ended, from a distance and in the rain. And it would certainly be impossible to see what was going on in front of the two men standing, casually looking out at the field. He reached his own hand down and covered Quinn's with it.

"It's like a mini-slicker-fort," he suggested.

"If you pull out a bowl of oatmeal, I'm going to be a bit concerned."

"Oatmeal is good for you—good for your heart. It says it right on the box."

"*You're* good for my heart. It says it right here." Quinn pointed to the smile on his face. And undercover lovers or not, Aaron had to kiss him, after he said something like that. But Quinn pulled away before Aaron even started to move. "Jesus Christ, did I really just say that? What the fuck, Aaron, I think hanging out with you is turning my brain into mush...."

But Aaron's hand on Quinn's cheek made him stop talking, and he didn't resist as Aaron tilted their heads enough for a quick, sweet kiss. Aaron would have liked more—a lot more—but when he moved to press their bodies together more closely, Quinn stepped back. "Respectable farm, Aaron."

"Yeah, okay." Aaron turned back toward the field. "Hey, your hands are freezing. Where are your gloves?"

"They're in my pocket. I needed my fingers free for work."

"Can you even feel anything with them? You might as well be wearing mittens, if your fingers are numb anyway."

"Yes, Mom," Quinn said mockingly, but then his face got serious as if the word had reminded him of what he was facing. "Jesus. How sure are you that they're coming?"

"None of the information is from *me*, man. But Mom said that Dad said that his cop friend said the cops had to send a report saying that the missing persons case had been closed. And when they did, apparently all hell broke loose—your family sent lawyers and private investigators and whatever else out to get details." Aaron frowned. "Actually, I thought Dad said that the cops would contact you, first, to see how much information you wanted released. Did they not do that?"

"Uh—no. But people have been calling my phone like crazy, the last couple days. I just didn't pick up, if I didn't recognize the number. I guess I should probably check the messages."

"Why do you even *have* a phone, Quinn?"

"To order food, mostly. But I picked up for you, yesterday."

"Yeah, you did. Thanks." Aaron wanted another kiss, but he managed to resist. "So, do you have a plan? For the family stuff?"

"Beyond... forts?"

"Yeah, a plan B, maybe."

Quinn looked back out at the pasture, and Aaron anticipated the next, "Fuck!" almost to the second. He didn't foresee the rapid turn that followed it, or the look of determination on Quinn's face. "Okay. You're right, I should get in front of this. I don't want them here, not if I can help it. So I'll give them a call? I can check in, say I'm okay, and that should be it. Right?"

"I don't know, man. I mean, that wouldn't be anywhere *close* to being enough for my family. But you guys are different, so... maybe."

"Yeah." Quinn looked thoughtful. "Is there a downside? To calling? Just how sure are we that all this is happening? Your dad wouldn't make it up as some sort of 'get Quinn talking' bullshit, would he?"

"No, he wouldn't lie about it. But why don't you just listen to your messages, and see?"

Quinn sighed. "Yeah, I guess." He patted his pockets. "I think my phone's in the barn. This is almost done, though. Can you just lift the far end of the gate? I was getting to the two-man-job stage, and Danny said he'd come down to help, but I haven't seen him."

Aaron wondered whether Danny had seen *them*, earlier, and had decided not to interrupt. He felt guilty for the triumphant thrill that came with the idea of Danny knowing. Danny would tease him, sure, but he'd be happy about it too.

They finished the gate together, and gathered up the tools and headed for the barn. Aaron followed Quinn into the office, and when Quinn looked like he was going to chicken out, Aaron burrowed through the pockets of Quinn's leather jacket and found the phone. He let his fingers touch Quinn's as he handed the phone over, and then headed for the coffee maker. Aaron tried to give Quinn at least the illusion of privacy as he listened to his messages, but Quinn didn't seem too concerned about Aaron's presence, so he didn't leave the room entirely. He wanted to be nearby in case he was needed.

Quinn had a lot of messages. He wrote down a few phone numbers on the pad of paper they kept on the desk, but otherwise he just listened. When he finally hung up, he looked over at Aaron and shrugged. "Yeah. Sounds like stuff is happening." He looked at the phone in his hand. "I guess I should call them."

"Do you want me to leave?" Aaron started for the door.

"No, man. I mean—I shouldn't do it here, anyway. I'm at work, and I've already wasted enough time on this today. I've got stalls to do, and you've got lessons and stuff."

"We can work it out, Quinn, if this is important. Danny and my mom can cover for us. Or just for you, if you want to do it on your own."

Quinn shook his head almost violently. His expression softened when he saw Aaron's look. "I just need some time to get it straight in my head, first."

"Yeah, okay. But—how far away is Calgary? They could be on their way here right now."

"Well, if they are, a phone call won't do much good." Quinn's smile looked a little strained, but at least he was still trying. "I'll just get started on the stalls, and worry about the rest of it later."

Aaron didn't argue anymore, and they both went about their day's work. It was frustrating, to have to put the good feelings on hold in order to let Quinn deal with all this new stuff, but

Aaron reminded himself that it wasn't about him. Sure, it would have been excellent if all he'd had to think about that day was finding ways to get Quinn alone, or wondering what they'd get up to that night, but this was real life. And he and Quinn were handling it, together, and maybe that was more important, and somehow more romantic, than if they'd been floating around on clouds together, totally detached from reality.

Late in the day, when they did find themselves alone together, out in the hay shed, Quinn moved into Aaron's arms naturally and without even a hint of caution. Their kiss wasn't playful, as Aaron had imagined that their early kisses might be, and it wasn't passionate, at least in a sexual way. It was just comfort, and affection, and acceptance. Aaron felt like he'd been an idiot to ever have thought that those other kinds of kisses were the important ones.

"You doing okay?" he asked, his lips only a breath away from Quinn's.

"Yeah, I'm fine. It'll be fine." Quinn didn't sound completely sure.

"Mom and Danny both asked if there's anything they should be doing. I caught Danny counting the cans of fly spray—I think he was planning to make them into Molotov cocktails, for when the siege commences."

"Good to know your whole family's mental." Quinn's fingers snuck in under Aaron's shirt and found the warm skin there.

Aaron wasn't sure if his shiver was from the cold or from the stimulation. He still couldn't quite believe it, that this was him, with Quinn. After all those months of wanting him, now he got to have him. "Whenever, wherever," he said, mostly to himself, but Quinn smiled in response.

"You making some plans?"

"Maybe. Is the offer still good?"

"I told you, man—no time limit."

Aaron was just about to ask whether it was a one-time offer or if he could have unlimited refills, but Danny's voice outside the shed cut off his idea. "Quinn! You around?"

Quinn moved away from Aaron a half-second before Danny stepped inside the doorway, out of the rain. It occurred to Aaron that his brother wasn't in the habit of yelling people's names out for no reason; it seemed like he'd been announcing himself, and making sure that he wasn't interrupting anything. Pretty smooth, for Danny.

"Hey, Danny. Do you want more second cut in the barn, or should I bring more of the first?" Quinn sounded totally casual, and Aaron wanted to laugh. They all knew what was going on, and they were all pretending that nothing was happening. It was silly. But when Danny didn't answer right away, Aaron took a closer look at his face, and the urge to laugh disappeared.

Danny was looking at Quinn. "There's some people here for you, Quinn. They say they're your family. Your parents, and your sister." He waited for a reaction, but Quinn didn't say anything. "They're waiting for you in the office."

Quinn nodded slowly, as if he wasn't quite absorbing the message yet. "Yeah, okay. Thanks." He looked back at the hay. "So, first cut or second?"

Danny frowned, but went with it. "Uh—some second, I guess. But I can do that, man. If you want to...." Danny stopped talking when Quinn grabbed a bale of hay and swung it over to the big wheelbarrow. Danny looked at Aaron as if for guidance, but Aaron was at a loss. He decided he'd just follow Quinn's lead. He picked up another bale and added it to the wheelbarrow, and saw Danny doing the same. There was only room for three bales on the wagon, and Aaron wondered belatedly whether it would have been better to have let Quinn handle them all, so that he could have a little more time to collect himself.

But Quinn didn't seem hesitant. He lifted the wheelbarrow and trundled off toward the barn as if it were any other day, and Danny and Aaron hurried after him. Quinn steered into the feedroom and deposited the bales of hay, and then, without stopping, without looking at Aaron or Danny, he headed for the office.

Aaron had no idea what to do. He wanted to help Quinn, however he could, but he didn't know where to even start. Should he be in there with them? It really didn't seem like Quinn had wanted him. Should he wait around outside, or would that be too obvious? He looked over to Danny, hoping for guidance, but Danny just shook his head as if he knew the questions Aaron wanted to ask. "No idea, Aaron. The whole thing's beyond me." He looked toward the office door, then back to his brother. "Help me with the feeding. Then you're in the barn, if he needs you, but you're not hanging around the door like a stalker."

Aaron was glad to have something to do with his hands. He thought about what Quinn had said, about his family's bad timing. Aaron needed Quinn, and it was becoming increasingly obvious, at least to Aaron, that Quinn needed him right back. He would just have to hope that this new development didn't get in the way of them both getting what they needed.

CHAPTER FIFTEEN

QUINN paused in the lounge before going into the office. He half-wished that he'd dragged Aaron in with him, but that wouldn't have been fair. The kid didn't need to get mixed up in all this. And if Quinn was being honest, it was easier, in a way, without him there. Aaron got in under Quinn's skin, and made him feel sensitized and hyper-aware. At times, it was a good thing, but in this situation, Quinn wanted to be as numb as possible. He only wished he had a bottle to help him out.

But he didn't, and waiting wasn't going to make anything better, so he forced himself to walk as far as the next doorway. And there they were. His mother was sitting at the table, her purse clutched in her lap, and his father was standing behind her with his hand on her shoulder. They looked so much older than he remembered. And standing by the desk, a beautiful young woman, long hair pulled back from a face that was familiar without being recognizable.

"Caitlin?" He stepped into the room. "Damn. You grew up."

She just stared at him, and he guessed he'd been wrong, hoping that she'd be the easy one to talk to. Or at least he hoped he'd been wrong—what if his parents were even more difficult? Still, they'd come a long way, so he guessed he had to give it a chance.

"Mom. Dad. Hi." Not exactly poetry, but it was more than any of *them* were managing.

Tears were rolling down his mother's face. He guessed it must be hard for her, to see him looking so much like the son she would never see again. He'd gone through a stage where he hadn't liked looking in the mirror, much, but possibly there were other reasons for that.

And still no one was talking. He decided that he'd give it one more try, and then go hide in the loft. "Sorry if it was hard to get hold of me. I didn't—I didn't know you were looking."

"Quinn!" Finally, his mother was speaking. Unfortunately, she didn't sound too impressed. "How could you possibly think that we wouldn't be looking?"

That was a bit surprising. He frowned at her, then at his father. They both looked equally outraged. "You...." He paused, and reviewed it in his mind. No, there was no way he was misremembering, or misinterpreting. "You told me to leave. You said—" He had to catch himself. Apparently he didn't have the old emotions buried quite as deeply as he had hoped. He took a breath, and continued in a calmer tone. "You said I was tearing the family apart, and I should go." He looked over at Caitlin. They'd all tried to shield her from the worst of their fighting, so maybe she hadn't heard that before. She was certainly looking a little shocked.

His mother's voice echoed the expression on his sister's face. "We were *upset*, Quinn! We were going crazy—we'd just lost a son, and you were... you were scaring us! You were acting like you wanted to join him!" She lifted her shaking hand to her shoulder, and her husband gripped her fingers tightly.

Quinn didn't know what to say. "I know. That's why—that's why you told me to go away." He frowned, and tried to control his irritation. "I seriously... I'm not getting this. I mean, okay, you changed your mind, or something. Fair enough. But... you thought I should just know that, somehow?" They didn't say anything, and he decided that maybe it was time for a shift in direction. "But okay, that's the past. Is there—" Was there a polite way to ask what the hell they wanted, now? "You came all the way out here. Did you, I don't know—what are you looking for?"

"They're looking for their *son*, Quinn!" Finally, Caitlin spoke, but from her tone, Quinn wondered whether her participation was really a good thing. "I'm looking for my *brother*!" She took a step toward him and looked almost threatening. "We're looking for some sign of actual emotion from you! After all you put us through, wondering if you were dead or alive for so long, and we finally find you—and you act as if we're an inconvenience, an irritation." She looked at her parents, then back at him. "I heard what you said to them, before you left. You said they'd only ever cared about Connor, not about you. But, Jesus, Quinn, isn't the same thing true for you? Obviously he was the only one *you* ever cared about, or you wouldn't have found it so easy to walk away from us."

Quinn wanted to fight that, wanted to argue, but he was tired, and there was no point anyway. "So ... say that's true. It just—it comes back to my question, doesn't it? If we all only cared about Connor, why are you all here? What do you want from *me*?"

"Oh, Quinn." His mother stood up and stepped toward him, but caught herself before she got too close. "It wasn't true then, and it isn't true now." She brushed the tears from her eyes. "We always loved you. We just—we didn't have much attention left for you. We were always so worried about Connor. And you were so good at looking after yourself. And then, later, so good at looking after him." She looked over at her husband as if inviting him to take over, but he was standing stone-faced and still, so she continued. "It wasn't fair of us—we know that. It was too much responsibility, and it never should have been yours. But that doesn't mean for a second that we didn't love you."

Quinn wasn't even hearing the words, he didn't think. Or he was hearing them, and storing them away to think about later, but he wasn't able to respond to them right away. He needed some time, and some peace. He needed some Aaron.

But he had to deal with this, first. "I work here." That wasn't what he'd meant to say, but it made sense, once he got started. "Can you—are you staying in town? Maybe we could meet up somewhere, later. Or I could call you." A phone call would be *much* better than another meeting. "But, you know—this isn't my office. We can't stay in here for too long." He was sure that no one would object, but he hoped his family wouldn't know that.

"What the hell are you doing, working in a barn?" His father finally spoke. "You were doing your master's at MIT, for Christ's sake. Now you're working in a barn?"

"Yeah. I work in a barn." He didn't owe these people his life's story.

"Your sister's working for the company, now. She's doing a co-op placement as part of her business degree. She's doing really well." He sounded as if he expected Quinn to be upset by this, as if he should think that she stole his rightful place.

Quinn just nodded. "Okay." He glanced at Caitlin. "Good work."

Caitlin's eyes narrowed. She looked at her parents, then at the door. "Okay. I guess we should get going, right? Quinn's spent as much time with us as he can spare from his busy schedule."

That stung, a little, but at least she was shifting things in the right direction. But his mother wasn't moving. She was standing almost exactly in the middle of the office, frowning like a toddler who'd been told that a beloved pet was dead. She looked like she knew something was very, very bad, but she couldn't quite understand what it meant. Then she shook her head. "No."

Caitlin turned to look at her, and her husband put his hand back on her shoulder, but she shook him off. "We are not walking away. Not this time." She was trembling, but she wasn't backing down. "We've always loved you, Quinn. We know that we made mistakes—lots of mistakes. And one of them was letting you do *this*, letting you shut yourself off from everyone around you. I know how much it hurt you when Connor... when he died. But it hurt us too! We could have been stronger, together, but you wouldn't let us." She was crying again, her voice shaking, but she wouldn't stop. "You wanted to wall yourself off, all alone with your pain. And your drinking, and your drugs, and your—"

She stopped, but Quinn continued for her, his voice quiet. "My whoring? That's what you called it, right? I mean, if it had been girls I was sleeping with, it would have been natural. But guys— obviously I was damaged, I was perverted." He looked over at his father. "It sure sucked for you, huh? I was supposed to be the one who could carry on the family business. Not Connor—he was fragile, he was artistic, better leave him to Mom, and *you* could take care of me. I was the apple of your goddamned eye, wasn't I? As long as I was *exactly* who you wanted me to be." He looked over at Caitlin. "A business degree—that's not bad, that's at least a little bit versatile. I went for Chemical Engineering, specialty in Geochemical Extraction." He shook his head. He couldn't believe he'd been so tractable. "Believe me, it wasn't an area of passionate interest. But a pretty near perfect fit for a petroleum company with a huge interest in the tar sands, huh, Dad?"

Nobody else was saying anything, and it was just as well, because apparently Quinn wasn't quite done. He knew he shouldn't have gotten started. There was no point in any of this, no reason to drag up past hurts. But, damn, it felt pretty good, in the same way it would feel good to press on a bruise or pick at a scab. He smiled at his sister. "If you get tired of working for the company, and you want a little freedom, I *strongly* recommend bringing home a same-sex lover. You'll get all the room you could ever dream of."

"That's not fair, Quinn." His mother was still crying, but she was standing her ground. "You could have told us earlier. Springing it on us like that, when we were already torn apart. That man, showing up at our home—obviously it was shocking for us. I'm sure it would have been lovely if we could have welcomed him with open arms, but we're only human."

"'That man' had a name. 'That man' cared enough about me to

fly across the continent to check in and make sure I was okay." Quinn wished he could blame his mother for everything that had gone wrong with Diego, but he knew that he had been the one most at fault for the end of their relationship. His mom had been right when she'd said that he'd wanted to just hide away with his pain, and not talk to anybody. Diego had tried to break through, but he hadn't gotten far. And Quinn had been happy to use his family's homophobia as an excuse to get rid of his first serious boyfriend. The only shred of self-respect Quinn could salvage from the whole situation was that the whoring hadn't started until Diego was gone. The drugs and alcohol, they were a different story.

Quinn's burst of anger was gone, and he was back to just being tired. There was a cheap plastic chair beside the door, and he sank into it and slumped forward, resting his elbows on his knees. He looked up, but didn't really focus on any of them as he asked, "So, this going about how you expected?"

"I was actually worried that it might be a little tense," his sister said dryly.

He shot her a look, and grinned in spite of himself. She smiled back, tentative but true, and he remembered her as a little girl, trailing around after her big brothers, trying to do everything that they were doing.

"You seeing anyone?" she asked.

Quinn frowned, but answered. "Kind of. I mean, yeah, I am—but it's new." He wasn't sure where this was going. "You?"

"Just broke up. He was cheating on me, the son of a bitch." She was still watching him closely, as if she was trying to figure out just what she was dealing with.

"Do you need help getting rid of the corpse?"

She smiled, and swept her hand up her body, ending with it framing her face. "He's been denied access to all this. Surely that's punishment enough?"

"Yeah, okay." He wasn't sure just what they were doing, but he didn't mind it. It was kind of fun, really.

Caitlin seemed to have made up her mind about whatever it was she'd been considering. "We're staying at the Sutton Place Hotel, downtown. Why don't the three of us go down there and get settled in, and then you and your guy can join us for dinner?"

Quinn wasn't sure he liked the sound of that, and it looked like his mom wasn't too enthusiastic, either. But Caitlin stepped over and put an arm around her shoulders. "We know where he is now. He'll give us his cell number before we leave. He could still run away, I guess, if he wants to give up his job, but... he's not *that* much of a selfish, cowardly bastard. Right, Quinn?"

He nodded obediently. He was beginning to be a little afraid of his sister. She handed her phone over, and he keyed in his number, and then she hit a button and watched him jump as the phone in his jacket rang.

"Okay, then. Hotel restaurant, say... seven thirty?"

That wasn't great. Quinn was pretty sure the Sutton Place was a pretty classy hotel. He wasn't sure that he had clothes that would be suitable for its restaurant, not anymore. And he had no idea about Aaron—he'd never seen the guy in anything dressier than a button-down. Not that he was sure he was going to pass the invitation along to Aaron, or that Aaron would want to come if he *was* invited. Damn it, why wasn't anything simple?

"Maybe somewhere else?" he tried. His sister gave him a blank look, and he got exasperated. "I've been asked not to return to the Sutton Place, after a series of incidents involving nudity and oatmeal."

Caitlin looked like she didn't know or care whether he was serious. "So where would you suggest?"

That was a good question. It briefly flashed through his mind to take them to the East Hastings restaurant he'd been kicked out of the other day, just to see if the service had improved at all, but that was probably an unnecessary complication. He didn't know where would be better, though. Most of his food came from take-out spots or dives—nowhere his parents would be comfortable.

"There's a bar in the hotel that serves food." His mother seemed to have herself back under control. "It's more casual, but still quite pleasant, as I recall. Have you been banned from there, as well?" He remembered this about her, her strange flashes of perceptiveness.

"Uh, no, I think I'm okay there."

His sister raised an eyebrow but didn't object, and his parents gave him stilted good-byes and then allowed themselves to be shepherded out of the office. Quinn had stood up when they were leaving, but he sank back down into the chair as soon as they were gone. He leaned back and closed his eyes, and he didn't know Aaron had come in until he felt the comforting hand on his shoulder.

"You okay?"

Quinn nodded slowly. "Yeah, I guess. It's just a lot."

Quinn heard the door shut gently, and then Aaron was kneeling before him, his hands on either side of Quinn's face, and the kiss was gentle and healing. Quinn knew what he wanted.

"Any chance you're free for dinner, tonight? With my fucked-up family?"

Aaron pulled back a little, and Quinn opened his eyes to see Aaron's concerned frown. "Are you sure? I mean—yeah, I can be there, if you want. I *want* to be there, if you want. But you don't have to. If it's going to make things awkward, or something."

"No, it'd probably make things better. But if I was you, I wouldn't want to go. It was pretty tense in here."

"Yeah, we heard a bit." Quinn jerked his head up, and Aaron looked guilty. "Not words, just volume."

Fuck. Quinn was really not going to make Employee of the

Month. "Sorry. It might be more of the same at dinner. Probably quieter, I guess, because they're usually pretty concerned about manners. Or at least, they used to be." He shook his head. "Nah, you shouldn't come, man. It'll be nasty or just boring. Either way—"

Aaron's quick kiss caught Quinn by surprise, but he didn't object. Aaron smiled at him. "Either way, it'll be better if you have somebody in your corner. And I just happen to be absolutely, positively, in every conceivable way, on your side."

"Yeah?" Quinn leaned back and let his eyes close again. "That's good to know." Aaron's hands were warm and strong as they rested on his thighs, and he brought his own hands up to tangle fingers together. It had been Quinn's idea to keep things with Aaron quiet, and he still didn't want to go parading around the barn holding hands, but this—this was nice. He needed a little of this. And Aaron didn't seem to be in a hurry to go anywhere, so they stayed like that for quite a while.

CHAPTER SIXTEEN

AARON checked himself in the mirror, for the seven-millionth time. He looked about the same. Unfortunately.

He squirmed a little, and resisted the urge to loosen his tie. Then he resisted the urge to rip the damn thing off his neck and set it on fire. He didn't think he was going to be a fan of the meeting-the-family dynamic. Which was just one more of the many, many reasons he was coming up with for wanting to spend the rest of his life with Quinn. This could be the last time he'd ever have to go through this torture.

The buzzer sounded, and he picked up the phone for the intercom. "Quinn?"

"Yeah. You ready, or should I come up?"

"What are you wearing?"

"Aaron, this really isn't the time for phone sex."

"I'm serious, man—are you dressed up?"

"Dress pants and a shirt. Don't worry about it, Aaron, just wear whatever's comfortable."

"No tie?"

"Me? No, no tie. Why, are you wearing one?"

Aaron ripped the fabric from his neck and gleefully tossed it on the couch. "Nope."

"Damn, too bad. Ties are sexy. They're like—leashes."

"And leashes are sexy?" Aaron looked at the tie doubtfully.

"Dude, you get turned on by *oatmeal*. Compared to that, fuck, yeah, leashes are *hot*. Now are you coming down or not?"

"Yeah, I'll be right there." He left the tie on the couch, and undid his top two buttons in the elevator. He was nervous about the whole thing, right up until he saw Quinn standing in the foyer, waiting for him. Then it all faded away, and all he wanted was to make things okay. He was there to help Quinn, and anything else was unimportant. "Hey," he said. It still felt weird to be able to lean in for a kiss whenever he felt like it. Well, not quite whenever, because then he'd get nothing done all day. But whenever, within reason. And Quinn's return kiss was sweet and open.

"You ready for this?" Quinn laced his fingers through Aaron's.

"I'm fine. You?"

"I'm sober. It's a fucking mistake, I'm pretty sure. But I thought I'd give it a try."

"Well, you said we were eating in the bar. So, you know, if things go straight to hell, the liquor's handy, right?"

"I like the way you think, man." Another quick kiss, and then they were out the door.

Aaron was still getting used to living downtown, and being able to walk almost everywhere. The hotel was only a few blocks from his apartment, and the night was clear, although chilly. It gave him a good excuse to keep hold of Quinn's hand—for the warmth. Not that Quinn had made any attempt to retrieve it.

They paused briefly outside the hotel, for Quinn to collect himself. Aaron played with Quinn's collar, amazed again that he was allowed to take such liberties. Quinn was fidgeting, and Aaron smiled at him. "This may be a good time to tell you about my escape plan."

"Your escape plan. Yeah, that sounds like something I should know about."

"Well, I don't have details figured out, exactly. 'Plan' may be a little generous. But I figure we can take my truck, and put the bike in the back. In case. And we could head East, because—well, because I don't want to mess with the border, and the truck wouldn't do too well in the ocean." Quinn was smiling a little, so Aaron figured he was doing his job.

"Not North?" Quinn asked.

"Too cold. If we escape in the summer time, we can talk about North. But, for now... East."

"How far are we going?"

"All the way, baby. I've never been to the Maritimes. Have you?"

"Uh—Halifax. And Newfoundland. Actually, I've been to P.E.I. too. So, yeah, I guess I've been to the Maritimes."

"Excellent. Some local knowledge could come in handy."

Quinn nodded slowly. "Yeah. Okay." He nodded toward the hotel doors. "You ready for this?"

"I was born ready."

"You were born backward—Danny told me."

"Well, Danny wasn't there, so he doesn't know for sure. Maybe my kind of 'ready' looks like 'backward' to the uneducated eye."

"Sneaky."

"Exactly." Aaron let Quinn lead the way into the hotel, and they found the bar without too much trouble. Quinn's family was already there, and Aaron got his first good look at them. If he had to describe them in one word, he was pretty sure the word would be 'rich'. He couldn't say exactly what it was, but he'd noticed the look before, especially at horse shows. There were some people who could wear jeans and a T-shirt and still look like they were made of money, and Quinn's family absolutely had that quality. Part of it was the quietly impeccable grooming, but there was also a sort of confidence, bordering on arrogance, an assumption that the world was there to serve them. Aaron wondered whether Quinn used to be like that, and how long it took for it to wear off.

Quinn's dad stood up as they approached, and Quinn nodded to the ladies, then shook his father's hand. He stepped aside, bringing their attention to Aaron, who tried not to hide. "Mom, Dad, Caitlin—this is Aaron Miller. Aaron—my parents, Carol and Ted Donahue, and my sister, Caitlin." Aaron saw Quinn's mom frown a little. He got the impression that Quinn had messed up the introduction, somehow, but he had no idea how, or whether it had been accidental or on purpose. There was a lot to figure out about the dynamics of this family.

"It's nice to meet you, Aaron." Ted's handshake was firm and businesslike. He was wearing dress pants and a shirt with no tie, but he had a sports coat on, and Aaron kicked himself. He didn't actually *own* a sports coat, but, damn, he should get one. It looked just right. Then again, as he'd already remembered, there were some people who managed to look rich and comfortable no matter what they were wearing. And powerful. Quinn's father seemed powerful, here in the hotel, in a way that Aaron hadn't noticed in the barn. Maybe he'd been a fish out of water there, but he was clearly in his element in this environment.

A server was waiting unobtrusively as they found seats, and she stepped forward as soon as they were settled. Quinn glanced around at the drinks on the table, then at Aaron. "Beer?"

"Sure, yeah."

"Two Pale Ales, please."

Aaron wasn't sure about the "ordering for him" thing, but he thought maybe he liked it. He felt like Quinn was looking after him, and it made it crystal-damn-clear that they were together, in case anyone was wondering. Aaron was absolutely in favor of any public acknowledgement that Quinn was off the market.

"We ordered an assortment of appetizers, to share," Carol explained. "We thought we'd wait a while for dinner." She smiled at Aaron. "I hope you're not too hungry. You work at the barn, don't you? Physical labor must give you a good appetite."

"Oh, I'm fine. I just sort of snack all day long. Thank you." Aaron was even more nervous than he'd expected. Was snacking all day long acceptable, or had he just made himself look like a boor with no self-control? And did it sound bad, that he worked in a barn? Was she thinking that he wasn't good enough for her son? He thought about trying to correct her. He could explain that he was a trainer and instructor, not a lowly barn hand, but that didn't seem right; making Quinn's job seem unimportant wouldn't likely win her over, and more importantly, it wasn't fair to Quinn. He settled on just smiling.

The awkward small talk continued through appetizers and another round of drinks. Most of it was directed at Aaron—it seemed like the family had decided that he was safer, less explosive, than Quinn. Aaron couldn't really argue with the strategy; Quinn was so tense he was practically vibrating, and anything he said came out sharp and brittle, although Aaron didn't think that was intentional. He wanted to take Quinn somewhere private and kiss him until he relaxed, until he was as sleepy and boneless as he'd been the night before. Hotels would have lots of extra blankets— maybe he needed to find their linen storage, and build Quinn his fort.

Quinn and Ted were both finished their second drinks long before the others, and when Ted suggested that Quinn switch over and join him in taste-testing the bar's assortment of Scotch, Quinn agreed with the first enthusiasm Aaron had seen from him all night. So that was another thing to worry about. Aaron had only seen Quinn be aggressive once, when he was denied alcohol in the East Hastings restaurant, so maybe he wasn't an angry drunk, just an angry-when-he-can't-be-drunk. Mostly, alcohol seemed to make Quinn slutty, which seemed unlikely to be a problem in this environment. Still, drinking wouldn't help to really solve any of the issues at the table. Aaron saw Carol send a worried look her husband's way, and realized that he wasn't the only one with concerns.

By the time they ordered their main courses, they'd covered the weather, recent movies they'd seen, Caitlin's education and plans, and pretty much every detail about Aaron's own family and ambitions. Quinn's mother had gushed about the Spruce Meadows equestrian facility near their house in Calgary, and Caitlin had joined in with her own tales of riding as a girl. Quinn was mostly silent, as was his father. Aaron was happy to help by making conversation and trying to keep things relaxed, but he was beginning to wonder what he was helping with. What was the goal, here? Were they just going to have an awkward family dinner and then go on with their lives as they had before, or was there something else that they should be working toward?

Part way through the main course, Quinn's father made his goals pretty clear. He started off almost innocently, asking about the horses. And Quinn responded with the most genuine enthusiasm Aaron had seen from him all night, talking about Clay, and how riding was harder than he'd thought it would be, but more rewarding too. Aaron wished he could tape record the conversation for his mom, as a reward for her support for the new relationship.

"So, it could be a good hobby, some day." Ted nodded as if he had found the solution to the world's problems.

Quinn looked wary. "Well, it's a good hobby, right now. I'm enjoying it, but there's no way I'm good enough to be making a living from riding."

Ted frowned. "A living? Is that what you call what you're doing?" He shook his head, and frowned back at the face his wife was directing his way. "I don't understand you, Quinn. Do you want to know how much I made last year? Between salary and stock options and investments?"

Ted seemed prepared to give them a number, but Quinn shook his head. "I don't really need details, Dad. I know you make a lot of money."

"And you—you're working hard, slaving away every day, for, what? Minimum wage?"

"A bit more than minimum. But, yeah, I get it—you make a lot more than I do." Quinn finished his drink, and nodded to the waiter, holding up his empty glass. "So I won't worry about running up your bar tab."

"Minimum wage." Ted said it like it was a new and particularly disgusting species of maggot. "At minimum wage—I did the math, once—at minimum wage, you'd have to work ten years to make as much as I made every *week*, last year."

Quinn raised his newly filled glass. "You did the math, huh?"

"It's not because I'm better than you, Quinn." Ted leaned forward as if about to say something confidential. "Maybe I'm better than a lot of the people who work menial jobs. Maybe I'm smarter, and certainly I'm better educated, and have more drive. But... not better than *you*, Quinn. You were on track to do just as well as I have." He paused for a sip of his Scotch, and Aaron watched Quinn closely. He didn't really seem to be responding to his father's words at all. Ted sat back in his chair, and continued. "I already had a place in mind for you, at the company. I had a path all mapped out for you, straight to the top. Especially if you'd done that MBA after your first master's, like we'd discussed. Everything was in place." He finally stopped talking, and looked at Quinn for a response.

Quinn took a sip of his drink, then swirled it around in the glass. "I think I like this one—it's a bit smokier, maybe? Less fruity than the last one?"

His father frowned. "That's all I'm getting? After all the work I put in, you're just going to ignore it, and talk about the Scotch my money is buying?"

Quinn's smile was sharp and cold. "Not bad—you surprised me. I thought you'd have started in on the 'my money is buying all this' bullshit a lot earlier."

"All right, enough." Quinn's mother sounded genuinely upset. "Ted, we just got him back—leave him alone for a while, can't you? And, Quinn." She sighed. "I know things have happened fast; they've happened fast for us, too. We're all a little off balance, here."

Aaron could see Quinn trying to relax. The chairs were too wide for easy contact, but Aaron scooted around a little and took advantage of his long legs, stretching out until his calf pressed against Quinn's. The reaction was instant, as Quinn's foot hooked around his ankle and nestled in. Aaron liked being the life raft that Quinn could cling to, but he hated it that Quinn was feeling so storm-tossed in the first place. He wondered how much longer the evening would last.

They went back to their safe small talk, after that, Quinn and his father letting the others carry the conversation. When the main course was cleared away, Quinn edged his chair over closer to Aaron's, and the contact between their legs got a lot more comfortable.

They all declined dessert and coffee, thankfully, and Quinn started squirming, obviously ready to leave. Thankfully, his family seemed equally ready to end the evening, and it wasn't long before they stood and said good night. They were planning to stay in town at least another day, and promised to call Quinn to set up another meeting. Aaron was surprised when Caitlin leaned in to hug him, and even more surprised when she whispered in his ear. "Keep him here. I'll be right back."

They all headed for the door together, and when Caitlin and her parents turned left, Aaron stood still, and Quinn gave him a cautious look. "Your sister said to wait—is that cool, or have you had enough?"

Quinn leaned back against the wall. "I've had way more than enough. But she's not as bad as they are."

"They're not really all that bad either, Quinn." Aaron wasn't sure how much of this he could get away with, but he felt like he needed to try. "I mean, your dad was a bit intense, but he wasn't evil or anything. And your mom and your sister, they're trying to make it work."

Quinn looked like he was maybe going to argue, but then made a face instead. He reached out and looped a finger around a couple of Aaron's. It was funny—for someone who'd been as obviously nervous about holding hands as Quinn initially had been, he sure seemed to like doing it now. Not that Aaron was complaining, at all. He shuffled a little closer, and looked around. They were in a bit of an alcove, out of the main traffic area—it was worth the risk. He leaned in for a quick kiss, and wasn't too surprised when Quinn responded enthusiastically.

He pulled away before things got too heated. "Respectable hotel, Quinn."

"You started it, man."

"You were the one who got your tongue involved."

Quinn grinned. "I wonder what else my tongue could get involved with, tonight." He looked over to see his sister returning, and raised an eyebrow at Aaron. "Rain check on that."

"What, it's not one of your 'anytime, anywhere' promises?"

Quinn pushed off the wall and let himself fall into Aaron, a little. "Nah, it pretty much is. I just like to pretend like I'm hard to get."

Then Caitlin was back. "Thanks for staying, guys. I just wanted a chance to sort a few things out."

Aaron had no idea what that meant. She seemed friendly enough, but the words were a little ominous.

Quinn seemed equally unsure, but he nodded. "Yeah, okay. Do you want to go back into the bar, or is it quick?"

"Oh, it probably won't take long, but I definitely want to go back into the bar. Mom keeps giving me speeches about moderation and being a lady, so I can't drink much around her, but I want alcohol, and I want it now."

Aaron hid his smile. At least Quinn and his sister had one thing in common. Caitlin led the way into the bar, but Aaron held Quinn back. "Do you want me here for this? I mean, I'm still fine being here, but if you want some brother-sister time, I totally understand."

Quinn didn't say anything, but his fingers tightened around Aaron's as he turned and followed his sister.

They found a smaller table in the corner, and the server smiled to see them back. "Charged to the same room?" she asked.

Caitlin nodded, but Quinn said, "No, thanks. Can you just start a tab here?"

"Sure. What can I get you?"

Caitlin looked at Quinn. "Did you actually like that scotch? The one you said was smoky. Or were you just being a pain in the ass?"

"No, it was pretty good."

"Okay. Aaron, you in?"

"Sure, I guess." Aaron didn't know much about Scotch, but he was willing to be educated.

Caitlin nodded in approval. "Okay, three...." She looked at Quinn.

"Taliskers, I think."

The server nodded, and left, and the three of them sat in silence. Caitlin finally spoke. "They really have been looking for you. Ever since you left. Private investigators, and police, and anyone else they could think of. They must have looked through most of Europe, and South America. I guess they didn't bother to look too hard so close to home." The drinks arrived, and she took a deep swallow of hers. "The number of times I've been here to go shopping, or stopped by on the way to Whistler...." She trailed off. "But that wasn't what I wanted to talk to you about. I want to figure out where we're going from here."

Aaron nodded enthusiastically, and then felt like a bit of an idiot. This was between Quinn and his sister; he was an accessory, at best. But Quinn's fingers were still wrapped tight around his, so at least he was a valued accessory. And Quinn didn't seem to be inclined to disagree with his sister.

"Okay. But, seriously—are we the ones who should be talking about this? It seems like Dad, at least, has his own agenda."

Caitlin waved a hand dismissively and took another deep swallow of her Scotch. She wasn't finished yet, but she nodded to the server and pointed at her glass to request a refill. She glanced at Quinn and Aaron's essentially untouched drinks and shook her head. "It *is* good. You should enjoy it. And I can charge it—Mom and Dad still pay my credit card bills, so don't worry about me having to spend my hard-earned pennies."

Quinn shook his head. "I can pay."

"If you insist. But, yeah, what I was saying was, we *are* the ones who should be talking about this. You've been away for a while, Quinn—you don't know what things are like, now. All Dad cares about is work. Not that it wasn't always his priority, but it got worse, after you and Connor bailed. Personal stuff—it's barely a blip on his radar. And Mom, she's pretty much been on autopilot for seven years." She finished her drink. "Jesus, seven years you've been gone."

The server was back, and Caitlin exchanged glasses with a smile, and took a sip from her new drink. "I used to worship you, Quinn. Typical little sister stuff, I guess. But more than most, maybe, because you were so good with Connor, and because you were so good-looking. All my friends had crushes on you. And Dad thought you were the great hope for the next generation, of course. Bragging to his friends all the time, and I was just soaking it all up, believing that you were perfect." Another deep drink, and this time Quinn was drinking along with her. She paused, had another drink, and when she spoke, her voice was vicious.

"You didn't just leave *them*, Quinn. Maybe *they* told you to go, but *I* sure as hell didn't!"

Quinn drained his glass. He let go of Aaron's hand and hunched forward, his elbows on his knees, his hands holding the empty glass, his fingers clenched as if he were praying. Apparently he had no response, and was just bracing himself to take whatever else Caitlin wanted to dish out.

But she seemed to have used up her anger. She was still frowning, but now it looked more like confusion than aggression. "What was so bad, Quinn? The things they said—I'm sure it hurt. But it was so bad that you just walked away and didn't look back? You just forgot about all of us?" A bit of frustration came back as she reached out and pushed at his shoulder. "Tell me, Quinn!"

Finally, he looked up. "I don't know what you want from me. It wasn't—it wasn't their fault. It was mine. Everything they said, they were right. I *was* being stupid, and reckless. I was drinking too much, and smoking or swallowing anything I could get my hands on. They were *right*. There wasn't much left of the family, but what there was, I was tearing apart. So I left."

He looked over at Aaron, and he looked like he was facing his executioner. He clearly didn't want to say any more, but he forced himself to continue.

"Connor—that was my fault, too. I should have known he wasn't strong enough to be on his own. He talked a good game, but I knew him. I should have known he was lying. He was my brother. He was my fucking *twin*, and I left him alone, and I let myself believe him when he said he was doing okay." It didn't really seem like Quinn was talking to Caitlin anymore. He was looking straight at Aaron, and he shook his head angrily. "I was in love. Head over heels." He sounded disgusted with himself. "I'd messed around a bit, at home, but Diego was the first guy I was serious about. And I told Connor all about him, of course." His voice was bitter. "I just couldn't keep my big mouth shut. So when Connor started feeling off, and he knew he needed my help—he must have known, he could always feel it coming—he didn't tell me. He just kept saying everything was fine, everything was great, he was good. So that I wouldn't have to mess up my stupid *romance* to go take care of my brother." Quinn looked down again, but it was too late; Aaron had already seen the tears in his eyes. "Fuck," Quinn said. "Why the fuck...." He looked up at Caitlin, not even trying to hide the tears now. "What do you people want from me? I screwed up, I know that. I—there's nothing I can do, not ever, to make it better. What the *fuck* do you want me to do?"

Quinn stopped and waited for an answer, as if he honestly thought that his sister would have one. She just shook her head, and Aaron could see that she was crying too. "That's all—okay, A, it's all bullshit, but, B... I just want you to be my brother. Mom and Dad, they just want you to be their son. We lost Connor, Quinn. It wasn't your fault. It wasn't anybody's fault, not yours and not Mom's or Dad's, no matter how much you all blame yourselves. It was just... bad chemistry, or something, in his brain." She was almost sobbing, but she took a moment and collected herself, then spoke through her tears, and she was back to being fierce. "It was a fucking miracle that he made it as far as he did. And every happy day he had, they were all because of you! Because you were there for him, and you understood him, and you helped him out." She reached over and grabbed Quinn's forearm, and pulled it away from his face a little. "Did you ever think that maybe it was a *relief* for him to finally be able to let go? For him to know that you had somebody who could take care of you, and help you through losing him? Jesus, Quinn—maybe it wasn't his death that was a tragedy. Maybe it was his fucking *life!*"

"Bullshit." Quinn wasn't loud, but he sounded determined. "He was happy. Sometimes, he was really happy."

"Oh, Quinn." Caitlin tried to smile at him, but she didn't really make it. "He was twenty-two years old. And I'll bet you could count the times that he was happy on one hand. All the rest of the time... drugged into oblivion, or miserable with fear and anger and confusion." She was crying again, or maybe she hadn't ever really stopped. "I talked to him the night before he did it. And I asked him how he was, and he said he was tired." Her face crumbled, but she managed to keep talking. "That's what he was, Quinn. He was just too tired to keep fighting. You helped him last longer than he ever could have on his own, but in the end... it was a mercy for him to be free. If you'd been there—you're right, maybe you could have stopped him. Maybe you could have gotten him to the doctors, and they could have worked out some new mix of drugs to turn him back into a zombie, and maybe he could have made it for another few months, or another few years of existence. And that would have been easier for all of us, for sure. But do you really think it would have been better for *him*?" She shook her head and brushed impatiently at her eyes. "Jesus Christ. I'm a fucking mess. Let's get out of here."

Aaron looked around the room. The rest of the crowd was still enjoying their evening, but their server was watching them closely, as if wondering what to do. Quinn pulled out his wallet and threw some bills on the table. And apparently he wasn't interested in change, because he and Caitlin both hurried out of the bar, their faces low as if they were ashamed of their emotions. Aaron followed after them a little more slowly.

Quinn and Caitlin were waiting for him in the lobby, and when he appeared, Caitlin nodded toward the front doors. "I need some air. And it's probably not a good idea for me to be walking around alone at this time of night. Can you guys give me a spin around the block?"

Quinn nodded, and Aaron followed along obediently. He was definitely feeling like a third wheel, but he was reluctant to leave. He wanted to have all this information, to help him understand Quinn better, and he didn't think Quinn would be interested in going through it all again. Even if Quinn were willing, Aaron wouldn't want to put him through it. Caitlin rested her hand on Quinn's elbow like a Southern lady, and then Quinn reached his other hand back to take Aaron's, and he was happy that he'd stayed.

They walked in silence for a while, and then Caitlin said, "Do you remember that hill we used to toboggan down? The one by the creek? We'd spend all day there, sliding down and trudging back up. Must have burned seven million calories. And we went home and melted chocolate chips in the microwave and pretended it was hot chocolate."

Quinn nodded, but then he said, "But—that was you and me, wasn't it? I don't remember Connor being there."

Even in the dim light, Aaron could see her smile at her brother. "That's right, Quinn. It was you and me."

They walked on, and Quinn was the next one to speak. "Do you still have that rabbit? What was his name? Mr. Donaldson? Why the fuck did you name a stuffed bunny Mr. Donaldson?"

Caitlin raised her chin in mock indignation. "He was a very distinguished bunny, so he needed a distinguished name." She grinned. "I think it was a character from a book, maybe. And, yes, I still have him. He's on a shelf, now, instead of my bed, but he's still around."

"Does he still smell like sour milk?"

"You were the only one who could still smell that, after he was washed."

"I think I can still smell it from *here*. That was a stinky rabbit." Quinn squeezed Aaron's hand, as if apologizing for not including him in the conversation, but Aaron didn't mind. He was just happy to hear them coming up with some happy memories, even if the bunny was a bit odd.

They made it back to the hotel, and stood outside. Caitlin stretched up and gave Quinn a kiss on his cheek. "I meant it, Quinn. I want my brother back. The rest of it—there's going to be shit to work through. I know that, and so do Mom and Dad. But... we want to be a family. We want to do the work. We just need you to want it too."

Quinn looked like he was signing his life away, but he nodded.

"Yeah, okay." He glanced over at Aaron, as if aware that he was about to steal one of his lines. "But—can we take it a bit slow? This is... it's a lot." Another look at Aaron. "There's good stuff happening out here, and—it's important to me. You guys are too, but...."

"Yeah. Slow is good. I'll talk to them, make sure they understand." Caitlin stepped backward and got a little more businesslike. "Maybe we could meet for lunch tomorrow, or something a little less intense than dinner, and then I'll get them home? We can talk on the phone, or come out again in a couple weeks. Or you could come to us, you know." She nodded toward Aaron. "I know Mom was being a bit pushy, but she was right, Spruce Meadows is worth a visit, for horse folks."

"Yeah, it's on my to-visit list, for sure," Aaron agreed. He'd been quiet for so long that it almost felt strange to hear his own voice.

"I could behave myself, if I had to. If Mom and Dad want dinner again tomorrow." Quinn sounded a little defensive.

"Yeah, you're a big talker. Wait until Dad starts in on the damn tar sands, and how they need good engineers. Or maybe he'll take a longer term approach, and tell you that he's been looking into the MBA programs at the Vancouver schools." She shook her head. "I think you were right—slow is good. There's no rush. None of us are going anywhere." She gave him a hard look. "Right, Quinn?"

"Yeah, yeah." Quinn took a step backward, and his hand found Aaron's again. They stood and watched as Caitlin went into the hotel, then turned and started their walk home.

"You okay?" Aaron asked.

"Fuck, I don't know. Maybe." Quinn squeezed Aaron's fingers. "Ask me tomorrow."

"Yeah, all right. Hey, you staying at my place tonight? You know—to make the tomorrow-asking easier."

"That's a pretty smooth sales pitch you've got there. I mean, some guys, they might try to seduce with big talk about their sexual prowess, or their accomplishments, or their money. You, you're going with 'convenient question asking'. That's sexy, man."

"You want sexy? Wait until you see the tie I left on my couch. Very leash-like."

"Well, okay, then. I'm in."

Aaron wasn't sure how it was happening. They were all *saying* that they wanted to take things slow, but somehow, everything seemed to be happening really fast. Just a couple days ago, he'd been pining over Quinn and sure that they would never be together. Now, they were casually joking, and Quinn was going to spend the night at his apartment almost as a matter of routine. He wasn't complaining. Not at all. He just wanted to make sure that he was paying attention, and appreciating everything as it happened.

CHAPTER SEVENTEEN

QUINN was exhausted. He didn't know what he'd been thinking, when he'd agreed to go to Aaron's. He guessed he'd just wanted more of the kid's calming, comforting presence. But Aaron had already been a damn saint; it wasn't fair to expect him to keep putting up with Quinn's crap. Aaron didn't seem to agree, though. He was walking happily toward his apartment, holding tight to Quinn's hand, and Quinn had no idea how to get himself out of the situation. And he didn't really want to, for himself. He didn't want to be alone, and he couldn't think of anyone he'd rather be with than Aaron. He was just tired of letting people down, and really didn't want to add Aaron to the list of people he'd disappointed.

They got to the building and Quinn thought about trying to make a break for it. He could say he was tired, or that he needed to get stuff from his apartment in order to work the next day. Both of those excuses were true enough. But Aaron looked at him and smiled, and didn't let go of his hand for a second, and Quinn let himself be guided upstairs. Hopefully Aaron would be satisfied with a quick blow job or something. Quinn really didn't have the energy for a marathon session.

"Do you want a beer? Or some juice, or water?" Aaron asked as soon as they were inside the apartment. Aaron headed for the kitchen, but Quinn shook his head.

"I'm fine, thanks." He unzipped his jacket and hung it over the back of one of the kitchen chairs.

Aaron filled a glass of water for himself, then walked over to stand in front of Quinn. He smoothed the tips of his fingers over Quinn's face. "You look tired."

Quinn nodded. "Yeah, I guess. I might—I might go to my place. You know, after. Instead of sleeping here."

Aaron frowned. "After... oh. Oh, yeah. I thought you might be too tired, but—hey, you said I could practice my blow jobs on you. Maybe this is a good time?"

That didn't sound quite right. "No, I'm fine. I thought... I thought I could do something for you."

"I invited you here to sleep. I mean, we can fool around if you want, but I just thought you might not want to be alone. I don't—" Aaron ran his fingers down Quinn's face to the back of his head, and tilted his face up a little. "Last night was about me, I figure. About what I wanted. Tonight can be about you."

"Last night wasn't exactly unpleasant for me, you know. You don't owe me anything."

"And tonight hasn't been unpleasant for me. And it's not like I'd be doing you a favor to have you stay over. As far as I'm concerned, any Quinn-time is good-time." Aaron's kiss was gentle, and almost chaste. "If you want your space, I totally understand. But if you want to stay... you could go have a shower, and then borrow some sweats to sleep in. I can set the alarm for early, so you can go home and get work clothes, if you need."

That sounded just about perfect. It was scary, how fast Quinn was coming to depend on Aaron. Quinn wanted to be the strong one; he wanted to be able to help Aaron out. Instead, he felt weak and dependent. He didn't like it in theory, but in practice, it felt incredible to have someone looking after him. "If that's okay—if you're sure."

"It's excellent, Quinn. Seriously. The shower's optional, of course. My sweats are in the second drawer, there, or if you normally sleep in something else...."

"My apartment's barely heated—I normally sleep in as many clothes as I can find. Sweats would be great. But, yeah, if it's okay, a shower would be good too." This seemed too easy, but Aaron seemed happy as Quinn burrowed through his dresser and pulled out a pair of sweatpants and a T-shirt.

The shower felt good, and Quinn turned it on so hot it almost burned. Aaron's shower gel smelled familiar and comforting, and Quinn made a note of the brand. When the kid dumped him, maybe he could buy a bottle of it for himself and sit around inhaling the scent. Pathetic, but Quinn was pretty sure he'd be happy for any sort of comfort, when the black day came.

Aaron stuck his head into the bathroom when Quinn was just thinking about getting out of the shower. He kept his eyes carefully aimed at the ceiling, as if to preserve Quinn's modesty. "Uh, there should be an extra toothbrush in the medicine cabinet, if you want it. Do you need anything else?"

"No, man, I'm good." Quinn was tempted to invite Aaron in, just for the company if nothing else, but there wasn't really room in the tub. And even as tired as he was, he didn't think he could be naked with Aaron without it turning into something else. Something satisfying, but exhausting.

Aaron didn't seem to have been fishing for anything, though, and Quinn finished his shower and then opened the toothbrush package and brushed his teeth. He thought about asking to borrow a razor, going for the full renewal package, but he decided it would be overkill. He'd shaved before dinner, and his beard really didn't grow all that fast.

He went out to the main room and froze. Aaron looked up and grinned self-consciously. "Stupid?"

"Jesus, Aaron—no, it's not stupid." He walked over and inspected the structure. Aaron had suspended a quilt from the four posts on the corners of his bed, and it hung a couple feet above the mattress like a canopy. There were extra pillows on the bed, too, and the covers were turned down, waiting. Aaron nodded in invitation, and Quinn crouched down and crawled in. Aaron was close behind him, and they lay on their backs and looked up at the quilt. "My fort," Quinn started, but he stopped when he heard how close his voice was to breaking. He rolled over onto his side, and Aaron twisted around so they were facing each other. "Thank you," Quinn managed, and Aaron kissed him gently.

"Go to sleep, Quinn." He pulled the covers up and snugged them in under Quinn's chin. "Tomorrow's a new day."

Quinn let his eyes close, and he felt warmer and safer than he had since he could remember. It didn't take long for him to drift away.

QUINN slept right through the night, and woke the next morning to a gentle kiss on his nose. "Wake up, Quinn. The alarm's about to go off."

Quinn opened one cautious eye, and remembered where he was. He smiled up at the canopy still stretched above him. "You are weird in an excellent way."

"That's a nice way to start the day." The alarm went off, then, a blast of radio noise that had Quinn flinching backward. Aaron shook his head. "I warned you—it's always best to be awake before the alarm." He scooted out from the fort, and Quinn saw that he was already fully dressed.

"What time is it?"

"Seven. I let you sleep in a bit - I can do the first feedings, and you can just come up when you're ready. Or if you need to do family stuff, me and Danny can cover for you all day."

"No, man, you've done a lot already."

"What, had a fancy dinner and made a fort?" Aaron's kiss was boisterous, with no apparent concern for Quinn's morning-breath. "Just wait, man—there's *lots* more I want to do." He leaned over and turned the radio volume down, then sat on the edge of the bed and started playing with Quinn's hair. It was a bit weird, but Quinn didn't complain.

"You're going to see your family again today?"

"I guess. You know as much about the plan as I do." Quinn didn't want to start thinking about all that until he absolutely had to.

Aaron nodded, and kept playing with Quinn's hair. It was a little too relaxing; Quinn knew he needed to get up and get the day started. But it felt so good, to lie there under Aaron's gentle touch.

"So, your dad," Aaron started. "He really makes that much money? I mean—that'd be millions of dollars a year, right?"

"Yeah. I never really asked, but he's the CEO of Canada's second-largest petroleum company. And my mom's grandfather started the company, so, you know, the family still owns a good chunk of it. He makes a lot of money."

Aaron's fingers were still playing, but his voice seemed distant. "We had a guy come out to the farm last year—he wanted to buy it, and develop the property. He offered almost four million dollars. We thought he was crazy. Mom was totally tempted. She thought we could always move farther out, buy a whole new property, and save the left-over money. She only said no because she didn't want to see the mountainside get any more development on it."

Quinn wasn't sure where this was going. "It's a great property. And it's not likely to go down in value, so it's nice to have that to fall back on."

"Yeah, it's great. It's just... your dad, he could buy the property, my family's whole—everything, like, a couple times over, with just the pay from one year. That's kind of crazy."

Quinn pushed himself up on one elbow and made sure Aaron was looking him in the eye. "He can't buy it if it's not for sale,

Aaron. Money is power, sometimes—but it's not *total* power, you know?"

Aaron nodded slowly. "Yeah. Okay." He snapped back to himself. "And I don't care how rich your daddy is, you're still not allowed to work in dress shoes. It's unsafe. So go home and get changed before you come up. Understood?" He shrugged. "Or, you know, don't come up at all, if that's better for you."

"Damn, you were a hard-ass for, like, five seconds, there. It was pretty impressive."

"I'm gonna try for ten seconds, tomorrow." He kissed Quinn's nose, and then his forehead, and then tip of his ear. "Be afraid."

"Yeah, I'm petrified."

Aaron grinned and headed out the door. It was a little strange to be alone in Aaron's apartment, but it wasn't uncomfortable. A big part of Quinn wanted to crawl back to the middle of the bed and hide in the fort all day. Aaron would come home eventually, and slide in with him, and they'd catch up on all the fooling around they hadn't done the night before. It sounded pretty much perfect, but he groaned and pulled himself out of bed. For one thing, he had to go to the bathroom. But he also needed to get his life in order; he wanted to *deserve* Aaron, or at least be working toward it.

He found the mug of coffee Aaron had left for him, and sipped it while he made a plan. He needed to go home and get changed. He knew he should leave Aaron's clothes behind, but he really didn't want to. He rationalized that he needed to wash them before returning them. He didn't have an excuse for his decision to keep them on for his trip home, rather than changing back into his clothes from the night before, but he let himself get away with that one.

He was changed and on his way out the door when his phone rang. He didn't recognize the number, but that didn't mean much these days. The circle of people who seemed to think they had a right to his time had grown pretty damn quickly recently. He picked up and heard Caitlin's voice.

"Hey, Quinn. Just checking in." She sounded bright and unreasonably cheerful.

"Yeah, hi." Quinn had no idea where to go with this conversation. "You guys all up?"

"Up, dressed, and ready for breakfast. We were hoping you might be able to join us." Her voice got quieter, and he realized that she was no longer speaking for her audience. "If you're still down with the give-everyone-a-little-time-to-think plan, I can get them on a flight at eleven thirty this morning. But they're not going to go anywhere without seeing you first."

"Yeah, okay." Quinn was glad she was coordinating things. He wasn't really sure what to make of his sister, but he was pretty sure his life would go more smoothly if he went along with her on most things. "Let me call work and see if I can get a bit of time off."

"All right. Call me back in five minutes, or I'll track you down." He heard the click of her phone shutting off.

He thought about calling Aaron, but he already knew the answer he'd get there, so he dialed Danny's cell.

"Hey, Quinn. What's up?"

"I know it's late notice, man, but Aaron said he could cover for me this morning with feeding and turn-out, and I can work late to finish the stalls—would it be a total pain if I came in a few hours late? It's a one-time thing, I promise."

"You want to come in a few hours late, and you've already figured out a way to make it work?" Danny sounded like he couldn't believe what he was hearing. "Jesus, Quinn, seriously? Is that all?" He laughed. Quinn would have liked to join him, but he had no idea what was funny until Danny explained. "Aaron called half an hour ago and said I had to give you whatever you wanted. He said no matter what you asked, if you called, my answer *had* to be 'yes'. Damn, Quinn, I thought you were going to ask for a kidney, or something. That boy is a bit dramatic, sometimes. You sure you want to take on the trouble?"

Quinn didn't know if the question was deliberate or not. He didn't know what Aaron had already told his brother, and he didn't know how much Danny wanted to hear. But he absolutely knew the answer to the question. "Yeah," he said quietly. "I want to take on as much as he'll give me."

Danny didn't answer right away, but when he did, his voice was warm, and Quinn could almost see his smile. "Well, hot damn. It's about time. Look, Quinn, Aaron or not, there's no problem with you taking the morning off. But I'm really happy to hear that you two are giving it a shot. It's—you guys deserve each other."

Quinn didn't bother to correct him. "Thanks. For the time, and, you know... thanks."

"Yeah. Okay, then, we'll see you when we see you. It's about time Aaron did some damn work around the place instead of swanning around all the time, calling himself a trainer."

"Yeah, okay. Say hi to him for me." That was probably a little cheesy, but Quinn didn't care. Just thinking about the kid put a smile on his face.

He hung up and called his sister back, and they arranged to meet at a café across the bridge in Kitsalano, on the way to the airport. It was the wrong direction for Quinn, of course, but he had a feeling he might be happy to have a long drive after dealing with his parents. He didn't want to drag his emotional issues into the barn if he could help it.

He got to the café before his family, and immediately started second-guessing his recommendation. He hadn't wanted to make his parents uncomfortable with his work clothes if they'd met in one of their typical restaurants. But now he was worried that they'd be put off by the garage-sale décor of the place, and the multi-pierced servers. He thought about calling and making alternate plans, but then a sleek, black sedan pulled up in front of the restaurant, blocking traffic briefly as his family climbed out. His mother and sister were smiling at him, but his father's attention, after a brief greeting, was directed toward Quinn's motorcycle, parked a few spots down the street.

"You've still got it?" His father walked to the bike and laid his hands on it almost reverently, then gave it a quick inspection. "You're keeping it in good shape."

"Well, you know—a poor person like me, I can't really afford a new one." Quinn hadn't planned on keeping the bitterness going, but apparently his mouth had its own ideas.

His father just nodded. "Good point. I guess there are hidden benefits to poverty." Quinn honestly couldn't be sure whether his father was joking or not; it was unnerving.

"Boys—we're hungry!" His mother was standing in the doorway of the restaurant.

So they all went inside, and nobody seemed to have a problem with the décor, and everyone claimed to enjoy their food. The conversation was careful, but not painfully so. All in all, it was a much more pleasant meal than Quinn had anticipated. When they were sitting back over coffee, though, his parents got down to business.

"Your mother gave me hell last night," his father said. "About pushing you. She said you'd never been interested in the family business, and that you'd done your time pretending that you were." He poured cream into his coffee and then returned his gaze to his son. "I'm not so sure about that. You liked the science, Quinn—I know you did. The business, maybe not so much, but we've got Caitlin to take care of that, now."

Quinn couldn't really argue. He *had* enjoyed the science. Breaking things down to their most basic forms, building them back up, figuring out how they'd interact... it had been fascinating. And he'd loved the engineering component, the challenge of taking the ideas out of the controlled laboratories and making them work in the real world. "I don't really agree with what you're doing in the tar sands."

His father looked startled. "Well, okay. We have other projects, other business interests. Of course the tar sands are huge, but they're not all we're about."

Quinn didn't even know why he'd started the discussion. What did it matter what he thought about the tar sands, or any other aspect of the business?

When Quinn didn't respond to that, his mother took her turn. "Aaron seems lovely. I really would like to see him at Spruce Meadows. Wouldn't he love it there?" She turned to Caitlin for agreement, but didn't wait too long. "You should both come out for the next event. I can't think of what it would be, off hand, but it's always wonderful. All levels of competition—enough to really challenge him, but if he felt overwhelmed, he'd have a welcoming home base with us."

"You mentioned that last night—I'm sure he appreciated the thought." Quinn looked to Caitlin for help, but she seemed to be willing to wait things out.

And then it was back to his father. "The local schools here, they must have engineering programs. If you wanted to go back to your master's. I mean, they wouldn't be MIT, but if you're feeling committed to this location, I'm sure they'd be a good start." His father seemed to think that he was offering a generous concession.

Then back to his mother, who asked, "And what are your plans for Christmas? We've spent the last few Christmases on boats, strangely enough—the Caribbean, then the Mediterranean. We were thinking about somewhere more exotic, this year, maybe the Galapagos. Does Aaron want to have Christmas with his family, or would he be able to join us?"

Quinn thought about the jack-o'-lanterns. He hadn't ever talked about Christmas with Aaron, but he was pretty sure there'd be some sort of tradition associated with it. Probably a weird one.

"And how are your teeth, Quinn?" Caitlin had apparently decided to get involved. "Are there any medical conditions of which we should be aware? Well, we'll let the doctors decide that—you're booked for appointments all next week. And we'll need to get you in to a stylist immediately, obviously. And while you're there, we can have you measured up for your new wardrobe. Aaron can have one too, if that's what it takes to keep you sweet. In terms of business, I don't suppose you've managed to pick up any Cantonese while you've been out here? No? Well, we'll have tutors sent in to teach you while you sleep. And—"

"Enough." Their father didn't look too impressed. He sat back in his chair and composed himself. "But, point taken."

"We've been looking for you for so long, Quinn." His mother sounded like she might be about to cry.

He nodded. "Yeah. Okay. But...." He wasn't sure just how much detail he wanted to go into. "I've been living a life, out here. I didn't mean to hide from you guys, because I didn't think I had to. I thought you were happy I was gone. I—" He took a moment to choose his words. "I've made mistakes, and I haven't been everything I would have wanted to be. But that doesn't mean I want to go back to who I was, you know?" He looked at their faces, and he wasn't sure they understood, but at least they were listening. He smiled. "I—Aaron." He looked at his mother. "Good call on that. I want Aaron to be happy. I want to deserve him. I do. He's important." He frowned, and tried to figure out what he was trying to say. "You guys are important too, but you're complicated. It's—I need some time." He looked at Caitlin, hoping for inspiration, but all he got was a supportive smile. At least that was something. "I promise to keep in touch." He looked at his mother, then his father. "Is that enough, for now?"

"So, when you say 'keep in touch'—does that mean you won't object to us implanting a small but powerful satellite tracking chip in your shoulder?" His father's face was deadpan.

Quinn was ninety percent sure that he was joking, but ten percent freaked out. "I think that might be a little excessive."

"I see." And there it was, a quick twinkle in his eye that left

Quinn dumbfounded. Had his father always been funny?

"E-mail." His mother said. "And Facebook. And... what else? Texts and phone calls, of course. And visits. You might want to take your time, but I'm in Vancouver regularly, so I'll expect at least a courtesy meal. And probably more."

It sounded reasonable, but there was a problem. "I don't have Facebook. Or e-mail. I don't actually—I *had* a computer, but I dropped it, and I haven't really gotten around to getting another."

His father and sister stared at him like he was visiting from a prehistoric age, but his mother seemed delighted. "Excellent! I have a lovely boy who helps me with computer things. I'll have him put something together for you. Where shall I have him send it?"

Quinn didn't think it was a good time to start explaining his home address. He gave the barn address instead, and his mother smiled happily. She had a mission.

His father was a bit harder to deal with, but Quinn wanted to try. "It's November. It's too late for school next term, and too early for school in September. And... I know the money's not great, but I like my job. I like the people, and I like the horses. And you said you've got Caitlin for the business. I can—I'll think about things, okay? Is that enough?"

His father smiled sadly. "Quinn." He looked like maybe that was all he was going to say, but then he shook his head. "I'm sorry I wasn't there for you, Quinn. I should have—I should have done so many things differently."

This was alarming. This was not tying things up in a tidy package as he'd hoped. He looked over at Caitlin, then back at his father. "No, it was my fault. I was a mess. An idiot. Whatever."

"No, Quinn. We were all a mess, after Connor. But I meant before that. When you were growing up. If I made you feel like you had to be a certain way in order for me to love you. If I made you feel like you couldn't be who you were. I'm sorry." He waited for

Quinn's nod of acknowledgement, and then waited a little longer before adding, "That said, it's ridiculous that you're wasting your time working for peanuts in a menial job that could be done by a trained monkey! I'll buy the damn farm and you can use it to perform chemistry experiments, I don't care, but you should be using your brain!"

Quinn knew that his father was mostly joking, but he also remembered his conversation with Aaron. "To the best of my knowledge, the farm's not for sale." He was tempted to add "and neither am I," but it felt unnecessarily confrontational. He decided to save it for the next fight.

His father seemed to get the message anyway. Caitlin finally decided to be useful, pointing out the time and calling for the car to come back around to pick them all up. Quinn hugged his family good-bye on the sidewalk; it felt strange, but not wrong. He watched them drive away, and thought back over everything that had happened in the last couple of days. He'd been in a holding pattern for so long, and then suddenly everything had changed all at once. It was overwhelming, but he didn't think it was bad. He thought of Aaron, holding his hand and building his fort, and he couldn't keep the smile from his face. The changes absolutely weren't bad.

He got on his bike and headed off to find Aaron.

CHAPTER EIGHTEEN

AARON wasn't sure how many false alarms he'd reacted to before he heard something that sounded like a motorcycle and looked outside to see that, finally, Quinn really was riding into the parking lot. He tried to play it cool, staying in the barn, but he could feel Danny smirking at him and his mother watching in amused approval, and he gave up on the pretense. He headed out toward the parking lot, and when Quinn saw him, he nodded toward the equipment shed, and they both moved in that direction.

It was raining out, just a little, enough that Aaron had felt it on his walk, but Quinn had been riding his bike through it all, and his lips were cold and wet when they met Aaron's. His hands were cold too, one pushing up under Aaron's shirt to find the warm skin over his ribs, the other wrapping around his neck and pulling his head down to deepen the kiss. There was no hesitation, nothing but need and desire.

Aaron felt invaded, assaulted, and he wanted more. Quinn hadn't been this sincerely demanding since their first night together, back before he'd known Aaron was a virgin, and Aaron hadn't known how much he'd missed it. He wanted the tenderness, and the gentle, relaxing touches, but he wanted the passion too. He guessed the truth of it was that he wanted *Quinn*, in all his infinite variety. And he had him, straining beneath his hands, pushing against his lips. Aaron let his brain turn off as he spun them around, pushing Quinn against the wall of the shed. Somehow they ended up with Aaron holding Quinn's arms up above his head, and when Quinn tried to move them, Aaron held him tight, held him still. Quinn jerked harder, then, and his eyes widened with something other than lust. Aaron came back to reality with a crash, and released his hold immediately.

"Shit, Quinn, I'm sorry. I wasn't thinking...." How long had it been since Quinn had been tied up and assaulted? How had Aaron let himself forget about that? Jesus, what must Quinn be feeling?

Quinn frowned, and reached out one hand to run it gently over Aaron's face. "No, man, it's okay. It just caught me by surprise."

"Quinn, no! You don't have to—"

"Don't have to *what*, Aaron? Don't have to get on with my damn life?" Quinn shook his head. "Fuck that, man. And fuck *him*. He doesn't get to affect me, not like that." Quinn's hands had lowered as he was speaking, but he lifted them back up again, put them in the same position over his head. Aaron hesitated, but Quinn's face was determined. "Do it, Aaron. I trust you."

Aaron lifted his hands slowly, and gently placed them over Quinn's. He leaned in for a kiss, but Quinn jerked his hands impatiently, easily shaking Aaron free. "Fuck you, Aaron—do it. Hold me down. Trap me. Don't treat me like I'm fragile, or damaged...."

Quinn's voice was lost as Aaron kissed him, hard and demanding. His hands tightened on Quinn's, and held firm as Quinn tried to push away from the wall. Aaron pulled his face back to make sure that this was really what was wanted. Quinn stared at him, eyes wide and dark, and his lips mouthed Aaron's name, silent but clear. "*Aaron*," a little louder that time, with the word ending on a moan as Aaron wrapped his tongue around Quinn's, tangling them together in a passionate knot.

They were both hard, straining against each other, desperate for friction, and it was the wrong place, the wrong time, but Aaron just didn't care. He left one hand holding Quinn's while the other fumbled with Quinn's fly and then his own. Finally, their cocks were free, hot and pulsing in the cool air.

This was stupid, and reckless. They were out of sight, and nobody but staff was allowed in the equipment shed, but it was still a totally crazy place to be letting himself get out of control. Somehow, that made the whole thing hotter. Aaron released one of Quinn's hands, and in an instant it was tight around Aaron's cock, jacking him fast and rough, and Aaron tried to match Quinn's pace. It would have been easier if he'd been able to concentrate on what he was doing, but the sensation from his own cock was enough to distract him, and when combined with Quinn's lips, tongue, and teeth, Jesus, even the hot current of his breath was enough to drive rational thought from Aaron's head. He could hear himself making a soft, grunting moan, and then it was too much, far too much. He pulled his face away from Quinn's and sank his mouth into the leather that covered Quinn's shoulder, biting to keep himself from yelling as he came, all over Quinn's hand and God knew where else.

When his body finally relaxed, he slumped and hung himself off of Quinn's strong body. He felt drunk, or stoned, or some other state of perfect lassitude, but for some reason Quinn wasn't being the still support that Aaron wanted. He felt Quinn's fingers grip the hair on the back of his head, but instead of being comforting and soothing, they were pulling, bringing Aaron's head back to look Quinn in the face.

It took a minute, but Aaron finally focused, and felt himself flushing. "Oh, shit. Sorry."

Quinn's smile was gentle, but there was still a hunger in his face, and Aaron knew what he wanted to do. He slid down Quinn's body, found his swollen cock, and took as much of it into his mouth as he could. He knew his technique still needed work, but he really didn't think Quinn cared right then. He'd watched enough porn to know the basics, and he did his best. It felt good, the flexibility of his tongue and lips against the rigidity of Quinn's cock, as if Aaron was adapting himself, using his body to give Quinn a safe, welcoming place in a cold world. He couldn't get nearly all the way to the base of Quinn's cock, and the whole thing was sloppier than he'd expected. And the deeper he was able to take Quinn, the harder it was to breathe. Yeah, Aaron definitely needed to figure out a few things here, but Quinn wasn't complaining. His fingers found Aaron's head and pushed him gently backward, and Aaron had been part of enough locker-room conversations to know what that meant. He'd be damned if he'd follow the suggestion, though. Still, it wouldn't be too sexy to choke to death, so he pulled back a little, sucked as hard as he could while still swirling and working his tongue, and then almost choked anyway when Quinn's hips shot forward as he came. Aaron managed to recover, though, and tried to remember how Quinn had handled this part with him. He swallowed, and kept the pressure up, and tried to resist the urge to jump up and do a victory dance around the equipment shed. The dance would have looked especially ridiculous considering that his own dick was still hanging half-out of his undone jeans.

Quinn's fingers tightened in his hair again, but this time he was being guided upward, and Aaron was absolutely ready for some more face-time with Quinn. He rose to his feet and leaned in, and didn't even try to hide his smug grin. "I made you come, man. That was me—I did that."

"Yeah? I thought it might have been you, but it's good to hear it confirmed."

Aaron kept his mouth close enough that he could kiss whenever he wanted to, which was pretty much all the time, but could pull away whenever he wanted to talk. Unfortunately, that was pretty much all the time too. He wondered whether they could learn that Helen Keller brand of sign language, so they could have a conversation with their fingers while their lips were busy. Then again, it was kind of hot, feeling Quinn's lips moving against his own as he formed words.

Unfortunately, the words themselves weren't always that sexy. "I'm sorry, man. This was a stupid place. I don't—I shouldn't have done that."

Aaron pulled back far enough to let Quinn see his frown. "You weren't the only one involved, Quinn." He glanced around him. "I mean, yeah, we shouldn't make a habit of it, but no harm, no foul, this time."

Quinn pushed him away far enough that they had room to tuck themselves in and do up their flies. "I'm already late for work, and then I take a break as soon as I get here. Excellent work ethic."

Aaron didn't know what to do with Quinn at times like these. He hoped that his strategy of joking him out of it was at least partly effective. "Yeah, you're taking your dad to heart, maybe? You think you're too *good* for our minimum-wage slavery? Is that it?" He ran his fingers along Quinn's ribs in an attempt at tickling, but Quinn just squirmed away. "How was, it, anyhow? With your parents?"

Quinn thought before he answered. "Actually, okay, maybe. I don't know. I mean... they want stuff. For me. From me." He looked like he wasn't sure how much more to say. Finally he shrugged, and kept his eyes fixed on the spot where one of his fingers was hooked through Aaron's belt loop. "And all I want is you."

Aaron felt like his chest would explode. He wanted to do another dance of celebration, one that would put his previous imaginary dance to shame. He wanted to pick Quinn up and spin him around, with a lot of extra swoops and dips and twirls. He managed to control himself, though, and just ducked his head down enough to find Quinn's hidden face for a kiss. "Well, you've already got that—so maybe they're just looking for what's next."

"I can't just have more of you?"

"You can have all I've got, Quinn."

Quinn ran his hands along Aaron's shoulders and down over his ass. "Well, that's quite a lot." He smiled, and then pushed Aaron away. "Damn. I've got to go do some work. Stop distracting me."

"Sorry." Aaron wasn't sorry at all. He and Quinn gave each other a quick inspection to make sure there was no evidence of their recent encounter, and then headed into the barn together. Danny waggled his eyebrows at Aaron, but thankfully didn't say anything out loud, and his mom was teaching a lesson, so he was saved from her scrutiny.

They worked through the day, Quinn so intent on making up for lost time that Aaron could barely get his attention at all. Aaron had late lessons, and Quinn stayed at the barn, stocking the feed room, sweeping the already-clean barn aisle, and finally cleaning the office and viewing lounge. Aaron wasn't sure whether Quinn was still feeling guilty about leaving early and arriving late, or whether he was hanging around until Aaron was done working. He hoped it was the latter, and by the grins Danny and his mom sent his way, he knew it was what they thought.

The last lesson was a group of middle-aged women who had just started riding, and usually they were a riot. They'd originally been given the latest slot because they were adults and were old enough to be out on a school-night; after a few lessons, Wendy and Aaron had agreed that it was lucky there were no kids around to hear them swearing like sailors, seizing on any possible sexual innuendo, and generally being disruptive. Most weeks, they were one of Aaron's favorite lessons.

This week, though, they just wouldn't *leave*, and it was driving him crazy. Sure, Tracey's story about her five-year-old's love of public nudity was funny. But it was *long*, and Aaron had some private nudity of his own that he wanted to get to. But the women were still grooming their horses, ostensibly, so there was really no way for him to get them out without making it seem as if he didn't care about the well-being of the animals. He made a couple comments, telling one woman, "Damn, he's clean enough for a show! He's just going to go roll in the mud, you know," and making a show of getting the rain sheets ready to go. There was no effect, and his presence just seemed to give them another distraction as they tried to bring him into the conversation. He gave up, and went to hide in the office.

That was where Quinn found him. It had been a long day, but one look at Quinn's face had Aaron totally revitalized. "Hey." Aaron tried to keep his cool. The equipment shed had been one thing, but grabbing hold of Quinn in the viewing lounge would be completely inappropriate. "Can we do something, after the ladies go? Or are you tired?" Aaron could feel his enthusiasm waning. "Of course you are. It's been an intense couple of days. We don't have to do anything, if you need some time on your own. Or we can just go back to my place—the fort's still up, right? If you just want to sleep. With me."

Quinn stepped closer, and glanced over his shoulder to be sure they were alone. "I want to do a hell of a lot more than sleep, Aaron."

"Yeah?" Aaron wasn't sure if he should push it; Quinn *had* gone through a lot in the last couple days. But some instinct suggested that the wound wasn't quite washed clean, yet, and that it would make sense to get that taken care of before it began its healing process. "Remember when you said 'anytime, anywhere'?"

Quinn nodded with a look of wary amusement. "Yeah. I think we already kind of tried that out, earlier. Have you got somewhere kinkier in mind?"

"No, not kinkier. But—it's okay if you don't want to, but I'd like to see your place. Maybe we could spend the night there, tonight?"

The wariness on Quinn's face confirmed Aaron's feeling that there was something worth investigating here, but he still wasn't sure it was the right time for it. Was he helping, or would it be better for him to be the one person who *wasn't* pushing Quinn for more than he wanted to give? "We don't have to. If you don't want to."

Quinn's expression was one that Aaron had only seen a couple times before, but that he wanted to see again as often as possible. It wasn't quite a smile, just a look of pure affection. "No, we can go there. If you want." And then the smile came. "There's no bathtub, but there's an excellent shower. Really big. Just, you know, in case you were feeling dirty." A thoughtful frown, and then another smile. "And the sweats I wore last night are still there, so there'd be something that would fit you to sleep in. 'Cause I wasn't lying about the place being really cold."

Aaron figured it was a sign of how far gone he was; a freezing apartment just sounded like a great excuse for wrapping himself around Quinn. Not that he really felt the need for excuses. "Sounds good. I'll just go check on the ladies, see if they're finally ready."

They weren't, of course, but Aaron made himself be patient. It was easier when Quinn came out and waited with him. They got the horses put away, finally, and the ladies left. It would have been more efficient to split up and do the barn-closing chores separately, but by mutual, undiscussed agreement, they walked around together.

They drove back to town together too, Aaron following Quinn's taillights through the dark, rain-damp streets. He wondered if he would have the courage to suggest that they start driving to work together. Their schedules didn't always coincide, but they often did. He'd asked Quinn about it before, and he'd been brushed off; apparently Quinn didn't always go home after work, and he liked to maintain his flexibility. But now that was sounding like an excuse, and Aaron thought maybe it was time to raise the issue again.

But it wasn't at the top of his mind as he pulled in behind Quinn, the bike parked sideways so they could share a parking space. They were in the West End, only a few blocks from Aaron's high-rise, but the feeling was totally different. Quinn was standing by an outdoor staircase, possibly an adapted fire escape, leading up the side of a stucco-covered house; it was hard to tell in the dark, but it looked like it might be baby blue. "I'm upstairs," Quinn explained. He started up the stairs and Aaron followed, but Quinn stopped abruptly halfway up and turned around, with his hands braced on the railings. "It used to be Connor's," he said so quickly that it took a moment for Aaron to understand.

"Connor used to live here." He supposed it wasn't exactly witty, but he needed to be sure.

Quinn nodded. "I didn't do it on purpose, exactly. I was looking for a place, and it was available, and I thought... I don't know. I just went to look at it. And the landlady—she lives downstairs—she saw me and she just said, 'Oh, good, you're back,' and she handed me the keys." Quinn shook his head. "Turns out she's a bit senile. She made me pay a month's back rent, actually."

"Crazy like a fox, sounds like." Aaron wasn't sure how to take this new piece of information. It didn't seem healthy for Quinn to be living in his dead brother's apartment, but if he thought about it historically, Aaron figured that generations of people had all lived in the same space. Maybe this was just one way Quinn had been looking for a home, or some continuity in his life.

Quinn shrugged. "Yeah, maybe. But, the thing is, Connor was an artist. That's what he was doing out here, going to art school. And he did some murals, in the apartment. The landlady painted over them, but I got most of that off. I mean, I'm not an art restorer, so there's lots of mistakes. But, yeah. There's murals. Just, you know... so you know."

Aaron nodded. "Okay." He reached up and took Quinn's hands. "It's *okay*, Quinn. Anything short of crucified kittens on the walls, and I'm still going to be crazy about you. And I mean actual kittens, not just a painting of them."

"Well, that's pretty sick, man." Quinn's fingers tightened around Aaron's. "No kittens."

They made it inside and Quinn hit the lights. It was a large, open space, easily three times the size of Aaron's apartment. The ceiling sloped on two sides where it was up against the roof, and Quinn had been right—the air was barely warmer than it had been outside. But Aaron didn't pay much attention to that. He was too fascinated by the murals. There was a huge one, covering all of one wall and spilling over the corners at either end, and a smaller one on the opposite wall. They were both abstract, swirls of color and texture, and Aaron wasn't sure if he really liked them, but he couldn't deny that they were powerful. There was no overhead lighting, just floor lamps, and they had been arranged to shine onto the walls, rather than into the room itself. Aaron could just make out a bed under the far window, and he could see a fridge and sink in one corner, but otherwise the space was open and bare. "How long have you lived here?"

Quinn shrugged. "Quite a while. But I'm not home all that much." He was back to looking defensive. "We don't have to stay here. Or, you know, if—"

"Do not even think about suggesting that I go home on my own, Quinn." Aaron felt real anger, and took a moment to collect himself. "I'm getting sick of you thinking that I'm that shallow. Or stupid, or whatever it is that makes you think that I don't know what I want, or that I'm going to wimp out at the first sign of trouble. I'm not going anywhere, Quinn. Not if I can help it." He took a deep breath. "And I want to do more than we've been doing. I mean... you know. I want to do everything. Sex. The whole thing." Aaron had decided that he wasn't going to use a swear word to describe anything that he wanted to do with Quinn.

"You don't have to, Aaron. I can wait. Or we don't have to do it ever, really—I read something somewhere, it said that lots of gay guys never fuck." He caught himself. "Have sex. You know, full-on."

"Well, that's fine for them, but I want to. You said 'anytime, anywhere'. Well, this is the time and place, buddy. Let's go." He held his arms out to the sides and beckoned with his fingers. "Bring it on, hot stuff."

"God, you're weird." Quinn smiled, but still seemed concerned. "Have you thought this through? I mean, do you even know if you want to bottom or top?"

"Quinn, I'm twenty-two years old. I've been thinking about this for almost a decade. It's not a passing damn whim." He lowered his arms. "I want to switch it up, and try both. But the first time, I want to bottom, if that works for you." Quinn looked surprised by Aaron's calm tone, so he decided to keep pushing. "I don't know what you'll do, but I think rimming sounds good. You know, as a warm-up. And then some stretching, I guess. If you don't have any toys here, I think fingers sound fine. For the actual sex, I read that doggie-style is probably easiest, for the initial penetration, but I think I might prefer some sort of modified missionary, just so we can still be face-to-face. There's a lot of other stuff I want to try, but judging by the look on your face, I think we should discuss it later."

"Jesus Christ, Aaron!" Quinn sounded scandalized, and Aaron didn't bother trying to cover his laughter. "It's not funny! You're supposed to be.... Well, I don't know what you're supposed to be, but that wasn't very fucking virginal."

"Oh, a new side to me. Something unexpected. Should I start making your excuses now, and telling you all the different ways that you can escape if you want to?" Aaron tried to make his face look stern. "Or should I calm the fuck down and realize that you're okay with seeing new sides of me, and it's all part of getting to know each other better?"

Quinn reluctantly took Aaron's offered hand. "Okay, well, you're assuming that I *am* okay with this new side of you."

Aaron wasn't sure where his confidence had come from, but apparently it was pretty strong. "Yeah, I am assuming that." He pulled Quinn in close. "Am I wrong?" He let his lips hover just above Quinn's.

"You know you aren't, you smug bastard."

Aaron rewarded him with a kiss, but then it was time to get down to business. "So, you mentioned a big shower?"

Quinn nodded, but he was clearly distracted. Aaron watched as Quinn strode across the floor to the wardrobe by the door and rooted around inside. He looked relieved when he turned around and held up a box of condoms and a tube of lube. "I don't really—I don't bring people back here. I wondered if maybe I was out. But it's all good."

"My mom'll kill me if I don't ask. Have you been tested, lately? For HIV, or whatever."

Quinn nodded. "Yeah. I go all the time. And I always use a condom. *Always.* I wouldn't put you in danger, Aaron."

"Okay." There was still an element of risk, Aaron knew, but he wasn't going to let it get in the way. "Duty to mother satisfied."

"Could that please be the last time you mention her, for tonight?"

"Absolutely." Aaron pulled his jacket off and threw it toward the front door. He didn't wait to see it land on the floor, just got to work on the laces of his boots. From the corner of his eye, he could see Quinn dropping the condoms off onto the bed, then starting to get his own boots off. "So, shower, yes?"

"If you want rimming, absolutely. I'm happy to do it, but I want you clean."

Somehow, *that* was what made Aaron shy. "You don't have to. I mean, I was saying it just to shock you, mostly. It's not...."

"Aaron, settle. It's a good idea. I like it. Just... let's shower, first." He took Aaron's hand and led him toward the door on the far side of the room. Quinn flipped a light on in the bathroom, and then hit another switch to turn on an overhead heat lamp. He saw Aaron's eyebrow go up. "It's a weird apartment. Most of it's crappy, but the bathroom rocks."

He wasn't lying. There was a glassed-in shower stretching along all of one wall, at least as long as a bathtub would have been, and twice as wide. The counter wasn't huge, but it looked like marble, and there were two skylights, although they weren't too effective at night.

"I think they started to renovate the place, and then stopped after this one room." Quinn pulled a couple of towels out of a glass-fronted linen closet and put them on the counter by the shower.

Then he brought his hands to the buttons of Aaron's shirt. "You still good with this?"

Aaron lifted his own hands and started on Quinn's fly. "Absolutely."

They undressed efficiently, and Aaron was amazed by how quickly he'd gotten comfortable with this. He was still excited by Quinn's body, and by the chance to be naked near him, but he wasn't self-conscious anymore, not even a little. When Quinn stepped inside the shower and started adjusting the spray, Aaron followed after him without hesitation.

Quinn's olive skin looked tan next to Aaron's paler body, and it was fascinating to watch the water play across the different shades. They were both almost completely hard, but neither of them seemed to be in a rush. Quinn had a washcloth and a bottle of shower gel, and he lathered up and washed Aaron all over. It was relaxing, and only vaguely sexual, although the rough texture of the washcloth against his cock was enough to get him fully hard.

After that, Aaron's arousal grew pretty steadily. Touches that had seemed casual before, Quinn dragging the washcloth along Aaron's back, or his side, became charged almost unbearably. Aaron felt as if there were a few places that he *needed* Quinn to touch. His lips, his nipples, his cock, and his ass all felt over-sensitized, almost aching, and they were the very areas that Quinn seemed to be avoiding. "Quinn," Aaron whined.

Quinn laughed softly, but he relented, bringing the cloth down between the cheeks of Aaron's ass. He slid it right under until it brushed against Aaron's balls, then brought it back, then under again. Aaron could feel his back arching involuntarily as he pressed his ass backward in a wanton invitation.

"Jesus, Aaron," Quinn muttered. He dropped the washcloth, but his hand didn't leave Aaron's ass, his fingers tickling around the hole, pressing and pulling and making Aaron feel nerves he hadn't known he even had. Aaron was almost dizzy, and he braced his hands against the wall of the shower and tried to maintain some sort of consciousness of the world beyond the sensations. That attempt was defeated at the first touch of warm, soft tongue. Aaron hadn't even realized that Quinn had dropped to his knees. The whole experience was almost too powerful—sexual, but somehow more. Aaron could hear his breath coming in ragged gasps, and he leaned forward a little more, letting his cheek find the relative coolness of the tile wall.

He wasn't sure how long it went on. Finally, he felt one of Quinn's hands reach forward, brushing past Aaron's balls to find his hard, aching cock. Then it was an impossible choice, pushing forward into Quinn's tight grip or back into the softness of his tongue. Aaron was suspended there, vibrating between the two sensations, until Quinn finally took mercy on him and jacked him hard, his grip tight and demanding. Only a few strokes and Aaron was coming in deep, pulsing spasms that washed through his whole body, then circled around and crashed through again.

Quinn seemed to know just when it was too much, when he needed to leave Aaron's cock alone. He didn't let up on his attentions to Aaron's ass, though, and for the first time Aaron understood the true beauty of this practice. His enjoyment wasn't over when he came, not anymore. The familiar lassitude was still there, but the stimulation overcame it without any difficulty. Quinn could go right on making him feel good—making him feel great—and it could last all night. Well, until Quinn's tongue cramped up, at least.

It turned out to be the hot water supply that ran out, not Quinn's energy. Aaron barely noticed it until Quinn kissed his way up Aaron's spine and then leaned over to shut off the water that had, Aaron realized, become tepid. "You don't want to go into that cold room out of a cold shower," Quinn warned. He guided Aaron out into the warmth under the heat lamp, and then picked up one of the towels and started drying Aaron off. A part of Aaron wanted to insist that he was fully capable of doing that himself, but a larger part was enjoying the pampering.

When the first towel was wet, Quinn wrapped it around his own waist and then picked up the other towel to wrap around Aaron. "Hey," Aaron protested. "You'll get cold."

"Nah, I'm used to it."

"We'll, you've already got one pretty huge goose bump." He nodded down to the tent in the front of Quinn's towel.

"That's just proof that I'm not too cold."

"I think it's proof that I'm too *hot*."

"Yeah, okay. You ready to go into the icebox?"

"I guess."

Aaron followed after Quinn, and the other room *was* cold, but some of the heat from the bathroom seemed to have reached it, because it was no longer absolutely freezing. Still, Aaron was glad to see the thick quilts on the bed. He was less happy to feel the cold sheets against his skin, but he dropped his towel and slipped in anyway. Quinn was right behind him; they snuggled up for warmth and neither of them complained.

They started kissing right away, but it was a while before the cocoon of warmth grew enough for them to feel inspired for any more dramatic movements. Soon, though, Quinn was back to his full-body treatment, his hands and lips visiting all the spots his washcloth had recently cleaned. Just like the last time, he frustratingly avoided the key locations, but still managed to get Aaron worked up pretty quickly. Aaron knew he was taking more than giving, this night, but Quinn didn't seem to be keeping score, so Aaron resolved to make up for it later. For now, he gave in to the feelings.

By the time Aaron finally started getting some attention to his most sensitive areas, his whole body was keyed up and ready. He felt like he was in a dream, one of the ones where he could breathe underwater, and his whole body was surrounded by welcoming warmth and gentle pressure. Quinn's tongue slid down the crack of Aaron's ass and it just felt like more of the same, until Quinn reached the center, the tight circle of nerve and muscle that quivered under Quinn's attention.

Aaron's back arched again, and he felt his breath catch and had to force himself to take another. This time, Quinn kept working with his fingers, and Aaron felt things get slippery and realized that it was lube. This was really happening. His body wanted it, wanted more of anything. He tried to ignore that for a moment, or at least work past it, in order to check on his emotions. Was he ready? Was this what he wanted, for sure?

He felt a finger playing around the edges, working almost but not quite past the tight muscles, and then Quinn slid up toward his head. "You sure on this? Absolutely?" The finger stayed where it was; it didn't stop its gentle movements, but it didn't go any further, either.

Aaron felt a warm bubble of joy rising from his gut. Yes, he was sure. This was Quinn. Of course he was sure. "Yeah. Absolutely." And since Quinn was there, it seemed like a good time for some kissing. Their lips were joined when Quinn's finger slipped inside for the first time, and Aaron knew that Quinn could feel his gasp, and then his smile.

They stayed like that, Aaron on his side with his shoulders and head tilted around almost flat, Quinn spooned in behind him. Quinn's free hand ran all over Aaron's body, but their faces stayed close, kissing and breathing and smiling together as Quinn eased Aaron toward their goal. When Aaron finally felt the larger, blunt pressure of Quinn's cock, he wanted Quinn inside him as much for the emotional completion as the physical sensation.

Quinn went slow, and Aaron was so focused on his own feelings that he barely noticed the way Quinn's face had tensed into a mask of fierce concentration. When Quinn finally bottomed out, his whole body relaxed for a moment, and Aaron realized how hard he'd been fighting the urge to go deep and fast.

"It's good, Quinn. I'm good." He wasn't lying. The stretch wasn't totally comfortable, yet, but it wasn't painful, and he felt safe and unafraid.

"I've gotta move, Aaron, please...." Aaron had never heard Quinn's voice like that, strained and tight.

"Jesus, yeah, Quinn, it's good," Aaron started, and then Quinn started moving and "good" didn't really seem like the right word anymore. It was gentle at first, just tiny waves against the stretched, sensitized skin wrapped tight around Quinn's cock, but as Quinn's movements got bolder, the waves turned into crashing, pounding surf. Aaron was pretty sure Quinn was still barely moving, by objective standards, but it felt more intense than anything he'd ever felt. He wasn't sure what he'd do if Quinn went any harder or faster; he couldn't imagine feeling any more than he already was.

He opened eyes that he couldn't remember closing and saw Quinn watching him closely, almost clinically. "Okay?" Quinn asked, his fingers roaming up from Aaron's chest to smooth the frown creasing his forehead.

"Yes." He stretched for a kiss, and Quinn obliged, and it was perfect again, the two of them joined in every way, making each other feel good all over. Then Quinn's hand wrapped around Aaron's cock and he realized he should stop using words like "perfect", because apparently there was always something better just around the corner.

It didn't take long after that. Aaron could feel his body tensing, could see where his fingers were clawing at the cool sheets over the mattress, but it was like he was somewhere else, watching but not feeling. He had a moment where he felt like he could catalogue every muscle in his body, every sensation on his skin, and then his orgasm hit, slamming him back into his body just in time to feel himself shooting come harder than he ever had before. The orgasm just kept going, spasm after spasm, until it was almost frightening. Quinn was still sliding in and out, still working that spot inside, and even after the orgasm had faded for most of Aaron's body, his cock was still jerking as every last drop of come was pushed out of his body.

Aaron was just back to himself when he felt Quinn tighten behind him, and the movement in his ass stopped, then jerked into motion, then held still. Aaron could feel the vibrations in Quinn's body and imagined that he could feel it pulsing through his cock as well. He hated the condom, wanted Quinn to be shooting his seed deep inside Aaron without a barrier. He didn't want *anything* between himself and Quinn.

When Quinn's body relaxed, Aaron kissed him, slow and gentle. Quinn's brain came back into service faster than Aaron's seemed to, and he frowned in concern as he cast his eyes over Aaron's face. "You're okay?"

Aaron just smiled. He was much, much better than okay.

AARON woke up to the smell of coffee and the sensation of a cold nose. The rest of him was okay, but his poor nose, sticking out from under the covers, was frozen.

He moved a little, and felt a few twinges of soreness as pleasant reminders. His stirring was apparently enough to get Quinn's attention. He looked over from his spot in the kitchen. "You up?"

Everything was sideways, but Quinn looked pretty good, walking toward him in sweats and a Henley, thick socks on his feet, and two coffee mugs in his hands. Aaron sat up a little, although he was careful to keep the blankets wrapped tight around him.

Quinn handed him a mug and set the other down on the floor beside the bed, freeing his hands for more carrying. He returned this time with two bowls, and Aaron could see fruit on top of something, but didn't realize what the "something" was until Quinn lowered the bowls.

"Oatmeal?"

"For *eating*. I've got to go to work, so I can't do brunch. Does breakfast count?"

"I guess." Aaron tried to look petulant, but he really didn't think he was pulling it off. He decided that he didn't even really want to try. "How're you feeling about your family stuff? I mean—are you okay?"

Quinn nodded for Aaron to scoot over, and they sat on the bed together, Aaron cross-legged with his bowl of oatmeal cradled in his lap, Quinn with his feet on the ground, looking over at the larger mural. "Yeah. I'm okay. I mean, they're my family. I love them. It's good to have them back, right? And I was thinking... I don't want to work for the company, I don't think, but maybe I'd like to get back to the engineering. Or science. There's some really cool stuff going on with alternative energies, and maybe I could be part of that. You know—I could look into it, at least."

Aaron tried to keep his voice calm. "So, would that mean going back to MIT? I mean, that's a really good school, right? Do you think you could get back in, now?"

Quinn frowned. "I don't—I hadn't really thought about it. I mean, I don't have any details at all. My head's still kind of spinning. It's just... a lot. You're a lot, and my family's a lot, and it's been a long time since I had anything, so—it's a lot of 'a lot', you know?"

Aaron wasn't sure how to feel about that. "Are you saying you want to slow down? I mean, if you need some space, I understand. You're right, this has all happened really fast, and I'm sure you're feeling pretty overwhelmed." He wasn't sure what he was doing, making it easier for Quinn to walk away from him, but he realized that he was saying it because Quinn's happiness had become more important to him than his own. Scary, but true. Luckily, Quinn was shaking his head.

"No. Not—not at all." He looked like he wasn't sure how much he wanted to say; it was a look that was becoming all too familiar to Aaron. Again, though, it was lucky that Quinn generally seemed to be finding the courage to open up. And he did this time, setting his oatmeal on the floor and turning so he had one knee up on the bed, facing Aaron head-on. "You're—you've been keeping me sane. Seriously. You're...." He trailed off, but it didn't seem like he was done, more like he was trying to find the right words. "I'm scared shitless. I mean, you can say that you're not going to change your mind, but when I worry about that... it's not that I think you don't know what you're doing, or that you're stupid or immature or whatever else. It's just that you're—you're new, and pure, and perfect, and it doesn't make sense for you to want to be with someone like me. Not in the long term."

It probably wasn't the best response, but it was all Aaron could think of on short notice. "Well, I'm not all that 'pure' anymore."

Quinn shook his head and smiled. "No, man—you're still pure. But, the thing is, when I'm with you, I can start to feel a bit that way myself. I've been feeling like I'm all washed up for.... I don't know. For way too fucking long. But spending time with you, even before the sex.... Don't get me wrong, the sex has been good, but—it's not the really important part. You know?"

Aaron smiled. He did know. He hoped he wasn't about to make a huge mistake, but he felt like maybe it was time. "I know it's another pile of 'a lot', so probably I should keep my mouth shut, but—you never seemed washed up to me. You always seemed perfect. I mean, even when you were being an asshole, you were still perfectly 'Quinn', you know?"

"I think maybe that's kind of an insult, man," Quinn said, but he didn't seem upset.

"No, it isn't, not at all. Quinn—I—" Damn, this was scary. Probably a terrible idea. But he wanted to do it. He needed to. "I love you, Quinn. I know we just started dating, or whatever, but I've known you for a long time, and I'm not stupid, and I know how I feel, and... I love you. So if you need to go to MIT, I'll just hope that we can figure out some way to stay together while you do that. And if we can't, then I'll still love you, and I'll still want you to be happy, and—"

"I don't want to go to MIT" Quinn's voice was quietly intense. "If I can't learn it at a Vancouver school, I'll just have to get by without it. I don't want to go anywhere. I—" He looked down at his hands, then back up, and his expression was raw. "I love you too, Aaron. I do. And I'm going to try really hard to not fuck this up, okay?"

"Okay." Aaron's voice sounded a little shaky, but he was just happy that any sound had come out at all. "And I'll try not to fuck it up too." He held up his hand to stop Quinn before he could start talking about how perfect Aaron was again. He really didn't need that kind of pressure. Quinn had said he loved him—that was more than Aaron had expected, and all he wanted to hear, for a long time. "We'll both try."

Quinn nodded, reluctantly, and then adopted a crafty expression. "Do you think Danny would be really pissed if I was a little late for work? I'm not opening, so the horses will be fed without me...."

"You more worried about my brother, or me?" Aaron put a little growl in his voice. He didn't want Quinn going anywhere, ever, without him. "Go in late. I'll help you get caught up later."

"Don't you kind of have your own work to do, later?" Quinn wasn't really arguing, though, and he wasn't going anywhere.

"I have lots of stuff to do later. With you." Aaron still wasn't sure that this was all real—he had always been sympathetic to the speed at which Quinn's world had changed, but he felt it even more now that he was experiencing a seismic shift of his own. "There's no rush, right? We've got all the time in the world."

Quinn still didn't argue, so Aaron moved forward, slowly, and tried to remember every detail of their first kiss after their declaration of love. It might be a little sappy, but he didn't care. He loved Quinn, and Quinn loved him back. That was all that mattered.

New Tricks

QUINN DONAHUE rolled and shrugged his shoulders as he trudged up the stairs. It had been a long, hard day at the barn, and he wanted to crawl into bed and sleep until the next morning. Or maybe have a hot bath first to soak some of the stiffness out of his muscles. He and Aaron had just moved into the new apartment, and they hadn't really had a chance to use the huge tub yet. He grinned to himself. He could soak the stiffness out of his muscles and transfer it to some other part of his body. Apparently thinking of Aaron had re-energized him.

He fumbled for his keys and unlocked the apartment door, then pushed it open. It was dark inside, and he felt a tiny, unreasonable twist of disappointment. It was Aaron's day off; obviously the guy had better things to do than sit around waiting for Quinn to show up. Just because *Quinn* had been looking forward to this all day, it didn't mean that Aaron was quite so pathetic.

He pulled his boots off and lined them up next to Aaron's on the mat, then shrugged free of his jacket and hung it on the only empty hook. He headed down the hall to the main room and almost jumped when he heard a familiar voice speak from the shadows by the window. "You're home." Aaron sounded—different. Quinn wasn't sure what the difference was, though, and he sure as hell wasn't sure why Aaron was sitting all alone in a dark room.

"You okay, man? Is something wrong?" Quinn worked at Aaron's family barn, and everyone had been fine when he'd left, so whatever the news was, it couldn't be too bad. Still, this was strange, and Quinn took a step toward the windows.

"Stop." Aaron's voice wasn't loud, but it was firm, and Quinn did as he was told.

"What's going on, Aaron?" Quinn wasn't worried, exactly, but he was definitely off balance. He tried to silence the nagging voice in the back of his mind, the one that suggested that maybe Aaron was tired of playing house, tired of Quinn altogether....

"Stay where you are and turn the kitchen light on. Don't adjust the dimmer, just turn it on." Aaron's voice was still quiet, still authoritative.

"Aaron..." Quinn started, but then he shook his head and did as he was told. The kitchen lamp wasn't bright, but it cast enough light for Quinn to see Aaron slouching in an armchair, a chair that he must have moved there just for that purpose. He looked like he was....

"Aaron, are you wearing a suit? What's going on, Aaron?"

"Stop asking questions. If you need to know something, I'll tell you. Otherwise—just trust me." There was a pause, and then Aaron's voice sounded more familiar. "Okay, Quinn? Will you trust me?"

Quinn was beginning to get some idea of what was happening. "Have you been watching porn again, Aaron?" He caught himself. Aaron had been a virgin when he'd hooked up with Quinn, and Quinn had been the furthest thing from innocent. If Aaron wanted to experiment a little, then it was damn well Quinn's *privilege* to be asked to participate. "I mean—sorry. No questions." He nodded slowly. "Yeah, Aaron—I'll trust you."

"Okay. Excellent." Aaron sounded like a little boy being told he was going to get a treat. But then he took a moment as if to collect himself, and when he spoke again his voice was back to being calm and firm. "Stay where you are, and take your jacket off. Throw it on the couch." A pause as Aaron watched Quinn obey, then, "Jesus, Quinn, on the *couch*, not the floor. How are you such a slob?"

"It's not easy to throw *fabric*, Aaron. Are we doing this or not?"

"No questions." Aaron was back on his game. "Take your socks off."

"My socks?" That didn't seem like the right order to Quinn.

"Quinn, if you can't stop asking questions, I may need to do something about that. Do you want me to tell you to put your socks in your mouth?"

"Aaron, this game is over if you tell me to put my socks in my mouth. They've been inside my sweaty boots all day, and...."

"Then you should stop asking questions." Aaron paused. "Unless you want the game to be over. Do you want the game to be over?"

Quinn thought about it, but not for very long. "No. I don't want it to be over."

"Good. Me neither." Quinn hadn't realized that Aaron was leaning forward until he shifted back and stretched his long, lean body out from the chair. Damn, Quinn liked it when Aaron stretched. "Take your socks off, Quinn. *Ball them up*, and then throw them *on* the couch."

Quinn tried not to grin and did as he was told. He looked down at his feet; it was strange how naked they looked. He wondered if Aaron was looking at them too.

"Now your top shirt. *Slowly*. Make it a show, Quinn. Make me want to touch you."

Quinn absolutely hoped he'd be able to persuade Aaron to touch him. As soon as possible. But he wasn't all that into putting on a show; he preferred to be the one watching and judging. Or at least, that had been his preference before Aaron; now, he liked to watch and *admire*. But this was Aaron's thing, and Quinn wanted to play Aaron's game. He unbuttoned the shirt, forcing himself to move slowly, but he was pretty sure that instead of looking sensuous and seductive, he was looking uncoordinated or possibly drunk. He forced himself to keep going, running a hand up his chest under the shirt and pushing it off his shoulder, then doing the same with the other hand on the other side. He held the shirt there, halfway down his back with the sleeves caught just above his elbows, and he remembered how stiff his muscles were and rolled his shoulders again.

Apparently that was enough; Quinn was lucky that Aaron didn't have much real-world knowledge of this sort of thing. *Lucky that Aaron didn't have much real-world experience about boyfriends in general*, that nasty voice in the back of Quinn's head added. But Aaron couldn't hear that voice, and he seemed pleased. "Very nice. Let it fall to the floor." Aaron's voice was a little husky, or at least Quinn hoped it was. "Now just stand there. Let me look at you."

It was strange; Aaron looked at Quinn all the time, but it didn't usually affect him like this. Well, it usually *affected* him; any attention from Aaron was good, and it tended to lead to sex, so that was good too. But there was something different about this, about Aaron looking at Quinn like he was appraising him rather than just waiting for Quinn to notice him. It was getting Quinn pretty hard, pretty fast.

"There's a new mark on the side of your neck. What did that?"

"How can you even see that? It's so dark in here...." Quinn caught himself. No questions. "It's just scratches. Your asshole brother hit me with a hay bale. He thought it was funny."

"Why did he hit you?" Aaron sounded more serious than usual; actually, he sounded like he might be about to get Quinn in trouble for fighting at work.

"We were just screwing around. He was tossing bales down

from the top of the loft, and I said something about how he was too slow, so he started pelting them down really fast...." If it had been a normal night, if they hadn't been doing whatever it was that they were doing, Aaron would have laughed at that. But things were different this night.

Aaron barely moved, just reached into his jacket's breast pocket and pulled out his phone, then hit a number and held it to his ear. "Danny? It's Aaron. I'm at the apartment. You were careless today, and you damaged my property. I don't like it, Danny. Don't do it again." He clicked the phone shut without waiting for an answer.

Quinn stared across the room. "Aaron, what the fuck! That's— Jesus, Aaron, that's a little much, don't you think? Why did you drag Danny into this?"

Aaron's gaze was fierce. "I'm not going to warn you again, Quinn. No more questions." He stood up and took a step closer, then another. It was *Aaron*, Quinn reminded himself. Big, goofy Aaron, who caught spiders and put them outside instead of squishing them. Just *Aaron*. But Quinn's skin tingled in an unfamiliar if not totally unpleasant way as the hair on his back and arms stood up on end. And his cock got a little bit harder.

"Put your arms out to the sides," Aaron ordered, and after Quinn obeyed, Aaron closed the remaining space between them. He stood close but didn't touch, and again he was inspecting Quinn, as if looking for more damage. He lifted one hand and brushed his fingertips along the scratches on Quinn's neck, and Quinn forced himself to stay still, to not move away from the tickling or toward the warmth. He did tilt his head a little to give Aaron more room when he leaned in and gently kissed each of the long, shallow scratches, and Aaron either didn't notice or didn't mind. "You're beautiful," Aaron whispered.

But then he stepped away. That wasn't at all what Quinn had been hoping for, but he managed to maintain his discipline and kept his feet still, his arms stretched out to the sides. Aaron smiled and reached out to run his fingers along the waistband of Quinn's jeans, just skimming the flesh before moving upward, underneath the fabric of Quinn's T-shirt. Aaron's fingers were cool against Quinn's warm skin, and when Aaron curled his hands so that his nails scratched a little, Quinn could feel the goose bumps rising.

Aaron shifted around and brought his other hand into play, pulling Quinn's shirt up and over his head while his hands were still in the sleeves. "Stand still," Aaron said, and he moved around until he was behind Quinn. "You still trust me?" he asked.

"Absolutely."

Aaron kissed the back of Quinn's neck before he twisted the T-shirt, knotting it around itself until it turned into a tight band holding Quinn's arms behind his back. "Okay?"

"Yeah," Quinn agreed. It was. He'd had bad experiences with this sort of thing, but none of that mattered, because this was Aaron. And letting himself be made helpless was *fine*, now, because he knew that Aaron wouldn't hurt him. Not on purpose, at least.

Aaron was tracing the muscles of Quinn's back, and as always, he bent to gently kiss the two long scars that marred the skin there. There wasn't actually much sensation left in the scar tissue, but Quinn appreciated the thought. He appreciated it even more when Aaron's hands snuck around Quinn's waist and ran down over the denim covering his hard cock. "You like this?" Aaron asked, his lips close to Quinn's ear.

"I like *you*."

"I want to do more—okay?"

If Aaron kept whispering like that, so close that his lips brushed Quinn's earlobe and sent shivers down his spine, he could do whatever the hell he wanted, but it probably wasn't part of the game for Quinn to be quite that enthusiastic. "Okay," he said instead.

Aaron shifted away, and Quinn would have been disappointed except that he soon realized Aaron was shedding a layer of clothing, which could only be good. Aaron tossed his suit jacket toward the couch and it landed perfectly on the seat; on a normal night there would have been gloating about that, but this night, Aaron's attention was apparently elsewhere. Quinn heard the rustle of fabric behind him, and then a blue stripe appeared in front of his eyes. Aaron's tie, held between Aaron's two strong hands, and moving toward Quinn's eyes. He kept perfectly still as Aaron wrapped the fabric carefully around his head, covering his eyes, then tied it snuggly, but not tight. "Okay?"

"Yeah, Aaron, it's okay." Quinn would have felt better if he hadn't heard the slight tremor in his voice, and even better if he could have fooled himself into believing that Aaron hadn't heard it.

Aaron was beside Quinn in a heartbeat, and he pushed up the cloth over one of Quinn's eyes to look at him more closely. "You're sure? We don't have to do this...."

"Aaron." Quinn made his voice firm. "It's fucking hot, okay? That's all. I'm not scared, it's just—intense." He tried to use his one functioning eye to convey sincerity and conviction, but he had a feeling he was probably glaring like a demented pirate. He fought back the urge to finish his sentence with an "Arr."

Aaron seemed convinced despite Quinn's limitations, and he let the fabric fall back down. "We're supposed to have a safeword. But, you know—you can just tell me to stop, and I will. Immediately."

"Aaron, I know that. It's good. The safeword is 'safeword', okay? But I'm not going to use it." Quinn wasn't sure what his role was here; it seemed like they were taking a break from Aaron's game, so maybe he was allowed to jump back to being the older, more experienced partner for a moment. "I trust you, and this is hot, and you can do what you want, okay? My body is yours. Seriously."

"Mine," Aaron said, and there was a little bit of a growl to his voice that let Quinn know that the game was absolutely back on. He felt Aaron kiss his shoulder, soft and open-mouthed, and then he drew in a quick breath as strong teeth closed on his flesh, nipping sharply before the tongue returned to soothe. Aaron kissed his way up to Quinn's neck, and he found a spot there, just in the hollow where neck turned to shoulder, and he nipped again, then sucked, long and hard. Quinn couldn't see, but he knew he was being marked. Claimed. He didn't even think about objecting.

He also had no objection to Aaron's decision to kiss his way up to Quinn's mouth. It had been too long since Quinn had been allowed to taste Aaron, to feel the smoothness of his tongue and the strength of his jaw. And when Aaron's hands moved to Quinn's chest and started stroking up and down his ribs, it didn't matter that Quinn was tied up, because he would never have wanted to move away anyhow.

He was a little less enthusiastic when Aaron broke the kiss off and used his hands not to caress but to keep Quinn from leaning after him. "Patience, Quinn," he said, and Quinn could hear the smile in his voice. "Come here." There was a gentle tug, and Quinn went with it. He let himself be led into what he knew must be the kitchen, and then Aaron maneuvered him around and pushed him gently backward. "Sit," he ordered, and Quinn did as he was told. He could feel the edge of the chair against the backs of his knees, but he trusted Aaron enough that he would have sat anyhow. "Stay," Aaron said, and the smile was back in his voice.

"Okay, we're not pretending that I'm a dog. I'm safewording all over that one."

Quinn could feel Aaron moving, falling to his knees, and then they were kissing again. Aaron pulled his mouth away far enough to say, "Really? It's absolutely out? Even if it's really important to me?"

Quinn groaned. "Fuck, Aaron. Seriously? You want to pretend I'm a dog?"

"Can I?"

"Jesus." Quinn hesitated, but there was really no doubt in his mind. If this was what Aaron wanted, then Quinn could give it to him. Quinn owed it to him. "I guess so. But it's weird, Aaron. Not nearly as hot as the other stuff."

"Oh my God, Quinn, I was totally joking! You'd actually let me treat you like a dog?" Another kiss, this one not as sweet because Aaron was laughing, and Quinn was still busy getting over his confusion. "Damn, Quinn, I didn't think I wanted to, but now that you've put it in my head...."

"I didn't put it in your head. You started it. And I'm finishing it. No puppy play. Not going to happen."

"But you just said I *could*. Damn it, Quinn, you're just being a tease." And then something in the atmosphere of the room shifted, and when he spoke again, the growl was back in Aaron's voice. "If you aren't careful, I'll have to punish you." He leaned down and trailed kisses across Quinn's chest, then paused and nipped, hard. Quinn gasped, and Aaron kissed the spot better, then moved on, with no discernible pattern, until he found whatever he was looking for and nipped again, just as hard. Another kiss soothed the soreness, another trail of kisses led to another sharp nip, and Quinn found himself teetering on the edge between pleasure and pain. His whole body felt alive, sensitized, and his senses strained to compensate for his lost vision. When Aaron finally pulled away and replaced his mouth with gentle, questing fingers, Quinn wasn't sure if he was relieved or disappointed.

"Have you eaten yet?" Aaron asked, and the question was so unexpectedly prosaic that it took Quinn a moment to understand it.

"Dinner? You mean, have I had dinner?"

"Yes, Quinn. Have you had dinner?" Aaron sounded amused.

"Uh, no. Not yet."

"Good." There was a rustle as Aaron rose to his feet. "I won't give you much; we don't want you too full to move, after all. But maybe a snack." Quinn heard the fridge door open, then shut, and there was a clatter as Aaron set something on the table.

Quinn waited patiently and was soon rewarded with the brush of something cold against his lips. He opened his mouth a little and leaned forward to capture whatever Aaron was offering, but it was nowhere to be found. "Aaron?"

No words, just a gentle hand on Quinn's chest, pushing him back until he was sitting straight. Damn. No questions, and now no movement? Aaron was taking this seriously. And that meant that Quinn would too. He made himself still and waited as patiently as he could.

The reward was another brush of whatever Aaron was offering, and this time Quinn didn't let himself move. Aaron pushed the food a little farther into Quinn's mouth, and he took a gentle, cautious bite. A burst of cold juice, and he knew what he was eating and bit the rest of the way through the strawberry. A bit of a cliché, maybe, but Aaron was a rookie. And they hadn't had strawberries in the fridge that morning, so that meant that Aaron had bought them today. Quinn had been off at work, thinking about Aaron, and apparently Aaron had been at the market, thinking about Quinn. That was good to know.

Quinn wasn't really convinced that there was a sexy way to chew food, but he did his best—mostly, he just slowed everything down. It seemed to be working on Aaron, anyway; Quinn could feel the hand that had been lightly resting on his thigh tighten, curving so Aaron's fingernails were in contact with the rough denim of Quinn's work pants. He swallowed the first mouthful, then sat and waited to see if Aaron would provide more.

Instead, Quinn felt Aaron's hand wrap around the back of his head almost roughly, pulling him forward into a deep, punishing kiss. The force of Aaron's lips overrode the pressure from his hand, and Quinn was pushed backward into the chair, Aaron's body following, wedging between Quinn's legs and crushing in. Aaron's tongue slid into Quinn's mouth as if it were chasing the last sweetness of the strawberry, and Quinn surged forward, not to escape the embrace but just to deepen it, to help Aaron in his quest to somehow fuse their bodies together.

He should have known better, he supposed, because it seemed to be his movement that brought Aaron back to himself and reminded him of what he was supposed to be doing. Aaron pulled his body away as his strong hand braced against Quinn's chest, and they both stayed still for a long moment. Quinn could hear the blood thumping through his ears, and he could absolutely feel it pulsing through his imprisoned cock. Finally, the strawberry returned, and Quinn obediently bit, chewed, and swallowed. Aaron's fingers played over Quinn's jaw and throat the whole time, gently pressing, testing, smoothing the skin. Quinn felt like Aaron was reading Braille, and wondered what message he was getting.

"Do you want more?" Aaron asked.

"If you want." Quinn wasn't just playing along; he felt like his own will had been drained away, and all he wanted was to make Aaron happy. Of course, it wasn't really Aaron's game that had left him with that lack of independence; Quinn had been feeling that way for months. In the best possible way.

Then Aaron left, and Quinn realized how full of shit he was. He *absolutely* had his own will and his own wants, and they both insisted that Aaron return to his side immediately. But he managed not to speak, and he was rewarded, eventually, with the pressure on his thighs from Aaron's hands. "Ready?" Aaron asked, and Quinn nodded, even while trying to figure out why Aaron's voice sounded a little strange. There was something against Quinn's lips again, and he repeated the process: bite, slow chew, swallow. Melon this time, a long strip of it. As soon as he'd swallowed, the melon was back, and when he was done with that bite, it was back again. Quinn felt the gentle brush of something against his forehead and realized that it was Aaron's bangs. And that Aaron's hands were both still on Quinn's thighs. Quinn opened his mouth for what he hoped was the last bite of fruit and allowed himself to lean forward, just a little, just enough to find

Aaron's lips, holding the melon. It was a bit awkward, kissing with the chunk of melon still half in each of their mouths, and Quinn took it as soon as he was able and swallowed it possibly a little too soon, but he managed to fight the huge chunk down and get back to the important stuff. Kissing Aaron properly was *definitely* more important than safe eating technique.

Aaron apparently didn't agree. "Jesus, Quinn, are you a snake? You're not supposed to swallow things whole."

There had to be some way to turn that into a sexual innuendo, but Quinn's brain seemed to be a little lust-fried. He just concentrated on kissing, on trying to make Aaron realize that it would be a good idea to quit with the food and get to something with more skin-on-skin contact. But Aaron was on to his tricks, and pulled away before Quinn could get much accomplished. "Patience, Quinn." His fingers ran over Quinn's face again, caressing each hollow and ridge. "I think I just want to look at you for a while. You're so beautiful."

"But I don't get to look at you?"

"That was dangerously close to a question, Quinn. We're not that far from the couch—your socks are not out of reach."

"I could just safeword."

"Yeah, you kind of blew that threat when you said I could treat you like a dog. You're not going to safeword anything, are you?" Aaron's voice was thoughtful. "Is that a problem, do you think? Like, should we not be doing this, if you're going to let me blow through all your boundaries?"

Quinn didn't like being blindfolded while having a conversation like this. Well, he didn't like having a conversation like this at *all*, but especially not when he couldn't see Aaron's reactions and couldn't use his eyes to convey his own sincerity. He tried to do his best with his voice. "Aaron. You're hot as hell, and you turn me on like I can't describe, but you're pretty fucking vanilla, man. Which is fine. Good, even—I like it. But I really don't think you need to worry that you're going to accidentally freak me out."

"Well, you don't know what I have planned," Aaron protested, but Quinn could hear the smile sneaking into his voice.

"No, I don't. But I'm looking forward to finding out. And I am *without* concerns about it, okay?"

A pause, and then, "I love you, Quinn."

"Yeah, okay. Now—you gonna show me what you've got?"

"I can't show you. You're blindfolded." Aaron's fingers tickled over the tie in front of Quinn's eyes. "But maybe I could let you *feel* something... oh, wait, your hands are tied. Huh. Maybe I'll just have to take a break and think this over." Aaron's hands brushed down over Quinn's bare chest, gently scratching at the spots that had been nipped earlier, and then, finally, thankfully, over the denim covering Quinn's aching cock. Aaron cupped the bulge almost thoughtfully, then rubbed up and down a few times, just the right pressure, just the right speed, and Quinn felt like he was a bit too old to be coming in his pants but he really didn't care about that right then, not if Aaron would just give him another couple... and then Aaron's hand was gone. "Yeah. I should probably take a little time and think this through," Aaron said, not even trying to hide the glee in his voice.

"Aaron, I swear...." Quinn wasn't sure if he was begging or threatening, but neither approach seemed likely to do him any good. Aaron's chuckle was low and sexy, the exact *last* thing that Quinn's cock needed.

But at least Aaron wasn't leaving entirely. Instead, he pressed forward on Quinn's shoulder. "Stand up, Quinn." Quinn did as he was told, trying to ignore the painful, erotic shift of his cock as he moved. "Those jeans seem a little tight. This isn't the seventies, you know."

"Aaron...." But there was nothing to say, not really. So Quinn just let himself be led, and the apartment was small enough that there was really only one place left for them to go. Well, assuming that Aaron wasn't going to take them to the bathroom. But he didn't, and Quinn soon felt the plush bedroom carpet under his feet.

"Stand still, Quinn." There was a rustle of something as Aaron moved around, and then nothing, although Quinn was pretty sure he could still sense Aaron moving. "I'm taking pictures of you, Quinn. I want to be able to remember every detail of this, but I'm sure I won't be able to. So I'll focus on remembering everything else, and the pictures will let me remember what you looked like. And I'll show them to you, and you'll see how beautiful you are." He came a little closer, and ran his hand thoughtfully down Quinn's chest to the button of his fly. "Can I, Quinn? Can I take these off, and take pictures of you then?"

The first part of the plan sounded perfect, but Quinn wasn't quite far enough gone to not hesitate over the second. "What are you taking the pictures on? You leave your phone lying around all over the barn, man—I really don't need Danny seeing that. Or, God forbid, your mom."

"I thought we had an agreement, Quinn. We don't discuss mothers when we're fooling around." He kissed Quinn's temple. "And it's on a camera. I'd be careful of them, I promise."

"Yeah? Careful like when you called Danny earlier?"

"Danny should have taken better care of my property." The growl was back in Aaron's voice. Quinn wasn't sure how much more his poor dick could take.

"Okay, yeah. Take my jeans off and you can do what you want with the camera."

Aaron rewarded him with a nearly-chaste kiss on the cheek. Then he whispered, "You can look at them afterward, and you can erase them if you want." Quinn nodded. That sounded fair. And maybe Aaron would let Quinn take some pictures, later. It would be nice to have something concrete to remind himself that this was all real.

And Aaron's fingers, deftly undoing Quinn's button and then his fly, were an absolute blessing. It got even better when Aaron put the camera down somewhere and used both hands to efficiently skim Quinn's jeans *and* underwear down. Quinn bit back a moan as his too-hard cock was finally freed, and he didn't even bother trying to keep quiet when Aaron caught the shaft in his hand and squeezed. It felt a bit like Quinn was in the supermarket, being tested to see if he was ripe, but he didn't complain. He was more than ripe, and absolutely ready to be....

Ignored, apparently. Aaron's hand left Quinn's cock and moved up to his shoulder. "Okay, step backward. Careful not to trip on your clothes. Good. Now another step, and sit down on the bed. Perfect." Quinn felt the mattress dip as Aaron leaned on it. "Now, I'm going to undo your hands. But that doesn't mean you're free. We're just repositioning, okay?"

"Okay." It was nice to have his work-stiffened arms free, at least temporarily, and Quinn took advantage of the opportunity to stretch them out a little. Possibly too vigorously, he realized as the back of his hand connected with what he was pretty sure was Aaron's nose.

"Ouch! Careful! Damn, Quinn, you're a menace."

"Sorry, man." Quinn really was sorry. But he couldn't take *full* responsibility. "My crazy boyfriend blindfolded me, so I can't really see what I'm doing."

"*Some* people, if they couldn't see what they were doing, would avoid making huge, sweeping arm movements. Maybe something for you to think about." Aaron didn't really sound hurt. "Now, in a more controlled manner... scoot yourself up on the bed, so you're lying on your back, in the middle. Yeah, good. Now, arms up over your head."

Quinn did as he was told, and felt something cool and smooth coiling over his wrists. It felt familiar. "Aaron, are those reins? Damn, have you got a leather fetish going on, too?"

"No, baby, it's not the leather, it's the horses. I hope you won't mind wearing a bit and a having a fake tail sticking out of your ass."

"Okay, I'm pretty understanding about all the porn, but you should probably stay off the fetish sites, okay? I really don't think you need any more ideas."

"I need *lots* of ideas. I've got a lifetime to look forward to with you, and I want to keep things interesting." He kissed Quinn's shoulder, then jerked the leather reins tight. Quinn tried to move his arms, and found that they were, as he'd expected, tied to the headboard. Aaron really wasn't missing a cliché. And every damn one of them was adding to Quinn's arousal.

Aaron's hands weren't doing anything to help Quinn calm down, either. He was acting as if he'd never seen Quinn's legs before and was tickling the skin, kneading the muscles, and then kissing all the most sensitive spots. Well, all but the one *most* sensitive spot, the only part of Quinn's lower body that *wasn't* being lavished with attention. He tried to shift a little, tried to subtly suggest that maybe Aaron would like to move up just a little bit, but if Aaron noticed, he didn't respond. Quinn thumped his head back into the pillow in frustration, then tried to make his body relax and enjoy the attention that it *was* getting.

But as soon as he started trying that, even that unsatisfactory attention went away. Aaron was gone, the mattress shifting as he climbed off the bed, and then just—gone. No noise, nothing. It was disconcerting. "Aaron?" Quinn tried. There was no answer. "Aaron? Did the aliens beam you up? Did you fall asleep? Go out for coffee?"

"You were warned, Quinn." Aaron's voice was quiet, but close. "No more questions." Something soft dragged up and over Quinn's face. "I love you, so I won't use your dirty socks. This one's clean."

"Oh, come on, Aaron...."

"Open your mouth, Quinn." Quinn thought about objecting, but did as he was told. Instead of having the sock stuffed inside, though, Aaron laid it crosswise in Quinn's mouth; if it had been longer, it could have been tied behind his neck. As it was, though, it didn't seem very effective. Then Aaron explained. "I'm just going to leave it there. You can spit it out anytime you need to. But if you spit it out, or if you try to talk around it—the game's over. I'll undo your hands, and I'll go make us some dinner while you jerk off in the shower, alone, and that's it for the night. You understand?" Quinn nodded silently; he understood too well. Aaron had made the gag pretty damned effective, after all.

"Okay, then. Before I was so rudely interrupted, I was taking pictures. I'm going to go back to that, now. You—relax. Be patient." A kiss on the forehead, and Aaron was gone.

It was hard to figure out what was happening. Quinn was pretty sure that Aaron wasn't taking pictures for the entire time. He'd climb back on the bed fairly frequently, for a quick kiss to one of Quinn's nipples, a finger's touch to some muscle somewhere, and, on one glorious occasion, a full-mouth kiss to the head of Quinn's cock. But Aaron always left again, left Quinn alone and aching for release. Aching for Aaron.

Finally, Aaron seemed to have mercy. He crept up the bed from the foot, sliding his body along Quinn's all the way, and then lay down gently on top of them. At some point, Aaron had lost his clothes, and they were both naked now, their hard cocks lined up perfectly. It would be so good, so easy…. Quinn shifted his hips, just a little; if he wasn't allowed to ask questions with his voice, he'd have to try to ask them with his body.

Aaron's answer wasn't quite what Quinn had been hoping for. "Not yet, Quinn. Almost. I promise. Just one more thing on my list, and then whatever you want. I'm yours after just one more thing."

That sounded pretty good. And chances were, Quinn wasn't going to exactly hate whatever the one more thing was, either. He nodded, not that Aaron had technically been asking for his permission. He waited for the new sensation, trying to trace through his memory, sorting through porn clichés that Aaron had likely seen, debating which ones would be next. But Aaron wasn't doing much. He slid most of his weight over so that he was lying on his side, snug up against Quinn's body, and he used his long reach to pet Quinn, smooth strokes from his face down to his thighs, sometimes skimming just beside his cock, but never giving Quinn what he wanted so much. Quinn tried to relax and enjoy, but then Aaron started talking, his voice right beside Quinn's ear.

"Quinn—I love you." Quinn's body froze, and for the first time he felt trapped by his restraints. Aaron's hand continued its soothing path, but Quinn knew that it was running over muscles that had been loose a moment earlier and were now tense. There was no way Aaron wasn't going to notice that. But he didn't comment on it. He just repeated himself, and then kept going. "I love you. More than I ever thought I could." A quick kiss to Quinn's ear, and then, "I've never been an unhappy person, not really. But I always felt like there was something missing. And I don't feel that way anymore. Because of you. Because I love you, and you love me back, and neither one of us is perfect, but we're perfect for each other." Quinn thought about spitting the gag out. It was torture to have to listen to all this and not be able to respond, to not deflect or joke his way out. He wondered whether Aaron had planned this all, right down to the punishment gag, or if that had just been lucky.

Aaron shifted so that more of his weight was on Quinn's body, and his hand slipped down to wrap around Quinn's cock, not working it, but not *exactly* still either. But Aaron wasn't done with his monologue. "I'm not going anywhere. Not until you kick me out, and if you do that, I'm going to spend a *hell* of a long time trying to fight my way back in. Okay? I love you, Quinn." His hand tightened on Quinn's cock, and now it started to move, slow and easy, but snug. Perfect. Except that Aaron was still talking, low and steady, right in Quinn's ear, as if he wanted to find the shortest route from his lips to Quinn's brain.

"I love you, Quinn." A soft, wet kiss to Quinn's jaw. "I love you." And Aaron shifted again so that his hard cock was lined up with Quinn's, and then Aaron's huge hand was wrapped around them both, still slow, but tighter now, and Quinn had been wrong to think that the earlier grip was perfect; he was wrong to ever use that word around Aaron, because as soon as Quinn thought things were as good as they could get, Aaron found a way to make them better. "I love you, Quinn." He kissed Quinn's temple, but that wasn't enough, it wasn't what Quinn needed. Aaron seemed to realize that.

"Still no talking," he said firmly, and then he lifted the sock away from Quinn's mouth, presumably with his teeth. One more "I love you, and I'm not going anywhere, ever," and then their mouths joined, and Quinn let his body arch up into Aaron's, hard muscle finding its match, hot skin melting together. As they reached their climax, their mouths broke apart so they could get more air, but Aaron didn't let up, murmuring "I love you, I love you," even as his hips began to move, driving into his hand, into Quinn, and Quinn could feel his own blessed orgasm wash over him just as Aaron's body tightened and shuddered above him.

Finally there was quiet, and Quinn tried to get his composure back, tried to re-center himself, but Aaron beat him to the punch. "I love you," Aaron said, and he brought his wet hand up between their bellies and played with the mess there, tickling and smiling as he said again, "I love you. More than anything. I, Aaron Miller, love Quinn Donahue." He kissed Quinn's nose playfully. "And he loves me back. And *he's* allowed to say it, but when *I* say it, he gets all weird. But not anymore, right?" Aaron shifted again, his full weight now on Quinn, pinning him to the mattress, and he used both hands to hold Quinn's head still, facing him. Quinn tried to ignore the come that he was sure Aaron was smearing on his face; he could shower soon. For now, he let Aaron have the attention he apparently needed. "I'm serious, Quinn. If the only way to get you to listen to me is to tie you up and gag you, then this is going to become a nightly routine. Okay? I love you."

Quinn nodded reluctantly. He *did* like hearing it. He did. It was just hard to let himself believe it.

Aaron seemed almost satisfied. "Okay, final quiz. You're allowed to talk now, and if you get the answers right, you're free.

But if you screw up, we're back to the very beginning. We'll do this as long as we have to, Quinn."

Quinn rolled his eyes and said, "Yeah, okay." It felt strange to use his voice.

Aaron braced himself on his arms and lifted his chest away from Quinn's. It put a bit of pressure on Quinn's groin, and damn it, he felt a stir of interest. Maybe he wouldn't mind too much if they started at the beginning again. Or maybe this time, it could be Aaron's turn to get tied up....

But Aaron's mind was not racing alongside Quinn's. Instead, he was focused on his damned quiz. "Okay, question number one—do you love me, and, in case you want to distinguish, are you *in* love with me?"

Quinn opened his mouth to answer, but Aaron held up a finger to stop him. "I changed my mind. You can't talk yet. Here, take the sock back."

"Are you serious? You just—" Quinn stopped abruptly as he felt Aaron's sharp teeth rest ever-so-gently on the tender skin between Quinn's nipple and his underarm. "Seriously? You're going to—Ouch! Jesus! Damn it, that—Ouch! Okay, shit, stop that! Give me the sock."

Quinn let his mouth fall open and accepted the sock between his teeth. He felt a little better when Aaron slid back down and kissed the spots he had bitten, but, still—this whole thing was getting out of hand.

Then Aaron was back next to his ear. "Okay, sorry I had to do that. But you need to stay obedient for just a little bit longer. And I think it's best if you just answer yes or no by nodding or shaking your head." He kissed the corner of Quinn's mouth. "So, we're back to it. No talking, just nod yes or shake your head no. The question is: do you love me, and are you *in* love with me?"

Quinn wished he could use words to elaborate on the

situation, but he settled for nodding his head up and down, and was rewarded with another quick kiss. Then Aaron said, "Okay, next question. And the reason this is only yes or no is because I don't want to hear any of your 'it's not really possible for me to answer that' or 'those words need to be defined' bullshit, okay? I just want a yes or no. And the question is: do I love you, and am I *in* love with you?"

Well, damn it, that was harder. He knew the answer Aaron wanted, but Quinn wasn't going to lie, and this was—well, damn it, he needed his words. He needed to explain how impossible it was to tell the difference between infatuation and real love, when it was the first time for both. He needed to clarify that he didn't think, not for a second, that Aaron was *lying*, he just thought maybe Aaron didn't know quite as much as he thought he did.

Then he remembered Aaron's words, whispered so intensely, so freely. Quinn knew they weren't just words, weren't something that Aaron said casually. Quinn had trusted Aaron without hesitation when it came to his body; maybe it was time to let himself trust Aaron with his heart as well. He moved his head slightly, and it felt right. It felt like something that he was strong enough to do. He moved it further, made it a clear nod, and as his head came back down his lips met Aaron's, waiting for him. The sock was quickly dragged away, and then Aaron's hands were on Quinn's, loosening the leather until Quinn could slip free and bring his arms down to pull Aaron closer. The blindfold was the last to go, impatiently pushed up over Quinn's forehead. "I love you, Quinn," Aaron said fervently.

Quinn fought back the disclaimers. Instead, he pushed with his hips and his shoulders, and rolled them over so that Aaron was flat on his back with Quinn hovering over him.

Quinn looked down at the beautiful, trusting, *loving* face that was looking back up at him, and he said the only thing he could think of. "Thank you." From Aaron's smile, Quinn was pretty sure that his words were enough.

ABOUT THE AUTHOR

Kate Sherwood, Cate Cameron, Catherine Dale... and probably a few new names, eventually. They're all one person.

One person who's lucky enough to get to live a bunch of extra lives through all the characters in her books, and who's trying desperately to keep all the lives organized into some sort of categories... so each name writes a different type of story.

But really, beneath the genre categories? All the stories will have some kind of humour, even in the darkest times. They'll all show characters who are far from perfect, but who are trying to be better.

Basic bio stuff? Kate/Cate/Catherine lives in Cottage Country, the water-filled world north of Toronto, Canada, the land where summers are sunny and crowded with visitors and winters are snowy and isolated. She loves it there. Not that she doesn't sometimes miss the city, especially when her internet is acting up or she wants something delivered!

She works full-time at a non-writing job but would love to shift into a more writing-centred life. There's a five-year plan. It might work....

OTHER BOOKS BY KATE SHERWOOD

For details, see www.booklives.com

Writing as Kate Sherwood (m/m)

All That Glitters – contemporary romance

Long Shadows, Embers, Darkness, Home Fires – four book contemporary action

Feral, Lap Dog, Twice Shy, Pure Bred – four book NA contemporary romance

Sacrati – fantasy/alt history

In Too Deep – NA contemporary romance

Chasing the Dragon – angst and adventure!

Mark of Cain – contemporary romance

The Fall, Riding Tall – two book contemporary romance

The Shift – contemporary fantasy novella – monster hunters!

Room to Grow – contemporary romance novella

The Pawn, The Knight – two book futuristic romance with plenty of angst

Poor Little Rich Boy – contemporary romance

More than Chemistry – light contemporary novella

Dark Horse, Out of the Darkness, Of Dark and Bright – three book contemporary romance with extras

Shying Away – NA romance

Lost Treasure – contemporary romance

Writing as Cate Cameron (m/f, YA)

The Billionaire's Forever Family – contemporary romance

Center Ice, Playing Defense, Winging It, Breakaway – contemporary YA hockey romance

Just a Summer Fling, Hometown Hero – contemporary small town romance

Shining Armor – contemporary romance (originally published under "Kate Sherwood")

Writing as Catherine Dale (YA, contemporary fantasy, general fiction—everything but romance!)

Dark Houses – Speculative YA

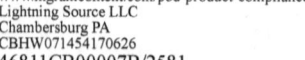